TELL ME
NO
SECRETS

Laurie.
Andrew

About the author

Julie Corbin lives in Sussex with her husband and three children.

Tell Me No Secrets is her debut novel.

TELL ME NO SECRETS

JULIE CORBIN

HODDER

First published in Great Britain in 2009 by Hodder & Stoughton
An Hachette UK company

2

Copyright © Julie Corbin 2009

A CIP catalogue record for this title is available from the British Library

ISBN 978 0 340 99381 1 (A)
ISBN 978 0 340 91988 0 (B)

Typeset in Plantin Light by Palimpsest Book Production Limited,
Grangemouth, Stirlingshire

Printed and bound by Clays Ltd, St Ives plc

Hodder & Stoughton policy is to use papers that are natural, renewable and
recyclable products and made from wood grown in sustainable forests. The
logging and manufacturing processes are expected to conform to the
environmental regulations of the country of origin.

Hodder & Stoughton Ltd
338 Euston Road
London NW1 3BH

www.hodder.co.uk

For my parents, Cynthia and Ian Henderson, who always encouraged me to dream.

ACKNOWLEDGEMENTS

It begins somewhere, and for me it was moving to Forest Row and meeting up with two great readers and fledgling writers, Helen and Yvonne – what fun we had!

Heartfelt thanks to Andie Lewenstein and Catherine Smith – two excellent teachers, writers and remarkable women who encouraged me to dig deep, be brave and never give up.

My writing friends for all their patient feedback and ongoing support – Mel Parks, Ellie Campbell-Barr, Liz Yonge and Jo Turner – I couldn't have done it without you. x

Sigi, Cristina, Jannine, Dorothy, Krys, Jane and Mike – how I miss those Tuesday mornings!

Parents, children and friends, past and present, at Ashdown House School – thank you for your interest and enthusiasm – most notably Sarah and Rob, Glenys, wise and wonderful Sue, Neville, Regan, Paddy, James and Julie, Anderley, Charlie, George, Haydon, Mike, Ed, Eifion, Bella, Carol, Lucy, Michelle, Ruby, Fiona Squire for her spot-on advice, Penny, Rachael, Liz, Helen Hill, all the children in the 1s and 2s – and yes, you George Breare! (Glenys – you're a star.)

Sandy Telfer for his timely input, Dave Morgan for being the first man to read it(!) and Helen Lewis for being my best friend and sounding board.

Jason Jarrett for his help setting up my website and for being the most interesting and entertaining apple mac expert ever!

My agent Euan Thorneycroft who picked up a lesser book and skilfully prompted me to rewrites. His input was, and is, invaluable.

My editor Sara Kinsella, Isobel Akenhead and Francine Toon – friendly, warm and generous – who knew publishing a book could be this much fun?

Thank you to my brother John, his wife Mags, my sister Caroline and her partner Roland with whom I share so much.

Last, but not least, for my husband Bruce and my three sons Mike, Sean and Matt – happy to live on tinned soup and sandwiches, with a wife and mother who mumbles or drifts off mid-sentence – who have cheered for me from start to finish without one single word of complaint. You are everything to me.

Prologue

They say that everybody has a secret. For some, it's a stolen extramarital kiss on a balmy evening after two or three glasses of wine. For others it's that girl, teased mercilessly about the shape of her nose or the whine in her voice until she has to move school.

Some of us, though, keep secrets that make liars of our lives. Take me, for example. The skeleton I fear isn't hiding in my closet. The one I fear lies underground. Her name was Rose and she was nine years old when she died.

I'm not going to make excuses for what I did. I'm going to tell my story as it is and as it was.

This isn't the beginning but it's a good place to start . . .

I

I live in Scotland, on the east coast a few miles beyond St Andrews. The east of Scotland is flatter than the west, the scenery less spectacular. We don't have the craggy peaks or brooding glens dour with dead men's stories. We have instead a gentle roll and sway of land and sea that lifts my spirits the way a mountain never can.

And the weather isn't great. After a couple of sunny days we're punished with the haar that rolls in off the North Sea, thick and cold until you can't see the hand in front of your face. But this evening it's exactly as I like it and when I've finished preparing the evening meal, I stand at the sink rinsing the knives and the chopping board and watch a couple walking along the beach, their faces turned up to enjoy the last of the day's sunshine.

The phone rings. I dry my hands and lift the receiver. 'Hello,' I say.

'Grace?'

I don't reply. I feel like I recognise the voice but at the same time, I don't. There's a tingling under my scalp and it spreads to my face. With my free hand I rub my cheeks.

'Grace?'

Still I don't reply. This time because I know who it is. 'It's me. Orla,' she says.

I put down the phone, return to the sink and lift the knives, washing and drying each one slowly and meticulously before putting it back in the knife rack. I rinse the spaghetti, toss it in oil and cover it with a lid then bend down and open the oven door. The juice from the berries has bubbled up through the crumble, running scarlet rivers over the topping. I turn off the oven and walk to the downstairs bathroom. I lock the door behind me and vomit so violently and repeatedly that I taste blood on my tongue.

The front door opens then slams shut. 'Mum?' I hear Daisy drop her school bag in the hallway and walk towards the kitchen. 'Mum?'

'I'm in here.' My voice wavers and I clear my throat. 'Give me a minute.' I splash my face in the sink and look at myself in the mirror. My eyes stare back at me, my pupils huge and fixed. My face is colourless and there is a relentless drumming inside my skull. I swallow two Ibuprofen with a handful of water and count slowly, from one to ten, before I open the door. Daisy is sitting on the bottom stair with our dog Murphy's head on her knee. She's crooning to him and rubbing the backs of his ears. His breathing slows and he gives a low, contented growl.

'How was school?' I ask.

Daisy looks up at me. 'You look hellish. Is it a migraine?'

'Must be.' I try to smile but my head hurts too much. 'Where's Ella?'

'Walking back with Jamie.' She rolls her eyes, stands up and kicks off her shoes. 'I don't know what she sees in him. What's for tea?'

'Spaghetti bolognese and fruit crumble.' The thought of food makes me want to be sick again. I distract myself by bending down to put her shoes in the rack then think better of it when the drummer in my head plays a five-stroke roll against my temples. I lean into the wall and try to calm myself but when the drumming stops I hear her voice: *It's me. Orla.*

I follow Daisy into the kitchen where she's taking a spoonful of sauce from the pot. 'It's good!' She smiles at me, reaches forward and kisses my cheek then wraps her arms round my shoulders. She's a couple of inches taller than me now and it makes me feel humbled, like somewhere along the way she became the adult and me the child. 'Why don't you have a lie down, Mum? Tea can wait.'

'I think I'll be okay. I've taken some painkillers. They should kick in soon.'

'If you're sure.' She rubs my back. 'I'll go and change.'

I tilt my head and give her what she calls my Oh-Daisy smile. Her shirt hangs out over her skirt, her tie is skew-whiff and her tights have a hole in them. The cuffs of her almost new sweater are already beginning to fray.

'I don't do uniforms,' she tells me, her cheeks dimpling.

I run my hand through her cropped hair and she leans against it for a moment before I gently push her away. 'Go on then. Back into the combats.'

She leaves the room, calling to Murphy who pads along

beside her, his tail thumping the air. I sit on a chair and try to think of nothing and no one. All I'm aware of is my breathing and I hold my hand over my chest, counting each breath as it first fills and then empties my lungs.

By the time Paul's car tyres crunch over the gravel on the driveway, I feel almost calm again. His door clunks shut and I hear the muffled sound of his voice and then Ella's in reply. When they come through the front door, Ella is half talking, half laughing. 'I didn't mean it like *that*, Dad!' she says. 'It's a play on words like two martyrs soup, tomato soup.'

Paul laughs. 'Don't tell me one of my daughters is developing a sense of irony. Whatever next!'

They come into the room; Ella is hanging on his arm. Paul bends to kiss me. 'Darling, are you okay?' He runs a hand over my cheek.

'I'm fine.' I stand up and rest my head against his neck. Immediately, tears flood the back of my eyes and I pull away. 'How was your day?'

'Usual procrastination at the departmental meeting but otherwise—' He stops talking. He is watching me. I'm making tidy piles of the letters and bills that are on the sideboard. He pulls me back towards him. 'Grace, you're shaking. What's wrong?'

'Just a headache.' I press my fingertips around my eyes so that he can't see the expression in them. 'It'll pass.'

'Are you sure?'

'Yes. Really.' I clear my throat. 'Combination of tiredness and dehydration.' I smile into the space between his body and the window. 'You know me – I never drink enough water.'

'Well, if I've told you once . . .'

'. . . you've told me a hundred times.' I manage to look into his eyes and see nothing but straightforward concern: no suspicion or irritation, just humour and a gentle kindness that comforts me. I risk leaning into his neck again. 'Thank you.'

'For what?'

I kiss below his ear and whisper, 'For being you.'

He squeezes me tight then releases me and looks around at the table and beyond that to where Ella is rummaging in the fridge. 'Daisy home?'

'She's upstairs changing.'

'How's my dad been today?'

'Fine. He went into St Andrews to the hardware store. Came back with a boot-load of supplies to repair the fence with.'

'No forgetfulness?' He tries not to look worried.

'Not that he mentioned.' I rub from his shoulder down to his hand then lace my fingers through his. 'Let's not cross bridges.'

'I know.' He gives me a tight smile. 'It's just that I hate to think about him getting lost and no one to help him. Anyway' – he opens the patio doors – 'I'll call him through.'

He goes outside to the small apartment that connects to our house and I mix some dressing for the salad.

'Are you getting tea?' Ella is eyeballing me over the

glass she's holding up to her lips, swigging back a huge mouthful of juice until her cheeks puff out.

'Yes. And it's ready so please don't eat anything.' I drizzle oil and lemon juice over the green salad. 'Are you going to change?'

She looks down at herself. She is wearing exactly the same uniform as Daisy but somehow on Ella it looks stylish. The navy skirt sits easily on her hips, the pleats swing as she walks then settle against the fronts and backs of her knees. She never has holes in her tights and her tie is always lying on centre. 'I'm not changing. I'm fine as I am.' She stuffs a piece of cold ham into her mouth, lifts the carton of juice, goes to pour it in the glass, changes her mind and holds it up to her mouth instead, slurping it back in exaggerated gulps.

I say nothing. My head still hurts, my nerves are strung tight – *It's me. Orla* – and, anyway, I pick my battles carefully with Ella. I edge past her and take the warm plates from the oven.

'. . . and that's when I said, "Don't bother, young man, I'll buy the brown one."' Ed comes into the house with Paul. 'What's for tea tonight then, Grace?' he shouts, rubbing his hands together. 'Best part of the day, this is.'

I smile at him. I love my father-in-law. He's one of life's gentlemen.

'You're looking a little tired around the eyes, my love.' He clasps my hands. 'What can I do to help?'

'You could toss the salad for me,' I tell him, hugging his wiry frame. 'I can manage the rest.'

We all sit down to eat. Paul and Ed are at either end of the table and the girls are opposite me. My stomach contracts at the sight of the food and I clench my jaw muscles hard until the wave of nausea recedes. I dish up, giving myself a small portion and hand the plates around. Everyone thanks me except Ella. She's busy under the table arranging Murphy's head on her feet. Paul looks down at the dog and orders him to his bed. Murphy ignores him.

'He's not bothering me, Dad,' Ella tells him. 'He's keeping my feet warm.'

Paul smiles. 'Just like Bessie, Dad, eh?'

'Now there was a dog and a half,' Ed says.

I spoon some spaghetti into my mouth and eat automatically, preoccupied with what's going on inside my head. Memories hatch like chicks in an incubator: Orla does handstands in the sun, her hair brushing over my bare feet as I catch her legs; arms around each other's back, running the three-legged race, giggling and jostling each other until we fall panting to the ground; summer afternoons, rolling up and over the dunes until our noses and ears are itchy and blocked with sand; cookery classes, flour on her cheeks, the rolling pin a weapon in her hand; trying on shoes, tops, trousers, skirts before finally parting with our pocket money. And then the last time we were alone together. The hard slap of her hand on my cheek.

'Is there any more, Mum?' Daisy is holding her plate towards me.

'Sure.' I load some on to her plate and pass it back to her. 'Anyone else?'

Ed reaches over and pats my hand. 'Delicious as ever, Grace. But I'll save some room for my pudding, if I may.'

I give Paul an extra spoonful and look at Ella. She seems to have more on her plate now than she did when she started. She is moving the food around, arranging like with like, separating out the tomatoes from the olives and the mozzarella from the basil. When she starts to pick the red pepper out of the bolognese sauce, I look away.

'Wait till you girls leave home,' Ed is saying. 'You'll appreciate your mum's cooking then. Won't you just.'

'I already do,' Daisy says, looking sideways at her sister.

Ella seems not to have heard and, pushing her plate away, looks around the table at us all. 'So guess who got the lead in the play?' she says.

'Now what play would that be?'

'*Romeo and Juliet*, Grandad.'

'Ah!' Suddenly, like a cloud drifting over the sun, Ed's eyes glaze over. He stares down at his fork, examines it from every angle and then puts it neatly beside his plate. 'I'm not sure what that's for,' he announces. Then, looking around him, says, 'Where's Eileen?'

'Eileen's not here right now, Grandad, and we're all having tea,' Daisy says.

'Of course we are. We're all having tea.'

He looks worried and I sense his rising panic. I rest my hand on his.

'But where is Eileen?' he says.

How to tell him that his wife has been dead these last five years? In the beginning we tried to orientate him to the present but all it did was make him relive his grief, acutely as a knife through flesh.

'Mum's busy right now, Dad,' Paul tells him. 'You're eating with us this evening.'

'Yes, right.' He nods to himself, trying to make sense of it, hanging on to the words. He looks at me. 'Is there pudding, Alison?'

'Coming right up,' I tell him. In these moments he often mistakes me for his daughter and I don't correct him.

'Anyway,' Ella says, turning to her father. 'I got the part.' She gives a broad, excited smile that lights up the whole table.

'Congratulations!' Paul and I say, both at the same time.

'That's fantastic! And who's playing Romeo?' I ask.

'Rob.' She shrugs. 'He wouldn't be my choice but Mr Simmonds seems to think he's the best.'

'And how many girls auditioned for Juliet?'

'About twenty.'

'And you were the best. Well done.' Paul reaches over and claps a hand on her shoulder.

'It's because she's good at flirting,' Daisy comments under her breath.

'I heard that,' Ella says.

'Well, it's true, isn't it?'

'For your information there's more to acting than meets the eye and at least I have boyfriends. Maybe if you didn't dress like a dyke—'

'Maybe if you weren't such a fashion victim, you wouldn't always be borrowing money from me.'

'Well, maybe if you were a better sister you'd be pleased for me,' she bites back. Her eyes well up with angry tears and she pushes back her chair and flounces from the room, banging the door behind her.

Daisy watches her go. 'With acting like that, is it any wonder she gets the parts.'

'Daisy!' Paul says with a sigh. 'Surely that was unnecessary.'

Daisy's face colours. I pass her some pudding.

'Be careful of sour grapes,' Paul continues, digging his spoon around in his crumble. 'It's not worthy of you.'

Daisy stops her spoon midway to her mouth. 'Why would I be jealous of her? We're identical twins. Capable of exactly the same achievements.'

'And that's why winding each other up makes no sense. I appreciate that you might have wanted the part—'

'I didn't audition,' Daisy tells him, enunciating each syllable. 'I don't like acting.'

'Is that any reason not to support Ella?'

'I do support Ella. More than you know.'

'Well, it doesn't look that way to me.'

His tone is mild but Daisy is bristling. I wait for her to raise the stakes but she doesn't, she calmly finishes her pudding and gives me the bowl. Her hands are steadier than her eyes and as she leaves the room she murmurs, 'What's the point?'

'Daisy!' Paul calls after her but she ignores him and he offers me an apologetic smile. 'Sorry, love. You've cooked a lovely meal and now they're both upset. I don't know what gets into Daisy sometimes. It was Ella's moment to shine and she spoiled it for her.'

'They're sisters.' I shrug. 'That's what sisters do. They bicker and they fight. Ella's just as bad when the mood takes her.'

'You're right.' He looks regretful as he passes me his bowl. 'I'll make it up to Daisy later. Whoever said being a parent was easy?'

'Not me.' I think of my own parents and the trouble I put them through. 'But at least you're managing to be liked by them both.'

'Not this evening. Or not by Daisy, at any rate.'

'Most of the time,' I acknowledge. 'And they respect you. Sometimes I think Ella would rather I wasn't around.'

'She'll change sides soon and then it'll be my turn to take the flak.' He leans over and kisses my cheek. 'We'll get there. We have each other. That's the most important thing.' His eyes meet mine. Soft, the grey of dove's wings, they are both wise and calming and it makes me want to tell him about the phone call. And more. But I can't. Not now, not ever.

He looks to the end of the table. 'How about a game of Scrabble then, Dad, eh?'

Ed, quietly finishing his crumble, brightens immediately and they both go through to the living room, leaving me to stack the dishwasher. While my hands do the work, my mind is elsewhere. Orla. Until this evening, I hadn't heard from her for over twenty years. So successfully have I locked away her memory that I have barely even thought of her. As young teenagers we were best friends. We went everywhere together, shared dreams and ambitions, triumphs and failures. And then, the year we both turned sixteen, everything changed. Rose died. And though we had our chance to be truthful, we didn't take it. We lied; each lie feeding the next until we had created a huge, irreconcilable secret.

The doorbell rings and I jump, drop a plate and watch it skid across the floor before coming to rest against the dog's water dish. I pick it up and put it in the rack then make my way to the front of the house. I have a horrible feeling that Orla will be standing there, her body materialising less than two hours after her voice. But when I open the door, I'm relieved to see that it isn't her, it's Jamie, Ella's latest boyfriend. He's standing on the doorstep looking sheepish. His hair is gelled up in spikes across the top of his head and he smells strongly of deodorant.

Ella clatters down the stairs and elbows me out of the way. She's wearing a tight, short denim skirt and a top that shows off her midriff.

'Ella, this is Scotland,' I tell her.

She's straightened her hair and it falls like a sheet, down from her forehead and over one eye. The other eye stares at me, belligerence glazing her expression. 'Your point being?'

'You'll freeze. Please wear something more substantial.'

'I'll keep her warm,' Jamie volunteers and Ella giggles. His gaze is frank, lustful. He licks his lips and I think of my beautiful daughter lying in a sand dune under his sweaty, adolescent body. I want to push him back through the door and ban him from the house.

'Is it just the two of you?' I say.

'No.' She shakes her head. 'Sarah, Mat, Lucy, Rob. The usual.'

'Where are you meeting?'

'Di Rollo's.'

'And then you're all going down to the beach?'

She gives me an insincere smile. 'Duh.'

I watch them walk away, their hips touching. His hands slide down her back and they kiss up against a lamppost. I turn away. Daisy is beside me putting on her boots. 'You know your dad didn't mean to get at you,' I tell her, stroking the top of her head.

'I know, Mum.' She shrugs and texts a quick message on her mobile. 'I'm going out for a bit. I'll be home before dark. And don't worry about Ella,' she shouts back over her shoulder. 'She's going to be careful.'

She's going to be careful? Unease creeps along my nerve endings and comes to rest uncomfortably in my stomach. I want to call after Daisy but she's already along the end of the street. I shut the door and rest my back against it then climb the stairs and go into Ella's room. Her dressing table is strewn with make-up, clogged tissues, cotton buds, small change, used bus tickets, empty cans of Diet Coke, spent candles. The floor is a muddle of clothes, clean and dirty mixed up. Schoolbooks are dumped in the corner. I open the drawer of her bedside cabinet and see a half-empty foil strip sitting on top of her hairbrush. I pick it up and read the name. The pills are called microgynon and each one is labelled a different day of the week.

I try to line up straight, coherent thoughts. I can't. All I keep thinking is that she's too young for the stuff of adult life: sex, responsibility, choices and consequences. A minefield. Rationally, I accept that she is hardly a child. She is in fact the same age as I was when Orla and I last saw each other: in the police station, both of us bedraggled, wrapped in blankets, complicit.

I put the pills back into the drawer. I'll talk to Paul. He is more level-headed than I am; his parenting skills are more assured. For me, mothering is instinctive and my instinct tells me that I should protect my girls from making mistakes. But short of locking them indoors, I don't know the best way to do that.

The mobile in my pocket starts to chirrup like a budgie. I look at the name flashing on the screen: Euan.

'Hi, Grace. Is Sarah there?'

'No. They're all down at di Rollo's.'

He sighs. 'Great. She hasn't come back from school yet and she needs to revise for her history tomorrow.'

'You could always go down and collect her but—'

'Might be more than my life's worth. What happened to only going out on Friday and Saturday nights?'

'Like when we were young?'

'Aye.' He starts to laugh. We have this conversation often. It goes along the lines of: when we were their age we wouldn't have dared . . .

'So how are things?' he asks.

'How are things?' I repeat with a laugh. It sounds like I'm being strangled.

'I missed you at work today.'

'I took some samples over to Margie Campbell in Perth,' I say, closing my eyes against thoughts of Orla and what she knows about me. 'She's commissioning me to paint the view from her family home in Iona.'

'Great stuff.' I feel him nodding. 'You're becoming quite the local celebrity.'

'Maybe. But, Euan—' I stop, balance the phone on my shoulder and fold my arms over my chest. 'Remember Orla?' I say in a rush.

'Yeah?'

Tears collect behind my eyes and I press my fingers against them until I see stars. 'She called me earlier.'

'Shit.' He whistles. 'What did she want?'

'I don't know. I cut her off before she had a chance to tell me.' I try to rub out a pen mark on the wall with my fingertip. 'The sound of her voice, it freaked me out. I thought I'd never hear from her again. I *hoped* I'd never hear from her again.'

'Do you think she'll call back?'

'I don't know.'

He turns from the mouthpiece and I hear him talking to Monica, his wife. 'She's down at the beach. Okay, you go. Yup.' He speaks back into the receiver. 'I wonder why she would call you after all this time.'

'Twenty-four years bar six days,' I say. 'I counted.'

'Grace. Don't,' he says. 'Don't go over old ground.'

'Do you remember when we were kids?' I'm whispering now. 'Do you remember how Orla always managed to get her own way, no matter what?'

'Yes, I remember.' He's silent for several seconds and I wonder whether he's thinking what I'm thinking. 'Are you coming into work tomorrow?'

'Yeah.'

'See you then . . . and Grace?'

'Yeah?'

'Don't worry.'

I don't answer. How can I not worry?

'Grace?'

'What?'

'We can sort this. Chances are she was feeling a bit nostalgic, spur-of-the-moment call and she won't repeat it.'

I wish I could believe that. 'How did she get my number? Do you think she's been talking to Monica?'

'Monica hasn't mentioned it and I think she would have. She never liked Orla. She would have asked you before giving out your number.'

I'm sure he's right. As children they were out-and-out enemies. It is unlikely that Monica would be willing to say hello to Orla never mind help her out by giving her my number. I finish speaking to Euan and stand by the door watching Ed and Paul play Scrabble. They don't notice me. They are locked into the game, father and son, enjoying time together. Paul is playing to win but, as ever, he is free of vanity and he laughs along with Ed, entering into the spirit of their supposed rivalry. He is a good man, an excellent husband and father and I love him more than I am able to express. The thought of living life without him is unthinkable. I wonder how much he could take before he was unwilling to stand by me. I wonder just exactly how far and wide his love for me stretches. I wonder but I don't want to find out.

15 June 1984

Rose shoves her way to the front, digging pointy fingers into the other girls' ribs. They don't grumble. They move out of her way because Rose's mother recently died and Miss Parkin has ordered us all to be extra kind to her. 'Rose is in your patrol, Grace, because I know I can rely on you,' she tells me.

I'm bored but trying not to show it. Almost sixteen and desperate to leave the Guides, I promised to go on one last camping trip. There are five girls in my patrol, all of them under twelve and Rose, the youngest, has just had her ninth birthday. That makes her a year too young for the Guides but Miss Parkin is her primary school teacher and has allowed her to join early.

The girls are all staring up at me, mouths agape, waiting for their instructions. 'Go and find some sticks,' I tell them. 'And make sure they're dry. Hang on, Rose.' I catch her arm before she scuttles off with the rest and point to her laces trailing on the ground. 'You need to tie those up before you trip over them.'

Her eyes look anxiously towards the other girls who are disappearing into the trees.

'Don't worry, you can catch them up in a minute.' I bend down to help her.

'Thank you, Grace.' She smiles, gap-toothed and tentative. 'I can't do double knots.'

'You'll learn.' I stroke her hair and give her a gentle nudge. 'Off you go then.'

'Have you got rid of your shadow at last?' Orla comes over to join me. Her hands are in the pockets of her shorts and she is chewing gum, her mouth slightly open.

'She's not so bad. Just desperate to get everything right. We were like that once.'

'You maybe! I never was.' She pulls cigarettes and a lighter out of her pocket. 'Her dad's a bit of all right though, isn't he?'

'I hadn't really noticed.'

'Liar!'

'For God's sake!' I hiss, looking around to make sure no one is listening. 'His wife's not long dead.'

'So?' She gives a careless shrug. 'That doesn't stop him being attractive. You coming?' She waves the cigarettes at me.

I shake my head.

'Suit yourself.' She throws me a dirty look. 'Some friend you are.'

She stomps off, her boots kicking up the dirt and I hesitate, almost go after her but decide not to. For the last few weeks she's been acting weird. I don't know what's wrong with her and she won't tell me. I suspect it might be to do with her parents. They are having marriage problems and Orla, as an only child, ends up in the middle of it. I wish I could do something to help, but whenever I try I get a mouthful of bitchy mind-your-own-business comments.

I walk through the trees towards the campfire. Acorns and pine cones litter the ground and as I step, they spring back under my boots. The air smells sweeter than newly baked bread or Euan's baby nephew when he's been bathed and talcumed, and a cool breeze is blowing through the branches. The other patrol leaders are gathered in the clearing and we stand chatting for ten minutes before Miss Parkin comes to give us our orders. She looks harassed. Her hair is sticking up all over her head and her blouse is crushed like she's spent weeks sleeping in it.

Orla is back looking cheerful again. She sidles up to me and speaks into my ear: 'Give her another day or so and she'll be completely demented.'

'Always talking, Orla!' Miss Parkin barks, her glance including me. 'Both of you, see to the sausages.'

The sausages are wrapped in greaseproof paper, more than a hundred of them, tight and shiny in their skins. I tip the bundle out on to the tray. They are linked to each other and I swing them around my head like a cowboy with a lasso. Orla catches my eye and we start to giggle. Miss Parkin's antennae snap back in our direction. She shouts our names and we straighten up, rigid as telegraph poles. I hold the sausages steady and Orla cuts them into singles with the knife.

'What does this remind you of?' Orla asks me. She positions one of them in front of her shorts, points it upwards and waves it around.

'Callum when Miss Fraser bends over at the blackboard,' I say at once and we dissolve into hysterics, a sloppy tangle of weak legs and arms.

Miss Parkin slaps the backs of our bare legs as we fall. 'You should be setting an example to the younger ones,' she tells us. 'Now get on with it or there will be no marks for either of your patrols.'

We pull ourselves upright again and I squash bubbles of laughter with thoughts of starving children in Biafra and people who lose their toes to frostbite or dogs that are beaten and cowed.

The fire is lit and we place the sausages over the makeshift grill. My job is to turn them and I do so carefully, shaking off burning sparks that fly up on to my arms. Orla works around me, organising plates and cutlery. Every so often, when Miss Parkin's eyes are elsewhere, she lunges towards me and pokes me hard in the kidneys. The fourth time she does this, I push her backwards and she crashes to the ground, scattering a pile of sticks. She lies perfectly still, limbs twisted in a parody of death. I pay no attention. I've recently won my first-aid badge and I know pretend when I see it.

The sausages are almost done and I move some of them off to the side. The smell draws saliva into my mouth faster than I can swallow and I want to spit like a boy but Miss Parkin is watching, her eyes fixing on each of us in turn.

Monica and Faye, heads together, are deep in concentrated effort. One splits oblong rolls with a bread knife, the other pours wavy lines of ketchup along the spines. As usual, Monica looks perfectly groomed as if she's just stepped out of the hairdresser's. I wonder how she does it.

Orla is back on her feet. 'I could have been dead,' she says with a huffy pout.

'I should be so lucky,' I mouth back at her.

She takes one of the sausages and bites the end off it. 'How about we sneak off and join the boys tonight?'

I don't answer. The youth club is camping about three hundred yards away, through the trees and beyond the pond. Several boys from our school are there, including Euan whom I've been going out with for five weeks and six days. He's my next-door neighbour and we've known each other for ever but that hasn't stopped me falling for him. The thought of joining him in his tent sends my heart racing but I don't want Orla there as an audience. Euan is mine and I'm not about to share time with him.

At last we sit down to eat and for the first time that day we are all quiet. The sausages, wrapped in white bread rolls, taste like a small piece of heaven. Bread melts on to my tongue, hot sausage breaks open and slides salty, succulent pork to the back of my throat. We each have three fat helpings and lounge back against rocks softened by sweaters and compare the size of our stomachs.

Dusk is creeping through the trees, casting shadows behind us and blowing a cold wind over our tired bodies. When Miss Parkin's back is turned, Orla reaches for the ketchup bottle, tips it up and makes words on the tray, slowly and deliberately, letter by letter as if she is icing a cake. I sit up to read what she's written: *Rose! Mummy wants to talk to you.*

I meet her stare. She is bold and brazen as a wolf on the hunt. Without shifting her eyes from mine, she nudges Rose with her feet. Rose, already half asleep, is curled up like a kitten at my side. She rouses into a sitting position, one eye still closed.

'What?' she says, rubbing at her cheek.

'There's a message for you, Rose!' Orla shakes her fully awake. 'Look! It's from the spirit world.'

I grab an overcooked, blackened sausage and before Rose reads the words, I swirl it through the ketchup until all that's left is a mix of half shapes and splodges.

'Aw!' Rose wails and I pull her towards me.

'Just go back to sleep,' I tell her, settling her back at my side.

'But what's the spirit world and what did it say?' she asks.

'Nothing.' I glare at Orla.

She glares back. 'Spoilsport,' she says.

2

Next day I stay in bed until almost seven, hugging into Paul's back, lingering in the intimacy of the night before. After Orla's call, I was watchful and anxious, but by the time I fell asleep, the phone call was pushed to the back of my mind. As soon as the game of Scrabble was over and Ed went through to organise himself for bed, I told Paul about finding out that Ella was on the pill. His reaction was, as I expected, more measured and less fearful than mine. He reminded me that she is, after all, being responsible and is days away from turning sixteen: not quite an adult but most definitely not a child. Nothing would be gained by taking a hard line but something could be gained by quietly chatting about how she is feeling and what her plans might be. We agreed that I would speak to her after school, including Daisy in the conversation so that Ella doesn't feel like I'm picking on her.

Then the girls came home from their evenings out and we all retired to bed. Paul and I lay side by side talking about the possibility of a sabbatical in Australia. For the last fourteen years, Paul has been professor of marine biology at St Andrews University but he is due some research time and has applied for a position at the University of Melbourne. Fingers crossed he will be successful and in two months' time we will up sticks and move to Victoria. Paul's sister and family have lived there for over fifteen years and are looking forward to welcoming us all.

Paul and I spent time planning and imagining where we'll live and how we'll enjoy the holidays – scuba diving or horse riding? The Barrier Reef or the Blue Mountains? – and then, moments later, we were making love, the sort of married sex that takes ten minutes but leaves behind a residue of sweetness that endures for days.

Daisy is out of bed first and then I follow, prepare breakfast and see them all out of the door before I set off myself. I'm lucky. I can walk to work. I call on Murphy and walk to the end of our street and down to the waterfront. The harbour is empty this morning and the tide is going out. The fishing boats have already left for the deeper waters of the North Sea where they catch shellfish and crabs. The harbour wall stretches for over two hundred yards; its top is almost four feet thick and I walk along the inside edge of it, enjoying the strength of the wind that comes in off the sea and tries to blow me backward. Every so often Murphy finds a smell irresistible and stops for a longer sniff and I turn around to look back at our house. It's painted a duck-egg blue and sits basking in the summer sunshine. The front garden could do with some tidying up and the gravel driveway spills on to the road but to me it looks perfect.

When the wall ends, I drop back down on to a

single-track road with yellow gorse on one side and a sandy beach on the other. The sea is grey and heavy and it moves rhythmically beside me like a timeless, soothing companion. I breathe in a lungful of salty air then look up to the sky where clouds scud across the blue towards the far horizon.

I love the weather here. It isn't a backdrop to what's really happening, it's the main event. Sometimes it runs through all four seasons in a day as if auditioning for a part in God's play. Confused tourists climb in and then out of their macs, take sweaters off, remark at the heat from the sun, then twenty minutes later rummage in rucksacks to find layers to cover up their goose bumps.

The water never grows warm here. It just doesn't. That makes wetsuits a great invention. We never had them when we were young and as children we would run into the sea, pull our arms into ourselves, shriek, dance in the waves, hopping from one frozen foot to the other. But what we always have is wind and already some windsurfers are about a hundred yards from the shore; their sails point upward, slashes of primary colours run across the white cloth like the brushstrokes on a child's painting.

It's an optimistic sky and I feel like an optimistic me. Thoughts chase around my head – Orla, Ella, Ed, a triumvirate of worries – but I don't hang on to them. Instead I enjoy the walk, one foot in front of the other, Murphy at my heels and the sea breeze buffing my cheeks.

As I turn the last corner I see Monica placing her briefcase and jacket into the boot of her car. I slow my steps to a dawdle. It's cowardly, I know, but I hope she might be in the driving seat and away before I am close enough for conversation.

Monica is one of those women who illuminates my own inadequacies. She is a successful and popular GP. She dresses beautifully: silk blouses and well-tailored suits. She does Pilates, she runs marathons, she plays tennis and golf. She is clear, crystal clear, about what she has and what she wants. She is organised. Her children never forget their lunch boxes or PE kit and homework is always completed on time. And she isn't confused about how to bring them up. She knows exactly what they need: love, guidance and opportunities. She doesn't drink more than one glass of wine in an evening, she limits coffee to two cups a day and she always chooses the low-fat muffin.

We have a long history together, beginning in primary school when I stood, brand new and alone, in my new red pinafore, pulling at the white, starched collar around my neck. It was noisy. Boys jostled and pushed into the queue. My tummy hurt and I didn't like the look of the school dinners – lumpy mashed potatoes, cabbage that made me shiver inside my skin and an enormous metal container of oily sardines.

I wanted to cry. Monica made room beside her on the bench. She patted the space and gestured for me to sit next to her. I felt gratitude swell up through my chest and empty on to my face in a grateful smile. Then she told me that my shoes needed cleaning and I should make sure I did it that evening. Perhaps I even needed new ones?

That's Monica. What she gives with one hand she takes away with the other.

I see that she isn't in any hurry this morning. In fact she's waiting for me. As I draw close she turns to me, smiling into the sun. 'Hi, Grace. Congratulations are in order, I hear.'

I shake my head. 'How come?'

'Euan tells me you have another commission?'

'Oh, that.' I nod like I'm just remembering. 'Margie Campbell.'

'Yes, Margie.' She runs a hand over the lavender hedge. Murphy thinks she's about to pat him and moves in, his tail wagging. She pushes him aside and dead-heads the lavender with quick, deft strokes. 'She's a great one, Margie. Has a real sense of community. She likes to support local artists.' She looks up at me. 'For better or worse.'

'Mmm. She does.' I smile straight back at her.

'Tom's off school today. He was sick last night so he's upstairs in bed.' She opens her car door. 'Don't let Euan forget about him.'

'I won't.'

'And if he perks up have Euan remind him that he hasn't done his piano practice.'

'Okay.' I open the gate and walk through it.

'And the window cleaner will be here around eleven. His money is on the kitchen counter.'

I wave back over my shoulder and walk around the side of their house. It's built of huge, solid bricks of grey granite that have silver- and gold-coloured seams running through. It's the type of stone that weathers well and the climbing roses complete the picture of an ideal country house.

I follow the winding path of stepping-stones to the bottom of the garden. Euan is an architect and he and I share a workspace. He designed it himself, soon after they moved back from London. The cabin is modern, built from Scandinavian pine, and is all soft angles. The roof is made from layers of cedar shingles that blend in with the surrounding trees and it's pitched at an angle allowing five huge Velux windows to draw light from the sky into the rooms. There are two rooms: one we work in and the other is a guest bedroom with double bed and en suite bathroom.

I can see Euan through the side window as I walk towards the door. He is working on a barn conversion for one of the local solicitors and is standing in front of his drawing board. He's wearing a T-shirt with *Not now I'm busy* written across the front of it, jeans and a pair of trainers.

I push open the door. Murphy barks and runs over to Euan, launching himself up on to his chest. Euan wrestles him back to the ground, rubbing his ears from side to side until Murphy barks again. Meanwhile Euan's dog Muffin has come over to me. She is also a Labrador, a gentler, calmer version of Murphy and she pushes a ragged slipper into my hand. I take it from her and throw it across the room. She runs for it and Murphy joins her, then they settle down into their dog bed in the corner, resting their heads on each other's back.

Euan is swinging his arms in circles like an athlete warming up. 'Good walk over?'

I nod. 'It's the best sort of day out there. So Tom's not well?' I take off my jacket.

'Temperature, headache, up all night vomiting. What can I say?' He rubs both hands over his face. 'He's thirteen. I thought we were past all that.'

'What time did you start work?' I ask him.

'About six.' He sits down. 'Any more calls from Orla?'

I shake my head. 'I've been thinking on the walk over here. What's the worry?' I hang my jacket on the stand and look to him for confirmation. His face is noncommittal. 'Why would she want to rock any boats? What could she possibly have to gain?' I check the water level in the kettle then press the switch to on. 'What motive could she have for digging up the past? I mean really?' I let out a breath. 'Coffee?'

'Please.'

'I don't think she'll ring again.' I look at him and he raises his eyebrows, waits. 'But if she does, I'm going to make it clear that I don't want to hear from her. We're grown-up women for God's sake. What's she going to do? Harass me? Stalk me? Shout our secret from the rooftops?' I stop ranting, sit down and look straight ahead. 'You know what? I think I overreacted.'

'Well . . .' Euan looks doubtful.

'No, really, I do. She's probably embarrassed by the whole thing and—'

He cuts in. 'She was never that easily embarrassed.'

'She might have changed.'

'Have you? Have I?'

'Changed?' I think about it. 'Yes . . . and no.'

'Don't be fooled by her. You know what she's capable of.'

I think back to some of the lies she told and the people she hurt and I give an involuntary shiver. 'Do you think she's intending to come back to the village?' I swallow the lump in my throat. 'Do you think she's going to say something about Rose?'

'I don't know.' His face is concerned. 'But unless she's had a personality transplant, I think that anything is possible.'

It's not what I want to hear and I slump back in my seat. 'So what should I do?'

'Act friendly. Find out what she wants.'

'Keep your friends close and your enemies closer?'

'Exactly.'

'You really think she might be my enemy?'

'Think about it. Think about how she used to behave.'

I think about it. 'She wasn't all bad.'

'She had you dancing to her tune.'

'Not always,' I say slowly. 'Sometimes it felt like a tug of war between the two of—'

The boards in the hall creak and we both look towards them. Somehow Tom has managed to come down the garden and through the door without either of us noticing. His feet are bare and he's scratching his crotch.

'Grace, I'm not well.'

'Poor you.' I give him a sympathetic look. 'Feeling rotten still?'

'I'm a bit better.' He squints at me. 'It's too sunny outside.'

'Spoken like a true Scotsman! Do you want to sleep down here?'

'Is that okay, Dad? It's lonely in the house.'

'Sure.' Euan claps him on the back and I walk him through to the bedroom. The bed is already made up and I pull back the covers.

'Climb in, laddie,' I say, adopting a nurse's jollity. 'Sleep is the best medicine.'

'It's a shame this bed never gets used.' He throws himself on to it, grabs a pillow to hug. 'Whenever we have guests they always sleep up at the house. I'm hoping Dad's going to let me have the cabin as a bachelor pad when I'm eighteen. There's enough light for him to work in the two rooms at the top of the house.' He opens one eye. 'And you too, Grace. You see, I'll be needing my own space by then because I'll be coming in late and stuff like that.'

'You might find Sarah trying to beat you to it, Tom. She has two years on you.'

'She's not going to hang around at home. She'll be straight off to uni.' He gives a yawn. 'Mum gets on her nerves.'

'Well, being a mother isn't easy,' I say, tucking the covers around him. I think of Ella and an extra weight is added to my chest as I breathe in. 'Sometimes you can't do right for doing wrong.'

'I feel really hungry.'

'It's a bit soon for food. I'll make you some lunch when you wake, I promise.'

'Thanks, Grace. You're wicked.'

I stroke the top of his hair flat. His lashes are long and rest on the crest of his cheeks, freckles scatter across his nose and his mouth is wide and tilts upward in a permanent smile. He looks so much like Euan did at thirteen that it makes my heart ache.

I arrive home after the girls. They are in the living room. Ella is lying on her front on the sofa, her eyes closed, her face resting sideways on a textbook. One hand hangs down near the floor and reaches for Murphy as he pushes into the room ahead of me; the other is twisting her hair around her index finger. Daisy sits sideways in one of the easy chairs, her legs dangling over the end of the armrest, a science book on her lap, and when I come into the room she looks up at me.

'Mum, did you know that a chemist called Antoine Lavoisier was guillotined during the French revolution and he told friends that he would keep blinking for as long as possible after being killed?' She looks back at the book. 'His last blink was fifteen seconds after decapitation.'

'Astonishing!' I smile. 'Painful too, I should imagine.' I rub my hands together. 'Changing the subject, girls! I thought this might be a good time for the three of us to have a chat.'

'Sure.' Daisy closes her book.

'Ella, can we have a chat?'

She lifts herself up on to one elbow and frowns up at me. 'I'm doing some revision.'

'I see that.' I nod encouragement. 'But perhaps you could just leave it for five minutes or so. Could you?'

She gives a laboured sigh and hauls herself up into a sitting position. 'If this is about the state of my room then I'll tidy it up at the weekend. I don't need a whole lecture about it.'

'No, it wasn't about that,' I say, sitting on the arm of the chair. 'It was more about boyfriends. You know, like you and Jamie and what your intentions might be.'

'Oh, Jesus! You have to be kidding.' She stands up and folds her arms across her chest. She is wearing jeans that are frayed around her feet. Murphy puts out a paw to try to catch the threads dragging on the floor. 'I'm not about to listen to you giving me advice on boys.'

'Please, Ella.' I hold out my hands, palms upward. 'Please just hear me out.'

She laughs. It's a derisory snigger that sets my teeth on edge. 'I bet you were a sweet little virgin until you were eighteen. What could you possibly have to tell us about boys?'

'I may have been a little backward at coming forward where boys were concerned but I'll have you—' I bite my tongue and take a breath, remind myself that this isn't about me and I need to get past Ella's antipathy and reason with her. 'The point is, Ella, that you're growing up fast and . . .' I pause, try to find the right words.

'And?'

'And it isn't always a good idea to rush the process,' I say. 'Sometimes we want to be grown up before our time and that's when we might get into trouble.'

'We? Who's we?' she snaps back.

'You, Ella. You.' I stand up alongside her. It doesn't particularly help – she is after all taller than me – but it gives me the opportunity to pace. 'I know that you don't want to be spoken to like this but the fact is that you are only fifteen.'

'Sixteen on Saturday,' she points out. 'We're having a party, remember?'

'The fact *is*,' I continue, my voice sharpening, 'you are *my* daughter living in *my* house and I would like you to behave like any decent girl should.'

Daisy shifts on her seat and starts to click her tongue on the roof of her mouth.

It distracts Ella, but only for a second and when she looks back at me it's with a brittle stare that leaves me in no doubt that I am standing on ground that is tilting and at any moment I'm about to slide. 'You've been snooping in my room.'

'I have been in your room but I don't believe I was snooping.' I watch her face move from incredulous through hurt and then anger. 'You're my daughter and I love you. All I want is what's best for you.'

She's still glaring at me when the phone rings and Daisy jumps up to answer it.

'Time out, you two,' Daisy says, holding the phone out to me. 'Mum, it's for you.'

I whisper, 'Who is it?'

She shrugs and I look back at Ella. 'We'll talk more later?'

She doesn't answer. She throws me one last filthy look and then I watch her retreating back and hear her feet hammering on the stairs as she goes up to her room.

I take the phone from Daisy's outstretched hand. 'Hello?' I say.

'Your daughter sounds nice.'

Hearing Orla's voice again makes my stomach tighten and all my earlier resolve evaporates quicker than drops of water on a hot griddle.

'Grace?'

I hang up and, taking the phone with me, walk through the kitchen and down the three steps into the utility room. Within seconds it's ringing again. I don't answer. I turn the ringer off and watch the display flash like a beating pulse and then stop. I stand with my arms folded and wait. Within seconds the display is flashing again until the call times out. The cycle is repeated several times and it becomes obvious that she isn't going to stop. When the pulse starts up for the tenth time I answer it.

'What do you want?' I sound calm but my knees are wobbling and I'm sliding down the wall. I drag myself upright again.

'Your daughter sounds just like you did. Does she look like you?'

'What do you want, Orla?'

'To catch up,' she says lightly. 'What else?'

'I'd rather not,' I tell her. 'Please stop calling me.'

'Grace, don't be like that.' There's bewilderment in her voice. 'Why can't we spend some time together? Weren't we friends once?'

'Once,' I agree. 'Twenty-four years ago.'

'But we *were* friends. We connected. Good friends are hard to find, aren't they?'

'I have enough friends. I'm happy as I am.'

'I want us to meet up,' she says, more definite this time and I sense steel behind the apparent friendliness.

'Well, I don't,' I say firmly. 'And I don't want you ringing me again.'

'I don't understand.' She breathes in and then out, loudly, the out breath ending on a sigh. I wait and, finally, she says, 'We have history together? Don't we?'

'Ancient history. Long' – I'm about to say dead and buried but think better of it – 'ago,' I finish.

'Just once. Meet me just the once. For old times' sake.'

'What old times would they be exactly?'

'Are you saying that we didn't have any fun together? Does our whole relationship have to be coloured by what happened at the end?'

I think about Rose. How much she trusted me. I feel the familiar sadness ripen inside me like a bruised, inedible fruit. 'Yes, I think it does.'

'Grace, I've changed.' Her voice drops to a whisper. 'I have. Truly, I have. I can't explain it all to you over the phone. It sounds dumb and I don't think you'll even believe me.' She laughs and the sound grates in my ear.

I move the phone away from my head and hold it at a shaky arm's length so that her excited voice is muffled.

'I know how this must seem, me getting in touch after all this time but please, just listen. I'm back visiting my mum. She's living in Edinburgh now. In Merchiston. My dad, you know, he passed away a few years back.'

I bring the phone up to my ear again. 'I'm sorry.' I

mean it. 'I liked him. He was always very kind to me. And your mum.' I think for a moment. 'I liked her too.'

'I know. It was sad. Dad was very sick and was in a lot of pain but towards the end he was peaceful and, well . . . I guess we all have to let go eventually.'

'You sound American.'

'Do I?'

'Your intonation. Some of the words.'

'Canadian. I lived there a while.'

'How is your mum?'

'She's good. She remarried. Is happy with her new husband. Murray Cooper. He's what you would call a good bloke.'

I strain to catch an edge of bitterness in her voice but there's none that I can hear. Perhaps she has changed? I shake off the thought and think about what Euan said: *Find out what she wants.* 'Why do you want to meet me?'

'It's a long story. And better told face to face.'

'Why would your story have anything to do with me?' I try to keep my voice light but my jaw is trembling and my mouth is dry, each word seeming to stick to the insides of my cheeks.

'Relax, Grace. It's not what you think,' she says darkly, her tone edged with mirth. 'How about I drive up tomorrow?'

'No,' I say quickly. 'I'll come to you. And not tomorrow. Thursday is better.'

'In Edinburgh?'

'Yes. I need to shop for supplies: brushes, acrylics, that sort of thing.'

'You're still painting?'

'Where shall we meet?'

'There's a small restaurant, on the left-hand side, halfway up Cockburn Street. One o'clock?'

'Fine.'

'I look forward to that.' I can hear her smile. 'See you then.'

As the line goes dead, so do my legs and I crumple down on to the floor. I sit in a heap for five minutes or more, trying to work out how scared I should be. On the one hand she sounded friendly and interested, on the other, pushy and determined. Perhaps she does just want to be friends but it seems unlikely. Orla always had her own agenda, and as Euan reminded me, she wasn't one to give up before she got what she wanted. Thinking back, it doesn't take long for me to come to the conclusion that even if she is only half as reckless and manipulative as she used to be then I should be afraid. I have to tread carefully. I can't let her back into my life. She is a living, breathing reminder of what happened all those years ago and I don't want her near Paul and the girls – not least because of what she knows about me.

June 1978–1982

Orla's mother is French. She wears neat black suits with fitted skirts that fall just below her knee and short, boxy jackets with square pockets and large buttons. She wears patterned silk scarves that she wraps three times around her neck and tucks into her collar. She wears stockings not tights and slides her feet into shoes with three-inch heels. Her lipstick is red and she keeps it in the fridge. Her perfume is both earthy and exotic and it draws me to her. She sings mournful songs as she does the washing-up. She smokes cigarettes, openly, defiantly, dropping her head back to make smoke rings curl up to the ceiling. She calls me '*mon petit chou*' and strokes my hair as if I am a cat, long luxurious strokes that make me smile up into her face. She kisses me on both cheeks whenever I come to visit. She has flashes of anger, stamps her foot, says '*merde*'. Then, in the next second, she will laugh like the world is once more a happy place. When Orla's father comes home from work she kisses him on the mouth and strokes her hand down the front of his trousers just as she strokes my hair.

'She's a right selfish madam,' my mother says.

'A fish out of water,' Euan's mother says.

'God knows what Roger sees in her,' my father says. 'She's as flirty as a flea in a bottle.'

I think she's wonderful. When I'm ten I ask her if she always wanted to live in Scotland. She throws back her head and laughs like this is the funniest thing she's ever heard. Then she looks at me mysteriously. 'Be careful whom you fall in love with, Grace,' she says. 'There are so many ways to live a life.'

I am allowed to call her by her first name. 'On-je-line,' I say, sounding out each syllable.

She claps. 'Such a perfect accent,' she says.

To Angeline, I am clever, I am pretty and I am the best friend her daughter could ever have.

Orla is allowed to drink wine. It's mixed with water – half and half – but she has it in a proper wine glass, sits with her parents around the table and is listened to as if she were an adult.

Both Orla and I are only children but whereas I am often kept at home or weighed down with 'too dangerous', 'be careful', 'mind you don't fall', 'you'll catch your death out there', Orla is allowed to swim in the sea in winter, dance in puddles, camp outside under the night sky.

When I'm ten I see Angeline in the back garden, topless. 'In this country,' she says, 'when the sun comes out you should always take advantage of it.'

I stare at her. Her skin is the colour of caramel and gleams with oil that smells strongly of coconut. She leans forward to kiss me on the cheeks and her nipples brush my arm.

And she is a Catholic. She wears a black lace mantilla over her head. She reminds me of Scarlett O'Hara in *Gone with the Wind* and when her dark eyes flash my way I feel blessed. Sometimes my mum allows me to go to church with her and I watch her pray like her life depends upon it. She prays in French, murmuring the words in a fast, breathy monotone, her fingers rubbing each pearl in her rosary beads as she moves along the chain and all the way back to the beginning. She lights a candle in front of a statue of the Virgin Mary and crosses herself. Then she turns to me and takes my hand. 'Ice cream?' she says and I nod, smiling up into her eyes.

At home we eat plain food. 'Get that down you,' my mother says, passing me a steaming plate of stovies. 'It'll bring the colour to your cheeks.'

Angeline wrinkles up her nose at the mention of corned beef and cabbage or mince and tatties. She says haggis is hardly fit for dogs. She travels to Edinburgh once a week to buy courgettes, aubergines and peppers, olive oil and anchovies. Sometimes they eat in front of the television. Dried fruits, apricots and figs dipped into Camembert melted in its box.

Orla spends a lot of time ignoring her mother. 'I'm more of a daddy's girl,' she says. By the time we're both teenagers, they have out-and-out screaming matches. Orla swears and shouts in rapid, hectic French. She throws cups and glasses until her mother grabs her wrists and shakes her. It's at times like this that Orla turns up at my house, unannounced, just barges in like she lives here. It doesn't matter what I'm doing: having tea, soaking in the bath, asleep even, she just comes straight in and has hysterics. My mother calms her down, mops her tears, listens to her complaints and feeds her home-baked biscuits and cakes. Then my dad drives her home. If it was me, I'd be told to stop the nonsense, but Orla gets away with it. 'She's highly strung,' my mother pronounces. 'It'll be the French blood in her.'

When I'm fourteen, I'm on a trip to Edinburgh with my grandmother. Gran is in the toilet in Jenners department store and I am waiting for her. I walk a few yards into the lingerie department and run my fingers through a rack of silk nightdresses with elaborate lace around the bodice and sleeves.

I see Angeline. My heart lifts and as I open my mouth to shout hello, a man walks towards her. It's Monica's father. I wonder why he's there. I watch him as he wraps his arms around her from behind and she leans back into him so that he can kiss her neck. She whispers up into his ear and his arms tighten around her waist.

She sees me and one of her eyebrows arches just a little. She places a finger vertically over her lips and leaves it there until I raise my own to mimic her. Then she smiles and blows me a kiss.

I don't know what to think.

3

There is no one in the graveyard but me. Windswept trees afford some shelter from the briny air that evaporates up from the sea but still many of the headstones have fallen over and others are faded or covered in moss, succumbing to weather and neglect. But not this one. This one is upright, gold lettering legible on a background of pink marble.

Rose Adams
1975–1984
Safe in God's hands

The grave in front is well tended. I have brought some delicate yellow roses, twelve of them, wrapped in a cream silk ribbon. I put them in the vase and pull a few small weeds from the ground. Then I kneel down, clasp my hands together and close my eyes. Guilt, regret, sorrow and remorse: over the last twenty-four years I have known them all but now, with Orla's phone call yesterday, I am mostly afraid. Afraid of being found out. I try to come up with a prayer but God and I have never been close and I don't feel I have any right to call on Him now. Instead, I speak directly to Rose. *Please, Rose. Please. I have done my best. Please.* It's not much but it's all I can think of to say to her.

Orla's voice is still in my ears and I find myself going over and over what she said. And the more I think about it, the more I realise that she was leading me in the direction she wanted, keeping me talking until I agreed to meet her. I am disappointed with myself for falling in with her plans but at the same time I am not sure what else I could have done. She wasn't about to give up. If I hadn't answered her yesterday then she would have called back today and tomorrow and the day after that until I spoke to her. All I can do is listen to what she has to say and hope that she will leave again without causing any damage. One thing is for sure: I don't want her to meet Paul and the girls. I have a life, a good life, and there is no place for Orla in it.

On the way back to my car, I pause in front of Euan's mother's gravestone.

Maureen Elizabeth Macintosh
1927–1999
beloved wife, mother and friend

It strikes me, as it always does, that the dash in between both dates says nothing about the life that was led. Mo was the original earth mother, universally loved and as much involved in my upbringing as my own parents were.

She gave birth to six children of her own: four boys and two girls. My own parents, on the other hand, tried for a baby for almost twenty years and when their marriage approached the end of its second decade with still no sign of the longed-for baby, they quietly gave up. Each month had become a time of mourning, a curse, and they couldn't live that way, my mother said, so they let go of their dreams and immersed themselves in work – my mother in the university library, my father as a carpenter with the local firm of builders.

Mo and her husband Angus lived next door and their children, a healthy, happy brood, spilled over the fence and into my parents' lives. A balm of sorts, perhaps. My mother would bake cakes with the girls while my father taught the boys how to work with wood, how to measure and use the electric saw, how to join and sand, how to make bird boxes, wooden spoons, letter racks and shelves.

So it was in the giving up that somehow I came into being and I was born on my parents' twenty-first wedding anniversary. But what with all the waiting and the hoping and the praying and then the letting go, my mother found that the reality of a child was often more than she could take. So when I refused my dinner again or ran away from the potty only to wet myself, Mo scooped me up and took me next door where I was absorbed into the crowd. I was propped up in the pram alongside Euan, her youngest and just three months older than me, or in the playpen in the kitchen where she talked to us while she chopped vegetables or prepared a chicken.

When I started nursery school my mother went back to work. Every day I escaped the intensity of parental interest that shadows the only child and walked home with Mo and Euan to spend the afternoon with them and any other stragglers who needed a place to go. Often I stayed for tea, Euan and I bolstered with cushions until we were tall enough to hold our chins above the level of the table.

I wish I'd brought two sets of flowers: one for Mo's grave too. Instead, I have to be happy with brushing spots of earth and stray leaves off the stone. She's been dead almost nine years but I can still remember her voice. *Some things we're not meant to know, Grace. Some things we're meant just to accept.*

I wonder at the things I accepted and the things that I didn't and I hope that wherever she is, she understands the choices I made.

I'm two minutes from my parents' house and I drop in on them on my way back from the church. My dad is up a ladder. He's closer to ninety than eighty but he won't slow down: *I'll be in my box soon enough and up till then I'll carry on as normal.*

I keep the ladder steady and shout up to him. 'Hello, up there!'

He looks down between the rungs. 'Oh, it's you, hen. Shouldn't you be working?'

'I've been out taking photographs.'

'Nice work if you can get it. What brings you here then?' He climbs down, putting one careful foot after the other.

'Of course, it's the birthday cakes. For the party.' He cuddles me tight. 'Your mother has been fretting over the icing for days. Should she make it pink for Daisy and Ella or just for Ella?'

'Ella.'

'That's what I said.'

I follow him over to the bench where he throws himself down, landing heavily on his backside, his feet flying up in the air.

'Look at that view.' His breathing is hoarse and he pulls a handkerchief from his pocket and coughs into it. 'No amount of money can buy a view like that.'

My dad has the bench positioned on the crest of the hill with an uninterrupted view of the sloping land and the water beyond it. The air is crisp and clear and, out at sea, an oil tanker tips over the horizon. The wind whips the waves into frothy white peaks that wash the rocky shoreline clean while up above gulls caw, flock and hover on the wind then dive into the water for fish.

I breathe in deeply and smile. 'I love it here,' I say, then notice that a small red stain is spreading across his handkerchief. 'Is there blood on that hankie, Dad?'

'What's that?' He pushes the evidence deep into his trouser pocket. 'You're as bad as your mother. Looking for problems where there aren't any.'

'Dad?'

'What?' His face contrives innocence but behind it his eyes flicker with anxiety.

I want to hug him to me but I don't. I am on the edge

of my own tears, ready to blurt out my own problems. 'Shall I get us a cup of tea?' I say.

'She won't want you interrupting her.' He gives a derisory hiccup. 'I tried to steal myself a cup a minute ago but was given short shrift.'

I lay a hand on his shoulder then go into the house. My folks have dozens of photos in the hallway: Euan and I sit end to end in a Silver Cross pram dribbling ice cream on ourselves; me and my dad holding up a shelf I'd just made; my parents' wedding photo, an impossibly young couple standing in front of the church, shyly holding hands.

And at the end of the row there's a photo of Orla and me. We are just thirteen and are standing together in front of a high wooden fence. Our inside arms are wrapped around each other's back, our riding boots and jodhpurs splashed with mud. We are grinning like mad. I remember the day well. We were both competing in the village pony trials and managed to come home with four rosettes and two cups between us.

I bend down and scrutinise the photo. There is no mistaking that we are the best of friends, tired legs and arms are slumped against each other and my forehead is resting on her shoulder. I caught up later on, but at that point she was almost six inches taller than me. And looking at her face, the black curly hair, dark eyes and open smile, I feel something unexpected. I feel happy. Tomorrow, for the first time in twenty-four years, we will lay eyes on each other. With a few chosen remarks to the right people she could blow my world apart and yet there is a small corner of me that is looking forward to meeting her.

I stand up and lean against the wall, shocked, and remind myself that there is no room for sentiment. I have to keep my wits about me and deflect Orla away from me before she pushes her way back into my life. I can't afford to make a mistake with this.

I take the photograph off the wall and go into the kitchen where my mother is spreading pink icing over the surface of a twelve-inch cake. As I open the door, she looks up, startled. Her face is flushed a raspberry hue and she's breathing hard as if she's just been running.

'Oh, it's you, Grace,' she says, moving around the table to greet me. 'What on earth are you doing here?' She gives me a perfunctory hug then steps back and looks at me, exasperated. 'If you've come for the cakes then I haven't finished them yet.'

'I know they won't be ready until Saturday.' I kiss her warm cheek. 'I'm not here to rush you.' I show her the photo. 'Do you mind if I borrow this?'

'Of course not.' She waves the palette knife. 'Keep it.'

'Thank you.' I slip it into my handbag, not really sure why I want it.

'Wonder how Orla's doing now,' she says casually.

I shrug. 'No idea. She just upped and disappeared.'

'She did write to you, Grace.' She gives me a sharp look. 'You were the one who let it slide.'

There's no arguing with that. I lift a couple of mugs off the hooks. 'I've just been chatting to Dad. I came in to get us a cup of tea. Why don't you stop for a minute and join us?'

'No, no, no! I'm busy with the finishing touches.' She examines the smoothness of the icing from several angles. 'You go and talk to him. He has some ridiculous notion about painting the house. I have the cakes to do and lunch will be ready soon. You're staying, I take it?'

I hesitate. 'Only if it's convenient.'

She frowns at me. 'Since when have I given my own daughter the impression that her visits are inconvenient?'

'I didn't mean it like that, Mum.' I put teabags in the mugs. 'Of course, I'd love to stay for lunch. I know it's a lot with the cakes, that's all.'

'I've been making the girls' cakes since they had their first birthday.' She reaches over and takes the teabag out of my father's mug. 'Not *those* teabags, Grace! Give him some peppermint. He's been having trouble with his stomach.'

'What sort of trouble?' I try to sound casual, add the boiling water to the mugs and look her full in the face. 'Mum, is Dad not well?'

'Oh, you know your father.' She breezes past me and takes another knife from the drawer. 'Always in denial.'

I wonder whether to mention the blood on the hankie but she's left the kitchen and is inside the pantry, humming purposefully. I take the tea outside and sit down on the bench beside my dad. 'I hear your stomach's giving you gyp?'

'Who, me?' He looks behind him as if there might be

someone else around. 'Fighting fit and raring to go, I am. It's just an excuse for your mother to get me started on a health kick.' He takes a sip of the tea and screws up his face. 'So how are my granddaughters?'

'Why not have the doctor check you over, Dad? One of those well man clinics, you know?'

'I know I'm getting old, toots. That much I know. No point in digging around. It'll only stir it all up. Look at Angus. Never a day's worry until the hospital got their hands on him. And Mo.' He gives a weary shake of his head. 'She was the same.'

'Please?' I take hold of his hand and bring it on to my lap. 'Please, Dad. For me.'

'Well . . . I don't know, lass.' His face moves through reluctance and irritation, eyebrows meeting in a frown and then rising again as he settles on maybe. 'You were always one for getting your own way.'

'I'll take that as a yes, then,' I tell him, smiling.

'So how are the girls? Keeping you busy?'

'The girls are great.' I nod, remembering that since I confronted her yesterday, Ella is acting like I don't exist. I have yet to resume the conversation about 'boys' and I know that when I do it will be an uphill struggle. 'Ella has the lead part in *Romeo and Juliet* so that will be one for your diary.'

'I'll look forward to that.'

A car draws up next door and a young couple climbs out. We all wave. They walk up the path and my dad pulls his chest up and sighs. 'It's never been the same since Mo and Angus passed on. Spring comes around again and the house changes hands.'

'I'll never get used to it either, Dad.' I rest my head on his shoulder and we watch the sea grab at the shore, then retreat and gather strength to try again. 'Time and tide wait for no man, huh?'

'Aye, it's a bugger.'

'I'm going to Edinburgh tomorrow. Is there anything you want while I'm there?'

'What would you want to be going all the way to Edinburgh for?' My father is deeply suspicious of all journeys. He can't imagine why anyone would need to travel beyond a ten-mile radius of St Andrews. 'Anyway, I thought you could get everything delivered over the Internet these days?'

'I like to browse the art shops and galleries. Gives me ideas.' I pause. In my head I say the words: *Remember Orla, Dad? She called me twice. She wants to meet me. I don't know why, but I do know that I'm scared. How much do you love me, Dad? How much?* I want to blurt it out and I almost do but just then my mum sets a tray down in front of us.

'Don't stand on ceremony, you two. Tuck in.'

My mother knows how to make a good sandwich, and when it's time for me to go, my stomach is full. As I drive off, I watch them in the rear-view mirror, their inside arms around each other, their free hands holding on to the gate.

It's already two o'clock by the time I round the path to work.

Euan is on the phone and watches me as I come in. 'Sure. No bother. We'll catch up next week.' He puts the phone back on to the cradle. 'Morning off?'

'I was taking photos. Then the churchyard. Had lunch with my mum and dad.' I drop my bag down on the floor. 'Is Tom well?'

'Yeah. He's fine now.' He pushes his chair away from his desk and the wheels spin on the hardwood floor. 'Back at school.'

I walk over and sit on the edge of his desk. 'She called again.'

His eyes widen and then focus on mine. 'Did you ask her what she wants?'

'She wouldn't say.' I sweep some crumbs off his desk and into the bin. 'She said she has to tell me face to face.'

'So how did you leave it?'

'I'm meeting her in Edinburgh tomorrow.'

He looks down at the floor, thinking.

'She also said it wasn't what I thought.'

He looks back at me. 'She'd say that to get you to go.'

That thought has been at the back of my mind all morning and my heart sinks to hear Euan say it out loud. 'But there's really nothing else I can do, is there? I have to go. And when she finds out who I married . . .' I try to laugh. 'She wouldn't say anything then, would she?'

He stands up in front of me, hands in pockets and moves his shoulders forward and then back again. 'I wouldn't put it past her.'

His chest is level with my eyes and I resist the impulse

to rest my head against it and cry with fear and frustration. 'You really don't have much of an opinion of her, do you?'

'She's trouble, Grace. She always was.' He lays a hand on my arm. 'Do you want me to come with you?'

'No.' The palm of his hand feels warm, his fingers firm around my upper arm. Safe. I shrug him off and move away, put the desk between us. 'I'll be fine. I'll manage.'

'I might be better at talking her round than you.'

'I doubt it, Euan. She never liked you. I think I can do it.' I take a purposeful breath. 'I know I can do it.' I go over to my own desk and sit down. There's a stack of photographs for me to look through. They are views from Margie Campbell's home in Iona: my next commission and one I was looking forward to. I love painting the sea in all its colours and moods and she has given me free rein to interpret the photographs however I want. The canvas is primed and I hoped to start today but I already know that I won't be able to concentrate. Orla's intentions loom large in my head. I just want to know what I'm up against and can't wait for tomorrow to be over so that I can get back to my life.

June 1976

Euan and I are playing in our den at the edge of the forest. He's just joined the Scouts and now he always carries a penknife and string in his pocket. He's been practising his knots and I have both my wrists tied together and then the string is looped around the trunk of the tree. 'I'm going to go back home and get us something to eat,' he says, running off. 'Wait for me.'

I wait for him. There's not much else I can do, tied up as I am, so I rest my head against the bark and watch ants crawl up and over my hands. I drift off into the gap between sleep and wakefulness and the next thing I hear is the sound of my mother's voice.

'What in God's name?'

I jump guiltily. 'Euan's coming back in a minute.'

My mother wrestles with the knot. 'What sort of a game is this, Grace? Look at the state of you!' My skirt has ridden up almost to my waist and she yanks it down. 'And those are your new sandals!' When the knot comes loose, I try to wipe the dirt off them but my mother shakes me roughly and gripping on to my arm marches me back up the road.

Mo answers the doorbell, wiping her hands on her apron. The smile dies on her face as my mother speaks. 'I have just found Grace.' She jerks me forward. 'Tied to a tree down at the far end of the field. By herself. Her skirt practically up around her neck. *Anyone* could have found her. *Anything* could have happened to her.'

Euan appears at Mo's side. 'I was going back.' He holds up a bag of sandwiches, some home-made gingerbread and two bottles of lemonade. 'I've got the supplies.'

'Next time, Euan, bring Grace back with you,' Mo says, stroking his sticky-up hair flat.

'But I was guarding our den,' I say.

'Yeah.' Euan is frowning at both our mothers. He drops the food on to the ground and pulls the ends of his fingers until his knuckles crack. 'We weren't doing anything wrong.'

'He had her tied to a tree, Mo.' My mother is shouting now and Mo takes a step backwards. '*Tied* to a *tree.*'

'Now, Lillian, a wee bit of freedom doesn't do them any—'

'*You* have the cheek to tell *me* how to raise a child? With Claire hanging out with the local boys and George drunk of an evening – and Euan! What of Euan? Never out of trouble!'

Mo's face turns whiter than her freshly laundered sheets that buffet and bounce on the line.

My mother looks down at me. 'You're not to play with Euan any more.' She looks back at Mo. 'I'll be making other arrangements for after school.'

My mother turns and I am half walked, half dragged down the path. I look back and see Euan still cracking his fingers and then he punches the doorframe and Mo urges him to come inside.

At school the next day, he won't speak to me. 'I'm a bad influence on you.' He kicks dirt up on to his trousers. 'Mum says I have to give you a wide berth.'

I am mortified and I try to explain that I'll win my mother round. He's not interested. I feel angry and then unbearably sad, my chest aching as if I've been punched. I don't join in with the skipping. I scuff my new sandals along the ground and watch Euan play football with the other boys.

I spend the next month going to Faye's after school. She won't play outside or climb trees. She says the sea's too cold to paddle in. She doesn't have dogs or chickens or Effie the goat and her sister is always correcting me. 'It's not shined it's shone . . . Don't put your elbows on the table . . . It's please *may* I, not *can* I!'

We have tea at five but I won't eat so I spend evening after evening with a full plate in front of me. After a couple of weeks of this, I grow tired and listless and my mother has to do the thing she hates most – take time off work – because I can't go to school.

I move three peas on top of a pile of potato and pat it down with my fork. 'I hate Faye and I hate her sister,' I say. 'I'm not going there any more.'

'How about the new girl, Orla?' my mother asks, in her too bright voice.

I shake my head. 'I don't know her yet.'

'How about Monica? She's a lovely, clever girl.'

I scream so loudly that my father comes through from the living room. 'What's going on in here?'

My mother is scouring the pots. She doesn't turn around, just carries on scrubbing. 'She's acting up again.'

'Then perhaps we should listen,' my father says to my mother's stiff back. 'What sense is there in all this misery?'

'Misery? Who's causing the misery?' She bangs the pressure cooker down on to the draining board. 'Always wanting her own way.'

'Lillian!' my father bellows and I force a forkful of food

into my mouth. It catches in my throat and makes a lump as if I've just swallowed a gobstopper. 'She's eight years old. She's making herself ill. Now climb down from that high horse of yours and go next door to Mo.'

'I will not!' my mother shouts back, turning round at last, her mouth twisted, her eyes wide open and fierce. 'I will not, Mungo! She will *not* run this house with her tantrums and her temper.'

Before my father has a chance to shout back, I bolt from the table and up the stairs, spit the potato into the toilet and sit with my hands over my ears until I can no longer hear the muffled sound of their voices.

Minutes later, the kitchen door bangs shut. I run to the back window and watch my mother walk down the path and into Mo's garden. I can only hear snatches of words . . . *wilful . . . wearing me out . . . was wrong.* Halfway through my mother puts her hands over her face. Mo reaches out and hugs her like she does with children. She gives her a handkerchief and my mother blows her nose then comes back to the house. I hold my breath. She comes into my room. She doesn't speak, just looks at me. I clutch her around the waist, tight as I can, then run down the stairs. My father glances up from his paper and I catch his smile as I whizz past him. I run through the gate and into Mo's arms.

She laughs and pushes me away from her. 'You'll be knocking me over next.'

I jump up and down. 'Where's Euan?'

'Down by the cove. And don't forget your bucket!' she calls after me.

Still running, I lift the pail and shout back, 'I love you, Mo,' then head off down the beach. The wind whips at my dress, my hair. I run barefoot, making squidgy footprints on the sand, my arms aeroplaning either side of me.

I see him along the shore bending to look at something in a rock pool. I call out to him but the wind lifts my voice up and away. When I reach him I can barely speak I'm so excited and I jump up and down and turn around on one leg. 'Euan! Euan! Guess what? We can play again! My mum gave in. I went on hunger strike like they do in Ireland and my mum gave in!'

He squints up at me. His face has sand stuck all over it in little clumps. 'Who says I want to play with you any more?'

I stop, deflated, feel tears sting at the back of my eyes. 'But you do,' I say. 'Because we're best friends.'

'Aye, maybe. But no more crying and no more showing your knickers.' He grins at me. 'Unless you want me to pull them down.'

'That's rude!' I push him and he pushes me back. I fall over and he sits on top of me, holding my arms. Seawater laps at my feet and I try to dig my heels in but they slide away from me.

'Do you submit?'

'Never!' I struggle and push as hard as I can but he holds my wrists into the sand and ignores my knees kicking into his back.

'Do you submit?'

His weight is pressing down on to my stomach. 'All right, all right! I submit!' I grumble. 'This time. Only this time, mind.'

He climbs off and lies beside me, lining up his head with mine. We stay together, catching our breath, squinting up at the clouds.

'Those big round ones that look like cauliflowers' – he points up and to the left – 'are called cumulus and those ones over there, see, really high up, are called cirrus and they're made at thirty thousand feet from ice needles.'

'Who told you that?' I ask him.

'Monica.'

'Monica!' I turn to face him and giggle. 'You played with Monica?'

He shrugs. 'She kept on following me around. She knows a lot of stuff. She even knows about fishing.'

I pinch him hard on the arm.

'Ow!'

I jump up and start to run.

'I'll catch you,' he shouts. 'I will.'

4

I take the late morning train through to Edinburgh. I try to read a magazine and flick through articles jauntily titled, 'My Husband Left Me for Another Man' and 'Babies Who Never Learn to Breathe' before settling for a piece on foods with a low glycaemic index. After a couple of minutes, I throw the magazine aside. I can't concentrate. I'm impatient to get there and get it over with.

I pace up and down the aisle. The carriage is empty apart from one teenager who is attached to an iPod and spends the entire journey texting on her phone. As the train crosses the railway bridge over the Firth of Forth, I stop and look out of the window. The water is a gunmetal grey. A container ship has just passed underneath the bridge and I start to count the multicoloured boxes on board, stacked high like building blocks. It reminds me of the game I played as a child; the one that was meant to break up the monotony of a long journey. Count the number plates beginning with V or the number of caravans driving north. Count the red cars, the hatchbacks and the cows that are lying down. Count the number of times I have thought of Rose since she died. Thousands. Tens of thousands. Too many to count.

The train arrives and I alight first. Waverley Station is buzzing with people and the hum echoes up into the steel rafters high above my head. I have five minutes to spare and I go into the bookshop to choose a book for Paul's birthday which falls just two weeks after the girls'. I know the one to buy. It's an autobiography by a famous musician, an entertaining and revelatory account of his life. I pay for the book and walk out into the wind, stopping for a minute to fasten my jacket and look up at Edinburgh Castle. Built on a plug of volcanic rock, it watches over the city and the Firth of Forth beyond. Sometimes sunlit and benevolent, today it is brooding. Gloomy grey clouds cloak the ramparts, casting long shadows on to the jagged rocks below.

I dodge a throng of tourists heading towards Princes Street Gardens and make a slow climb up Cockburn Street. My stomach grumbles and grinds, as if eating itself, but behind the anxiety I feel curious. I want to see her. I want to know what she's been doing with herself for the last twenty-four years. And most of all, I want to know why she got in touch.

I'm about ten feet away when I spot her, just inside the doorway. I'm surprised by how she looks. She isn't wearing any make-up and her black curly hair is pulled back in a plain band highlighting the grey that spreads at her temples and forehead. Her clothes are simple – a pair of jeans, a white T-shirt, a navy blue cardigan and flat lace-up shoes. Up in the castle, the one o'clock gun goes off and it startles me so that I automatically step towards her and she sees me, calls my name, rushes forward and kisses me on both cheeks. She smells of lavender.

'You look wonderful,' she tells me, standing back and holding on to my elbows.

We are the same height and our eyes are level; hers are deep brown, almost black, like cocoa-rich chocolate.

'You haven't aged a bit.' She laughs, looks me up and down and shakes her head. 'Adult life suits you, Grace. Come!' She gestures behind her and starts to walk backwards, almost tripping over a chair leg. 'I've bagged us a table in the corner here.'

We sit down. I feel happy, sad, nervous, but most of all I feel awkward. She looks so much like herself and yet the spark is missing. Even at fifteen she was glamorous, mischievous, sexy. Boys trailed behind her, bug-eyed and tongue-tied, and she would flash them smiles so sultry, so promising, that they would melt into puddles of hormones.

She takes a breath, holds on to it as she looks at me, then lets it out slowly. 'It's so good to see you! I've thought of you such a lot over the years.' Her eyes grow wistful and then warm again. 'Do you have any family photos with you?'

I haven't spoken yet and now all I can do is shake my head. I don't know how to articulate my way past the strangeness.

'Well, never mind. Hopefully, I'll be able to come up and meet them in person sometime soon.' She gives me a playful smile. 'Let's play catch-up. Last twenty-odd years.' She leans her elbows on the table and her chin on her hands. 'Start wherever you want.'

Her stare is piercing and I pick up the menu to occupy my eyes while I think of a reply but before I have a chance to read it, she snatches it from me and says, 'I've ordered for us. I hope you don't mind.'

I do mind. It's presumptuous of her. She has automatically assumed the right to make decisions for me, just as she did when we were children. It ignites an irritation in me. It's a small flame but hot enough to power me past my silence and into speech. 'You ordered for both of us?'

'I didn't want to waste any time. The food can take a while to come. You know how it is in these little places; they can't always afford enough staff.'

I sit back and look pointedly around the room. There are a dozen tables and three waitresses. I debate with myself whether to take a stand and insist on choosing my own lunch but decide not to. It will only delay matters and I want to get to the crux of the meeting as soon as possible.

'So how have you been?' I say.

'Good.' She gives me a Gallic shrug that reminds me of her mother. 'I've lived all over, kept myself busy. Nothing as meaningful as having babies. So tell me! I know you have at least one daughter. Any more children?'

'So you've spent the last twenty-four years on the move? That's a long time.' I swallow down some water. 'And a lot of travelling.'

'I guess so,' she acknowledges. 'Far East, Australia, Peru, Italy, Mumbai, all for three years or so and then time in Canada where I settled for twelve years.'

'And is there a man in your life?'

She rolls her eyes. 'Let's not go there. Me and long-term relationships – always a disaster; until now, that is.' Her face softens and she smiles into her neck.

'Until now?' I'm interested. Maybe this is why she's come back. 'Are you in love?'

'I suppose.' She grows thoughtful. 'Yes, I am. But please! Now you! Tell me how you are.'

'I'm good. I'm fine.' I reach for some bread and tear it in half. 'Not much happens in my life. Same old, same old – you know how it is. Time moves slowly in the village.'

'I don't believe you for a minute!' She makes a petted lip. 'Come on! Tell me about your children. How many? What are their interests? How old are they?'

'I have two girls, identical twins but Daisy has short hair and Ella's is long. They have their dad's eyes, and smiles that are all their own. Daisy is good at science and likes to make things with her hands. Ella loves to act. She's more outgoing than Daisy.' I stop talking while the wait-ress places a salad in front of us: buffalo mozzarella, melon and watercress. 'They'll be sixteen on Saturday,' I finish.

'Sixteen? Wow!' She shakes out her napkin and places it on her lap. 'Are they having a party?'

'Yes. In the village hall. It's been repainted since you left but otherwise it's no different. We've hired a DJ, ordered lots of food and drink.' I shrug. 'All the kids do it now. It's just a round of parties from one weekend to the next.'

'Do you remember my sixteenth?'

I nod. 'I was thinking about it yesterday. First the fight

with your mother and then all that business with Monica. I'm hoping we get away with a bit less drama.'

'I never did forgive my mother.'

'What, even now?'

'She always had to be the centre of everything.' She wrinkles her nose. 'But, yeah, sure. It's all water under the bridge.' She finishes her salad and pushes the plate away. 'So, two girls? Almost grown-up.'

'Well, Ella would like to think so.'

'Is she difficult?'

'Not exactly but she knows her own mind.'

'Like her mother then.'

'I was never difficult.' I give her an appraising look. 'I would have had to work hard to catch up with you.'

'I did have my moments, didn't I?' she concedes. 'Thank God we don't stay fifteen for ever.' The waitress clears our plates and Orla reaches down into her bag and brings out her mobile phone. 'I need to make a quick call,' she says and steps outside the restaurant.

It's a good opportunity to watch her and I do. She is relaxed and smiling as she talks into the receiver. She looks completely harmless. There's not a hint of the conniving or spite that she used to be capable of and I'm beginning to wonder what I was nervous about. She's not the dangerous, impulsive Orla that she once was. She's a calmer, more civilised version, I think.

She comes back to her seat. 'So what about the old gang? Monica, Euan, Callum, Faye.' She reels them off. 'What happened to them?'

The restaurant is in full lunchtime swing. The waitresses weave between the tables, plates held high above their heads. Our main course is red mullet with spring vegetables and I take my first mouthful before answering. 'Tastes good,' I say, pointing with my fork.

'My mother comes here. You know how fussy she was . . . and is.'

'Is she well?'

'Yes, very. In her element, actually. New husband, lots of money, busy social scene.' She shakes her head. 'Sometimes I wonder why my father put up with her for all those years. She was the reason we left the village, you know.'

'No, I didn't.' At the back of my mind I had always thought it was because of Rose, because Orla and I could never have lived together in the same village, looking each other in the eye day in and day out, after what we'd done.

'Did you think it was because of Rose?'

I nod. She was always in the habit of second-guessing me.

'It wasn't.' She looks beyond me. Her eyes are still her most stunning feature. A cocoa and caramel blend. 'Anyway, tell me about the gang.'

'Faye left the village . . .' I think. 'It must be twenty years ago now. She lives on the Isle of Bute. She married a sheep farmer. Has four bairns last I heard. Callum runs his dad's business now. Employs half a dozen people on the boat and in the fish shop. Hasn't changed. Talks non-stop and is still into football. His son Jamie is Ella's boyfriend. Euan is an architect and Monica is a GP.'

'So Euan's still in the village?'

'Mmm.'

'You didn't marry him, did you?' Her eyes widen. 'Tell me you did!'

'No!' I look at her as if she's mad. I knew this was coming. 'God! That would have been like marrying my brother.'

'Grace, you don't have a brother and the looks you used to give each other had nothing to do with sibling love.'

'Really, Orla.' I fake a bored expression. 'That was a hundred years ago.'

'So is he married? Do you still see him?'

'He married Monica.' I say it casually, let it slide off my tongue like cream off the back of a warm spoon.

'What, Euan and Monica?' She sits back in her chair and frowns at me. 'I don't believe you!'

'Mmm.' I swirl some mineral water around in my mouth. 'They have a couple of kids, boy and girl. Monica works in the practice in—'

'Wait! Wait!' she interrupts me. 'Euan and Monica? *Are married?* That just doesn't make sense!'

'Love doesn't always, does it?'

'Euan didn't even *like* Monica.'

'How do you know?'

'It was obvious!'

'Well, sometimes that's the way it is, isn't it? You think you don't like someone, in fact you positively dislike them and then wham!' I bang my hands together. 'Cupid's arrow strikes and you're lost.'

'How did you feel?'

'Me? I was happy for him!'

'You didn't feel jealous? You were inseparable!'

'No, we weren't. You and me.' I point to her, then back to myself. 'We were inseparable.'

'Euan loved you,' she says quietly. 'Even at sixteen I could see that.'

I laugh. This is harder than I thought. 'As I said. We were like brother and sister. Still are.'

'So who did you marry?'

'Paul. He works at the university. He lectures in marine biology.'

'Would I know him?'

Our desserts have arrived and I swallow a spoonful of pavlova, sweet meringue breaking into the sharp taste of the raspberries. It occurs to me not to tell her my husband's surname, to fudge it or even make something up but my marriage is not a secret; she can easily find out for herself. And I'm hoping that Euan is wrong. If she intends to tell the truth about Rose's death, then this will surely stop her. 'I married Paul Adams.'

She stares at me. I watch as her jaw slackens and drops open. I don't look away. I am prepared for this. I have rehearsed it. I knew she would take issue with my choice of husband. She's not the first. Why do people think they know me better than I know myself?

I stare her down and at last she looks away, lifts her glass of water to her mouth. Her hand is shaking and she tries to steady it with the other one. 'I won't pretend I'm not surprised,' she says quietly.

'I'm sure.'

She lets out a breath. 'Paul Adams?'

I don't respond.

'Grace?'

'What?'

'The same Paul Adams?'

'Yes.'

'Rose's dad?'

'Yes.'

'I don't know what to say.' She sits back and pulls at her hair. 'I just don't know what to say.'

'You think he's a poor choice. Why? Because of what happened to Rose? We fell in love. We got married. We have the girls. I love him – still. That's it.' I fold my napkin into a tidy square on my lap. 'Now drop it, please.'

'You're happy?'

'Yes. I am.'

She smiles at me. 'Then I'm glad,' she says. 'I am, really. You deserve to be happy. We all do.'

I can't believe she means it. I wait for her to throw something else my way but it doesn't come. We finish our desserts and I sit back and rub my stomach. 'Good food.'

She gives me a watery smile.

'Are you staying with your mum?'

'No. At a convent in the Borders.'

'A convent? A Catholic convent? With *nuns*?'

'Yes.'

'Never!' I laugh.

'You're surprised?'

'Well . . . yes. I seem to remember your mother couldn't get you to church for love nor money. By age twelve, you were calling yourself an atheist, weren't you?'

'Mmm, I was. But I've changed. I'm joining the order as a novice. I want to become a nun.'

'Great . . . good.' I shrug. 'Whatever presses your buttons.' I smile like I mean it. I realise I do mean it. It seems completely out of character but I want to wish her well. 'Surprising but good.'

'More surprising than you marrying Paul Adams?'

'What?'

'You expect me to say nothing? You drop a bombshell like that and I'm supposed just to smile and congratulate you?' Her voice grows harsh. 'Paul Adams? What the fuck possessed you? *Rose's father? You married Rose's father?*'

I sit back in my seat and fold my arms. 'Interesting language for a would-be nun,' I say quietly. 'But then I have been wondering when the old Orla was going to make an appearance.'

'Well? I've found God, not so unusual for someone our age. While you . . . ?'

'You know very little about the grown-up me, Orla, as I know very little about you.' I feel tired suddenly. I push my hair back and force myself to sit up straight. 'So how about we just stop the pretending and you tell me exactly why you got in touch.'

'Okay.' She takes a breath, pushes her water glass to one side and leans elbows and forearms on the table.

'You're not going to like it but I want you to remember that I bear you no malice.'

'Just spit it out.'

'I need to put my wrongs to right. And I need to make peace with those people I hurt.'

Ice starts in my fingertips and freezes a path beneath my skin, travelling inwards until I shiver. 'What exactly are you saying?'

'I've made my confession to the priest. Now I need to confess to the people who were affected by my actions.' Her tone is light as candyfloss. 'What happened to Rose: it was cruel. What we did was wrong and then we compounded it by lying to ourselves and to the police.'

'You're telling *me*?' I don't know whether to laugh or cry. 'Since when are you entitled to take the moral high ground?'

'Don't be angry, Grace.' She tries to take my hand. I pull away. 'This is not about you and me. This is about doing what's right.'

'I have paid my dues, Orla. I have.' I keep my voice low. 'I may not have been honest with my family or the wider community but I have always been honest with myself.' I pause; choose my words carefully. 'I have made good any sin that I committed.'

'There is a penance to be paid.'

'I'm not a Catholic,' I remind her. 'And this isn't about religion for me. This is about doing the right thing.'

'Me too.' She lets her head drop to one side. 'I need to do the right thing. Surely you can see that?'

'And what would that entail, exactly?'

'Telling Paul.'

'Why? Why on earth would you do that?'

'To give him some closure.'

'At the expense of his marriage?' My voice is getting louder. I sense the women at the next table glancing across at me. 'His daughters' happiness?' I am horrified. 'We agreed to keep this a secret.' I bang my fist against my chest. 'Paul is my husband. We have two girls together. If you tell the truth about what happened that night, you will ruin all of our lives. Is that really what your priest advised? Is that truly what your God wants?'

'Put yourself in my shoes.' Her voice is silky smooth, her eyes black and shiny as hot tar. 'I need to join the convent with a clear conscience.'

I stand up and lift my handbag from the floor. 'I knew you hadn't changed. You almost had me fooled but I bloody knew you hadn't changed. You are your mother's daughter. Everything is always about you.' I rummage in my bag, find my purse, pull out thirty pounds and slap it down in the centre of the table. 'Go back to where you came from, Orla. Stay away from me and stay away from my family. I'm warning you.'

As I turn away she grabs hold of my wrist. 'Ten days. That's all you have. Either you tell Paul or I do. The choice is yours.'

I wrench her off me and, careless of the other lunchers, say loudly, 'You come near my family and I will have you, Orla.' I hold her eyes for several long seconds. Her look is fearless. 'I won't hesitate to hurt you. I mean it. *That* choice is yours.'

I leave the restaurant and hurry along the road back to the station. I realise that I've forgotten the book I bought for Paul but I can't go back for it. I know that I'm crying but I don't care. I board the first train back home and wonder what the hell I'm going to do now. Always, always, I knew. I knew that this would come back to haunt me. I drive home from the station, rigid, gripping the wheel.

By the time I pull into the driveway my head is so full of fear, remorse and what-ifs that I want to bang it against a wall and knock myself out. Instead I open a bottle of pinot grigio and watch it glug-glug into the glass. I stand leaning against the counter and drink one full glass down then pour myself another, and another. My life, my girls, my husband, my house, my dog, even my armchair all look like the best anyone could ever have and I know I'm going to lose all of it.

Ella comes into the kitchen. 'Where have you been?'

'Edinburgh.'

'Jesus! You might have said. You could have bought me those jeans I wanted.' She kicks the fridge closed with her foot and looks me up and down. 'What, drinking already? It's only four thirty.'

My head is starting to fuzz over. A blessed distance is opening up between myself and the words in my head. Sure, Orla is a bitch but I will find a way to shut her up. I will. Perhaps Euan will help me. I wasn't entirely truthful with Orla. After Rose died, we made a pact not to tell anyone, but I did. I told Euan. I told him a couple of days after I'd done it. I couldn't keep it to myself. As a secret, it was so much bigger than me.

My limbs feel heavy and loose and I roll my head around on my neck to ease the tension in my shoulder muscles.

'So?' Ella is watching me. 'What's with the drinking?'

Suddenly I feel like everything is within my control. 'Ella.' I smile. 'We still need to talk.'

'Well, *obviously* you've been in my room, so what is there to talk about?' She leans back against the counter and folds her arms across her chest. 'So you know I'm on the pill and you don't like it and you don't like Jamie. Big deal!' She sneers down into my face. 'This isn't the nineteenth century. Girls choose their own boyfriends. And by the way, it was Daisy who suggested I go on the pill. She's not as perfect as you think.'

'That's great. I'm glad you girls have been giving each other advice. Sisters should support each other, and you know what? You're right.' I wave the glass at her. 'Why should it matter what I think? You go right ahead! Do what you want, live your life any way you want to, see where that gets you.'

I pour my fourth glass of wine, toss the empty bottle into the bin and when I look back at her I see that disquiet is edging in at the corner of her eyes, forcing her to speak.

'What's the matter with you?'

'What's the matter with me?' I laugh. 'What's the matter with me? I know! I'm tired of your attitude. You want to be an adult? I'll treat you like one.' I turn my back to her and scrabble about in the back of the cutlery drawer until I find what I'm looking for.

'You *smoke*?' She is incredulous.

'What? You think you have a monopoly on that too?' I hold the packet out to her. 'You want one?'

'Mum!'

I light up the cigarette and inhale, holding my breath for several seconds before I blow smoke up towards the ceiling.

She starts to add up my symptoms on her fingers. 'You've been crying, you're smoking, knocking back the wine like there's no tomorrow?'

'No tomorrow?' I laugh. It sounds maniacal. 'Well, now you've hit the nail on the head!'

'Jesus, Mum, are you ill? Shall I call Dad?' A tear trickles down her right cheek and she pushes it into her hair.

I wave her away. The wine is lulling me, relieving me of inhibitions and it makes me want to confess. 'No, I'm fine. I'm not sick. It's just—' I stop. Articulating what I feel will involve the truth. And I can't do that. I look at my daughter and know that she must never find out. Never. 'Really, I'm fine. Just wallowing in a little self-pity.' I shrug. 'It happens.'

She hugs me hard and I feel her woman's body press against mine.

'All part of being an adult.' I make an apologetic face. 'Every so often you feel a failure or a bitch and wish you'd done something differently.'

'But you *never* do anything wrong, that's why you get

on my nerves!' she shouts. 'You're always patient with me even when you should be grounding me or telling Dad. You never lose it with Grandad even when he's confused as hell and you have to repeat things a hundred times and you're kind and you laugh and you can paint – you're like the best artist I know and you look good! You're a milf!'

'What's a milf?'

Her eyes widen. 'Oh, don't make me tell you!'

'Well, you'll have to now – and as we're both adults.'

'Mother I Would Like to Fuck.' She screws up her face. 'Jamie said it.' She starts to laugh. 'I'm sorry, Mum, but really it's a compliment.'

'Yes, I can see that.' Somehow I'm being allowed to stroke her hair. 'So will you come and visit me in prison?'

'Oh, Mum, stop it!' She pushes me away. 'Like you ever did anything wrong!'

15 June 1984

Lightning wakes up the sky and I count the seconds – one . . . two . . . three . . . four – until thunder cracks across the tents. It's raining so hard that the water stings my cheeks. I pick my way over exposed roots and fallen branches keeping my torch pointed down, just ahead of my feet, shining a path. It takes me only a couple of minutes but by the time I reach Orla my hair is plastered to my head and my boots are sopping wet. She is waiting for me close to the pond. The pond is out of bounds because it's less than a hundred yards from where the boys from the youth club are camping. Somewhere, just beyond the trees, Euan, Callum and several other boys from our year are in their tents, most likely getting drunk.

Orla is throwing stones into the water. I watch one skim along the surface half a dozen times before it sinks. 'This better be good,' I shout to her as I draw within earshot. 'Parky will have our guts for garters if she catches us out here at this time of night.'

'Live dangerously, Grace, why don't you?' she shouts back, lobbing another stone. 'What's the worst she can do? Throw us out of the Guides?' She turns and looks at me. 'Would either of us care?'

'I don't suppose so,' I admit.

Orla often accuses me of playing it safe; that, and caring about what other people think. I don't share her 'fuck-em' approach. I wish I did but I am burdened by expectations. I am the longed-for child, the apple of my parents' eye. I am Grace. I am polite. I am kind and considerate. I never make trouble at school. My grades are good. I always do the right thing.

It's close to midnight and as the clouds blow across the sky, the moon is revealed, full and bright as a silver coin. But still the rain pours down, filling the forest with watery sounds: dripping, gurgling, bubbling, swirling, hammering on the leaves until they bend with the weight and shed their load in a puddle on the ground. Water slides off my hair on to my cheeks and down on to my lips. It tastes cold and fresh. I tip my head back and drink it in, ignoring the wet that misses my mouth and runs down my neck inside my clothes. Soon I'll be freezing.

'So what, Orla? What?' I shout to her. 'What did you want to tell me?'

She comes right up beside me and whispers loudly into my ear. 'It's about Euan.'

'What about Euan?'

'I tried him out for you.'

I frown, confused. 'What do you mean?'

'I tried him out for you. He could be a better kisser but otherwise . . .' She stops talking, looks upward as if contemplating the universe and all its secrets then glances back at me and shouts, 'Otherwise he was a pretty good shag.'

I stare at her, my stomach hollow as if scooped out with surgeon's metal. I am wet through to my skin and yet still a fire sparks up in my throat.

'What's with the face?' She laughs. Water drips off the end of her eyelashes, nose, hair and off the end of her smile which is both knowing and sly. Sleekit, my father would say. 'You look like your dog's just died.' She pushes me on the shoulder and my feet slip on the muddy bank. I fall down on to my knees and catch myself just before my face hits the ground. The wet earth smells bitter and I cough into my hand then stand upright again, plant my feet firmly between a rock and a clump of heather and push my hair out of the way behind my ears. Orla is skimming stones again. Not a care in the world. I shout across the space between us.

'You had sex with Euan?'

'What?' She holds up her hand to her ear. 'I can't hear you!'

I reach forward, grab her and pull her towards me. 'You had sex with Euan?' I repeat. Her eyes look straight into mine. I see spite, anger and something else that I don't recognise. 'How could you, Orla? You could have anyone! *How could you?*'

'He's nothing,' she says to me. 'Shag him and get it over with.'

I feel someone tugging at my back. I keep hold of Orla and turn around. Rose is standing there. Her lips are moving but I have trouble making out what she is saying. I hear the words lost and sleep but that's it.

'Go back to the tent, Rose!' I bawl into her face and she is startled, draws away but doesn't let go of my jacket. I turn back to Orla.

'He doesn't matter! Forget him!' she shouts. She is laughing, her features harsh and feral in the moonlight. She shakes her head and water sprays around in all directions. I realise she is enjoying this. She has planned this quite deliberately and has chosen this exact moment to tell me. We're in the middle of nowhere. I have no one to turn to.

'You bitch.' I say the words so quietly I can't even hear them myself. Rose pulls at me again and I turn and push her hard, backwards, down the muddy bank away from me and swivel round to face Orla again. 'You bitch. You fucking, fucking bitch!' I slap her hard. She reels sideways, almost loses her footing, but at the last second finds her balance and stands upright. I hit her again and this time she falls down into a kneeling position and stays there. She doesn't slap me back. She lets me hit her over and over until my hands are sore and the strength is gone from my arms.

I head back to the camp, tripping over boulders and fallen branches. Twice I slither on wet ground and fall down, bang my shins and scrape my cheek. I stand up again and keep going until I reach the campsite. Monica is standing outside the supplies tent. 'I thought it would be better to put these under cover,' she tells me, shifting plastic boxes of breakfast cereal, and cooking utensils under the awning. 'There's no point in them getting wet. You can help if you like.'

I ignore her, unzip my tent and feel my way through the darkness to my sleeping bag. I take off my wet clothes and throw them into the corner. My towel is right at the top of my rucksack. I dry myself and climb into my pyjamas. All around me is the sound of heavy, contented breathing. My knuckles are sore and I rub them. I do it automatically, not wanting to think, holding off the point when I start to cry.

In my sleeping bag, curled up like a foetus, I think about what just happened. Orla is – was – my best friend. We were friends, weren't we? How could she? And Euan? How could *he*?

I pull the bag tightly down over my head. I resolve never to speak to either of them again. I don't need Orla and I don't need Euan.

5

Sophie, the community psychiatric nurse, is coming for a visit this morning so neither Paul nor I have gone into work. Paul is marking papers in his study and I'm in the kitchen making flapjacks, Ed's favourite. It's keeping me busy. But not busy enough. I can't get yesterday out of my head: the disastrous lunch in Edinburgh, Orla and her revelation. She wants to be a nun. Of all the unlikely people in the world, Orla has decided to take holy orders. As a teenager, not only was she irreligious but she was also a consistent bully and often a liar and a cheat. There was nothing sensitive or gentle about her and looking back, I am amazed that I remained friends with her for as long as I did.

I can't forget her parting shot: ten days. I have ten days to tell Paul how Rose died otherwise Orla will come and do it for me. But I have no idea how to tell him and I'm driving myself mad with the worry of it. The optimist in me hopes that she'll reconsider without persuasion. Before we met yesterday, she didn't know that I married Rose's father. Surely that will change her mind. I know it would change mine; but then the pessimist in me reminds me that I'm not Orla. And while her words spoke of closure and conscience, her tone and facial expressions said something else altogether. She was smirking by the time I left. I'm sure of it.

I try to focus on the positive – somehow Ella and I ended the evening closer than we've been in ages. She and Jamie haven't got as far as actually having sex but she was worried that it might happen and wanted to be careful. They are planning on using the 'Double Dutch' method: condoms and the pill. The doctor explained the side effects but she was feeling fine. She'd only been taking it for two weeks and she felt a little bit tearful but then, 'I'm not exactly an easy person, Mum, am I?' she said.

'I admire your frankness,' I told her. And we laughed like we were the best of friends.

I don't expect it to last but it's such a leap in the right direction that I want to enjoy it, wallow in it, celebrate the fact that for once I'm getting it right with my daughter. And of course, I can't because of Orla. I know that I dealt with her badly: losing my temper and walking out of the restaurant was not the best plan. And now everything is left hanging.

Through the kitchen window I can see Ed weeding one of the flowerbeds. He is kneeling on a mat, every so often shifting his weight to the opposite knee. He has arthritis in his joints and I know that gardening is painful but he loves to do it. 'I can't just sit in a chair idling away the hours,' he says. 'I may be down but I'm not out.'

I admire his courage and his sheer bloody-mindedness.

One day at a time is his maxim and at the moment it seems like a good one.

Paul comes into the kitchen and starts to fiddle with the toaster. 'Ella says it's broken.'

'She set off the smoke alarm when you were walking Murphy but I think it's just blocked,' I tell him. 'She keeps putting those thick teacakes into it.'

He takes it to the back door and tips it upside down in the compost bin, shaking all the crumbs out. I stop what I'm doing and watch him. He is twelve years older than me, but aside from the fact that we grew up liking different music, I can't say the age difference has ever been apparent. It has simply never been an issue for us. Like most couples, our marriage has had its share of ups and downs, but through it all I have never doubted my love for him or the choice I made to marry him.

When he puts the toaster back, I grab both his hands. 'Why don't we go to Australia early? Now? This weekend?'

He laughs. 'I haven't had word from the university yet.'

'But there's no way you'll be turned down. The acceptance letter is only a formality.'

He laughs again. 'I don't think we should jump the gun, sweetheart.'

'Why not?' I keep pushing. Suddenly it seems like the easiest solution. Surely Orla wouldn't follow us to Australia. 'Let's be spontaneous!'

'But the girls haven't finished the school year. Ella has yet to dazzle us with her performance as Juliet.'

'I don't think she'll mind so much. And it's their birthday

party tomorrow. They can say goodbye to their friends.' I hug him tight and then draw back to look up into his face. 'Just think! We could live out all those dreams we've been sharing.'

'And we will! But not for another couple of months.'

'Please.' I force a smile. 'I just want us to be together as a family.'

'But we are together as a family and you have Margie Campbell's painting to complete and we have to rent out the house.' He puts his hands either side of my face and kisses me. 'And I have to finish up at work. There are all sorts of ends to tie up, aren't there?'

'Paul. I . . .' I stop, not sure what I'm going to say next. After all these years, I can't just come out with it. When I was first married, I had this theory that I would be able to tell him about what happened to Rose and that we would be close enough for him to forgive me. There would be a moment, an opportunity, an opening up in time and space, a redemption gap for me to slide into. But, of course, although we talk about Rose, that moment of truth never comes and gradually I had to accept that I would never be able to tell him.

He is waiting for me to speak, his look unhurried. I remember reading once about the necessary attributes for a lasting marriage: patience, humour, kindness . . . and forgiveness. I know that Paul is blessed with the first three. But forgiveness is a tall ask and I know how he feels about responsibility. He has always wanted to know who was responsible for Rose's death and I know that if he ever found out, he would want that person taken to task. What I don't know is what he would do if that person was me.

'What's up? I can see you're worried about something.' He tugs my hair playfully. 'Tell me.'

'Paul . . .' I hesitate, remind myself that once out in the open, the truth can never be put back. I will have to live with the consequences for the rest of my life. My marriage will be over, my life will change for ever and the girls – what about them?

'Grace?'

I have to say something but I'm not sure what. I can't risk telling him about Rose and my part in her death, yet somehow I have to warn him about Orla. 'There's a threat – not to our lives,' I assure him quickly, knowing how he feels about the girls' safety. 'But to our happiness.'

He smiles uncertainly and gives a small shake of his head. 'What sort of a threat?'

'The past. Something from the past.'

'What?'

'Just a moment. A moment in time when I did the wrong thing.'

He thinks about this. 'You're not secretly in debt, are you?'

'No. I—'

He tips my chin up so that our eyes meet. 'And you're not having an affair?'

'No. I'm just . . . I. Well . . . hypothetically, if someone came to talk to you about me,' I say in a rush, 'to tell you something bad about me, something you didn't know and hadn't imagined, would you listen?'

He starts back. 'Is this a serious question?'

'Yes.' I lean back against the worktop and wait for him to think. He is a scientist. He thrives on facts, proof and evidence. I haven't given him much to go on but still he does me the courtesy of thinking about it.

'So hypothetically?' He raises his eyebrows and I nod. 'Someone comes and tells me something that you did when?'

'A while ago.'

'Before we met?'

'Yes.'

'Is it an offence? In the eyes of the law?'

'Probably.'

'But you got away with it?'

'Yes – actually no!' I say quickly. 'I didn't get away with it. It might *look* that way but I *have* made up for it.' I take a hesitant breath. 'I believe I have made up for it.'

'Then that's good.' He strokes the back of his hand down my cheek. 'And no, I wouldn't listen to what anyone has to say. If you choose not to tell me then I respect that.' He shrugs. 'I find it odd though, Grace.' His smile is confused bordering on hurt. 'I didn't think we had any secrets from each other, but still.' He gives a definitive nod of his head. 'It happened before we met and I respect your right to privacy.'

'Thank you.' My eyes well up and I blink fast to keep away the tears.

'What's brought this on?'

'Thinking back . . .' I shrug. 'You know how it is. Age and time.'

'Just one thing.' He frowns for a moment. 'You don't have to give me the details but I'm interested to know why – why can't you tell me?'

His eyes are gentle, encouraging. We have been together for more than twenty years and I can count on the fingers of one hand the times we have wounded each other. There was the day I lost Ella on the beach in France and he was angry at my carelessness and then there were the months following our move back to Scotland when I sank into a depression and I would catch him watching me, wary of challenging my lethargy in case I might break completely. 'I can't tell you,' I whisper. 'Because I'm afraid you won't love me any more.'

Immediately, he reaches for me and I cleave to him like a barnacle to the hull of a fishing boat. We stay like this for a minute or more until I cry myself quiet and then he holds me at arm's length so that he can look right into my eyes. 'Listen, I know you. I know you are a good person. Whatever this thing is – it doesn't matter! I will never stop loving you. Never.'

His words slide deep into the well inside me and for a moment my fear is diluted, but almost at once I know that the feeling won't last.

He looks beyond me towards the front of the house. 'Sounds like Sophie's car. Are you up to her visit? Shall I ask her to come back another time?'

'No. I'll be fine.' I give him a watery smile. 'I'm sorry to make such a fuss.'

'I expect this is something that has assumed a greater importance than the sum of its parts.' He gives me a quick hug. 'So let's just forget it.'

He walks away, leaving a cold space where he stood. I splash my face in the sink then go to the back door and take a couple of deep breaths, blink back the tears and have a smile ready for Sophie when she comes into the kitchen.

'So how's it been, Grace?' Sophie is small and dark and exudes calmness and capability from every pore. She tips her head to one side. 'Are you all right? You're looking flushed.'

'I'm fine. Nothing to do with Ed. Trials and tribulations of raising teenagers. You know how it is.' I feel guilty blaming the girls but it's the easiest thing to say.

'I'm a bit behind you there. Mine are only two and four right now. Two boys and the one in here.' She strokes her bump protectively. 'Another football player by the feel of it. Makes it nice and easy for hand-me-downs.'

'Two sugars, isn't it?'

She nods.

'Enjoy them while they're young.' I pass her a mug of tea. 'It's gone in a flash. One moment they're running around in nappies and the next they're towering over you telling you, in no uncertain terms, just where to get off.'

'How are you, Sophie?' Ed comes in through the door and holds out a hand to her. 'Just been finishing a spot of gardening. Weather like this is too good to waste.'

We all sit down and Sophie takes Ed's details from her bag. 'Now last month we were discussing the memory lapses and different strategies you could use to help.'

'Yes.' Ed takes his notebook from the back pocket of his trousers. 'I keep notes so that I remember who's been to see me, what's been said, that sort of thing. And Grace very kindly wrote me out some lists. I have them here.' He opens a page. 'This is a copy of all the phone numbers I might need.' He puts on his reading glasses. 'This page reminds me what to do if I am lost. And this one reminds me what to do before I go to bed, switching off the television, locking up, that sort of thing.' He gives a wry laugh. 'Of course, it's not much help if I *forget* that when I forget I need to look at my notebook. What happens then?'

Sophie has a repertoire of reassuring expressions and she uses one now. 'I hope you find that doesn't happen, Ed. It's all about rhythm and routine.' She changes tack. 'And have you been getting out and about?'

'Yes. Two or three times a week I play bowls.' He looks at me. 'I have a lot to do here.'

'Ed is invaluable to our family,' I say. 'Gardening, handles on doors, helping with the shopping – he fills in all the gaps. I'm not too sure how we ever managed without him.'

Ed smiles gratefully and Sophie writes a few words in his file. 'And how have you found your memory?'

'Well, I have lapses, of course. I'm hardly the man I was but, mostly, I think I'm managing. Adding up is difficult and sometimes I don't know who people are.'

'We play Scrabble most evenings,' Paul chips in. 'That helps Dad's confidence with words.'

'And we have Australia to look forward to,' Ed says. 'I'm not forgetting about that! Letter should be here any day now.' He smacks a hand down on Paul's knee. 'I've every confidence that Paul's application has been successful and then we'll be living close to my daughter Alison. Both families will be able to spend lots of time together.'

Sophie starts to ask questions about Australia and I tune out, find I can smile and nod in the right places without really listening. But the voice in my head is more persistent and much as I keep pushing the thoughts away, back they come like a boomerang. I try to work out what I know for sure and what is merely a possibility. Orla is joining a convent and, before doing so, wants to salve her conscience. If she tells the truth about that night, I will be found out. The result will be catastrophic.

Trying to tell Paul was a mistake that I can't repeat. It's automatic for me to seek comfort from him but this is not something he can help me with. I have established that he loves me and is completely on my side but it is cold comfort because the fact is that I am deceiving him. He has given his support without full possession of the facts. Were he to know the nature of my secret, I am sure he would feel horrified and betrayed. It's doubtful that he could ever forgive me. Instead of reassuring myself of his love, I have made myself feel worse than before. Compounding one deception with another – I feel like I am on a slippery slidey slope and I have to haul myself to safety before it's too late.

16 June 1984

One of the junior girls lands on my head. 'Ow! Angela!' I push her away from me and massage my scalp.

'Sorry, Grace.' She starts to giggle. She has one leg in and one leg out of her trousers and is hopping around in what little space there is between the sleeping bags. 'I'm just trying to get my jeans on.'

'Well, sit down then before you land on someone else.' I take some clothes out of my rucksack and put them on. Lynn is asleep. Mary and Susan are getting dressed. 'Where's Rose?'

'She must have gone to the toilet,' Angela tells me. She now has both her legs in one side of her trousers and is inching across the tent. She falls full-length on to the sleeping Lynn who starts to flail around, knocking a mug of water over the notes for Mary's camping badge. That sets Mary off. I'm not in the mood for this. I hardly slept and when I did Orla's face was there in my dreams, larger than life and twice as cruel.

My own face feels puffy, my skin tight with dried-on tears and I grab my soap bag, unzip the tent and go outside where the sun is just beginning to warm the ground. The heavy rain has left puddles all through the campsite. The pile of firewood is soaking. It doesn't bode well for breakfast.

It's already seven o'clock and most of the patrol leaders

are up. Last night seems unreal. *Could I have imagined it?*
I look around for Orla. Somehow she's found dry wood
and is building a fire with some of her patrol. She is bent
down next to it trying to blow it into action. One of the
girls asks her a question and she looks up. Her face has
the beginnings of a bruise over one cheek and she has a
scratch at the side of her right eye where my ring tore the
skin. I didn't imagine it then. My stomach lurches as her
words come back to me. *I tried him out for you. He could
be a better kisser but otherwise he was a pretty good shag.*

I feel like I want to start crying all over again and am
grateful when Miss Parkin blows her whistle. 'Fall into
patrols please, girls. Who's on breakfast duty?'

Faye's patrol raises their hands.

'Bacon butties all round, I think. Get started. You'll find
everything you need in the supplies tent.' She eyes the
rest of us. 'Sandra, your shirt should be tucked in. Angela,
stop giggling. Grace? Where's Rose?'

I look around and notice for the first time that she isn't
part of the circle. That's odd because she has stuck to me
like glue since we climbed into the minibus. I glance over
the other girls' heads expecting to see her coming towards
me, trailing through the woods carrying sticks or water.
Something helpful. And then the details of the night before
come back to me. I remember ignoring her when she came
to speak to me. And I pushed her. I remember now. Quite
hard and if she'd skinned her knee or banged her elbows
I wouldn't have heard her cry above the sound of all that
rain. Maybe she's in a huff somewhere.

'I'll go and find her, Miss Parkin.' I move out of the circle. 'She's probably cleaning her boots or something.'

'Be quick about it, Grace. Orla, you go with her.'

I'm already at the edge of the wood. 'I can go myself,' I call back. 'She won't be far.'

The last person I want to spend any time with right now is Orla. I think of Euan with his tongue in her mouth, his hands all over her. And the rest. I shudder. What the hell? How could he? We are supposed to be going out.

Orla runs to catch me up. 'Wait!'

She's almost alongside me. 'Fuck off, Orla.' I push her backwards. 'I'm never talking to you again.'

'For God's sake!' She rights herself and grabs hold of my arm. 'I was just winding you up! I didn't really have sex with him. He fancies you! Everyone knows that.'

I fold my arms and face her. I want to believe her but on countless occasions I've watched her lie: to teachers, to parents and to other children. She does it seamlessly. There is nothing elaborate about her lying and it's the straightforward aspect that makes it so believable.

'How do I know you're not lying?' I say.

'Because we're friends. Best friends.' Her hair is wild around her shoulders, curls jump out all over her head. Apart from the bruise and the scratch, her face looks paler than normal and it occurs to me that she probably didn't get much sleep either.

But it's her eyes that give her away. They are uneasy. Sad, even. I remember something else. 'Why didn't you fight back last night?' I ask her.

'Because you were right to hit me.'

'But you've just said you didn't do it.'

'I didn't.'

'So why didn't you tell me that last night?'

'Because. Because . . .' She puts her hands in the back pockets of her jeans, lifts her shoulders and shrugs. 'I deserved it.'

She's not making sense but still I feel sorry for her. She looks miserable, bloody miserable. 'We can talk about this later. We need to find Rose. I'll look over by the pond.'

I trudge off over the squashed ferns and tangled brambles and Orla holds up her hands on either side of her mouth and shouts, 'Rose! Breakfast time.'

My chest feels lighter and I take some deep breaths. I'm not totally convinced that she's telling the truth but it doesn't look as black as it did last night. I decide to give my face and hands a quick wash, so kneel down at the edge of the pond and take my soap out of the bag. My mother has packed me off with Yardley's lily of the valley: *With no proper facilities you'll want something that smells nice.*

I dry myself on my T-shirt and sit back against a rock. All is quiet apart from Orla's voice and the intermittent calls from one blackbird to another as they busy themselves in the trees. The air is unusually still and the sun warms my face. I feel myself sliding back towards sleep and quickly stop myself, stand up, automatically brush both hands over my backside and look all around the pond but can't see any sign of Rose.

About twelve feet into the water ahead of me I spot a jacket. I can't see the front of it but it looks like one of ours. We all have the same navy blue waterproofs with the Girl Guide motif and our unit number printed over the left breast. Angela's mum works in the factory and got us a special deal.

Orla pushes through the woods behind me. 'She isn't out in this direction. Let's go back before we miss out on the bacon butties.' She stops beside me. 'What's that nice smell?'

'Lily of the valley soap.' I touch my wash bag with my foot. 'You know my mum – good at the details.'

'Unlike mine,' Orla says, her expression cloudy. 'She won't even notice I'm gone this weekend.'

I point ahead of us. 'One of the girls has lost her cagoule.'

'We can come back for it later,' she says, but I am already picking up sticks and discarding the shorter ones until I find one long enough.

'I think I can reach it with this,' I say. I take off my shoes and socks, roll up my jeans and wade in. The stick catches at the body of the jacket. I try to give it a tug but it doesn't shift. 'It's lodged on something. I'll have to go in deeper.' I come back out and take off my jeans.

'You really hurt my face, you know.' Orla is lying back on a rock, rubbing her cheek. 'It bloody hurts like hell.'

'Serves you right. You shouldn't go around making up stuff like that.' I throw my T-shirt down on top of my jeans and wade in some more. The cold water reaches up past my knees and makes me gasp. 'I hope whoever's jacket this is appreciates it.'

'We'll make her scrub the pots,' Orla says. 'Parky has Irish stew planned for dinner. Stew on a camping trip! She's completely barking.'

When the water hits my thighs I stop. I'm only a few feet away now and the movement in the water sets up a small wave. The arm of the jacket slides out to the side. I go to grab it with the stick then stop, blink once, twice, three times. Each time my eyes open I see the same thing. There are fingers coming out of the end of the jacket.

'Hurry it up!' Orla is growing impatient. 'She's probably back at the campsite by now eating the last of the bacon.'

I turn back. 'Orla, in . . . I . . .' My voice gives out.

'What?' She frowns and looks to the end of the stick. 'What the . . .' She splashes in behind me and we grab the body, haul it back to the bank then up on to the flat ground.

When we turn her over we both let out a scream. It's Rose. Beautiful, blonde Rose. Her face is greyish-blue and bloated, her hair tangled with weeds and small splinters of wood.

'Fuck, fuck, fuck. Grace! Fuck.'

She is stiff and cold. I roll her on to her side and press down on her back to expel the water from her lungs. Some dribbles out. I roll her on to her back again and thump her heart once. Then I feel the bottom of her sternum and begin cardiac massage. I pump her chest counting as I go . . . five, six, seven and then blow air into her mouth. The stench from her mouth is nauseating but I manage not to retch. 'Get Miss Parkin, Orla!' I say between breaths. 'We need help.'

'Grace! She's dead.' She pulls me away from her. 'Can't you see? She's long dead.'

'She can't be.' I frown, back off, rub my hands on my bare legs, stare at Rose, now merely a body. Her eyes are blank, empty, devoid of the spirit that made her Rose. I can't think. There is nothing in my head. No words to help me make sense of this. I look round at Orla.

'It was . . .' Her limbs are jerking and her body is contorted. She grabs her hair and howls.

I place my T-shirt over Rose's face. It doesn't feel right; her eyes open watching this.

'It was you.' Orla claps a hand over her mouth. 'It was you.'

'What are you talking about!' I am horrified.

'When you pushed her!'

'What?'

'Was she in the tent when you went back?'

'I don't know.'

'Think, Grace.' Her eyes are wide and feverish. 'Think.'

I think back. I didn't check that Rose was in her sleeping bag. I didn't check on any of them. It didn't even occur to me. I was too upset. And before that, the memory of Rose's hands on the back of my coat. I see myself turn around on the very spot we're standing on now. She was trying to tell me something but I couldn't make out the words and I didn't give her the chance to repeat them.

I look down at my hands. A heavy weight drops down

into my pelvis. 'Christ! I pushed her. I pushed her down the bank.'

Orla moans and starts to pace, huge long strides that cause her to trip over boulders and clumps of grass, wobble and then steady herself. 'Think, think, think.' She is banging her head with her fist. 'We have to get our story straight.'

There's a singing in my ears. 'She's dead.' I realise the enormity of what I've just said and I start to tremble then turn towards a bush and throw up. After half a dozen retches my stomach is empty; acid burns in my throat.

'We have to stay calm.' She holds my shoulders, her fingers gripping my skin. 'You could be done for murder.'

'Murder?' I wipe my mouth with the back of my hand. In my mind's eye I see my future: my parents' faces, my name in every newspaper, prison bars. My insides drop, my legs give way.

Orla catches me, props our hips together then pushes me back against a tree.

'But it was an accident. Jesus, Orla. It was an accident,' I tell her. I look down at Rose's body on the ground. 'I would never do something like this.' A tremendous pressure builds in my chest, leaving no room for air. I start to choke, hold my neck and try to cough but I can't.

Orla slaps me hard across the face. My teeth bite into my tongue and I wince then cry out with the pain.

Orla shakes me. 'Listen! You can still be prosecuted. Say nothing about last night. Nothing. Grace?' she hisses. 'We saw nothing. We heard nothing. Do you hear me?'

6

The DJ is set up at one end of the room. Lights flash behind him, change colour and make shapes on the ceiling. Daisy is in jeans and a plain black halter-neck top and her face is glowing with a kind of iridescent happiness. Ella is wearing a pair of faux leopardskin footless tights, flat gold shoes and a black pelmet skirt. Her T-shirt is a shocking pink and says 'super bitch' on the front in sparkly letters. Her hair lies down her back, hooked up on one side of her head with an imitation tropical flower. They are both surrounded by friends and are opening presents. Daisy folds the wrapping next to her on the table; Ella throws it down by her feet.

I leave them to it and arrange the food on to plates next to bottles of drink and paper cups. Then I take a bag of rubbish outside and light up. I'm halfway through the cigarette, and growing tired of batting away the anxiety that's mushrooming inside my skull, when I hear Euan's voice behind me.

'What? You haven't started again?'

'Only in moments of stress,' I tell him.

He comes down the steps to join me and I offer him

the packet and the lighter. He takes one out, lights it and looks up into the sky. It's bursting with stars that shimmer and gleam and feel almost close enough to touch.

'So what happened in Edinburgh?'

'It was bad,' I say. 'Think of the worst-case scenario and double it.'

He blows a ribbon of smoke out through his mouth and over my head. 'She's going to tell Paul how Rose died?'

'Yup.'

I feel him recoil. 'Shit.'

'I know.' I shrug like it's hopeless. 'It's all part and parcel of clearing her conscience. She's becoming a nun.'

He gives a dry laugh. 'That's bullshit. She's no closer to becoming a nun than I am.'

'I'm not sure I believe her either but probably some nuns do start out as troublemakers until they see the light.'

'She was more than a troublemaker. She was cruel and bitchy and dangerous. She was dangerous, Grace.' He points his cigarette at me. 'And she was always the girl you could have behind the bike sheds.'

I turn to him. 'You had Orla behind the bike sheds?'

'I might have done.'

I jerk up straight. 'You *might* have done?'

He has the wits to look sheepish.

'Well, did you or didn't you?'

'I think I might have. Well, not behind the bike sheds . . .'

'You *think* you might have?'

He sighs. 'I did.'

'You never told me that. God, Euan! What the fuck?'

He tries to touch me but I move out of his reach. 'It meant nothing to me and even less to her, believe me. Anyway, what difference does it make?' he shouts.

'Keep your voice down!' I look behind us, up towards the steps but all is quiet. 'When exactly did you have sex with her?'

'It was twenty-odd years ago! I was a virgin. I was horny.'

'When exactly, Euan?'

He shrugs.

'Was it before Rose died?'

'I don't remember.'

'Well, *try!*'

'What is this?' He reaches for me, strokes the goose bumps on my arm. 'What's going on?'

'Please.' I force myself to stay calm. I wonder why Euan and I have never discussed this before. And then I know. Because I believed her. I believed her the next day when she said she had made it up. She didn't have sex with Euan. Why would she? 'Just try.'

He looks off into the distance, thinks for a few seconds. 'It was when we went potholing in Yorkshire for geography O-level. We stayed in tents in a field next to the youth hostel. Usual thing, no mixing with the opposite sex after lights out but we did and then' – he raises an eyebrow – 'somehow Orla and I fell on to the sleeping bags together. The others were outside messing around. I was having a bit of a grope.' He stops. 'She seemed to know what she was doing. Guided me inside her. It was—'

'She planned it,' I tell him. 'She knew how much I liked

you.' I start to pace up and down past the bins, counting off the dates on my fingers. 'So in March you turned sixteen. In April you went potholing. On 5 May we started going out. Rose died on 15 June.' I sit down on the bottom step because my legs are not going to hold me up. 'Why didn't you have sex with me?'

'You didn't do geography.'

'I don't mean then *exactly*,' I say. 'I mean at any time. Back then,' I add.

'Grace.' He looks at me sadly, reaches his hand towards me but I am too far away and it drops into the space between us. 'When Rose died? That was it.' He shrugs. 'You were off on a mission.'

He's right but it hurts to hear it out loud. I can't look at him. 'I'm going to the loo.' I climb the steps, smile my way past a couple of teenagers and go into the bathroom. When I'm washing my hands I see myself in the mirror. I look like I haven't slept in days. My eyes don't stay still. They are darting from side to side as if I'm working out in which direction to run. Why is it that the course of my life ended up hovering on such a mundane decision: geography or history? If I had been there Euan wouldn't have slept with Orla. I'm sure of that. And then there would have been nothing to argue about.

But even if he had, what about the night Rose died? If it hadn't been raining so hard, I'd have heard the splash as she fell into the pond and I'd have dragged her out again. If Miss Parkin had put her in another girl's patrol, Monica's or Faye's for example, she wouldn't have come looking for me. If I'd had flu – it was doing the rounds – and missed the camp or if I'd never joined the bloody Guides in the first place, Rose would still be alive.

A series of incidents, a series of choices and finally a consequence so appalling that it has haunted me the whole of my adult life.

I go back outside again and find Euan still there. 'We were arguing about you,' I tell him. I rest my head back against the cold stone of the wall and lean into him until my shoulder touches his upper arm. 'She said that she'd had sex with you. And then the next day she denied it. Said she'd only been winding me up.'

'She was always a good liar.'

'I tried to tell Paul yesterday.' The memory fills me with a new sort of terror and I start to hyperventilate. 'I couldn't bring myself to say it, but if I can't change her mind then I'll have to tell him before she does.'

'Don't. Don't even *think* about going down that road.' He grips my shoulders tightly and steadies me with his eyes. 'First we have to talk to her.'

'I handled it really badly, Euan.' I feel empty, like there's no fight left in me. 'You know what? Maybe it's time for me to stand up and say I made a horrible, horrible mistake. I pushed a little girl over and she died.'

'She may not have died because you pushed her, Grace.' He's said this to me before and like all the other times I wish I could believe him but there's too much room for doubt.

'I'm just so tired of hiding this. Really and truly, I am.'

I start pacing again. 'Don't you think Paul deserves to know the truth? She was his daughter, Euan. His *daughter*.'

'Confession may be good for the soul but it's not always good for your relationships. Think about what would happen.' He looks at the ground then back at me. 'You love Paul, don't you?'

'Yes.'

'So you have to preserve your marriage,' he says flatly. 'Your love for him and his love for you. The girls' happiness. Your family has to be your priority.'

He is right and it does me good to hear it. I nod, pull my shoulders back and take a few breaths. 'So how can I stop Orla?'

'Let me help you. Two heads are better than one.'

Relief floods my bloodstream and is quickly followed by a reminder, a warning. Euan and me: we're not always good for each other. 'You're sure?'

'Yes.' He stands opposite me and says softly, 'We're friends, aren't we?'

His leg is touching mine and I move away at once, almost trip up in my haste to keep my distance.

'We have to keep this kosher.' I try to make my voice light. 'You know—'

'I know,' he cuts in and his eyes narrow for a second. 'We had an affair. But that was years ago.' He shrugs. 'It's all behind us now.'

'Okay.' I put my hands in the back pockets of my jeans. 'I just don't want us to misunderstand each other.'

'Orla is threatening you and you need help. That's it.' He shrugs again. 'That's all. No ulterior motives.'

'Then I appreciate your help.' I give him a quick hug. 'Thank you.'

'You're welcome.'

'So how? How can we stop her?'

'We'll think of something.' He throws out his arms. 'Whatever it takes.'

Several feet apart, we stare at each other for what seems like minutes and then I catch the sound of Paul's voice behind me and I shift away from Euan and start to tie a bin bag, my shaky hands more thumbs than fingers.

'I think she's just outside. Yes, here she is! Grace!' He's smiling broadly. 'Look who I found.'

Orla appears out of the back entrance of the hall and stands on the top step next to Paul. I stop breathing and stare at her for the longest moment until I am forced to inhale. She is smiling down at us, and then she runs down the steps, has her arms around me, hugging me to her like we are long-lost sisters. 'Grace! It's so wonderful to see you!'

I keep my arms flat to my sides and say nothing. Truth is I am too shocked, too completely blindsided to have any idea what to say.

She lets me go and throws her arms around Euan then steps back and looks him up and down like she's about to buy him. 'Euan Macintosh!' she says. 'Hasn't life been treating you well? You haven't changed a bit!'

'Orla? What a surprise!' He gives her a half-smile. 'What brings you to the village?'

'Oh, you know how it is. I've always loved a party and I was passing through, reacquainting myself with old haunts when I met Daisy outside. One look at her and I knew she had to be Grace's daughter!' She grins at me. 'It was like going back in time.' She lets go of Euan and grabs hold of my hands. 'It seems like only yesterday that *we* were both sixteen.'

I pull my hands away. There is bitter saliva in my mouth. I can't look at her. I know that if I do I will grab her hair and shake her, rattle her until her teeth fall out and her spine is reduced to jelly.

Paul searches our faces, sensing the tension. 'So, I'll leave you three to catch up, shall I?' He looks at me enquiringly.

I look back. I want to protect him. I want to hold on to him and tell him that whatever Orla says he's not to believe it, that he's not to be alone with her, that she is the worst sort of person. That she will pretend it's all for the sake of honesty and closure.

I take hold of his arm and push him ahead of me. 'I'm coming inside too.' We climb the steps and find the girls milling around in the kitchen.

Ella gives a shriek when she sees Paul. 'I wondered where you were! Come on, Dad, you're allowed a dance.' Ignoring his protests, she drags him off and Daisy, already flushed from dancing, turns to me.

'Your old friend seems really nice, Mum.' She drinks back a glass of Coke. 'Dad's invited her to lunch Sunday week.'

'He's *what*?'

Daisy laughs. 'Chill, Mum! What's with the yelping?'

'Dad invited her to lunch?' I say, hoping I heard her wrong.

'Well, she kind of invited herself really. She said something about wanting to catch up with you and perhaps we could all have a meal together and Dad said she was welcome to pop in some time and then she said how about Sunday and Dad said okay.'

My mouth is slack. I can hardly believe it. Orla has wheedled her way into an invite to Sunday lunch and that will be exactly ten days since we met in Edinburgh. She means it. She means to tell Paul about that night. For the first time I realise just how serious this is. Dizziness spreads through me in a powerful wave and I fall back on my heels, bump my head on the cupboard door.

Daisy pulls me upright again. 'What's up with you, Mum?' I am holding my hands across my temples and she moves them away so that she can see my face. 'Is everything okay?'

'Fine. I'm sorry.' I take a deep breath and make myself smile. 'Dad and I are going to walk back home soon. Leave you both to it.'

'Cool. Want to come for a dance first?'

'No, you go on though. Give your dad a run for his money.'

I follow behind her and stand in the shadows watching her join Ella and Paul. They have a quick conversation, the girls laughing and excited while Paul shakes his head and makes his most reluctant face. Undaunted, Daisy shouts a request to the DJ and a rhythm and bass beat brings most of the teenagers on to the floor. The girls hold one of Paul's arms each and begin to teach him some dance steps. Within minutes, he's picking up the moves but he looks awkward and lumpy and the girls stifle their giggles and pull him this way and that until he gets the hang of it.

I want to join them but I know I can't. I don't deserve them. My hands are shaking and I force them into the pockets of my jeans. Immediately the tremor spreads to the muscles in my thighs, down my legs and into my feet. This is my family. I am a wife and a mother but I am hiding a secret so huge that if it comes out it will negate everything good I have done these last twenty-four years, and to expect Paul's forgiveness would be to expect the moon to drop down on to my doorstep.

I watch my family and I know, in this moment, that I will do anything to preserve this. I go to the back of the hall to find Orla again. She is in the kitchen with Euan and Callum who was at school with us.

'But what about marriage and children?' Callum is saying. 'Won't you feel like you're missing out?'

'My spiritual life is everything to me. I really feel like I've found myself.' She laughs self-consciously, looks over at me.

I can't meet her eye. I want her to leave. Plain and simple. My fists clench and unclench by my sides and I feel like I'm ready to use them.

'I spent a lot of time roaming,' Orla continues. 'I was

lost. I lived with men who were . . .' She pauses, looks at Euan as she searches for the right word. 'Unsympathetic. So much time trying to make the unworkable work, and the unthinkable palatable but now, at last, I have a fit. In the convent.' She smiles like the revelation has come to her afresh. She has the same look on her face that she had in the restaurant. Like she's in love.

'So what about sex?' Ordinarily a shy, amiable bear, I'm guessing Callum is emboldened by a couple of Special Brews. He's leaning on the counter top, staring at her, seemingly memorising each of her features in turn. 'What are you going to do for nookie?'

She gives him a motherly look. 'There's more to life than sex, Callum.'

'I'm not saying it's the be-all and end-all. But it's an important part of life. Expressing yourself as an adult. Keeping all parts in good working order.' He holds up his hand. 'Not that *I* would know that much about it. Being divorced. Lead a simple life, I do. Not much time for play.' He's dissembling now and Orla laughs, clearly amused by him. 'What do you think, Euan?' He turns to Euan and winks. 'Back me up here, pal.'

'I think it's up to the individual,' Euan says. He is standing to the left of me. He has a sausage roll in one hand and a cup of tea in the other. 'You never struck me as someone who would be attracted to a life of self-denial, Orla.' He shrugs and smiles at her. 'But each to his own.'

'I know!' She gives a giddy, girlish giggle. While not exactly flirting – she's not quite the old Orla – she's clearly loving the attention. 'I've finished with all that worldly striving and competing and aiming and for what?' She throws out a challenge. 'A faster car, a bigger house, a room full of gadgets?'

'And having a faith sets you free from all that?'

'Yes, I think it does. It's real.' She clutches her chest. 'Don't you believe in God, Euan? Don't you feel there's a power behind all this?'

'I don't believe or disbelieve,' he tells her. 'Opportunities come like waves on the beach. That's the nature of things. Is there a God behind it? I don't know.'

'Master of your own fate, huh?'

'I believe in personal responsibility.'

'Really?' Her voice is light and I almost don't catch her next words. 'Personal responsibility and integrity go hand in hand, don't they?'

'I live my life as best I can. Keep moving forward.'

She glances at me, then back to Euan. 'No looking back, huh?'

He shakes his head. 'The past can't be relived, Orla. Nothing that was broken can be fixed. Nothing done, undone. What use is raking over old ground?'

'Reparation . . .' She thinks for a bit. 'Redemption.'

'Can redemption be healing when others are hurt by it?'

She leaves his question to hang in the air until it grows heavy around our heads. Seconds tick by and I find it increasingly difficult to breathe in.

'Am I missing something here?' Callum smiles uncertainly at them but isn't able to catch their eyes. They are staring at one another as if to look away will mean defeat. 'When did it start to get serious?'

'Callum, I think the DJ needs a strong arm to help him with some boxes,' I say, finding my voice at last.

'That'll be me then.' He stuffs his mouth with crisps and heads for the door. 'Back in a mo.'

'Twenty-four years have gone by, Orla. We're not the people we were. If you carry out your threat you'll not only ruin Grace's life but you'll take her family down too. Can you live with *that* on your conscience?'

The only sound in the room is the fan in the corner of the kitchen. Wind is blowing in from the outside and the blades are flapping backward and forward. Finally, her eyes tilt and meet mine. 'Still your knight in shining armour?'

I don't answer.

Her mouth twitches and she bites her lip, looks at her feet, points one foot, then the other and starts to revolve her right ankle as if warming up for exercise. Then she meets his eyes again. It's a look that says, do you really want to take me on? Euan doesn't falter. He stares right back at her and I love him for it.

'So what's to be done, Euan? What's to be done?'

I jump in: 'You leave. You walk through that door and never come back.'

'But I've only just got here.'

'This is my daughters' party that you're gatecrashing.'

'Daisy said there isn't a problem with me being here.'

'She is polite.' I say the words slowly and deliberately

and Euan's eyes flash a warning. 'She's hardly going to tell you to bugger off.'

'Steady on, Grace!' Callum is back. He gives a forced laugh. 'DJ sorted. Why don't we all retire to the pub?' He looks at his watch. 'There's happy hour down at the Anchor until ten.'

'I'm taking back Paul's invitation to Sunday lunch,' I continue. 'You're not welcome in my house.'

'Is it yours to take back?' She lifts her handbag off the floor. 'This is not going to go away, Grace.'

She leaves the kitchen and I follow her, watch as she walks straight on to the dance floor towards Paul and the girls. They all look pleased to see her. Daisy grabs her hand and Ella even throws her arms around her. Within seconds she is moving in time with the three of them and they are all laughing together as if they've known each other for years. Then, arms in the air, she shimmies in front of Paul, blatantly provocative.

'A lap-dancing nun,' Euan says in my ear. 'I've seen it all now.'

Anger cranks up the heat in my stomach and I move forward.

'Don't.' He holds my wrist. 'She wants you to make a scene. Don't give her the satisfaction.'

I grit my teeth and wait for the music to finish. When it does, she kisses them all on both cheeks, saving Paul for last, both her hands resting on his upper arms and then she rubs down to his forearms and clasps his hands, cleverly letting go just before he begins to look uncomfortable. She heads for the door and I follow her out and down the steps to her car.

'This is not going to go away.' She throws the words over her shoulder. 'You know that, don't you?'

'What happened that night will stay between the two of us,' I say. 'End of story.'

'Or would that be the three of us?' She looks back to where Euan is standing in the shadows. 'You told him, didn't you?'

I don't reply.

'Euan knows you did it. Am I right? And he's still fighting your corner. Or is it more than that?' Her voice lowers. 'He gave you a look just now. What kind of a look was it?' She turns her head skywards, muses for a bit, snaps her fingers. 'I know! Hungry. That's what it was. It was hungry.'

'You should set off.' My teeth are clenched tight. 'Even at this time you can meet traffic on the bridge.'

'Honesty really is the best policy.' She tries her best to look regretful. 'Set down your burden.'

'Oh please!' I'm fast approaching breaking point. 'Cut the sanctimonious crap! What are you suggesting? A cosy Sunday lunch where we all sit around the table and share our secrets? And when you make your confession to Paul, what *exactly* do you think is going to become of my marriage?'

'Paul is a reasonable man. I think you underestimate him.'

'And I think you should stop messing with my life!' I

am shouting now. I can't help myself. The cautionary voice inside me reminds me that others might hear what I'm saying but I'm too angry to care. I want to force her into her car and watch her drive far, far away.

'What makes you think you can stop me?' She unlocks the door. 'My reasons are for the best, Grace. While yours? Can you say the same?'

'Yes, I can. This is about my family.' I look away, distracted for a moment by Monica. She's watching us from the other side of the road, her arms folded tightly across her chest.

'Sooner or later children have to learn that their parents are fallible.'

'Oh really?' My eyes are back with Orla. I'm nodding. 'Is that what this is about? Fallible parents? *Your mother?* Is that it, Orla? Is it *my* fault your mother slept around? Is it *my* fault you went into competition with her? Just exactly how many boys did you shag in fourth year?'

She flinches.

I don't stop. 'There was Dave Meikle, Angus Webb, Alastair Murdoch.' I count them off on my fingers. 'Oh, and then of course there was Euan, wasn't there? That one was just for me.' We are right in each other's face, close enough to fight for the same molecules of air. 'If you want to take the blame for Rose's death, you go right ahead but you are not dragging me into it.'

'I don't have to drag you into it. You're already in it and I'm going to tell the truth whether you like it or not.'

She opens the door with a flourish and climbs into her

car. I want to kick the tyre but I don't. I deliberately take a step backward. I need her to leave. Right now. Retaliation is not an option. The engine starts up and she drives off.

'What is *she* doing here?' Monica has crossed the road and is standing beside me. She is pale, her eyes wide open and anxious. 'What did she want? Why are you mad with her?'

I want to say, *What's it to you, Monica? What's it to you?* But I take a deep breath and say breezily, 'You know Orla. Always likes to wind everyone up.'

'Me for sure,' Monica says. She is visibly trembling, her jaw judders and she tenses it still. 'We hated each other's guts. But you were her friend.'

'Well, not any more.' I walk away. 'You coming inside?'

16 June 1984

Miss Parkin is sitting on a wooden bench. 'She must have got up during the night to go to the toilet.' She shakes her head and more tears run down on to the collar of her blouse. 'I thought we were far enough away from the pond. I thought we were.' She keeps repeating this over and over. 'I thought we were. I thought we were far enough away. I knew she couldn't swim but I thought we were far enough away. A hundred yards or more; that's far enough, isn't it?'

Sergeant Bingham is a big man with hands twice the size of my dad's. He rests one on her shoulder. 'I'm sure you did your best, Miss Parkin. Accidents will always happen. Tragic, for sure. Absolutely tragic.'

'Grace?' She looks over at me, pleading. 'Why would she leave the tent? You didn't hear her, did you?'

I try to speak, to say something comforting, but I can't. We're in the police station. Orla is on the bench opposite me, Miss Parkin is to the right. They've wrapped us in blankets. Orla has shrugged hers off but mine is still tight around me because I can't stop shivering. Rose is dead. Sweet little Rose who wouldn't harm a fly. And I've killed her. I feel like my skull is cracking and will soon splinter into a million tiny pieces that will never find their way back together again. I'm holding my jaw tight, jamming my teeth together but it doesn't stop them from chattering. The policewoman tries to make me drink some sweet tea but I bring it straight back up again.

Orla looks perfectly composed. I want to collapse and let the words pour out, just tell the truth and take my punishment but Orla holds me with her eyes. Her will is like iron. Every time I feel myself falter, she draws my gaze back to her and encloses us both in her determination.

My parents arrive and my dad gathers me up in his arms. I shut my eyes tight and press my face into his tweed jacket. He smells familiar and strong, like he always does, of wood shavings and coffee and I start to cry again. He hugs me tighter, rocking me backward and forward.

'Your daughter and her friend Orla found the younger girl's body,' Sergeant Bingham tells them.

My mother gasps. 'In the name of God!' she says. 'How could such a thing happen?'

'It seems to have been a tragic accident,' the policeman

tells her. 'Your daughter did a sterling job of trying to resuscitate Rose but it was to no avail. Most likely she had been in the water all night.'

My mother gasps again and clutches her hand to her mouth.

'I'm afraid Grace is in shock and will need some time to come to terms with it.'

'Sarge?' The policewoman sidles up to him. 'Rose's father is here.'

I don't want to look. I don't want to see his face but something makes me open my eyes. My right eye is pressed into my father's coat but my left sees him. He is standing with his hands in his pockets. He is completely still. I watch as Sergeant Bingham breaks the news and as long as I live I will never forget what happens next. Mr Adams drops to his knees and when Sergeant Bingham tries to lift him to his feet again he resists and starts to bang his head on the floor. The sound is loud and hollow like the crack of an air rifle.

'Mr Adams. Please. Let's help you up, sir.'

Rose's dad is beyond hearing him. He has started to cry; gut-wrenching sobs that find an echo in my own chest.

I am allowed to go home. I climb into the back of the car and Sergeant Bingham has a final word with my dad.

'We may need to talk to your daughter again,' he tells him. 'It will be for the procurator fiscal to decide, of course, but it seems to be a straightforward case of death by misadventure.'

The story is covered in the local paper.

'GIRL DROWNS ON GUIDE CAMP', the headline screams, in inch-high bold print. And underneath:

Nine-year-old Rose Adams, only child of Paul Adams, drowned in a deep pond last night in a picturesque woodland close to St Andrews. The site is a favourite for Guides and youth club camping trips. Rose, a member of the Guides for less than two months, was out of her tent in the middle of the night. It's thought that, upset by the thunderstorm, she must have stumbled into the pond some time after midnight. Rose's body was discovered early this morning by Grace Hamilton, 15, and Orla Cartwright, 16. The girls made a valiant attempt to resuscitate Rose but were unsuccessful.

Miss Parkin, who leads the unit said, 'I knew that Rose was a non-swimmer but I felt we had taken the necessary precautions. I am deeply upset by this tragedy and my sympathy is with Mr Adams. Rose was a wonderful little girl, vibrant and helpful. She would have made an excellent Guide.'

This is a double tragedy for Mr Adams, a newly appointed lecturer in marine biology at St Andrews University, whose wife died last year.

To the left of the text, there is a small black and white photograph of Rose's father. He has a look on his face – both wild and blank. He is what my mum describes as distraught. To the right is a huge colour photograph of Rose. She is wearing a white blouse with a sweetheart neckline and a red cardigan. She doesn't have all of her front teeth and her gappy smile is wide and uncomplicated.

She looks very much alive and the memory of how she was when I last saw her makes my heart shrivel.

I lie in bed. I can't get up. I try but I feel dizzy. This goes on for over a week. My mum tries her best to stay patient with me but by the end of the third day I see that all she wants is for everything to be back to normal. She tries to persuade me to make an effort, have a bath, come downstairs for tea – but I can't.

On the eighth day, Mo comes to my room. She cradles me in her arms and I cry on to her pinny. 'What happened was terrible, Grace. Terrible. But what's all this about you not getting up?'

'I can't, Mo. When I walk I fall over.'

'That's because you've hardly been eating anything.' She reaches down into her shopping bag. 'I made you some cheese and onion scones and some melting moments.' She holds out the goodies towards me. 'Smell that and tell me you're not hungry?'

She's right. Hunger shouts in my belly and knocks my reluctance sideways.

My mum appears at the door with a tray of tea. 'Any luck?'

'She's just tucking in now, Lillian,' Mo says, squeezing my hand.

If my mum is insulted that my appetite has been re-kindled by Mo's food rather than her own, then she hides it well. 'Good! When you're finished eating I'll run you a hot bath. I can change your sheets while you're busy in the bathroom.'

Mo stands up. 'Shall I send Euan through later to cheer you up?'

'What an excellent idea!' my mother says, all bright and breezy. 'I expect you've missed out on some school work that he can help you with.'

'Yes,' I say to Mo. I dip a melting moment into my tea and catch the softened piece in my mouth before it falls. 'Please ask him to come through.'

Euan and I started going out on the night of Orla's party back in May. And the evening before Guide camp, I lay awake with the sensation of his kisses in my mouth and his hands on my hair and back. He's knocked on the door every day since the tragedy but my mother has told him I'm asleep. I'm not but it's easier to pretend. I am afraid to sleep because every time I do, the nightmare starts; every night the same one, the same outcome.

I know that I can't lie in bed for the rest of my life but neither can I go back to my old life and act as if nothing has happened. I know that when I explain what I need to do, Euan is the one person who will be on my side.

'And Orla called in several times this week,' my mum is telling Mo. 'Grace was sound asleep but we chatted for a bit. She's being sensible about it.' My mother glances over at me. 'She's putting it behind her and getting on with her life. She left you another letter, Grace. Have you read it yet?'

I don't answer. It's the fifth letter she's written to me. I've ignored all of them – I'm not even reading them now – but she still hasn't got the message. I don't want anything to do with her. The thought of seeing her again is abhorrent to me. It's not that I blame her. I don't. I blame myself. But Orla is a reminder of the worst person I can be.

I finish eating, have a bath and wait for Euan. As soon as I see him, my heart fills. I jump out of bed and throw myself against his chest, put my mouth into his neck and breathe deeply. 'I've missed you.'

He hugs me to him. I'm wearing a cotton nightie, not very thick. I am suddenly shy, knowing that he can feel every part of my body through it. I slide under the covers again, pull them up to my chin.

'I brought you some sandwiches.' He sits down on the bed and passes me one, egg mayonnaise and pickle, and bites into the other himself. We eat in silence for a few minutes.

When we're finished he leans over to kiss me. I hold his shoulders.

'I did it.' I say it quickly before I lose my courage.

'Did what?'

'I killed her.'

He frowns at me. 'Who?'

'Rose.' I remember that there has been no suggestion that Rose's death was anything other than accidental. 'It was my fault.'

'Just because you were her patrol leader it doesn't make it your fault.'

'No. I did it. I actually did it. It was a mistake.'

'You did what? What was a mistake?' He's shaking his head at me. 'How?'

'I pushed her, Euan. I pushed her hard and it was raining and she was tiny.'

He backs away.

'The ground was slippery and the pond was deep and she couldn't swim.'

He's staring at me as if I've lost my mind.

'I didn't know she'd fallen into the water. It was dark and Orla and I were arguing and—' I stop, remember what we were arguing about – Euan. But later, she told me that she was lying. 'The thing is . . .' I hold my hands out.

He's staring at me, waiting for the rest.

'I need to make it better.'

'Make what better? You didn't kill her!'

I climb out from under the covers, kneel on the bed and start from the beginning. I give him all the details: the depth of the pond, her hand on my jacket, me turning around, unable to make out what she's saying, bawling into her face, then pushing her hard, down the bank, going back to my tent, not checking that she was there. I tell him everything except what Orla and I were arguing about.

When I'm finished he says nothing for a few seconds and then, 'That doesn't prove you did it.' He is tense, his lips tremble as he speaks. 'It doesn't, Grace. You're making it sound logical but there are other scenarios that are just as logical.'

'Like what?'

'Like you pushed her away and she went back to the tent. Then later on, when you were asleep, she got up and went out again.'

'Why would she do that?'

'Because she wanted to talk to one of the other girls, because she was looking for something, because she was sleepwalking!' he says triumphantly. 'I watched a programme about it. Loads of people sleepwalk.'

I want to believe him but I can't. I know what I did and I know what I have to do now.

'If I didn't do it then why would she be visiting me?'

'Visiting you?'

'Every night since it happened, I have dreamed about her.' I screw up my fists and keep my voice steady. 'And every night when I wake up, she's standing at the bottom of the bed and is trying to tell me something.'

'For fuck's sake! This is bollocks.' He grabs hold of me. 'You're upset. You're imagining it. It's like the monster under the bed. It isn't real!'

I start to cry. It makes me angry – what use are tears? – and I bang my fists on the bed. I can't do this on my own. 'Listen, Euan, please. I need the dream to stop. You have to help me.'

'Help you how?'

I tell him.

Twice he draws away from me, once he says quietly, 'This is mad, Grace. Totally fucking bollocks.' But he strokes my hair as he says it and I know that he will help me. Maybe against his better judgement, but he will help me.

He leaves soon after and for the first night in over a week I am able to fall asleep without dreading it. The nightmare comes as it has every night since I found her body. I'm standing on the bank of a river. I'm surrounded by the ominous shadows of pine trees that stretch up as high as a five-storey building. The sky above me rumbles and rain buckets down on to my head but somehow I never grow wet. The water lingers briefly on my face and hair then rolls off to make a puddle around my feet.

I wait for her, patiently. I listen, turn a full circle, try to anticipate her shape in the gloom until suddenly she's there in front of me, wet through, the hem of her coat waterlogged and dragged low around her knees. She is trying to tell me something, but as she talks she slides away from me. I reach for her hand and catch hold of the tips of her fingers . . . for a second I have her . . . and then she slides down the bank, and into the water.

I throw back the covers, sweating, gulping a breath. My insides plummet but still I am compelled to look up. She is standing at the bottom of my bed, water dripping from the ends of her hair, eyes the colour of mud. Her mouth moves. I lean forward, concentrate, try to lip-read but still I can't make out what she's saying. But this time, I'm able to tell her something. We watch each other for the longest moment and then I blink and she is gone.

7

'Wasn't it funny Orla turning up like that?'

I don't answer. I'm round at Monica's. I'm returning the food containers she brought to the girls' party. We're at the breakfast bar in her kitchen. The work surfaces gleam. Utensils hang in regulation rows on hooks beneath the cupboards. Canisters are labelled – tea, coffee, sugar – and sit squarely behind the kettle. There's an absence of dust, of clutter, of spilled milk or peeling paint behind the rubbish bin. There's no egg clinging to the front of the dishwasher or mashed potato trodden into the floor tiles. It's like a show house. And Monica is perfect to show it off. Her hair is always sleek and sits on her shoulders, kicking up and out like a cheerleader's foot. Her make-up is carefully applied, her smile the same.

'Ground control to Grace.' Monica hands me a cup of freshly brewed coffee. 'I said wasn't it funny, Orla turning up like that?'

'I didn't ask her, if that's what you're implying.'

'What does Orla have on you?'

'I'm sorry?'

'If looks could kill, I'd have been certifying her death.'

'She gatecrashed the twins' birthday party. I didn't appreciate it.'

'You didn't know she was coming? Really?' Her eyebrows are plucked to within an inch of their life. She's trying to read me, catch hold of the lie and wring its neck. I guess it's part of the training. Doctors are used to patients being evasive.

'Has my dad made an appointment to see you?' I say, suddenly remembering about the blood on the hankie.

'If he had I wouldn't tell you,' she says. 'Patient confidentiality.'

'I realise that, but maybe you could prompt him into coming? I'm worried about him. When I was with him the other day he coughed some blood on to his hankie. My mum thinks it's coming from his stomach.'

'He usually sees another doctor in the practice but' – she gives a reassuring nod – 'I'll have a word.'

'Thank you.' I almost mention Ella and the pill but don't, because apart from the fact that I don't want Monica to have the opportunity to give me a lecture on parenting, I'm tired. I didn't get to bed until 2 a.m. and then I slept fitfully. 'Are you up in the middle of the night cleaning?' I look around the pristine kitchen and sigh. 'Seriously, Monica, I don't know how you do it. You put the rest of us to shame.'

She pulls her back up. 'I wasn't brought up like you.'

'Eh?' I have a sudden and intense craving for a cigarette and I wonder whether Euan has any hidden at the back of the cupboards.

'You were completely spoiled.' She pauses.

I don't say anything. I'm still thinking cigarettes. If he's hidden them anywhere they'll be down in the cabin.

'You had a surfeit of everything,' she continues, sitting down opposite me. 'Whereas I had to bring myself up. My parents' marriage was a shipwreck for as long as I can remember. All they had time for was their own self-indulgence and misery.'

'I'm sorry.' I take a mouthful of coffee and rest the warm cup in my hands. 'I didn't know.'

'And it wasn't just your own mother who looked after you like you were a princess.' She's glaring at me now. 'But you had Mo, *as well*. Mo. She was such a favourite with everyone. Everybody loved her.' She stops talking, looks into the middle distance and says quietly, 'I was glad when she died.'

'What?' That wakes me up and I jerk up straight, watch the coffee rise in the air like a wave and spill down on to the walnut worktop.

She looks at me blankly. 'How could I ever have competed with her?'

'You couldn't possibly have wished her dead!'

'I didn't say I wished her *dead*,' she shouts. 'I said I was glad when she *died*. No.' She holds up her hand. 'I wasn't *glad* when she died but I wasn't as bothered as I should have been.' She sighs. Changes her mind again. 'Oh, I don't know what I'm saying.' She drops her head into her hands and starts to cry. 'Jesus, don't tell Euan. He'd be gutted. Please.'

'I won't.' I'm genuinely shocked not just by what she's said but by the way she's breaking down. I haven't seen her lose control since Orla's sixteenth birthday party. I don't know whether I should go round the table and hug her. I settle for placing a hesitant hand on her shoulder; a couple of seconds and then I pull away. 'I think you need to rest more.'

'Listen!' She grabs my hands and looks at me with the kind of desperation that I associate with myself. 'Orla is bad news. I know that you were friends with her but you have to keep her away from the village.' She's squeezing my hands and I try to wriggle them free but she tightens her grip. 'I want you to know that if you need any help dealing with her then I'm willing.'

I don't need any reminding that Orla has to be kept from the village. My head has not let me forget it since I came back from Edinburgh. Orla turning up at the girls' party was just another nail in the coffin and now that she's wangled an invite to lunch, my fate is all but sealed. 'Please, Monica,' I say. 'Let me have my hands back.'

She lets go immediately, sits back and takes a few breaths. Her lips are still moving but now she's keeping the words to herself.

I wipe the coffee spill, rinse the cloth and put it back beside the sink. 'Do you have any cigarettes?'

'Garage. Top shelf. Behind the pots of old paint.'

I go into the garage and find the cigarettes. There're eight left in the packet. They look past their best but still better than nothing.

When I come inside again Monica hands me a lit match

and opens the back door. 'You know about Orla's mother and my father?'

I light up and draw the smoke into my lungs. It's not going to help my headache but when the nicotine hits my bloodstream I feel a different sort of energy that might just see me through the rest of the morning. 'I saw them in Edinburgh together. He was kissing her. It took me a while to put two and two together, though.'

'You *saw* them?' A shudder passes through her. 'Where? When? Why didn't you tell me?'

'I was fourteen. I know that for sure because my gran took me to Jenners for afternoon tea. And as for telling you?' I shake my head. 'I was a bitch at times. I hold my hands up to that. But I wasn't *that* bad.'

'It had been going on for about a year before I found out then.' She sits back in her seat and looks at the ceiling. Her cheeks are streaked with tears and she takes a piece of kitchen roll and blows her nose then goes to the sink and splashes her face with cold water. 'You'll understand now why I hate her so much.'

'But that wasn't Orla. That was her mother.'

'She's tarred with the same brush.'

'Monica, you're a doctor. That's hardly scientific!' I have to shout after her because she's left the room and is climbing the stairs. I stand by the back door and look down the garden. I can't see the cabin from here but I know it's there and it attracts me like iron filings to a magnet. I want to kick off my shoes and run down the path, lock myself inside and never come out.

'This is the three of us.' Monica is back and she is holding out a photograph.

I take it from her. It's black and white and is in a polished, silver frame.

'I keep it beside my bed.'

She is sitting on her father's shoulders, her hands resting on his head. His right hand is holding her feet and his left arm is around her mother's waist. Monica is laughing. They are all laughing. 'You look happy,' I say, passing it back to her.

'I was seven. We were in North Berwick on holiday.' She stares at the photo and her eyes fix as she drifts into a memory. 'Angeline took that away from me.'

'It doesn't do any good to dwell on the past,' I say, knowing full well that the past never really lets you go. 'You were a child. You couldn't have changed anything.'

'History has a habit of repeating itself.'

'Your parents are both dead, Monica.' I shake her gently. 'And Angeline lives in Edinburgh now. She can't hurt you any more.'

'Secrets are destructive, Grace. You know?'

I feel prickles of discomfort hurtle down my spine. I, of all people, understand the eroding nature of secrets; the slow drip of guilt and remorse that leaves a sticky residue over everything you do or feel.

I wave my thumb in the direction of the front of the house. 'I need to get back.'

'Sure.' She follows me along the corridor. There is a chart beside the coat rack with the children's timetables on it, their music lessons, sports practice and coursework deadlines. I stop to admire it.

'We could do with one of those,' I say.

'It keeps us right.' She's rubbing her hands together. She's nervous suddenly. It's coming off her like radiation. 'Grace?'

'Mmm?'

'I'd rather you didn't mention this to Euan. Any of it.'

It's on the tip of my tongue to say I thought you were tired of secrets but I don't because I am seeing parallels between her and me. I don't want to but I am. 'I won't tell him,' I say.

When I climb back into the car, I don't drive off straight away. I sit with my head back against the rest and my eyes closed. For the first time in years, I've seen a side of Monica that makes me remember she's human: flesh and blood, like me. We're not natural friends; we never have been. As children we rubbed each other up the wrong way and that has lasted into adulthood. But adultery respects no one, and when Euan and I were having the affair, I went out of my way to avoid her. It was easier to do that than acknowledge how hurt she would be if she found out. And Paul. What is the matter with me? I have been the worst sort of wife. I have deceived him and I have cheated on him and I have the feeling it will get worse before it gets better.

There's a knock at the window and I look up, startled. It's Euan. He climbs in the passenger side and I automatically draw my body closer to the door. 'What brings you here?' he says.

'I took some food trays back to Monica.' I give him a

half-smile. 'Thank you for yesterday. I appreciate your help. I do.'

'Pity about the argy-bargy at the end though.' He raises his eyebrows. 'I thought we agreed you wouldn't bait her.'

'I know.' I bang my hand on the dashboard. 'I'm sorry. I am. But she really winds me up. She's so up herself. Do you think she really intends to be a nun?'

'Not for one moment. She's not doing this for the sake of her conscience; she's doing it to make trouble.' He is looking thoughtful, sad even. 'She's out for blood.'

'How can you be so sure?'

'What priest would advise someone to behave like this? She didn't even push Rose. It's none of her business what happened that night. This is one hundred per cent Orla's idea.'

'I suppose.' I take a big breath. 'I've been thinking. I can't just sit here and wait for her to turn up again. I'm going to go to Edinburgh this afternoon and see whether I can have a chat with her mother.'

'How will that help?'

'Angeline always liked me. She might be willing to fight my corner and change Orla's mind. They often battled over Orla's behaviour, but in the end Orla always did what her mother wanted.'

'Do you have her address?'

'Not exactly but I know she's married to a man called Murray Cooper and that they live in Merchiston. Can't be that hard to find them.'

'It's worth a try. But what if Orla's there?'

'She's supposed to be at the convent but if she is there then . . .' I shrug. 'I'll talk to her, not lose my temper this time, see if I can find out why. Why come back now?'

He sighs. 'Raking over old ground will mean everyone has to relive the whole thing. That won't be good for any of us.'

I shiver. 'It's Paul's reaction I'm worried about.'

Thinking about Paul is difficult. I am so afraid that he will end up hurt by this, hurt so deeply that he will question everything – our love, our marriage, our memories – and he will look ahead and see an impossible future. Despite my secrets, I believe that we have a strong and loving partnership. Could I stand up in court and convince a jury of my peers? Could I take the jury on a journey that would make them understand my actions and so forgive my mistakes?

I think I could.

September 1984

It's over two months since Rose died and I'm back at school, going through the motions. I quickly realise that I have to pretend to be over it otherwise people watch me and whisper about me and I get no peace. So I do. I do pretend. I pretend to everyone around me but not to myself. Me, myself, I remember everything: her bloated face, waxy skin and staring eyes. And I remember the reality of her father's grief; gutted. Quite literally. As if someone had emptied him out.

At the start of the new term, Orla doesn't turn up for school and I find out that she has left the village. Her father has moved to the London branch of the company and they will now be living in Surrey. I didn't see her or speak to her but I overheard my mother and Mo talking about how Orla didn't want to go and locked herself inside the house. The police had to be called to break down the door and gossip has it that she was dragged, kicking and screaming, into her father's car.

I'm glad that she's gone. I'm glad I'll never have to see her face again. She sent me a letter with her new address on the back of the envelope. I tore up the letter without reading it. Five more have arrived. I tore them up too.

Euan is fed up with me. He thinks it's time to move on from 'all this mithering on about Rose'. I understand why he feels that but I can't move on until it's sorted, because if I do, the dreams will never stop. And when I wake she'll be there, watching me.

I have been reading about ghosts and how they can be laid to rest. A ghost will stick around and haunt the living until satisfied that justice is done and that their loved ones will be fine without them. Rose won't leave me alone until I make amends. I'm sure of it. As sure as I am of my own breath and my own guilt.

So what to do? I can't bring her back and I can't go to the police.

My plan is to find someone special for Mr Adams. In less than a year, he has lost the two people who mean more to him than anyone else in the world: Rose and, before that, his wife Marcia. Marcia died of cancer; the fast-growing sort that mushrooms out of nothing and extinguishes a life in less time than it takes for one season to change into the next. Euan found this out for me. Two evenings a week he washes dishes in Donnie's Bites, the restaurant opposite the university. Mr Adams and Rose were regulars there and at the time of the tragedy that's all people talked about. How hard it was for Mr Adams. Double tragedy: first his wife and then his daughter.

'I'm not doing any more spying,' Euan says.

'I'm not asking you to spy. Not exactly.'

We're sitting on the bed in my room. David Bowie is on the record player in the background. I prefer Elton John but I've put Bowie on for Euan. My mum and dad think he's helping me with my biology Higher. The autumn term has barely started but already I'm falling behind with schoolwork. I've had to make decisions about what I want to do when I leave school and I said nursing and the careers officer was pleased. She wrote that down and told me what subjects I needed and where I should be applying to.

Truth is I have no idea about what I will do when I grow up. I can't think beyond this problem. I can't think beyond the shadow of Rose at the bottom of my bed and how best to please her so that she will leave me in peace.

'He looks fine. He's back at work now.' Euan is toying with the LP cover, flipping it around between both hands. 'He came into the restaurant last night to have something to eat.'

'On his own?'

'Lots of people eat on their own and anyway' – he kisses me just below my ear – 'I'm giving up that job. There's one going on reception in the community centre. Better perks. I'll get to use the gym for free.'

'Have they replaced you yet?'

'No and no.' He shakes his head. 'I know what you're going to say and I won't put you forward for the job. You don't need a job. You get more than enough pocket money as it is.'

'Yes, but—'

His mouth stops mine. I let him kiss me for a few seconds and then I pull away.

'I won't ask you for anything else, ever again. I promise.'

'For fuck's sake!' He stands up. 'How long is this going to go on?'

'What?'

'Your one-track mind.'

'I'm not—' I stop and try to think of the best way to explain it but his jaw is set and I know that look. 'I just want to make it right.'

He sighs and stares at his feet. 'Mr Adams will be fine. He's a good bloke. He won't have any trouble finding another wife and having more children. All in good time. You can't replace one person with another just like that.' He snaps his fingers. 'You have to let this go.'

I don't answer. I am locked into it. Euan can walk away. I can't.

'Fine then. I give up.' Resigned, he turns the door handle and looks back at me. 'See you around.'

I jump up from the bed. 'Are you chucking me?'

His face is set hard. 'There's no talking to you any more.' He closes the door behind him. I hear him say goodnight to my parents and then he's gone.

Over the next few days I persuade myself that Euan and I are just on hold and I persuade my parents to allow me to apply for the job. It takes some doing. I promise to work harder at school, to finish my meals and to spend less time alone in my room. Then they say yes.

The dishwashing job is gone, Donnie tells me, but he can go one better. I can be a waitress. The hourly pay is lower but I'll get tips. 'Especially if you smile like you are now. Pretty girl like you.'

The first time I serve Mr Adams he looks at me twice and says, 'Grace. Grace Hamilton?' He stands up and shakes my hand. 'How are you?'

'I'm fine.' I feel embarrassed and ashamed. 'I'm sorry. I never properly said . . . I'm so sorry.' My face flushes and my lips begin to tremble. 'I know you came to see my parents and . . . I'm so sorry.'

There is a sadness in his eyes that makes my throat catch. 'Rose was delighted to be in your patrol. She looked up to you.' He sits down again and pulls in his chair. 'You have nothing to be sorry for.' He points to the blackboard on the wall. 'So what would you recommend from Donnie's specials this evening?'

'The mussels are popular,' I tell him. 'And treacle tart for pudding?'

I find myself watching him from the shadow of the corridor that leads to the kitchen. He is even more handsome than I remember. He has high cheekbones and soft grey eyes and when his mouth smiles, they smile too. He plays squash and often arrives with a hearty appetite, his hair still damp from the shower, combed back from his forehead in straight lines.

I also remember that Orla wasn't the only girl in the Guides who had a crush on him. Much younger than all the other dads, he affected us all, to varying degrees. He was always friendly, without being overly so, and had the ability to tune in and listen to us in a way that most adults didn't, and that made me feel both shy and eager to talk to him.

Days become weeks and I begin to call him Paul. Sometimes he eats with colleagues, mostly other men, but occasionally a woman called Sandra joins him and sits up close, barely eating her own food as she seems to hang on his every word. If he is alone and business is slow, I sit down beside him and we chat about school and his work at university, bus timetables and the weather. I keep my eye out for women to introduce him to, teachers at school who're single, and other customers in the restaurant but no one seems special enough and, truthfully, the few times he is joined by Sandra I feel jealous and find every reason not to like her.

The dreams become less frequent – I must be doing

something right – and my life settles into a rhythm. Euan does a good job of avoiding me and I let him and then, after the October half-term, he doesn't come back to school. A week goes by and still he isn't in class. I ask my mum whether he's sick.

'Not that I know of,' she says, then hesitates before adding, 'He's moved down to stay with his uncle in Glasgow.'

'Why?'

'Better options there for his exams.'

I know this can't be true. He was already doing the Highers he needed for university.

I go next door to Mo. I haven't spoken to her for a few weeks and she spends the first minute hugging me and asking me how I am. When she takes a breath I say, 'Where's Euan?'

'He's in Glasgow with family. Better for him down there.'

'He didn't even say goodbye.'

'It all happened fast.'

'Could I have his address?'

She strokes my hair. 'I'm sure he'll write to you when he's ready.'

'I'll write first.' I give a short laugh. 'I don't suppose he'll be much good at letter writing anyway.'

I expect Mo to smile and give me the address but she doesn't, she turns away. 'Best leave it, Grace,' she says. 'How about a lemonade? I've just made some.'

'But please, Mo.' I move around so that I can see her face. 'He's my friend. I want to write to him.'

'No,' she says. 'That won't be possible.'

'Why not?' Tears are already filling my eyes and I blink them away.

She sighs and looks at me sadly. 'He doesn't want to hear from you.'

My solar plexus pulls inward as if I have been punched. I run out of the front door and keep running until I get to the playground. I sit on a swing and move backward and forward, backward and forward, keeping my feet on the ground and my eyes on the horizon. I can't believe it. Euan has left the village. I'm not allowed his address. He doesn't want any contact with me.

I stay on the swing for over an hour. It starts to rain. I don't move. I come to the conclusion that there's nothing I can do about it. If he doesn't want to talk to me then that's that. I know that Mo won't give in to me and I know that Macintosh is too popular a name for me to try to look for him. But one thing's for sure: he'll have to come back and visit and then we can talk. I'll bide my time. Keep myself busy. I'm in the restaurant three evenings a week and working harder with my school work, as I promised. My art teacher thinks I should study art at the college in Edinburgh. She writes a letter home to my parents.

'You're a born nurse,' my mum says. 'Don't go changing your mind at this late stage.'

'Now steady on, Lillian.' My dad puts down his knife and fork. 'What do you want, Grace?'

I want it to be like it was. I want to go back to 15 June

1984 and live it differently. He's waiting for me to speak. 'I'm not sure, Dad,' I say at last.

'In that case stick with nursing.' Mum loads more mashed potato on to my plate. 'Much safer that way. You don't know what type of people you'll end up mixing with if you go to that art college.'

'No rush,' my dad says, patting my hand. 'There's plenty of time to make up your mind.'

By the end of fifth year we're all seventeen. To my knowledge, Euan has not been home. Not once. But I do find out that he's been accepted at university to study architecture. I have enough Highers to start my nursing course but I'm not yet seventeen and a half so I decide to stay on for sixth year at school. 'You're far too young to leave home anyway,' my mum says.

Sixth Year Studies biology is harder than I thought. I've been serving Paul for over a year now and feel brave enough to ask, 'Do you ever do extra tuition?' I place his sea bass and sauté potatoes in front of him. 'I'm struggling a bit.'

He looks up from the paper he's reading. 'I'd be happy to help you. Why don't you speak to your mum and dad? See what they say.'

My parents are glad that I'm taking my studies so seriously and Paul coaches me in his lab at the university. Soon it becomes the highlight of my week. He helps me with my project and I see him in a different context, engrossed in his research work and respected by students and colleagues. He is easier to be with than anyone I know. Every so often we talk about Rose and one day as we're finishing up he tells me about his wife Marcia. They met at university when they were both eighteen. She fell pregnant by accident and neither of them was comfortable with the reality of an abortion. So they married. When Rose was born he fell in love with her, he said. She was the perfect baby, a sweet and cheerful bundle. To lose them both was the hardest thing.

'Anyway, enough about me.' His hand shakes as he locks the lab behind us. 'Have you applied for your nursing course yet?'

'Not yet. I have the application forms. I just haven't filled them in.'

'What's stopping you?'

I shrug. 'I'm not sure I want to be a nurse. I don't like the sight of blood.'

He laughs. 'That could make it tricky then.' He presses the button for the lift. 'Your drawings are beautiful, you know. The details included in your fieldwork report show exceptional talent.'

'I like drawing and painting,' I acknowledge. 'I had thought about art college but my mother thinks I'll end up mixing with hippie types and be smoking pot and having rampant sex with all and sundry.'

'It's a mother's job to worry. Don't be too hard on her.'

I punch the edge of his shoulder. 'How do you know that I'm hard on her?'

'It's that look you get on your face sometimes – don't-mess-with-me-or-else.' We step into the lift and he glances at me sideways. 'Feisty.'

'Feisty?' I hold up both fists. 'Who's feisty?'

I start to think of him at night, in my bedroom. I'm still a virgin. I wish I wasn't, I'm almost eighteen, but it was always going to be Euan and now he's gone and not one letter, not one, and although I've been out a couple of times with other boys I've quickly lost interest. I start to think about Paul, to fantasise about him kissing me, making love to me. No cold hands or fumbling like with boys my age but the experienced, confident touch of a grown-up man.

I don't dream about Rose any more. Every day I think of her but being close to Paul has lessened the guilt. I'm not over it. I know what I did and I know that it will never sit comfortably inside me. There is no way to reconcile killing a child but I am able to function and smile and even laugh again. I have to avoid certain triggers: I've never been back to the Guides, I don't go anywhere near the pond and I cannot abide the smell of lily of the valley soap. It transports me straight back to the pond's edge, Rose bloated and blue, her body fatally altered by the water.

Towards the end of the school year I'm having my last lesson with Paul and feeling desperate. He's so much a part of my life now that I don't know what I'll do without him and I can't think of another excuse for us to spend more time together. We cross over the road to Donnie's Bites. This time I'm not waitressing. I'm taking him for dinner, as a special thank you.

We're eating our starters, prawn cocktail with Donnie's spicy sauce, when he tells me he's planning to go to America for a couple of years. He has a place to study with Professor Butterworth in Boston. He is the most respected scientist in the field of marine biology.

My heart plummets. 'I'll miss you.' I blurt it out, just like that. I'm surprised at myself and I blush.

'And I you, Grace.' He looks at me kindly. It's a look he always gives me: tolerant, understanding, fatherly. I hate it.

'I'm not a child,' I tell him. 'You always look at me as if I'm a child. I'm not.' I take a mouthful of food. 'I'm eighteen next month.'

'I know.' He pauses. 'I am well aware of you.'

'You are?'

'Of course I am. I'm a man and you're a very attractive young woman.'

'You find me attractive?' My heart is swelling like a balloon.

'Grace.' There's that look again. 'Don't.'

'Why not? Because of the age difference? Paul, it's only twelve years.' I throw up my hands. 'That's nothing!'

'Not just that. I've had too much tragedy. You're young. You have your whole life ahead of you. It would be wrong of me—'

'What happened was terrible,' I butt in. 'To lose Marcia and Rose. But please. Give me a chance.' I reach across the table and take his hand. 'Please.'

It's three months until he leaves for America and he

agrees that we can spend some of that time together. He is working on a PhD – toxicology and disease in marine mammals – and I join him in the lab either helping set up experiments or working on a project of my own: a portfolio for art college. Although I've yet to tell my parents, I've decided that I can't possibly be a nurse. It's one of those ideas that sounds good in theory but in practice, I know it wouldn't work. It's not just the thought of blood and needles and broken limbs, it's the thought of having to encounter death. I can't do it. I know it would remind me of Rose and what I did to her. And that hurts too much.

Three days a week, after the lab work, Paul teaches me how to play squash. I pick it up quickly and before long we're having proper games: not taxing for him but good enough to feel like exercise. We go to the cinema together and find we have similar tastes in movies and books. He introduces me to his close friends and, to my surprise, I find I can hold my own. I know enough about Paul's work to talk with confidence and I find his friends impressed by my own growing conviction that I can paint. As time passes, I see Paul looking at me differently. I become less of a teenage girl and more of an equal and finally, towards the end of the summer, he kisses me and I know that at last he is seeing me as a woman. 'What man could resist loving you?' he says.

Before he goes to Boston he asks me to marry him. I tell my parents. Silence. My mother's mouth falls open into an O shape. My father is staring at me, newspaper poised above his knee, his head to one side, frowning, as if he hasn't heard correctly.

'Look!' I hold my ring finger towards them, moving it slightly so that the diamonds catch in the light from the standard lamp.

My dad clears his throat. 'It'll be a long engagement?'

'No, Dad. Paul starts work in America next week. I want to be married by Christmas so that I can go out and join him.'

'What? What is this madness, Grace?' My mother rises to her feet. 'You can't possibly be married!'

'Lillian.' My dad drops his paper and stands up too. 'Grace, as you know, we are very fond of Paul, but he is a man who has suffered two great losses in his life.'

'But that's the thing, Dad.' I take hold of my father's hand and swing it towards me. 'I can make him happy again.'

'Grace, you found his child.' His voice lowers. 'His dead child. I can't help but think that this has caused you to have feelings for him, feelings that you would never otherwise have had.'

I drop my dad's hand and step backward. I've thought of this too but I truly believe that what Paul and I feel for each other has nothing to do with Rose's death. I feel sure that if Rose was alive, we would still be in love. 'I love him.'

'Then I'm asking you to wait. Just wait a little while.'

'But I want to join him in America.'

'You can visit each other.'

'Two or three times a year,' my mum chips in. 'The time in between will fly by.'

'He might meet someone else.'

'If he loves you then he'll be happy to wait.' My dad walks towards the telephone. 'I'll have a word with him.'

'No!' I shout. I have a horrible feeling he will put Paul off. 'Paul makes me happy. I thought you would understand that.'

'Grace.' My dad rubs his hand across his forehead. 'What about Euan?'

'What *about* Euan?'

'I always felt that you two would end up together.' He looks pained. 'All through your childhood you had a bond.'

'But I'm not a child any more and I haven't seen Euan for ages and I haven't even thought about him in weeks.' That isn't entirely true. I think of Euan most days. It isn't deliberate. It's just that he pops into my mind. I eat a sandwich and I think about how Euan doesn't like tomatoes. I play some music and I remember the concert we went to in Edinburgh. I walk along the beach and I think of us jumping the waves. I take the bus into St Andrews and automatically look towards the back row in case he's sitting there.

But none of that matters. Euan is gone. My childhood is over. I'm eighteen now and ready to get on with the rest of my life. My father insists that Paul comes to have a word with him. Paul readily agrees. He had wanted to do the traditional thing and ask for my hand in marriage but I wouldn't let him. I didn't want my dad to have the opportunity to say no. I feel a sense of rightness, a rounding off – Paul and I sharing a life together.

Paul talks to my dad. He agrees to wait for a year but I do not. I insist, persist, push and pull until we all make up our minds to a compromise – six months. My mother grumbles and groans. She doesn't have long enough to plan the wedding. I am to wear her wedding dress: ivory silk with antique lace at the sleeves and neckline.

'Six months is surely enough,' I tell her.

'It feels rushed,' she says.

'I just want to be married and join Paul in Boston.'

'You've been over twice already.'

'Yes, but I want to be there full-time. As his wife.' I smile into the mirror and swish the skirt of the dress one way and then the other. 'Can you imagine, Mum? We can pop down to New York for weekends and everything.'

'Yes, yes. Although God knows your father will miss you.' She has her dressmaking pins on a strap around her wrist. She takes a couple out and tucks in the bodice. 'You're much thinner than I was. I hope Paul knows how difficult you are with food.'

'You will both come and visit me, won't you?'

'On a plane? I'm not sure your father would agree to that. We're quiet people, Grace. Not ones to make a fuss. You know that.'

I let it go, decide that I'll work on my dad later.

Paul and I are married on 15 April 1987. When I see him standing at the altar, all the love songs in the world fall short of what I feel. The ceremony is profound, permeated with the love that passes from his eyes to mine and back again. The reception is small – just close family and friends. Mo and Angus are there but Euan is not. He is at university in Bristol studying architecture. 'Exams,' Mo told me. 'But he sends his good wishes.'

I can see in her eyes that this isn't true but still I smile because, strangely, it doesn't hurt. I belong to Paul now. And he to me. I feel different. More grown-up, certainly, but also a fuller, better person, someone who has a clearer sense of direction and of herself. For the first time since Rose died I believe I have a future and that, at last, I am truly making it better.

8

By the time I get to Edinburgh it's already well past midday.
A search through the telephone directory confirms that
there's only one Murray Cooper living in Merchiston, in
a detached, early Victorian house, one of only a few that
hasn't been divided up into separate apartments. I park
on the street and walk between two stone pillars, anchors
for the iron gates that swing wide into the rhododendron
bushes either side. A gravel driveway sweeps around to
the entrance. An estate car has the driver's side open and
a golf bag resting next to the boot. The front door is part
wooden, part stained glass in the style of Rennie
Mackintosh: a single red poppy with green leaves on an
opaque beige background. My fingers feel along the
copperfoil squares at the edges of the panel before I ring
the doorbell. It sounds a prolonged ding-dong and a
balding man with ruddy cheeks comes almost immediately, steps into the porch and closes the inner door behind
him then opens the outer one, stares at me, says nothing.

'I'm sorry to disturb you but I'm looking for Angeline.
I wonder whether she might be home?'

'And you are?'

'Grace Adams. My maiden name was Hamilton. I was a friend of Orla's.'

'Ah.' He absentmindedly scratches the protrusion of fat around his middle then points a hand towards the car. 'I'm off out for a round of golf but I expect that Angeline will be free for a chat. Come inside.'

I follow him into the hallway. Black and white tiles stretch to the bottom of the wide stairs and beyond. A glass cupola provides natural light that fills and warms the space.

'You say you were a friend of Orla's?'

'As children, yes.'

'I expect she's alienated you too then, has she? With all her antics? I can't imagine what Angeline did to deserve such a daughter.' He tips his head to one side. 'But judging by the father I suppose it's hardly a surprise.'

I wonder whether I've heard him correctly but before I can ask, we are interrupted.

'Murray?' The voice is melodic but with a commanding undertone, unmistakably Angeline. 'Do we have company?'

'Indeed we do.' He holds on to the walnut banister and calls up. 'A young lady friend of Orla's. Grace is her name.'

'Grace?' Angeline comes to the top of the stairs and stands there. 'Grace?' She takes the steps quickly, elegantly, considering the height of her heels. Her face lights up. 'Look at you!' She throws out her arms and kisses the air either side of my cheeks. 'Aren't you looking fine!' She steps back and examines my eyes, my skin and down my body before coming back up to my face. She lifts the ends of my hair, rubs them between her fingers. 'You know I have a fabulous hairdresser.' She touches my forehead. 'And it's never too early to start with some simple cosmetic work.' She leans in closer and slips her arm through mine. 'It's a woman's obligation to keep herself attractive.'

'Thank you, but I'm happy as I am.' I can't help smiling. She looks almost exactly as I remember her and I'm catapulted back to ten years old again: chumming Orla home from school, dressing up in Angeline's old blouses and scarves, singing and tap dancing our way around the house, Angeline leading the way; chopping vegetables in the kitchen, learning how to make ratatouille, how to roast a duck and make authentic fish stock for bouillabaisse. And then the holiday in Le Touquet where she disappeared for two whole days, Roger and Orla steadfastly pretending everything was normal, everything was fine, nobody worried except me.

She is still beautiful, her bone structure is strong, her nose straight, her eyes as deep as her daughter's. Her clothes are classic, understated. She is wearing a simple, black cocktail dress and black suede stilettos. Delicate pink pearls lie around her throat. Her lipstick, though, is bold, the same pillar-box red that I remember.

'You've met Murray?' She gestures manicured nails towards him. 'We've been married almost five years now.'

'Each one happier than the last,' he says, staring intently at his wife as if alert for his next cue.

'Murray was in insurance but now he's retired. We love to travel. Three journeys abroad already this year.' She lets go of my arm and takes hold of his instead, smiling up into his face before turning back to me. 'Are you still living in Fife, Grace?'

I nod. 'Still in the village.'

'Fife has some excellent golf courses. Do you play?' Murray asks.

I shake my head.

'Husband?'

'Yes, I have a husband but no, he's not a golfer.'

'Pity. Waste.' He purses his lips. 'Would like to move up that way myself but Angeline has too many unhappy memories.' He pats her hand. 'Not all men are meant to be faithful.'

I try to catch Angeline's eye but she is busy with the collar of Murray's polo shirt. *What has she been saying?* Roger, with his tartan braces and endless patience for the low-key rhythms of family life – I can't imagine any man less inclined to adultery. 'I don't follow,' I say.

She turns her back to me. 'Murray, my darling, enough chatter! You will be late.' She steers him towards the door, hands him his golf shoes, his car keys and bundles him outside. He waves a hand backward in my direction and allows himself to be settled into the car, hair smoothed down, both cheeks and then his mouth kissed.

I watch them and think about Roger, salt of the earth, hard-working. He was kind, respectful, a quiet man who was bowled over by his exotic wife – a wife who never held back when it came to showing off. As a child I loved her exuberance, her caution-to-the-wind behaviour that so directly opposed my own parents' take on life, but standing here now, I see how much she exerts her will.

She waves Murray to the end of the drive then comes back inside.

'Roger wasn't unfaithful, was he?'

'There is more than one way to be unfaithful, Grace.' She wipes her feet and offers me her knowing look, the one that used to hold me in her thrall. 'He didn't give me the life he promised me.'

I look around. Half of my home could fit into Angeline's hallway and with Edinburgh house prices as they are, this property has to be worth more than a dozen of mine. 'Because he didn't earn enough?'

'I like powerful men, Grace. Men who are successful. Money is a part of that. I make no secret of it.'

'Yes, but—'

'But? But?' Her tone slides from melodic to clipped. 'Is it a crime for a person to reinvent herself? Or is the crime success itself, perhaps?'

'I don't mean to criticise,' I say, backtracking now, mindful of why I'm here. 'It's just that I remember Roger as a good man.'

'But memory can be faulty, don't you find? And there are so many things that children don't see.' She walks ahead of me and I follow her into a square sitting room with French doors leading into the back garden. The walls are painted a sunflower yellow and the carpet is a subtle shade of blue. A large painting hangs above the fireplace. Simple, wide brushstrokes suggest an African landscape at sunset, the outlines of stalking cats in the foreground, retreating wildebeest moving into the distance.

'So what brings you here?' she says.

'I had lunch with Orla earlier in the week and last night she came to the village to see me.'

'Well! And I thought she'd gone on her retreat.' She makes a tutting noise with her tongue. 'She was always unreliable. Entirely selfish. Sit down, Grace.'

I sit down on a cream leather sofa that swallows me into its middle. Holding on to the arm, I pull myself forward and perch on the edge. 'I came here to ask you about her.'

She sits opposite me on a high-back chair and holds herself straight. 'Why?'

'She could potentially make a lot of trouble for me.'

'What kind of trouble?'

I hesitate, look up at the chandelier then back at Angeline. 'It's complicated.'

'So complicated that you can't explain it to me?'

I try to smile. 'She knows something about me that could ruin my life. She is planning on telling the one person who will be most hurt by it.'

'Your husband?'

'Yes.'

She inclines her head. 'She knows that you are unfaithful to him?'

'Worse than that.' I briefly close my eyes. 'Much worse than that.'

She is frowning. She crosses one ankle over the other. 'You have children?'

'Two girls.'

'A mother will do anything for her children. You can judge me harshly—'

I go to speak but she holds up her hand.

'*Ça ne fait rien.* A mother will go to the ends of the earth for her child, dirty her hands, sell herself even if that's what it takes. I stuck with Roger because of Orla. Whatever my mistakes – and there were many – I tried to be the best mother I could.'

'I'm sure you did, Angeline.' I'm not about to argue that point. 'I just wondered whether you could help me understand Orla. Now. What's brought her back to Scotland? Why she wants to rake up the past? Is she really joining a convent?'

She shakes her head impatiently. 'Her head is full of nonsense. She has a mind to exorcise the past. But she'll come round.' She strokes a hand across her skirt, removes some imaginary fluff. 'Eventually.'

'Eventually won't be soon enough.' My voice wavers and I take time to breathe then lean further forward. 'She is coming to the village next Sunday and says she will tell my husband what I did. I can't stress how damaging this will be for my family. Is there any way you can talk to her for me?'

'No.'

'No?'

'No.' She sits back.

'Angeline.' I steady my hands on my knees. 'I would never have come here if I wasn't desperate. I'm appealing to you as a woman and as a mother.'

She thinks about this, looks up at me through eyelashes that are long and sleek and curled up at the ends. They have to be false. 'Shall we have coffee?'

'Please.' I feel like I've been given a stay of execution and when she leaves the room I stand up, start to walk the floor, moving around occasional tables and ornaments. A grand piano has pride of place close to the French doors. Photograph frames are arranged across its lid. A younger Murray with three girls: a smiling toddler holding a watering can, a teenager with braces on her teeth and an awkward tilt to her body, another girl doing a cartwheel. Three wedding photos, the same girls grown-up: off-the-shoulder dresses, tiaras, laughing bridesmaids, bouquets, new husbands in kilts. Then there's Murray and Angeline's wedding: people all around them, sunshine, a horse and carriage, electric smiles. I look closely at the family and friends' faces but Orla isn't there.

Angeline comes back with the tray. 'We honeymooned in Turks and Caicos. Have you ever been there?'

'Orla isn't in your wedding photos,' I say, this time sitting on a hard-backed chair to the side of Angeline.

'No.' She pours coffee from the pot into two bone-china cups with wide brims. 'She wasn't able to make it.'

'Oh?'

'Life is a series of choices, Grace. Sometimes we go right and sometimes we go left. But always we need to be moving forward. Orla does not have a talent for this.' She lifts the jug and holds it poised over my cup. 'Cream?'

'Thank you.'

'She made an enormous fuss when we left Scotland. She wrote to you, you know?'

I nod.

'But you never wrote back.'

I say nothing. I refuse to feel guilty about that too. After all, Orla wasn't even the one who killed Rose – it was me. I was the one who had to live in the same community, walk the same streets, feel Rose's presence both day and night and carry it still to this day, the secret lurking in my blood like a cancer.

'Does she have any proof?'

I keep my tone light. 'Proof of what?'

Angeline takes a sip of her coffee, returns the cup to the saucer and draws her back up straight. 'You strike me as a woman of experience, Grace. Would you say honesty is always the best policy?'

'If possible.'

'And yet you have a talent for concealment, do you not?'

I don't answer straight away. I wonder how much she knows, Angeline with her searching eyes and quick wits, her own margins wide enough to include blatant affairs and self-serving lies. Would Orla, all those years ago, have told her about Rose? Unanswered letters, a new school, a dearth of friends, would she have been pushed to confide in her mother? I doubt it. And likewise I'm not about to be pressured into saying something I'll regret.

On the tray there is a silver bowl heaped with misshapen brown sugar lumps. I use the tiny tongs to grab a lump and drop it into my coffee. Bubbles escape to the surface and I stir it slowly then take a sip. All the time Angeline watches me. She's waiting for a sign of weakness. I'm not about to buckle. 'So when you left Scotland, Orla was unhappy?'

'She had a breakdown. She made a foolish mistake, had to have an abortion and as if that wasn't bad enough' – she forces a sigh – 'when she was admitted to hospital, she threw herself from a window, ended up with concussion and a fractured femur but still very much alive.'

She looks across at me, primed for my reaction. I wonder why she's telling me this – and with quite such frankness. I feel a rush of questions – *Abortion? Suicide attempt? Why? What happened?* – but I keep my face impassive. I feel sick for Orla the teenager and for the woman she's become but I have a feeling that if I push too hard for answers, Angeline will clam up and I will be dismissed. 'That must have been a worrying time for you.'

'It was a dramatic stunt, nothing more.' She dismisses it with a flick of her wrist. 'Shortbread?'

'Yes, thank you.' I take a bite. It might as well be sawdust. 'What happened to Roger?'

Her eyes dart to mine.

'Orla told me he died.'

'Roger isn't dead!' She is bristling now. 'I divorced him ten years ago.'

'Orla lied?' I say at once, not quite believing it. Why would she do that? I can almost hear Euan's voice giving me the answer: *She wanted you to meet her and she was prepared to lie to get you there.*

'Perhaps she lied, perhaps you misheard her.' Angeline is unconcerned. 'It's of no importance. What *is* important is that my daughter was forty this year and what does she have to show for it? No husband, no children, no property, just debts and addiction and . . .'

She stops talking and re straightens her back, then moves her head around on her shoulders, eyes shut, chin dipped. It strikes me that each one of her movements is studied, meaningful. All for my benefit?

'Addiction?' I say, quietly.

'Yes, Grace. My daughter is a drug addict . . . was a drug addict,' she corrects herself. 'But then we only have her word for that. What does it matter what happened years ago? Bad things happen. It's how we deal with them that counts.'

That resonates with me. Rose died twenty-four years ago and how have I dealt with it? By hiding it. I have tried to make good with Paul, I have tried to be a good wife and mother but mostly I've coped by keeping it covered up.

'How are you anyway?' She treats me to an open smile. 'Tell me about your husband and children.'

Her mood has shifted again but I can't match it. I am

not about to be drawn into chitchat. 'My family are well and happy. I'm here to ensure it stays that way.'

'Your tone is harsh.' She pauses, lets the air freeze. 'Must I remind you that you have come to see me? That this is my home?'

Her expression seethes with hostility and I feel uneasy, afraid even. I have a horrible feeling that she can read me, just as Orla can. I'm out of my depth and the child in me wants to dissemble then retreat. But the adult is determined to leave this house with as much information about Orla as possible. 'You're playing with me, Angeline. I don't appreciate it.'

She laughs at this. It's deep and throaty and involves her tossing her head back with a younger woman's abandon. 'Grace! *Tu es si grave!*' She stretches across to touch my knee but I move to one side.

'This *is* serious.'

Her eyes heat up. 'Very well.' She settles her mouth back to neutral. 'Perhaps the truth will enable you to help both my daughter and yourself. She liked you once – very much – perhaps you can like each other again.'

I doubt that but I say nothing.

'Orla has spent several years in prison. She has been free for four months now.'

Everything inside me stops. The room itself seems to wait, hold its breath along with me. 'Prison?'

'She has yet to find her bearings. All this business with the nunnery. Nonsense.' She brushes the palms of her hands together. 'She could do with a friend, someone to help ease her back into society. Scotland has a special place in her heart.' She holds a finger out towards me then puts it against her lips. 'But I hope I can trust you to be discreet. I have protected Murray from the nuisance of it all.'

'*Nuisance?* Surely a prison sentence is more than just a nuisance?'

'Is that the wrong word?' She tries to communicate surprise but her eyebrows can't dent her unlined forehead. Her command of English is near perfect. I know that and so does she.

'What was she in for?' I blurt out. 'Was it serious?'

'Yes. Well . . .' She stands up. 'Orla was always attracted to the meanest sort of men . . . The details? I will leave her to tell you herself. But really, Grace! I think we've spent enough time catching up, don't you?' Arctic smile. She starts a brisk walk to the front door and I follow her. 'It's for the best that you don't come here again. I've moved on with my life. Perhaps you need to too. A new chapter. Delving back into the past is never a good idea.'

'But we're all a product of our pasts, are we not?' My legs are shaking as I go down the front steps.

She chooses to ignore this. 'Orla's married name was Fournier. Quite a scandal.' She half closes the door. 'And Grace?'

'Yes?'

'All this nonsense about the convent? I'm sure that were they aware of her past, she would be shown the door.' Her eyes are blank. 'So now you have what you came for?'

I turn away before she does – a small victory – and just about manage to resist the urge to run down the driveway. I drop my keys on the ground, pick them up again, unlock the car door and look back at the house. Bloated clouds are suspended over the roof, low and heavy, ready to tip and smother it. Angeline is standing at the window. She is too far away for me to see her expression but still it unsettles me and my skin crawls. I climb into the car, start the engine, drive about two hundred yards then pull into a parking space and just sit there, thinking, trying to make sense of everything that was said.

It's as if she's given me the colours – abortion, suicide attempt, addiction and prison sentence – dark colours with which to paint a picture of Orla's life. I don't know what to make of it. It's all much more dramatic than I expected. I wonder how much Angeline is twisting the truth, making brutal statements about Orla while leaving out any details that might help me make sense of her.

It strikes me that even Orla's memory isn't loved; no photos on the piano, no tender words or empathy. Angeline's fine speech about a mother doing anything for her children? I don't believe it. Not this mother.

I ring Euan. 'Can you talk?'

'Give me a sec.'

I hear him close the door behind him and walk outside. 'How was it?'

'Worrying. If Angeline's to be believed, Orla sounds like a loose cannon. But then Angeline is no doting mother. If I had to sum her up in one word it would be utterly ruthless.'

'That's two words.'

'I almost feel sorry for Orla,' I say quickly.

'Why? She's out to ruin you. Don't get sidetracked, Grace.'

'I know. I know. But listen, if I ever complain about my mother again just remind me of Angeline.'

'That bad, huh? But did you find out anything useful? Anything that might persuade her to back off?'

'Maybe. Are you near a computer?'

'I can go down to the cabin. Why?'

'Wait for it.' I take a deep breath, not prepared to believe what I'm about to say. 'According to Angeline, Orla had an abortion then tried to kill herself, was a drug addict and was in prison.'

'Shit. What the hell for?'

'I don't know. Angeline wouldn't say. She made a point of pretending to be open but then pulled back on the details. I wouldn't be surprised if she was exaggerating. Downright lying, even. Are you there yet?'

'I'm just switching it on.'

'And talking of lies, Orla told me that her father was dead and he isn't. How weird is that?'

'Sounds like a woman who'll use anything to get what she wants,' he says drily.

'Can you Google her? Her married name was Fournier.'

'It's warming up.'

I think about connections, threads that link one event with another. When did it start to go wrong for Orla? With Rose? Or was it before that? 'Have you found anything?'

I hear him typing. 'Nothing coming up so far.'

'It can't have been anything major then, can it?'

'Who knows. I'll keep trying. You coming into work tomorrow?'

'Yeah.'

'See you then. And Grace?'

'Yeah?'

'Don't worry. We'll fix it.'

5 May 1984

'You will be coming to Guide camp, won't you, Grace?' Miss Parkin says.

'Well, I was hoping . . .'

My mother gives me a look.

'When is it again?' I say.

'Six weeks' time. And with Rose recently joining your patrol, it will be such a boon to have you there. I know she's very young but she really is a sweet child and her father is a wonderful man. Very handsome too.' She looks wistful. 'He won't stay a widower for long.'

Miss Parkin is around at our house because my dad is making her a rocking chair. It's bad timing for me because I had hoped to avoid the Guide camp in June, but now, with my mother breathing down my neck, it's impossible to say no.

'Grace will be happy to come along, won't you, Grace?'

I nod and then try to smile. 'I'm off to Orla's. I'll be home around eleven.'

'No later!' my mum shouts and I resist the urge to bang the door on my way out.

It's a ten-minute walk to Orla's house which is pretty in a fairytale kind of a way and sits back from the road in a natural hollow as if sprouting from the rock behind it. It's early evening and I've come around to hers so that we can get ready for her sixteenth birthday party. This last couple of days she's been moody or distant and I'm hoping that she'll be back to her old self and that we can have a good time tonight.

When I knock on the door I hear Orla and her mother arguing. That's not unusual. They often go at it hammer and tongs, until one or other gives up. But this time it sounds particularly fierce. I ring the bell and seconds later Orla throws the door wide, doesn't acknowledge me but turns back to her mother and continues her rant.

The French is so rapid I can barely make out what they're saying. I catch phrases like 'none of your business', 'how dare you!' and 'your father is a gentleman' from Angeline while Orla hurls insults: *Salope! Garce! Putain!*

I don't stop in the hallway. I know there's no point in getting between them. I tried that before and ended up catching the tail end of a punch. Instead I climb upstairs to Orla's room, sit on her bed and read an old copy of *Jackie* magazine. We're really too old for it now but one or other of us still buys it for the Readers' True Experiences. I start to read 'I Knew He Was Married But I Didn't Care' and am halfway through when Orla comes crashing into the bedroom, banging the door so violently that a shelf of books tilts to one side and drops on to the bed beside me. The right side of her face is red where her mother has slapped her.

'Jesus, Orla!' I put *Jackie* aside and start to gather the books into a tidy pile. 'What on earth were you fighting about this time?'

'You couldn't follow it?' She pushes me aside, scoops at the books with her arm and tips them all on to the floor where they land in a heap of twisted spines and crushed pages.

'I don't think those were the sort of French words Madame Girard would normally teach us,' I tell her, trying to straighten the shelf back on the wall.

'Will you leave that!' She grabs the corner of the wood and hurls it across the room. It hits the edge of the window-pane and cracks the glass. Several jagged lines fan out from the crack. One stretches halfway across the window.

'Fuck's sake, Orla!' I hold on to her shoulders and shake her. 'Calm down! You'll end up not being allowed to go out. You can't miss your own party.'

She pulls away from me and rummages in the cabinet beside her bed. Behind the hair ties, make-up and loose change she has hidden a packet of cigarettes. She throws herself down on the bed and crosses her legs. The bed shakes as she uncrosses them, bangs her fist on the wall, re-crosses her legs, then agitates her left foot backwards and forwards. 'My mother is a bitch, a *putain*, a whore.'

'Look, everybody hates their mother sometimes.' I hold on to her wayward foot. 'It's only natural. God, sometimes

I want my mother to *die* she's so bloody annoying but it blows over.'

She looks at me and I see there are tears in her eyes. My own eyes automatically fill up in response. I have rarely seen Orla cry. She has never to my knowledge been even close to tears since she fell off the harbour wall when we were ten and broke her arm in two places. She is fierce and feisty and will take anyone on, suffer anything. It's part of the reason I like her.

She looks away, picks at the wallpaper and says quietly, 'You don't know the half of it. My father is an arse for putting up with that bitch.'

I am reminded of Edinburgh, standing in Jenners department store and watching Orla's mum, her lipsticked smile, her body leaning into Monica's dad. 'Orla, it's your birthday!' I reach forward and hug her. 'Let's just forget all this and have a great time.'

'Yeah, exactly.' She heaves in a shuddering sigh. 'On my fucking birthday, as well.'

'Let's make each other up.' I find some rouge, eye shadow and mascara. Orla leans forward and closes her eyes.

'I can't wait to get out of this dump.'

I paint two shades of green over her lids and up as far as her eyebrows. 'There are probably worse places.'

'Like where?'

'Close your eyes!'

'There's a whole world out there,' she grumbles. 'And we're living in a place the size of a postage stamp where everybody knows everybody else's business.'

'Couldn't you go to your aunt's in France?' Orla's aunt is even more glamorous than her mother. She is a fashion buyer for Galeries Lafayette and whenever she comes to stay she oozes couture and elegance. 'I'd love to live in Paris.'

'It's not all it's cracked up to be,' Orla says, lifting the hand mirror to admire herself. 'America would be better. Wide open space. Cowboys. Men with muscles bare-back riding.' She pouts at her reflection in the mirror. 'Take me, I'm yours.'

By the time we get to the village hall she's back to her old self. The disco is set up and we spend the first ten minutes dancing then we stand back with some Irn-Bru to watch the others.

'Shall we get some fresh air?' Orla says. 'I've hidden some vodka under the second bush past the phone box.'

We go outside just as Monica comes around the corner. She is positively shimmering with animosity. She glows like the red forty-watt bulb in my bedside lamp and her chest is heaving like she's just run a mile. She stops in front of Orla. 'I want to talk to you.'

'Not *now*, Monica.' Orla gives a weighty sigh of boredom but I'm close enough to see that the pulse in her neck begins to beat faster. 'Can't you see I'm busy? I have a birthday to celebrate.'

'Your mother is a filthy French whore.'

'Monica!' I move in front of Orla. 'What the hell? Go away! You're not even invited!'

'This is between me and Orla,' she shouts. Her eyes are

wild and her hair is standing up on end like she is possessed. 'Now move out of the way.'

I look back at Orla for an answer.

'It's okay, Grace,' she says, shrugging, nonchalant. 'We've already had a run-in about this. Looks like she's come back for some more punishment.'

'Don't think you'll get away with this.' Monica points a shaky finger into Orla's cheek. 'May you rot in hell, Orla Cartwright. May your whole family rot in hell! Every last one of you.' She throws the last words at Orla like a witch delivering a curse and I'm not surprised when she finishes it off by spitting on the ground at our feet.

As she turns away, Orla's hand moves out and grabs the back of Monica's blouse. It all happens quickly and I am slow to react. By the time I try to separate them Orla is sitting across Monica's back and is pulling her hair. The screaming and swearing is louder than my entreaties to stop and I can't match Orla for strength. I need Euan's help but he hasn't arrived yet. I know where he'll be – down at the harbour hanging about with Callum.

I run as fast as I can and hear them before I see them. They are sitting on one of the two picnic benches that are on the grassy area opposite the harbour wall. They have cans of lager next to them and are arm wrestling.

'Come quickly!' I am puffed and I lean my hands on my knees. 'Monica and Orla are fighting.'

They both jump up and we run back together to the village hall. Callum hauls Orla off and holds her back while

Euan helps Monica to her feet. He tells her that she should see a doctor about her head. There's blood trickling down the side of her cheek on to the collar of her blouse. She touches it with her fingers. 'I think it's just superficial,' she tells him. 'I want to be a doctor, you know. I'm going to get out of this place.'

'Right.' Euan takes a few steps backward to stand level with me.

Monica's face twists. She looks a complete sight. I wonder how she's going to explain this at home.

'I'll walk you home,' Callum volunteers.

Monica looks him up and down. 'Don't bother,' she says. 'Enjoy your party.' Her eyes fill up. 'Don't let me stop you.' She turns and lurches off.

I watch her retreating back and I shiver.

'Show over.' Euan takes my elbow. 'Fancy a dance?'

We all go back into the hall. Orla wipes the back of her hand over her bloodied lip but otherwise she seems to be none the worse for her fight. She starts slow dancing with a boy from fifth year. His hands slide down across her bum and pull her closer. Euan takes my hand and leads me on to the floor. He puts his arms around me.

'I don't want to stay,' I tell him. I pull away. 'I think I'll just go home.'

'I'll walk with you,' he says. He looks around. 'Nothing much happening here anyway.'

I put my arm through his and we go down on to the beach so that we can walk home along the shore. We both have torches in our pockets and we shine them ahead of us.

'What was the fight about?'

'Orla's mother and Monica's father are having an affair.'

'Shit.'

'I know. Monica's never been my friend but I feel sorry for her.' I lean my head against his shoulder. 'I wonder how she's going to be able to show her face at school on Monday.'

'Wasn't a good idea to start a fight, though. Especially with Orla. Monica was bound to come off worse.' We're close to the water's edge where waves stalk us, stretch out and cover our shoes. Icy water splashes my ankles.

'It's freezing!' I shriek and pull him towards the sand dunes.

His arms circle my waist and he kisses me gently on the lips.

'What was that for?'

'Because you're the prettiest girl I know.'

'Simply irresistible.' I blow him a kiss and start to mime a model's catwalk. He's shining the torch at me and light reflects back up on to his face. I expect him to be smiling but he's not. His expression is serious as if he's working through a maths problem.

'Do you want to go out some time?' His voice is low. 'Grace?'

'We're always together.'

'I mean out. Out together.' He scrapes his right shoe in an arc across the sand. 'Properly.'

I frown. 'Like a date you mean?'

'Yeah.' He waits.

I think about it. Euan and me. Me and Euan. A couple. 'Okay then.'

'Okay then?'

'Okay then.' I start giggling and then I push him. He pushes me back and I topple, give a scream.

'Grace, is that you?' It's my dad's voice.

Euan pulls me up straight.

'What's going on down here?' My dad appears over the sandbank, shines his torch right at the two of us. 'Oh, it's you, Euan. I'm just on my way down to the social club for a game of snooker. Better head on home, the pair of you. It's too cold to be out gallivanting.'

9

When Paul leaves for work and the girls for school, I take Murphy for a quick run on the beach and then drive to work. Euan is already there. 'Was there anything on the web about Orla?' I say as I come in the door.

'Nothing. Whatever she was in prison for, it couldn't have received much press coverage.'

'Shit.' I start unbuttoning my coat. 'I was hoping we'd find out what she'd done.' I think back to Angeline's words. 'I thought she said her married name was Fournier but maybe I heard her wrong.'

'I'll try other spellings later but, in the meantime, I've been ringing round and I've found the convent she's staying in,' he says. 'St Augustine's. It's close to Hawick.' He logs off his computer and stands up next to me. 'Shall we go?'

'To the convent?' I stare at him. 'Now?'

'Why not? Like you said – we can't just sit around and let her make all the moves.'

'Are you sure?' I didn't expect this. 'It's a long drive. We'll be gone the whole day.'

'I wasn't planning on doing much work this week anyway.' He's already putting on his jacket. 'I won't say much. I promise.' He takes hold of my elbow. 'But I'll be there if you need me.'

'Do you think we should let someone know we're coming?'

'No. I don't want her spinning us a line about no visitors,' he says. 'Better just to turn up. That way she can't fob us off.'

He locks the cabin behind him and we start off up the path and past the house. Visiting Orla when she least expects it seems like a good idea and I'm glad that Euan is prepared to come with me. The clock is ticking, the seconds, minutes and hours bearing down on me. It's less than a week until Sunday lunch when Orla plans to – what? Make an announcement as we eat? *Oh, by the way, everyone! Has Grace mentioned that she killed Rose? Yes, really! She pushed her into the water. Left her there to drown.* Or is she intending to take Paul aside, into his study perhaps, where his research papers and textbooks are piled high on the desk and photos of the girls smile down from the walls; Ella, Daisy and Rose witnessing Paul's distress as he hears about the sorry fate of his first daughter. Will she even hold Rose's photograph as she tells him?

I won't let it happen. Sure, she's tougher and more streetwise than me and, like her mother, her margins are wide but this is my family I'm fighting for. There's nothing more important to me than that.

We travel in Euan's car and while we drive I tell him about Angeline. 'She behaves with complete authority. Like she's some sort of monarch. And she has no sympathy for Orla.'

'Well, neither have we.'

'Yes, but she's her mother! You'd think she'd at least express some love or understanding. Take the abortion for example. She described the pregnancy as a foolish mistake and Orla's suicide attempt as a dramatic stunt.'

'Lots of women have abortions. They don't throw themselves out of windows afterwards.'

'Yes, but it was obviously traumatic for her! And what about the man? I bet he didn't suffer.'

'Grace, you have to stop with the excuses!' He slows the car down and turns to stare at me. 'Orla is trouble. She'll tell Paul about Rose's death and life as you know it will be over. Don't go down the road of trying to understand her.' His tone is harsh. 'She's as manipulative as her mother. She's a conniving bitch. You know that.'

'I know. I know.' I'm surprised by his vehemence and I put my hand on his knee. 'It's just that if her mother had been—' I stop and think about my own girls, how I would move heaven and earth to protect them. Orla is a very real threat to their happiness. There's no room for weakness on my part. 'You're right. No sympathy. None.'

The convent grounds are close to the English border, off a long, straight road with rolling hills and sporadic clumps of conifers either side. When we see the sign, St Augustine's Roman Catholic Convent, we leave the main road and drive down a narrow single track, bumpy with dips and potholes, until we come to the front of a red-brick wall. The wall is upwards of thirty feet high and has a huge wooden door, shaped like the jawbone of a whale, positioned halfway along it. A smaller, person-sized door is cut into the bigger one. We use the iron knocker three times then stand back to wait.

Less than a minute later, there is the distinctive sound of someone dragging back the bolts. Then the door swings open, wide enough for us to see a smiling nun. She's short, five feet at the most, and her frame is as delicate as a child's. I imagine that even a moderate wind would fill her black skirts and lift her heavenwards.

'I'm sorry to bother you. My name is Grace and this is Euan. We need to speak to Orla Fournier. Urgently,' I add.

'Fournier?' she repeats, pursing her lips.

'Cartwright,' Euan says and looks at me. 'She's using her maiden name.'

The nun nods. 'Are you friends, my dear?'

'Not exactly but it's important that we speak to her.'

'Well now, Orla is here on a retreat and in those circumstances we—'

'It's an emergency. Family business,' Euan says, moving forward so that the toe of his shoe is just inside the doorway. 'We can't leave without speaking to her.'

Her smile doesn't waver. 'You're the young man I spoke to on the phone?'

'That's right,' Euan says. 'We're sorry to come without an appointment but there wasn't time to make one.'

'Orla will be leaving us on Friday. Could your business wait until then?'

'I'm afraid not,' Euan says. 'Time is of the essence.'

'In that case you must come inside.' She pulls the wooden door open wider. It creaks on its hinges before coming to rest against the back of the bigger one. 'I'm Sister Bernadette.' Her handshake is firm. 'Welcome to our convent.'

We step into a cobblestone courtyard with a grass square at its centre. The grass is neatly trimmed and edged with rose bushes.

'Let me just bolt the door behind us,' Sister Bernadette says, small fingers deftly drawing the heavy iron back into place. 'I'm told one can never be too careful.'

A black and white cat makes a beeline for me and weaves through my legs, his tail curling around my calves. Then he gives a plaintive meow and sits at my feet looking up at me. I bend to stroke him and he purrs loudly, his eyelids dipping with pleasure.

'I see Bubble is making friends with you,' Sister Bernadette comments. 'We're rather overrun with cats! And none of them any good at mousing.' She moves her long skirt aside to reveal a small grey kitten resting in its folds. She scoops him up and carries him close to her neck. 'Hard to resist though, aren't they?'

As my eyes grow accustomed to the scene, I count five more cats sleeping in neat circles in the suntrap on the grass. 'You have quite a collection,' I say.

'Thirty-six at the last count.' She frowns momentarily. 'We really must find homes for them.' Then shakes off the thought and says, 'Come along, my dears.'

We walk around the grass and through an open archway in the building diagonally opposite. Bubble runs along the flagstone corridor ahead of us. Treading lightly on silent paws, he stops in front of a door and waits for us to catch up. We are shown into a square room with three long windows facing south. It's almost midday and the sunlight catches the dust motes that hang in the air. The room is comfortably but sparsely furnished. Two well-used sofas face each other, and a solid oak coffee table is positioned to one side, underneath the window sill. Several books lie on the table scarred with the evidence of time and heavy usage.

'Sister Philomena is threatening a trip to Ikea but it suits us, I think.'

'It's homely,' Euan says, stroking the back of the sofa. Bubble jumps up beside his hand and waits for it to stray his way. 'People- and cat-friendly.'

'Exactly! A little make do and mend in places but we're here for the Lord's work. Let others worry about interior design.'

We both smile. I'm so tense, my face is beginning to feel like it will crack.

'Now to find Orla. At this hour she may well be helping in the dairy.'

'Before you go, Sister,' I say, my hand skimming her sleeve. 'I'm wondering – do you think Orla will join you permanently?'

'As a novice, you mean?'

I nod.

'There's been no suggestion of that. I think Orla's feet are very firmly planted in the outside world.' She gives me a conspiratorial nudge. 'A life of prayer is not part of her aspiration.'

'I thought she might be swayed by the sense of community and ambience here.'

She looks dubious. 'Sometimes a life of prayer and worship may seem attractive but in reality, it can be a challenge.'

Bubble leaves with Sister Bernadette and we are left alone.

'You were right,' I say to Euan. 'Another lie. So much for the becoming-a-nun story.'

'It should make it easier,' he says. 'If she's not doing it as a matter of conscience then we have a better chance of changing her mind.'

'My stomach is churning.'

'I'm here.' He briefly touches my cheek. 'Moral support.'

The next hour or so will dictate the course of the rest of my life and I'm terrified. Terrified, but at the same time glad to be taking action. Third time lucky. *I can do this.* I breathe deeply and walk up and down the room. I'm determined not to lose my head this time.

Five minutes pass and, finally, Orla walks in. Euan is standing by the window and I am sitting on the arm of the sofa, skimming through an edition of *The Imitation of Christ* by Thomas à Kempis.

'Grace. Euan.' She does a good job of smiling. 'This is a surprise.' She looks at the book in my hand. 'See, Lord,

I stand before You naked and poor, begging for grace and imploring mercy.'

'I hadn't got that far,' I say.

'Chapter 112.' She is dressed as she was before. Dark trousers and cardigan, white top, her hair tied back in a simple band and no make-up.

'Right.' I put the book back on the table. 'Look, I'm sorry we've interrupted your stint in the dairy but we . . .' I look at Euan. He's staring away from us, out through the window. 'I need to talk to you.'

'Take a seat.' She passes me a cushion embroidered with the words *God is light*. I wedge it into the small of my back. She sits down opposite, crosses her legs and waits. I am immediately reminded of Angeline. Both mother and daughter have a rock-hard stillness that radiates outward like a force field. They are entirely sure of themselves, as if their thoughts and motives are superior to everyone else's.

'So . . . I feel like we haven't had a proper chance to talk. The first time, in the restaurant, I was too shocked to respond sensibly and the second time it was my girls' birthday and well . . .' I see how it feels to smile at her. 'I was more concerned with being a mum.'

I stop there. She doesn't fill the silence. She just sits, her hands clasped on her lap, her eyes watching me. My smile feels misplaced, tactically weak. I remove it at once.

'Orla, I've come here to ask you not to visit my house on Sunday.'

She raises one eyebrow. 'You don't think Paul will be relieved to have some closure?'

'Paul accepted the pathologist's verdict.'

'He must have had questions?'

'It was an *unfortunate accident*,' I stress. 'Most likely caused by a combination of factors: the storm, unfamiliar ground, a child's natural curiosity putting her at risk.' As I'm speaking a memory comes back to me: Paul, several years ago, visiting Rose's grave, grief talking. *Why did she go into the water?* I blink the memory aside and push on. 'Your story would be—'

'My story?' she interrupts. 'The truth is not a story. The truth is the truth. Wouldn't you agree, Euan?'

All this time Euan has been standing by the window but now he comes and sits down beside me, his thigh resting against mine. 'The time for the truth was then, Orla.'

'The truth will out,' she says. It's almost a whisper, smooth as melted chocolate.

'Only because you're going to say something.'

'And not before time.'

'Dredging it up won't help anybody.'

She laughs at this. 'It will help me! Aren't my feelings worth considering?'

'Orla, we had our chance to be truthful,' I butt in. 'Now time has moved on and Paul and I' – I bring my hands together – 'our destinies are linked. We have two children. You have to understand how damaging this would be for us as a couple and as a family. In fact – that would be it! No couple, no family, not after that.' I'm managing to keep my tone even but only just. I take a few breaths, wait for Orla to answer.

She doesn't. She stares at Euan and then me and then back to Euan again.

'Let's be clear.' She leans towards me. 'I am going to tell Paul about that night whether you like it or not. What you think or feel is irrelevant.'

'But, Orla, you didn't even push her! It was me! You weren't directly involved.'

'I was there. Right next to you. It might as well have been my hand.'

'But it wasn't your hand. You were simply a bystander.'

'I see.' She looks up to the ceiling and then back at me. 'So a blind man is walking along the street. There's a manhole in the road but the cover has been left off. I see him walk towards it. I watch as he falls down into the hole. Who is to blame, Grace? The person who left the cover off? The man himself – perhaps he should have stayed home – or is the fault mine for watching him fall?'

'That's hardly the same thing,' Euan says. 'Nobody saw Rose drown.'

'So you're saying Grace is innocent?'

I hold my breath. I expect him to tell Orla what he's been telling me all these years, that there's no hard and fast evidence it was me. Coincidences happen. Just because Rose was found close to the bank where I pushed her – that doesn't prove anything.

But he doesn't cast doubt on my guilt, instead he says, 'Accidents happen. Tragic accidents that can't be undone.' He shrugs. 'The only option is to move on. Put it behind you and move on.'

Orla gives Euan the full benefit of her stare. 'We killed someone,' she says flatly. 'We killed a child.'

'It was dark, Orla!' I shout. 'We didn't know she'd fallen into the water.'

She turns back to me. 'And the next day when we found her? What about then?'

'Well, it was too late, wasn't it? She had been dead for hours.'

'We could have owned up.'

'We could have . . .'

'But I stopped you saying anything.'

'But I didn't have to listen to you!'

'Of course you did! You always listened to me.'

'I had free will. I chose not to exercise it. That doesn't make it your fault.'

'We wouldn't even have been there if it hadn't been for me.' She tips her head to one side and says softly, 'Seriously though, how have you lived with it all these years?'

'With difficulty,' I admit. 'And believe me – that's an understatement. But always, *always* I try to make things good and better whenever I can.'

'She was a child. We were cruel and careless and she ended up dead.'

'I know that, Orla! I fucking know that.'

Euan puts his hand on my arm.

I swallow, lower my voice and say, 'Believe me, there has not been one single day when I haven't thought about Rose and wished that I'd done it differently – but it happened. Confessing to Paul and dragging my family through the mud will not change the fact that we were there and Rose died.'

'It keeps you stuck in the past though, doesn't it?'

'What do you mean?'

'You haven't moved on. You straddle two time zones, keeping one foot planted in each. Isn't that uncomfortable?'

My heels start drumming on the floor. 'I have no idea what you're on about.'

'Are you sure? Are you sure you're not still living back where you left off? What about Euan?' She looks at him but he doesn't bite. 'The man you think you should have had. Your feelings preserved with first-love intensity. You hark back to a time when life was simple, before you loaded yourself down with guilt and remorse and family baggage.'

'My family are not baggage, Orla. They are the reason I'm here.'

'You're here for yourself.'

The rising temper inside me is so all-encompassing that I daren't speak.

'You're stuck, Grace. You're on a rubber band looping backward. You're continually pulled right back to that night and the horror that followed.' She blows out her cheeks and says, 'You even married her father.'

'I fell in love with him. I told you that already. I love him still.' My tone is staccato and my fists are clenched. I want to hurt her physically, pull her to the ground and stamp some sense into her. It's not an emotion I'm used to and my face is heating up from the effort involved in staying still.

She gives me a satisfied smile and I realise that getting me riled is exactly what she's after. In my mind's eye I see her on her knees in front of me, defeated, her cheeks tear-stained. It makes me feel better. I pull my feet tight into each other and hold them still.

'You know what, Grace?' She laces her fingers together and raises her arms straight up above her head. 'I think you'll feel much lighter when we get this out in the open.' She looks at Euan. 'I think we all will.'

'This is not a game to me.' My voice is steady again.

She widens her eyes as if she can't believe I would suggest such a thing. 'Me neither.'

I lean forward. 'You have to see how impossible my life would become.'

'But think what it would be like if you no longer had anything to hide.' She also leans forward. She is whispering. 'To an outside observer it would look as if we were sharing secrets. 'What would it feel like?'

I almost fall into her eyes. I can't help it. In direct sunlight they are smoky, large, fluid and soft as cashmere. I take a moment to think about what it would be like to journey through my life, free and easy, nothing nasty under any stones, or in the dark corners of the closet. How effortless it would be to live life without fear of discovery. How refreshing to embrace complete honesty. Wonderful. And impossible.

I break eye contact and look out of the window. An

ancient gardener is using a hoe to clear weeds at the edge of the cracked paving stones. He is slow and methodical and every so often he stoops to lift the weeds and throw them into his wheelbarrow. After a minute my mood has settled and I look at her again. She is sitting back in her seat, her legs stretched out before her.

'You know Euan thinks there's a distinct possibility that I didn't kill Rose,' I say.

She glances across at him. 'Does he now?'

'He thinks there are other explanations. She could have been sleepwalking, she could have been out looking for something—'

'Well, God forbid that we don't consider Euan's opinion.'

'He has a point.'

'He wasn't there. He was off getting drunk with Callum and co. Weren't you, Euan?'

He doesn't answer.

I grab her arm. 'We just automatically assumed that it was me.'

'It was exactly the same spot.'

'Coincidence.'

'I know what happened to Rose.' She shakes me off. 'There is absolutely no doubt in my mind. None.'

The room is growing darker. The sun is now fully hidden behind clouds that cover the sky and cast murky shadows on the walls. I pull my cardigan together and do up the buttons. 'What happened to your husband?'

She shrugs. 'What's it to you?'

'I'm curious.'

'It didn't work out.'

'How come?'

'We weren't suited. Sometimes that happens, doesn't it?' Her voice thickens. 'It seemed like we were compatible. We were both half French. We both loved rock music. He was sexy.' She pauses. 'We knew each other three weeks and were married in Las Vegas. It felt overwhelming, exciting. We were together a year before it dawned on me that he wasn't all he seemed.' Her eyes slide away from mine. 'That's it. There's nothing more to say.'

'And the drugs? And the prison sentence?' I say quietly.

She starts back but recovers almost immediately. 'Congratulations. You really have done your homework. Euan's idea, was it?'

'No, it was my idea. And your mother helped.'

She flinches. It's brief but acute and, in spite of myself, I feel for her. Even now she wants Angeline to put her first.

'You went to see her?'

'Yesterday.'

'She must have been delighted when you turned up! She doesn't dare talk about me to all her posh friends. She is denied the pleasure of gossiping about me because it would reflect badly on her. I am kept out of sight and out of mind.' She is visibly rattled, her foot shaking, her fingers tapping a rhythm on the arm of the sofa. 'I've no doubt she took great delight in telling you about all the bad men I've chosen over the years. The drug abuse. And then there's my stint in prison. Convenient for her – meant

I couldn't visit. And did she visit me, I hear you ask?' She raises her eyebrows. 'Not once.' She laughs. It's a discordant sound that makes me recoil. 'Kept you away from Murray, did she?'

'He went out for a round of golf. He's under the impression your father was unfaithful.'

'I know. My mother as a victim?' Her tone is acerbic. 'Can there be anything less likely?'

'I never noticed as a child quite how manipulative she was.'

'She has a patent on that al—' She stops short, seems to remember that we're not meant to agree on anything.

'So should I believe your mother?'

'I don't care what you believe.'

'Lying about your dad's death. That was . . .' I try to find the right word. 'Cheap. It was cheap and it was callous.'

'So? It got you to meet me, didn't it?' She says it without emotion. Her mood has oscillated from pent-up agitation to disengagement. She has the most disconcerting stare – knowing and yet compassionless. It makes me realise that she's not the girl she was. I thought I was dealing with a grown-up version of the girl I once knew – a girl who was impulsive and head-strong, who could lie and cheat but underneath it all had a beating heart. This isn't that girl.

'I don't remember you like this.' I reach across and shake her knee. 'What has happened to you?'

'We all have to choose sides.'

'What sides?'

'Right and wrong. If someone does wrong they should be punished, shouldn't they?'

'Well, yes but—'

'What do you think, Euan?' she says loudly. 'Should people get off scot-free?'

'Rose's death was an accident,' he says. 'Punishment doesn't always have to be public or direct. There are many ways to make good.'

'And I have,' I say. 'I make Paul happy. I do. Telling the truth about what happened to Rose will not serve him well.'

'Are you entitled to make that decision for him? I wonder, if you were to lose one of your daughters, wouldn't you want to find out who was responsible?'

The thought of losing either of my girls is abhorrent to me. I'm not about to go there. And I won't explore Paul's lingering pain either. It's something that even in my quietest moments, when the family is asleep and I'm curled into Paul's back, I daren't think about.

I change direction. 'You're not becoming a nun then?'

'Says who?'

'Sister Bernadette. No suggestion of it, she said.'

Orla shrugs. 'So what?'

'So what you're a liar? So what you're a meddler? So what you don't give a shit about anyone except yourself?'

'Grace.' Euan rests his hand on mine and I sit back, take a deep breath.

'Yes! Listen to Euan,' Orla says, a sideways smirk on

her face. It makes me want to slap her. 'He'll keep you right.'

'What is this about, Orla? Twenty-four years later and you turn up to set the story straight. Why?'

She shrugs. 'Memories. Past lives. You know how it is.'

'No. I don't know how it is. I don't know how you get from that to this.'

'I don't have to explain myself to you.' She looks at Euan. 'Either of you.'

In my handbag, I still have the photo I took from my parents' wall, the one where Orla and I are dressed in jodhpurs and riding boots, splashed in mud, happy with our rosettes. For six years we were best friends. We spent almost all our free time together. We knew the other's likes and dislikes, could speak for one another and anticipate each other's thoughts. Surely that's still worth something.

'I brought a photo with me.' I dig around inside my bag to find it. 'Do you remember this?'

She glances at it and then away again.

'No, look!' I stretch to put it into her hands. 'Really look at it.'

I watch her eyes roam over the picture moving from one detail to another.

'You won that day, didn't you?'

'We both did.' I point to the rosettes. 'You over the jumps, me on the cross-country.'

'Bobbin never had the patience for cross-country. He always stopped to chomp on something.' She hands it back to me. 'We had some good times.'

'We did. We really did.' I smile, watch her face harden.

'But, in the end, we weren't such great friends, were we?'

'Orla—'

'My letters.'

'What letters?'

'The ones I sent after Rose died. You didn't read them, did you?'

She's right, I didn't read them. She sent about twenty letters in the space of three months – half of them were hand-delivered, and then they moved house and the other half were sent from England. At first I tore them up and tossed the pieces into the wind. Then I didn't even bother doing that. I simply binned them unopened.

'I took a lot of time over them. I was trying to make it up to you. You should have read them.'

'Orla . . .' I hesitate. 'I was really upset. I couldn't get out of bed. I could barely stand. I went about in a daze, terrified that someone was going to find out what I'd done and, at the same time, terrified that they wouldn't and I'd have to live with the guilt for the rest of my life.' She's looking down at her feet. I almost reach for her hand, then change my mind and screw up my fist on my lap. 'I'm sorry I wasn't there for you but I wasn't even there for myself! I was like a zombie. Wasn't I, Euan?'

Her eyes flick upwards. 'Why do you do that? Why do you look to him for verification?'

'He was there!'

'You always look at him like he knows and you don't.'

'He does know me. He has seen me go through it.'

'I bet he has.'

'Look! You're not the only one who has a conscience. But telling the truth won't change the outcome. There is nothing to be gained.'

'I'm looking for redemption. And I will have it.' She stands up. 'That night, what happened to Rose? It wasn't all about you. We could have helped one another. If you had shown me the slightest concern . . .'

I stand up opposite her. 'You're doing this to me because twenty-four years ago I didn't read some letters that you sent?' I almost laugh. 'Christ, Orla! I'm sorry I hurt you.' I clutch my chest. 'But—'

'It's too late. I don't need your permission to tell the truth. Or yours.' She throws Euan a malevolent stare. 'Now fuck off, both of you.'

She leaves the room. Euan is on his feet and after her before I have a chance to react. When I find them in the corridor, he is holding her arm just above the elbow. He is talking quickly, urgently and she listens and then she laughs, spits in his face and says something. He reaches for her throat and pushes her back against the wall. I hear the thud of her head as it ricochets off the stone.

'Euan!' I try to pull him away from her but it's as if I don't exist.

Their eyes are locked. She doesn't try to remove his hand from around her neck. And she doesn't look scared. In fact, weirdly, she is smiling. After a few moments he lets her go, turns and walks towards the front door.

I am stunned by his sudden aggression and even more by Orla's delight in it and I look to her for an explanation. 'Orla?'

Her eyes are glowing, bright and lively, as if she's having the best time. It is so at odds with what has just taken place that I back away and at once her attention shifts to Sister Bernadette who is coming towards us from the other direction. 'I'm so looking forward to Sunday lunch,' Orla says loudly, pulling me into her. 'Paul and I have such a lot to catch up on.' She kisses my cheek and murmurs, 'You're not fooling me with your I-love-my-family-more-than-anything crap.' She gestures towards Euan's retreating back. 'Just think yourself lucky I don't tell Paul about him too.'

April 1996

I open the door. Euan is standing on the step. He is wearing a dark brown leather jacket and has the collar pulled up around his ears. His hair is longer now and is being blown by the wind. Curls drift across his forehead and back again.

'Grace,' he says.

I stare at him. His eyes are so blue that I see the summer sky in them.

'Grace,' he says again and smiles at me.

I can't speak. The truth is I don't want to. I feel completely lost in the moment like I'm dreaming the best dream and if I blink or speak I'll break the spell.

'Can I come in?' he says.

I move aside and he climbs the steps. As he passes me I breathe in deeply and shut my eyes. We stand in the porch. It's square, less than five feet either side. He smells of the wind and the sea but mostly he smells of himself.

'Grace?'

I look into his eyes. I feel very brave doing this, like I am about to bungee jump off a bridge. 'You smell the same,' I tell him.

'I smell the same?' he repeats then laughs. 'I suppose I would, wouldn't I?'

I consider him. I drink him in. 'You look the same.'

'As I did twelve years ago?'

I nod. We haven't seen each other since we were both sixteen and he went to live in Glasgow.

'I have some lines now around my eyes.' He smiles. 'See?'

I nod again.

His hands are in his pockets and he swivels on his heels. 'Is it okay for us to go in?'

'Yes.'

He walks through to the back of the house and I follow him. He stops at the kitchen window, looks out over the view. 'Mum tells me you have twin girls now. Are they here?'

I shiver. I don't mean to. I reach across him and close the open window. 'Paul's taken the girls up to his parents in Skye,' I tell him. 'They're due back tomorrow morning. He's very good with them,' I add.

He looks at the mess of paper across the table, lifts one of my charcoal pencils and puts it down again.

'I was drawing. I was thinking.' I stop, breathe, and try again. 'I was hoping to draw. I was thinking of organising myself to paint. I want to paint again,' I finish, helpless in front of him.

He leans back against the worktop and crosses his arms. 'Haven't you been painting?'

I don't answer.

'You were good. What happened?'

I clear the papers into a tidy pile and shrug. 'Life, babies.'

'Do you enjoy your life?'

'Do you?'

He nods. 'Yeah. For the most part, I do.'

I avoid his eye, switch on the kettle, empty spoons of coffee into two mugs. I fill them with boiling water, top up with milk and slide along the bench seat, hugging my coffee mug. He sits down opposite me. His left leg touches mine under the table and I move further along.

'I'm sorry I don't have any biscuits,' I say. 'I was going to bake some this afternoon but—' I stop and look down into my mug. There's too much milk in it. I push it away. 'Truth is I'm not much good in the kitchen.' I think about the mess in the rest of the house. 'I'm not much of a housewife.' I laugh; it sounds shrill and I frown.

'Do you have any help?'

I screw up my face. 'Why would I need help? It's perfectly simple. I just have to apply myself.'

'So why don't you?'

'Because . . . because . . . I'm tired.' I shrug like it should be obvious.

'The girls. They're almost four now, right? Do they sleep?'

I nod. Then shake my head. 'It's not the girls.'

'What is it then?'

'What is what?'

He doesn't answer straight away. He just looks at me, like he's disappointed, like I should be pouring my heart out, then and there, all over the table, spilling my guts like a knifed corpse in an abattoir.

'You look thin,' he says finally.

I try to laugh. 'Thin is good, isn't it?'

'Is it?'

'So most women would say.' I feel like I'm choking and I cough into my hand. 'So why have you come to see me? I was under the impression you were avoiding me. Mo's kept me up to date, of course. Congratulations on your children, by the way. Mo tells me they're great wee bairns.' I try to imitate her good humour but it falls flat.

He is looking me up and down, measuring me with his eyes. 'You don't look well on it, Grace.'

I am hurt, devastated even. It takes all my effort not to cry and I dig my fingernails into my hand. I know what he means, of course. God knows I am the first to admit that I am a mess. My hair is unkempt. I cut the fringe myself with a pair of scissors. I'd had enough of it falling into my eyes so I hacked away at it and now it sits higher on the right than it does on the left. Fingerprints pattern my clothes. Four little hands. I never seem to be able to keep them clean. No sooner have I wiped yoghurt off one daughter's hands than the other has found a crayon, a puddle, a melted chocolate. And I'm thin, I know. My blouse hangs off me, my eyes look too large in my face, my cheekbones angle sharply under my skin. There is a mirror in the hall and in the two bathrooms. I see myself. But his words hurt because I want him to see me like I was.

He's watching me, waiting for me to say something, give him some explanation. What? That I can't be bothered eating? That I'm too tired to eat? That the very act of rousing myself to lift forkfuls of food up to my mouth is enough to kill my appetite? That, anyway, I can't taste it? And worst of all, that I don't see the point?

'Are you visiting your folks?' I say at last when the silence threatens to suffocate me.

'Yes and no. I'm moving back to the village with Monica and the children.'

I stop my hands shaking by sliding them under my thighs. 'Why? I thought you couldn't wait to get away from here?'

'Well, we decided it wasn't so bad here after all. Sarah is almost four, Tom just two.' He looks out of the window, past the climbing frame and garden hut, over the low picket fence to the sandy beach where the sea races up and down the shore. 'Didn't we have it good here?' he asks me. 'What better place is there to raise children?'

'You sound nostalgic,' I tell him and my own mind skips

back to beach picnics, treasure hunts, camps we built in the dunes. Running, running, running shoeless along the beach no matter what the weather. Rock pools, sand-castles in the rain, ice creams melting on to our fingers, skipping along the harbour wall. Dares and double dares. Bet I can climb higher up that tree than you, bet if you chap on Mrs Young's door you'll get caught. Chickenpox, both of us off school for two weeks confined to the living room playing Monopoly, letting each other cheat so that we can rush on to the hotel stage. I have all the reds and greens, the Strand, Trafalgar Square, Bond Street, Regent Street; he has Park Lane and Mayfair. We play snakes and ladders, down the ladders and up the snakes. We learn how to play chess and sit opposite each other locked in concentration until one of us finds the edge and beats the other.

'So you're coming back?' My voice is so quiet I can hardly hear it myself.

'Monica has been offered a position in a GP's practice up in St Andrews.'

'She's done well,' I say, wondering how she managed it with two small children. 'But then she was always the organised one.' It sounds bitchy. I don't mean it to.

He smiles. 'Monica was always more willing to apply herself than you or me.'

'But you're an architect?'

'Yes, but not a very ambitious one.' He laughs like it might be a sore point. 'So we're coming home. I will start a part-time business that fits around the children. Monica

will work full-time. We've bought the Jardines' old house.
Do you remember it?'

'Along Marketgate?'

'That's the one.'

'It needs a lot of work done to it.'

He nods, pushes his mug away and leans his elbows on
the table. I can hardly breathe. My head is buzzing, light-
hearted and joyous; like a funfair ride it abruptly jolts
forward ahead of me and I imagine having him in my life
again, the delicious possibility, years of bumping into him
in the newsagent's, Sunday lunches in the pub, PTAs, our
girls becoming best friends, New Year parties and maybe
even the odd summer barbecue.

'So, Grace, twelve years, huh? How's it going?'

His voice is gentle, like he's talking to a little girl but it
cuts through me like a chainsaw through oak and I try
not to choke. 'It's . . . yeah . . . it's . . .' I stop. Think. Stall
for time. 'How is what? Specifically, I mean.'

'How's life? Do you enjoy being a wife and mother?
How are you?'

I fiddle with a spoon, start to hum, pick up a pile of
tumble-dried children's clothes and fold them. I'm on my
fourth T-shirt when he stops my hand with his.

'How are you?'

I don't take my hand away. He feels so warm, so over-
flowing with heat that I want to take off my clothes and
sunbathe.

'Tell me.'

Of late I have been feeling bloodless, like there's nothing

in my veins but now colour rushes to my face and floods my cheeks. 'I'm managing,' I say at last.

'Look at me.'

I look.

'Tell me,' he says.

I shake my head.

'Grace?'

'What?'

'I'm your friend.'

'Are you?' It's a whisper and he leans forward to catch it, pushes my hair back from my face.

'Tell me,' he says.

'I don't lie to you,' I tell him. 'I don't lie. Not to you.'

'Oh, Grace.'

That's all he says – oh, Grace – and then he reaches across the table and I begin to weep, not to cry, but to weep heavy tears that crack me open like footprints on an icy pond. He stands up and lifts me off the bench, rests his back against the wall and holds me against his chest while I weep his shirt wet. He says nothing, just holds me, strokes my hair and when I'm finished he takes my hands, leads me into the living room and sits me on the sofa. He gives me tissues, hunkers down in front of me and rubs my knees.

'You're freezing,' he says. He pulls the blanket off the back of the sofa and wraps me in it, swaddling me up like a baby so that in spite of myself I giggle.

'You're a good dad,' I tell him.

'Mostly. Not always.' He smiles at me, smooths his

fingers over my swollen eyelids. 'So tell me. What's going on with you?'

'I see her,' I say at once. 'I see Rose. Mostly in my dreams and she's drowning and I can't save her but then other times I see her on the beach or in the garden and in my girls – I see her in my girls. I was fine until I came back to Scotland.'

'You're tired, Grace.' His face is solemn, his jaw tight. 'That's all.'

'It's not just tiredness.' I clutch his hand. 'I do see her, Euan. I do.'

'Ghosts don't exist. You're exhausted from young children. You don't eat enough. Listen!' He holds my face close to his. 'I would bet all the money I had that Rose didn't die by your hand.'

'You would?'

'Yes. I would. You're a good person. A better person than most. There is no one I know who is a better person than you. I mean that.' His tone is compassionate and urgent. It feels like balm, like forgiveness. 'You have to let this go. Otherwise it will destroy you. And it will affect the girls and Paul.'

I nod. 'I can't tell Paul. I've never been able to tell him. The doctor says I have depression.'

'You don't.' He looks fierce. 'You just need to be kind to yourself. You need to move on and you need to eat.' He goes into the kitchen. I listen to him as he opens the fridge and the cupboards. I rest my head against the back of the sofa and for the first time in years I feel like I can just be. I feel warm and cosy and I rub my cheeks against the soft edges of the blanket.

Euan comes back. He's made scrambled eggs for us both. 'Now don't say you don't like them,' he tells me. 'Because I know you do.'

My stomach gives an appreciative rumble at the sight of the food. I take the plate from him and swallow the saliva that fills my mouth. I sit the plate on my knee and look at it. It's one of Paul's mother's plates, willow pattern, exquisite blue and white. The eggs are sunshine yellow from our own chickens that peck around in the run Paul made for them at the bottom of the garden. The toast is granary. It looks perfect but I don't want to eat it. Instead, I toy with rearranging it so that the eggs sit neatly on the toast and the sprig of parsley is dead centre. (Parsley? I didn't know we had any. I have no idea where he found it.)

The room is so quiet I can hear the ticking of my own watch. I turn my fork around in my hand. He's waiting for me to start. 'Tuck in,' I tell him.

'Not until you do.' He lifts the fork to my mouth. I keep it shut. 'I can do aeroplanes,' he says.

I take a breath. 'I think I'll manage.' I close my eyes and open my mouth. I want to spit it out but I don't. I chew it. Slowly. It tastes good. He's grated cheese through it. He feeds me some more. 'I think I'd like to be your baby in a high chair,' I tell him.

'You need that much looking after? Then I'm your man.'

When I've finished my eggs, he hands me his plate and

pats his flat stomach. 'My mum's taking every opportunity to stuff me full. You'd be doing me a favour.'

This time I feed myself. I finish his eggs, stop short at licking the plate. Then I lean back and puff out my cheeks. 'That was good. I never knew how hungry I was.'

He touches my arms, runs his hands the length of them and clasps my hands again. 'Okay, Grace, here's the deal,' he says. 'You're going to let go of Rose and start remembering stuff. You're going to remember that we're friends and that you can draw and paint. Do you promise?'

'Yes.'

'I can't hear you.'

'Yes,' I say, a bit louder.

I look at him. He holds a hand up to his ear.

'Yes, yes, yes.' My insides are smiling. 'I promise.'

We talk and we talk, about everything and nothing: what it's like being parents, whether he still listens to the radio in the dark, whether I still have to draw everything I see. He leaves around midnight. He holds me on the step and we hug then he turns me around and pushes me indoors. 'Meet you down on the harbour wall tomorrow?'

I nod.

'Two o'clock? Bring the girls. It's time I met them. I'm practically their uncle.'

I watch him walk to the end of the street and then I come inside. My heart is floating behind my ribcage and my face is sore from so much smiling. Euan is the closest I've ever had to a brother. When we were growing up he was my constant companion. Sure, sometimes we fought, but mostly we had fun sharing our childhoods. And still, even now, he makes me feel good about myself, reminds me that I am the person I want to be. And as the only other person who knows about Rose, he is a counterpoint to my own fear. Having him back in the village will be a gift. All my Christmases and birthdays rolled into one.

I rise early in the morning, shower, wash my hair and dry it into something that resembles a shape. I find a top that highlights the green of my eyes. I layer it over a white long-sleeve T-shirt and a pair of casual trousers with deep pockets halfway down the leg. I rummage through my make-up tray and find eye shadow, an almost dried-up mascara and a lipstick. I empty the dishwasher, write *hairdresser appointment* on the whiteboard in the kitchen and lay out a bowl and a spoon on the table. I pour some muesli from the container and cover it with milk. I lift my spoon and hesitate, close my eyes, take a deep breath. I eat slowly and carefully, as if to make noise and draw attention to myself will trigger an alarm. I finish a whole bowl and want to cry with relief. Instead I stand in front of the mirror and smile at myself, refamiliarise myself with my face. I'm still too thin, too tired-looking, but behind that there is a light in my eyes that I haven't seen in a while. If I had to give it a name I would call it hope.

When my family arrives back home I'm drawing – simple, charcoal sketches of the girls, partly from memory, partly from the photographs that line the wall in Paul's study.

Paul comes into the kitchen alone; the girls have fallen

asleep in the car, and I hold the drawings up for him to see. 'What do you think?'

'I love them.' He examines each one, lifts them up to the light, angling them in his hand. 'Can I keep them?' He looks at me. 'I'd like to have them framed.'

I lean against the top of his arm and smile. 'They're not good enough for that, Paul.'

'I beg to differ. And what's more I can tell the girls apart.' He points to each of the drawings and picks out one child from the other.

'That's right. Their posture isn't the same.' I think about it. 'Ella just has a different attitude.'

He hugs me suddenly and speaks into my hair. 'I've been so afraid that we might have lost you,' he says, his voice thick with emotion.

I pull up my head so that I can look into his eyes. 'Paul, I know I haven't been the best wife and mother lately.' He goes to answer me and I put my hand over his mouth. 'No, really, I know I haven't. But I think I can change. I'm sure I can.'

He starts to kiss me and I lean into him, relax my body against his, breathe in his familiarity and close my eyes to everything except the feeling that I am loved and wanted much more than I know.

After a few moments he moves away and I try to draw him back to me. He looks beyond me to the front door and when I listen too, I hear cries from outside. 'Daddy, Daddy now!' Hand in hand we walk outside and find the girls struggling to free themselves from their car seats.

'You woke up!' Paul lifts Ella out and they rub noses. I go around the other side and undo the buckle on Daisy's seat. She slides into my arms and settles her cheek against mine.

Just before two o'clock I load them into the buggy. They're old enough to walk but still Ella insists on having her own place to sit. They're wearing tights and skirts, wellington boots and home-knitted cardigans and hats in a Fair Isle pattern: greens, pinks and cream for Ella, blues, reds and cream for Daisy. My mum is never happier than when she's knitting and the girls have more woollens than even Scottish weather can do justice to.

I give them each a bag of breadcrumbs for the gulls and we head off along the path to the harbour. The road is cobbled and the girls giggle and squeal as they're bounced up and down over the stones. It's a beautiful day. The sea is calm, its surface like polished glass broken by gulls as they dive into the water for fish.

When I reach the beginning of the harbour wall, I stop. I don't really expect him to be here. I wonder whether I've imagined the whole of the previous evening; a kind of intense wish-fulfilment brought on by an empty stomach and a lack of sleep. I hold up my hand to shield my eyes and look along the curve of the wall. My eyes focus and within seconds I spot him. He's standing about fifty yards away talking to a group of fishermen who are mending their nets in a patch of sunshine. He glances up and sees me, climbs up on to the wall and jogs towards me, one leg perilously close to the outside edge. When he reaches me, he looks like he's going to topple over backwards and I scream, grab hold of his trouser leg.

'Chicken.' He grins at me and jumps off the wall down beside us. The girls are regarding him with cool, serious eyes.

'Man being silly,' Ella says, pointing at him.

'Out of the mouths of babes.' I am smiling so much that my face is in danger of splitting in two. We rest our backs against the wall and he starts up a conversation with the girls. It goes like this:

'I'm Euan and you must be?' He waits, his eyebrows raised quizzically.

Neither of them deigns to answer him.

'This is Daisy.' I gesture in her direction. 'And this is Ella.'

'And I thought I was seeing double.'

They don't speak.

I whisper next to his ear, 'They hear that one a lot.'

'Is this for the gulls?' He reaches for Ella's bag of bread and she pulls it tight into her stomach. He turns my way with a help-me-out face.

I giggle and shake my head.

He stretches back, looks up and around the sky then leans forward again. 'I know!' He rubs his hands together. 'Who wants an ice cream?'

'Me!' they both cry out at once and start waving their arms and banging the backs of their boots against the wheels.

'Shouldn't we feed the seagulls first?' he asks them.

'No,' Ella shouts, fingers working at the straps around her shoulders and waist. 'They're not hungry.'

'She takes after her mother,' I say, bending to help her and then Daisy. 'No patience.'

They both run off along the path to di Rollo's, their boots splashing through the briny water that has leaked from the boxes of fish being loaded on to a lorry. Euan lifts my arm and puts it through his and pushes the buggy with the other hand. We get to the shop as Ella is pointing to the largest cone.

'It will be melted before you can eat it,' Gianluca is telling her. 'And look who is here!' He comes around the counter and shakes hands with Euan. 'You back for a visit?'

'Coming back here to live,' Euan tells him. 'Can't get a decent ice cream in London.' He looks down at Ella and Daisy. 'So what will it be, girls?'

Ella holds on to his jeans and jumps up and down. 'Chocolate chip, chocolate chip!'

He glances over at me and winks. 'Why am I not surprised?'

Gianluca loads two scoops of ice cream on to a cone and passes it to Euan who hands it down to Ella. She looks at it with a kind of startled awe then starts to suck the top of it, slurping it into her mouth with satisfied smacks of her lips.

'Daisy?'

Daisy is standing to the side watching. She goes to speak but no sound comes out. She looks at me uncertainly.

Euan lifts her up and she leans on the glass and frowns down into the trays then, overwhelmed, turns back to me again.

'You usually have mint,' I remind her. 'Like Daddy.'

She nods and Euan puts her down. She runs to stand beside me, wraps her arms around my legs and pushes her thumb into her mouth.

'Are you sure they're identical?' Euan asks me, pulling money from his pocket.

I shrug. 'I don't get it either. They're so different.' I rest my hand on the top of Daisy's hat. 'Always have been.'

'Daisy is the shy one,' Gianluca says, leaning across the stainless-steel counter to give Daisy her cone. 'And there is nothing wrong with that, huh, *bambina*?'

She smiles at him, and settles back in the buggy to enjoy the ice cream.

I put napkins around both their necks while Euan holds my cone and then we say goodbye and go back out into the sunshine. We walk over to the fishermen and sit down, like they are, on upturned boxes, Ella squeezing between Euan and me. Seagulls wheel and caw above our heads then land on the pavement beside us where they squabble over an abandoned ham sandwich.

'Making a right racket, they are,' Callum says. He frees his net of tangled seaweed and tosses the weed over his shoulder. 'What do you reckon to that noise, Daisy?'

Daisy likes Callum and by way of an answer, she hands me her cone and places her hands over her ears. He laughs at her, leans forward to tickle her knees and she wriggles out of the buggy and tries to lift up an empty lobster net and bring it close to the others.

'Business good?' Euan asks him.

'Can't complain.' He threads the needle through the netting, weaving a criss-cross pattern through the tears. 'As many lobsters and crabs as we can catch, we can sell. For all those fancy restaurants down your way.'

'Not my way any more,' Euan tells him. 'I'm coming back here to stay.'

'Well, good on you, pal. Come to his senses at last, eh, Grace?' He looks over at me. 'What do you think to that? Euan's coming back where he belongs, north of the border.'

'I think it's great.' It's an understatement so huge that I start to tremble with a kind of bottled-up hysteria, like a fizzy drink that's been shaken and is about to pop. I stand up and help Daisy carry the lobster net. When I look back, Euan is smiling.

10

I follow Euan out of the convent. He is fuming. His hands and legs shake as he climbs into the car. Neither of us speaks until he overtakes a lorry too close to a bend and I ask him to slow down. He says nothing, just pulls into a lay-by. Clouds gather on the horizon ahead of us, the wind blowing them inward and then outward as if they are breathing.

'Look, this isn't your battle.' I rub his left hand through mine. 'I don't want to drag you down with me. Maybe you should cut me loose.'

He gives a short laugh. 'How would I go about doing that? You're more a part of me than my own sisters. You're in here.' He taps the side of his head. 'Letting go of you isn't an option. I think we have to outmanoeuvre her.'

'How?'

'Say we were with each other on the night Rose died. Brazen it out. She doesn't have any proof. Who's going to believe her? Look at her history – mental illness, drugs, prison. That makes her about as far away from a reliable witness as you can get.'

'But if we say we were with each other then that will be lying. Isn't that perjury?'

'It won't go to court, Grace.'

'But still.' I think about it. I'm not sure I could pull it off. In spite of the way I've lived for the last twenty-four years, lying does not come easily to me. The fact is, I was never properly questioned about Rose's death. It was presumed that her death was an accident, unseen, unheard. I have never had to defend my position and I am absolutely sure I couldn't stand in front of Paul and fake innocence.

'I can't believe she has become this person,' I say. 'There's nothing of the girl left.'

'She was always like that. Just not with you. Now you're seeing her other side. I'm going to have a cigarette.' He opens his door. 'You want one?'

'No.' I've had my mobile phone on silent and when I check it there is a missed call from Paul. I can't speak to him – not yet. I text him instead: I'll be home later. Dinner in oven.

I sit back and chew on my nails, frustrated and dismayed with the turn of events at the convent. Nothing either of us said made any difference. In fact, it seemed like the opposite. The more she saw I wanted her not to tell Paul, the more determined she became to do it.

Outside the heavens open and Euan comes back into the car. We both stare through the windscreen. Water pours down from a heavy sky, flattening grass and making quick puddles in the hollows. Half a dozen sheep, necks tucked in, bodies up close, cling stoically to the hillside, their hooves sliding on the rocky slope.

I rub my hands over my face. 'I wish I'd read those bloody letters.'

'This isn't about letters,' Euan says. 'It's about control and it's about revenge.'

'Revenge for what?' I watch two more sheep move in close to the hillside huddle. 'I honestly don't get why she would come back after all this time.'

'It's like that sometimes for people, isn't it?' He turns to look at me. 'Grievances fester for years. Then a catalyst comes along and bingo.'

I drop my hands and turn sideways too so that our faces are close. 'What did you say to her?'

'When?'

'Just now. Before you had her by the throat.'

'To back off. Crawl under the nearest stone.'

'And what did she say?'

He shrugs. 'Nothing worth repeating.'

'The bit that made you really mad? When she spat at you?' I say.

He shakes his head. 'Swearing. Nonsense. She isn't a rational human being.'

I have to agree with him. Her eyes, just before we left, were lit with an unhealthy euphoria; the kind that speaks of madness rather than joy.

'Rain's easing off,' Euan says. 'We should head back.'

'I'm not going to let her anywhere near Paul on Sunday,' I say. 'I won't stand by and watch her say it.'

'One step at a time.' He turns the key in the ignition. 'It's not over yet.' We rejoin the road and he settles to a reasonable speed. 'Not by a long way.'

I try to relax back in my seat, silent, prey to my own thoughts. I feel like the past has caught up with the present. It's as if the last twenty-four years have been reduced to a single day. I'm right back where I started. I've just killed Rose. I feel the push of my hand against her chest as if it were yesterday. I am the fifteen-year-old me in the body of a woman. I feel panicked and scared and ready to jump from the car and run.

I look at Euan, now in the body of a man, but still very much the boy I remember at sixteen. For all his sober driving and fancy car, for all his money and success, his loss of control back at the convent – that wasn't Euan the husband, father and upstanding member of the community, that was Euan at sixteen, impulsive and headstrong.

Neither of us speaks until we drive across the bridge and into Fife.

'Do you want to stop for something to eat?'

I look at my watch. It's just gone three o'clock. 'I mustn't. I have to get started on the piece for Margie Campbell. I'm already days behind. It might even take my mind off this.'

He nods his agreement and carries on driving.

When we get inside the cabin I sit down behind my desk and immediately stand up again and start to pace. Euan has the kettle on and is making a sandwich in the small kitchen between the workroom and the bedroom. 'Maybe I should go for a walk first,' I say. 'Clear my head.'

'Suit yourself.' He points to the breadboard. 'Do you want some?'

'No, thanks.' I open the front door and realise I don't want to go for a walk. I want to talk. I go back to Euan and blurt out, 'Orla was right, you know, about me living with one foot in the past.'

He glances at me quickly then away again.

'Do you ever feel like you're still sixteen?'

'No.'

'Not even a wee bit?'

He thinks about it. 'I have some of the same feelings I had when I was sixteen but I don't feel like I'm sixteen.'

I hate it when he does that – splits hairs and corrects me, as if I'm simple. My stomach heats up. 'Do you know what she said to me when we were leaving just now? She said I should think myself lucky that she doesn't tell Paul about us.'

He stops pouring milk into his cup and gives me his full attention.

'How can she know about us? How can she know we had an affair?'

'She doesn't know!' He shakes his head at me, exasperated. 'She's just taking a punt and no doubt the look on your face told her she was right.'

'It's not just *my* face that gave it away. At the girls' party she said you gave me a hungry look. That's what she said.'

He throws out his arms. 'So what if I did?'

'We had an agreement.' I bang the flat of my hand on the work surface.

'I haven't broken any agreement.' He moves past me to

the sink. 'Look at yourself! She winds you up and you're off across the floor like a tin soldier.'

'Well, she had you pretty bloody wound up by the end! You had her by the throat. You could have hurt her!'

'Would you care, Grace?' He is speaking quietly, his face up close. 'Would you really care?'

I think about how angry she makes me: when she stood at the top of the steps at the girls' party; when I left her just now at the convent, a catlike smile denting her cheeks; when she sat in the restaurant smiling her way through a meal only to threaten to blow my world apart. Was my threat to hurt her an empty one? I can't answer that. Would I step forward and save her? No, I wouldn't. I definitely wouldn't save her.

'I just want her out of my life,' I say lamely.

'Well, that won't happen unless you take measures to stop her. Wake the fuck up.'

I flinch. 'Don't swear at me.' I point my finger at him like I'm talking to Ella and he laughs. 'It's not funny, Euan.'

'No, it isn't funny,' he says. 'And look! She's got us fighting now.'

'I hate it when you swear at me. You sound nasty. You don't sound like yourself.' I press my fingers against my temples. Thoughts are flocking around inside my skull, not in the socially orientated way that birds have but in an altogether uncoordinated way, banging into each other, screechy and chaotic. I feel like it's only a matter of time before my head shatters completely. I press my hands against it and start to rock backward and forward.

'Come here.' Euan puts his arms around me and at once I feel something else: something sweet and familiar, deadly, to be avoided. I push him away from me.

'Don't,' I say.

He draws back, sighs.

'I'm sorry,' I say quickly. 'I'm confused. I can't think straight. Fucking hell, I don't know what to do.'

'Well, when you make up your mind, let me know. In the meantime, I'm having something to eat.'

He goes through and sits down behind his desk and I try to stop pacing, shaking, going over the same worries – but I can't. My head is full of fear and reproach, a treadmill of what if and what now and how to save myself before it's too late. There's some whisky at the back of the cupboard. I pour some into a glass and swallow several mouthfuls down quickly, shivering involuntarily as it burns its way down my throat. Within minutes I experience a deadening in my limbs but the voices in my head are still raging. Seeking oblivion, I pour myself another glass. More minutes pass, a comfortable fuzz swells through my skull and I am able to shut out the noise and tune into quieter thoughts: a memory.

I am seven years old and my dad and I are out on our bikes. It's summer time and every evening we come to the neighbouring field to feed the horse carrots and then his favourite Polo Mints. He comes running across and lets me stroke his velvet muzzle and then laughs, showing me all his teeth and it makes me giggle until I can hardly catch my breath. But this day, just as we arrive, we witness the horse being shot in the head. The instant the bullet makes contact with his skull, he drops to the ground, the sound splits the air and crows scatter and cry up into the sky. I fall off my bike and start to scream. My dad helps me up then speaks to Mr Smith, the owner, and to the vet.

'He was sick, Grace,' my dad explains to me. 'The vet had to put him out of his misery.'

'He wasn't miserable!' I shout and it's the first time I realise that adults aren't always to be trusted, that they don't tell the truth.

I have nightmares. I see blood and guts and all sorts of things that didn't even happen. The only person who comforts me is Euan, not by anything he does or says, just by letting me sleep beside him in his bed. For three whole nights I lie beside him. I think of nothing, just lie there with an empty head, my sore heart soothed by the sound of his breathing.

My limbs feel heavy but I can just walk without falling over and I go through to the room and look at Euan. There's a ringing in my ears and my heart is pounding against my ribcage as if it's trapped inside. What I am about to do is wrong but I truly believe that I am doing it for the right reason.

'Remember when Smithy's horse had to be shot?' I know my lips are moving but my voice sounds far away. 'You let me sleep in your bed.'

He has finished eating and is leaning back on the seat, his feet up on the desk. 'What age were we?'

'Seven.'

'I didn't take advantage of you then?'

I resist the temptation to banter. 'On the fourth night you got fed up and kicked me out because I was making you hot but for those three nights you were everything to me.' I move closer, pulled towards him on an invisible rope. 'And when Rose died you were the only person I could tell.' Closer still. 'And when you came back to Scotland, you set me right again. I know we're married to other people and I know I shouldn't be saying this—' I stop, sway, try to swallow but my tongue is taking up too much space in my mouth. 'But you've always known how to fix me. Always.'

His face softens. 'Grace?' He stands up.

I tune in to the detail on his shirt. I focus on the buttons. There are six of them, pale blue and ridged around the edge. The top one is undone. I unbutton the next one and slip my hand inside, just below his collarbone. His chest is covered with soft hair that curls around my fingers. My face follows my hand. He smells like ginger biscuits and warm chocolate and something else that makes me feel crazy. Relief. I'm not thinking – instead I am sliding into the groove of a deep and powerful connection. I kiss the quickening pulse in his throat and whisper, 'Please.'

He says my name again but this time it isn't a question and I feel the last of my inhibitions fall away. He turns me around so that my back is against his chest. I look through the window back up the garden where Muffin is lying full stretch in a patch of sunshine. He puts his arms around my waist. He rocks me from side to side and I lean back against his chest. When he starts to kiss my neck, I close my eyes. His hands travel up my back, unhook my bra and cup my breasts. He pulls my trousers down, slides his hand to the inside of my thighs and separates me with his fingers. He hooks them inside me and I gasp, lean forward and when I hear him unzip his jeans I start to moan. At first he moves in short, shallow strokes and when I ache for more he pushes hard and deep until I tell him I'm coming and he stops, kneads the back of my shoulders, waits for me. I am relaxed to my fingertips and I smile from the relief and wonder of it. I murmur no as he withdraws and I turn around to catch him in my hand.

He backs away from me and into the bedroom. He sits on the bed, leans against the headboard and I ease myself down on top of him. 'I've missed you.'

'More.' He looks at me quickly, holds my hips and pulls me further on to him. 'I've missed you more.'

We don't rush it. We linger and we prolong the moments and then, when we're both satisfied, we lie back on the bed: me on my front, Euan on his back. I lean on my elbow and look up into his face. I feel languid and soft in my bones. His hand strokes me lengthways, from the small of my back up into my hair. We lie like this for several minutes and then he says quietly, 'We have to decide what to do about Orla.'

Memory crawls up from the pit of my stomach and bites me. 'We do.' I rub my face across his chest. 'Any ideas?'

'We could buy her off?'

'I don't have any money.'

'I do.'

'No.' I frown at him. 'I'm not taking your money. Not that. God knows I take everything else.'

'Don't be daft.' He lifts my fingers and kisses them. 'If she's about to wreck your life and some money will keep her quiet then let's just give it to her.'

I am grateful to him. Tears are never far away and I blink hard, climb out of bed and pull his shirt on. 'I would pay you back.' I nod my head. 'I would.'

He smiles. He looks relaxed, free, like the boy I remember.

I lean forward and kiss him. 'I'll get us a drink.' I go through to the kitchenette, fill a pint glass with ice and orange juice then go back to bed. We both sit with our backs against the headboard. I take a drink then pass it to him. We sit like this for a while, passing the glass backward and forward.

'When I was in the graveyard the other day,' I say, 'I was trying to work out what Mo would think of all of this.'

'My mum was a practical woman. If she'd known a phrase like damage limitation I think she would have used it.' He looks at his watch and stands up. 'Let Orla come to Sunday lunch. Get Paul out of the village. All of you, the whole family, should go out for the day.'

'And when she turns up?'

'I'll meet her,' Euan says. 'I'll offer her money.' He bends down to pick up his clothes. 'I'll get rid of her.'

I stand up alongside him. 'But what if—'

He puts his hand over my mouth. 'Trust me,' he says. 'I'll deal with her. Then we can all go back to normal.'

Normal. Normal is good. Normal is fine. Normal means we return to nothing more than childhood friends, grown-up workmates. Normal is Paul never imagining that I know anything about Rose's death. Normal is going off to Australia for a year, more, for ever.

'Euan?' I bite my lip. I haven't told him about Paul's sabbatical in Australia. I haven't told him because I had a feeling he would try to talk me out of it and now that we are intimate again it's even more important that I go away.

'Yeah?' He is half dressed, disappearing back into his clothes. And then he'll be gone. It makes me want to push him on to the bed and climb on top of him.

'Thank you.' I pull his shirt off, over my head and hold it out to him. 'This is yours.'

He looks me up and down, slowly.

I watch his eyes move and focus. I wait. And when he pulls me into him, I breathe into my relief.

'Forget the shirt.' His hands are everywhere, roaming, along my spine, my neck, my hair and down again. 'This is mine.' He takes my hand and puts it between my legs. 'Don't forget it.'

I smile. 'Actually, that's mine.'

'You were never any good at sharing.' He kisses my neck and I grow taller inside. 'Only-child syndrome.' He tugs my earlobe. 'I'll soon tease that out of you.'

I don't resist and an hour later when he leaves me at

the gate, I look up and down the street, don't see anyone and risk turning my head back for a last kiss.

My family are at home. They all shout hello as I come in. Daisy and Ella are either side of Paul. They are watching a film.

'Where's Ed?' I say.

'Out at bowls.'

Paul goes to stand up but I wave him down again, manage to kiss his cheek and hang back at the same time. 'I've had a hectic day. Do you mind if I go straight up to bed?'

He looks concerned. 'Can I bring you anything?'

'No, thank you.' I drop my head as if I'm tired. 'I just need to sleep.'

I say goodnight and go upstairs, shower and then lie in bed and stare at the ceiling. My head is quiet. All thoughts have disintegrated. They are ephemeral, see-through, powerless. I am simply a feeling machine. My body is still resonating with the aftershock of what I've done. My limbs are pliable, softened to the bone and my core is not made of blood and tears but of air and music. Self-loathing lurks in the background – I haven't forgotten that adultery is a sure road to misery – but for now, I feel like I've been rinsed through with honey.

Hours later, when Paul comes to bed I'm still awake. He moves in beside me and the length of his body lines up with mine. I love him – that has never been in any doubt – but at the moment he can't help me. I need to protect him from the truth, as much for his sake as my own. Some memories are like cuts that never heal. The skin above them remains so fragile that one little scratch makes them bleed. Rose is that memory for both of us and we share the same sorrows: a deep regret, a sense of disbelief and a heartfelt wish to live that time again and this time live it differently.

19 June 1984

It's three days since we found Rose's body and I'm in bed. I've spent the day lying here, hardly moving. Whenever my mum or dad come into my room I close my eyes and deepen my breathing, make it long and slow. Shortly before teatime I hear Orla at the front door. My mum tells her I'm asleep and then says, 'But join us for tea! I'm sure Grace will get up when she knows you're here.'

No, I won't. I absolutely, bloody won't.

Orla says no, she can't come in. Her parents are expecting her back any minute. But she's written me another note – her third since it happened. My mum brings it in with my tea.

> *Dear Grace*
> *Please! I'm so worried about you. Please stop ignoring me. I'm upset too. I'll drop in again tomorrow at four o'clock. Please speak to me. I have something to tell you. I think we'll be able to help each other.*
> *Love*
> *Orla xxxxx*

When my mum leaves the room I tear the note into tiny, insignificant pieces, stand at my window, open the palm of my hand and watch the pieces blow away.

Just before seven thirty the doorbell rings again.

'I'm so sorry to disturb you—'

'Mr Adams,' my dad says. 'Please come in.'

I lie completely still in my bed. I daren't blink or move a muscle.

'First,' my dad says, his tone grave, 'my wife and I wish to express our heartfelt condolences for the loss of your daughter.'

'Indeed.' My mother has joined them in the hallway. 'We are so terribly sad for you.' Her voice catches and I know she will be leaning into my dad for comfort.

'Come through,' my dad says. 'Sit with us for a moment or two.'

They leave the living room door open but although I strain my ears, all I can hear is the slow murmur of Mr Adam's speech and my parents making sympathetic noises. I get out of bed and go to the top of the stairs. It's better – I hear words like 'disturbing' and 'beautiful' – but it's not enough to follow the gist of what's being said so I creep down several steps and sit just above where the banister starts, pulling my feet in so that I can't be seen from the living room.

'And I want to thank Grace. I want to thank her for trying to save Rose.'

'We'll pass on your message, Mr Adams.' It's my father who's talking. 'Unfortunately, Grace is not up to visitors at the moment. The doctor has been round and he says she's in shock.'

'I was hoping she could help me understand why Rose was out of her tent.'

'She's told the police everything she knows,' my dad says. 'She's an honest girl, a sensitive girl.'

I wince at this.

'Of course, and I wouldn't want to bother her. Not at all. Rose was delighted to be in her patrol. The night before she left, it's all she could talk about, how kind Grace was and how much fun they all had together.'

I wince again, draw up my knees to my chest and press hard to stop myself from crying.

'Shock affects people in different ways. She's not saying much.'

'Not saying much,' my mum echoes.

'I understand,' Mr Adams says. 'There're just so many unanswered questions and I wondered whether Grace could help me make sense of what happened. You see, Rose couldn't swim. She was afraid of water. She would never have gone into it without a very good reason.'

'It was the middle of the night. She must have slipped. That's what the police think, isn't it?'

'Yes, but why would she be out of her tent? She was nine years old. She was a good, obedient girl.'

'Perhaps she needed the toilet and didn't want to disturb anyone,' my dad says. 'And then she must have lost her way in the dark.'

'She wasn't in the habit of getting up to the toilet during

the night. Never. I feel sure she must have been out of her sleeping bag for another reason.'

'Why don't I make us some tea?' my mum says with forced lightness. 'And I baked some macaroons this afternoon.'

As she walks below me to go into the kitchen, I sit further back on the step and hug into the wall. Mr Adams has thought this through. Like me he is obsessed by the detail – detail he doesn't and can't ever know. For how can I tell him? Tell him that Rose was out of bed at midnight because she had something important to say to me. Tell him that I wasn't interested in what she had to say. Tell him how she ended up in the water. I imagine walking downstairs into the living room and announcing, *It was me! I killed Rose. I pushed her into the pond.* I imagine my mother screaming, my father frowning, asking me why I would make up something like that. The ruckus it would cause. Orla and I questioned again by the police. Both of us branded as cruel and heartless – the worst sort of girls.

My mother comes back with the tea and I am still glued to the stairs. It's too late for honesty. I have set off on the journey of a lie and there is no going back.

'Have you got someone looking after you?' my mum asks him.

'My parents have come to stay.' The teacup rattles on the saucer. His hands must be shaking. 'They live in Skye, close to Portree.'

'They must be devastated too. Their little granddaughter. Such sadness.'

'Yes. Rose meant a great deal to them. We spent a lot of time up there especially after my wife died.'

'Such awful bad luck,' my mum says and I don't have to see her face to know that she will be holding her mouth tight to stop herself from breaking down.

'I wish I'd never let her go to Guide camp. I wish I'd been there,' Mr Adams says, sounding distressed. 'I was at home reading or sleeping while my daughter was drowning. She was young and vulnerable and I wasn't there for her.'

My dad murmurs something soothing and then there is an awkward silence, a full minute or more, until Mr Adams clears his throat and says, 'I won't keep you back. Perhaps if Grace is ever able to talk about what happened, you might get in touch with me.'

'Of course,' my dad says.

As soon as they all stand up, I sneak back upstairs, pull back the edge of the curtain and watch Mr Adams climb into his car. He doesn't drive off straight away. He sits there in the dark, thinking. I know that, like me, he is tormented with thoughts of her last moments. Did she struggle and fight before she slid under? Did she cry out? When her lungs filled with pond water instead of air were the pain and fear overwhelming? Did she drown because she became tangled in the weeds or did her body float and settle there after she was dead?

Finally, Mr Adams starts the car's engine and drives off, slowly, like he's lost his way.

11

The village I live in is tranquil and slow. Nothing much happens here beyond the simple activities of daily living: shopping, cooking, raising children, a pub lunch on a Sunday or a weekend picnic down on the beach. People are friendly – nosey some would say – and as in any small village, gossip is currency to be exchanged as a mark of friendship and belonging. The weather is always the first thing to be discussed, and then people move on to who has just had a baby, who is on their last legs and who is responsible for any vandalism. Invariably, it's either one of the McGoverns or the Stewarts. Two families – that's all it takes – and with four sons each and none of them good citizens, they keep the gossips going for days with which one of them is responsible for the graffiti on the church gate, who smashed bottles atop the harbour wall and are they bringing drugs into our midst?

When we were young, the village felt constrictive and boring and we used to fantasise about moving to the lively streets of Edinburgh or Glasgow – even Stirling would have been better than this – but now I love it. Every day, come rain or shine, wind or sleet, I walk along the cliff

path and enjoy the sensation of salty air in my lungs and
the wind cutting in from the North Sea, lifting my clothes
and hair as it tries to carry me away with it.

But life can turn on a sixpence, as Mo used to say and
my life as I know it is under threat. Why couldn't I, all
those years ago, have done the right thing? Fifteen was
surely old enough to face up to what I had done. Old
enough to recognise that the consequences of keeping such
a hulking great secret would far outweigh the pain of
confessing at the time.

My body is aching for Euan and a repeat of yesterday
afternoon but I'm ignoring it and I'm ignoring him. He
called me twice this morning. I didn't answer so he sent
me a text: I know you're avoiding me. Come
to work. I'm barely there this week anyway.
Nothing will happen.

There are advantages to someone knowing you this well:
they anticipate your needs, they know exactly where your
funny bone is and they can lift you when you're down.
They know what to say to make it better. They know how
to boost your confidence.

And the disadvantages? They are the flipside of the
advantages: Euan can hold me in the palm of his hand.
He makes me feel simultaneously powerful and helpless,
pliable as play dough.

I know him and I know myself. If I go to the cabin
today we will make love. All it takes is a millisecond of
unguarded desire and I will be pulled back into his orbit.
Once was an emergency, a last-resort bid to escape the

chaos in my head – and it worked. I feel clearer, less afraid, more able to see a way through this. But twice would start a pattern and lead us both back into an affair. I've been there before, and for the love of Paul and my girls I've worked long and hard to haul myself back from it.

The sign reads *Mind yer heid!*. I duck obediently and walk through the doorway into Callum's fish shop.

'Here she comes! My favourite customer,' he says. 'Much mess after the party?'

For a moment I wonder what he means. The twins' party seems like weeks ago. 'No, it was fine. We had it cleared up in no time.'

He crosses his arms over his waxed apron. 'So what was Orla doing turning up like the ghost from Christmas past?'

'You tell me. I didn't know she was coming.'

'You were good mates once, you two.'

'Once. Yes.' If only that friendship had been enough for Orla to change her mind. Yesterday's visit to the convent has taken away any hope of that. 'Many moons ago.'

'No love lost there then, eh? The aggro was fairly brewing. Thought Euan and I might have to separate you both.'

'Even worse, Paul invited her to lunch this weekend.'

'Just tell her she can't come! Simple, innit? Make something up. You're going to Aberdeen to visit a sick friend or your stomach's upset from a dodgy curry. White lie never did anybody any harm,' Callum continues, scrubbing down his work surface. 'So what are you after?'

'I was thinking of making crab pâté. Family picnic.' *For Rose. In her memory. Remember her, Callum? I killed her. Me. How can that be? How could I have done that?*

'Just want the white meat then?'

I nod and he starts preparing the crabs.

'Couple be enough?'

'Sounds good.'

'Don't forget a grating of nutmeg. Brings out the flavours.'

'Aye, chef,' I say, saluting him, but, truth is, my heart's not in it. Tomorrow is the anniversary of Rose's death. It's exactly twenty-four years since she died. It's a special day for our family and since the girls were small our routine is to take a photograph of Rose up to the cemetery and remember Paul's daughter and the half-sister the twins never met. As the years have gone by, I have learned not to dread it but this year, with Orla ready to blow the safe open, I feel more on edge than ever.

'Euan got a lot of work on?'

'He's working on a barn conversion, for the Turners.'

'Thought he might fancy a fishing trip. Busman's holiday for me but I'm up for it. There's some good salmon to be caught up near Inverness.'

'He's doing a lot with the school this week. They're having organised activities for the fourth years.'

'Jamie's signed up for sailing right enough. Teenagers, eh? Who'd have them?'

He starts telling me about his son's wasted opportunities and I nod in the right places. Fishing? It sets me thinking. It's a while since Paul and Ed have been to Skye. The house Paul grew up in is still in the family. It stands close to Portree with the Cuillin Hills behind it and the sea in front. I'll suggest it. The girls and I can go down to Edinburgh for a shopping spree. They never turn down an opportunity to shop, especially when I offer to treat them. Orla will still come to lunch but she will meet Euan instead of Paul.

Callum hands me the crab.

'Cheers. Put it on my tab, will you?' I say and another customer comes into the shop behind me. Mrs McCulloch. A good friend of my mother's, we exchange hellos.

'Wind's not quite as bitter as yesterday,' she says. 'But still, it should be warmer than this by now. I only hope we get a decent summer. Give me that piece of haddock there, Callum.' She turns to me. 'Of course! You'll remember her, Grace! Roger Cartwright's daughter. Bonny girl, her mother was French.'

My heart skids to a halt. 'Orla?'

'That's her! An Irish name. I knew that! And she has a foreign-sounding surname. Must have married but I didn't see any sign of a husband. The rundown cottage at harbour's end – the one that's inaccessible by car – she's renting it. She's moving in soon.'

My stomach contracts and suddenly the smell of fish threatens to make me vomit.

'Apparently she came up the once, a couple of months ago, to have a recce round. She didn't stop by to see you then?'

I push through the door, not caring that my hasty exit will be seen as something to speculate about, and run up the steps to the High Street. I need more shopping: milk, bread and tomatoes but I don't stop. I keep on running until I get home. Once inside, I lock myself in the downstairs bathroom and sit down on the lid of the toilet seat to think.

So. Orla is moving back into the village. Came a couple of months ago to have a look around. If Angeline is to be believed, that would have been soon after she left prison and weeks before she called me. She has clearly been planning this. I wonder how much she knows about us. In fact, I would bet every last penny I have that when I met her in Edinburgh, she knew exactly who Euan and I had married, how many children we both had and that we were working together in his cabin. And more besides. She has played us both for fools. Euan is right: she is conniving and spiteful and out for blood. I ring his mobile. 'It's me. Can you talk?'

'Mum!' Daisy giggles. 'I have Euan's phone. He's windsurfing. It's really funny actually cos—' She breaks off. More giggling. 'No, you're wet!' she shouts.

I hear a boy's laughter in the background. 'Daisy? Ask Euan to call me when he has a moment, will you?'

'Yup.' She's still laughing when I hang up.

I come out of the bathroom. Ella is lying on the sofa watching MTV. She is eating her way through a packet of custard creams, scraping the cream in the middle out with her teeth and giving the biscuit to Murphy. He is lying by her side, his head positioned beside her trailing hand waiting for the titbits.

She sees my face. 'I only like the creamy centre.'

'It's not good for him.'

She leans her cheek on his furry back. 'Doesn't she just spoil everyone's fun?'

I grit my teeth. As I thought – our getting along was short-lived. 'Have you walked him?'

'He doesn't need walked! He's fine.' She stands up and throws him the empty packet. He takes it to his bed, starts ripping it up.

'Did you at least stack the dishwasher?'

'I'm going to Sarah's in a minute. Monica's giving us twenty quid to clean out her attic this week.' Her mouth drops down in a huffy pout. '*She* doesn't expect slave labour.'

I have an almost overwhelming urge to hit her: for her insolence, her carelessness and her don't-give-a-shit attitude. I flex my fingers and call on Murphy. I'm better off outside. Big skies, endless sea, perhaps my problems will shrink and I won't feel so bloody desperate.

I walk briskly, the coastline stretching ahead of me to St Andrews. Orla moving back to the village is one thing but Orla moving back to the village with the intention of coming clean about how Rose died is too much even to contemplate. I try to walk my thoughts into some sort of order but it doesn't work. There is no way to reconcile this. Orla can't live here. She has to be made to see that.

There's a figure walking along the sand towards me.

At first too far away for me to make out whether it's a he or a she, as we draw closer I see that it's Monica. 'I forgot how strong this wind can be,' she shouts to me, holding her hair down into her neck. 'Do you mind if I walk with you?'

'No.' My face is smiling. Yesterday, I made love to her husband but somehow I'm behaving normally. She falls into step beside me. 'Ella tells me she's going to help Sarah clean out your loft.'

'I haven't been up there in years and with Euan off doing activities this week, I thought I'd take a couple of days off myself and clear out the junk. Some of it's his stuff. He can't possibly want it after all this time.'

We are at the end of the sandy beach and we climb up and over the grassy hillocks that border the pathway to a ruined cottage. It's even windier up here and we both hold on to our coats. We're puffing by the time we reach the top and I turn to breathe in the view that stretches out before us. The pewter sea roars, yawns and bites at the shore while the blue sky above is almost completely obscured by huge dirty white clouds that are being chased eastwards by the wind.

'This place is so *depressing*,' Monica declares. 'Dark, brooding, dour. Everything I hate about the Scottish character is reflected in the landscape.'

'Hardly!' I turn towards her profile. 'It's exciting and dramatic and when the sun comes out there's nowhere like it in the world.'

She grabs my arm and propels herself around to face me. 'Do you believe history repeats itself, Grace?'

She said this to me already, the other day, after the girls' party. I take a moment to think. Monica waits. Her eyes are wide and seem to reflect my own sense of foreboding. She is expecting me to say something profound, satisfying, solve a puzzle for her. 'I believe that, eventually, what goes around will probably come around,' I say at last.

'Did you know that my father killed himself?'

'Well . . .' I suspected as much. When I was sixteen, I overheard a whispered conversation between Mo and my mum.

'Over Angeline.' She climbs up on to some fallen stones and looks down at me. 'Do you think there's a suicide gene?'

'I don't know.' I'm out of my depth with this.

'But what do you think?'

'I'm not a scientist! And I'm not an expert on human behaviour. Sometimes . . .' I hesitate. 'There might be an explanation.'

'My father committed suicide and my mother drank herself to death. How else could that be explained?'

'Neither of your parents was able to cope with their lot but that doesn't mean it will happen to you.' Then I remember that, like me, she is an only child. But, unlike me, she lost her father at sixteen and her mother at twenty. How hard must that have been? I reach for her hand.

'Look, Monica, I feel for you, I do. And I wish I had done something to help you when we were young.'

She turns blank eyes to mine. 'So now you know why I hate Orla so much?'

'Yes . . . and no.'

'She didn't care, Grace. She didn't care that her mother was destroying my family.'

'I think she did, you know. On the evening of her sixteenth birthday party she had a huge fight with Angeline. She really didn't approve of what her mother was doing. In fact—' I'm about to tell her what Orla said at lunch in Edinburgh. How she never forgave her mother. But I don't, because let's face it – nothing Orla says can be believed and I'm the last person who should be sticking up for her. 'Your father's suicide was hard on you.'

She shrugs. 'It wasn't his fault.' Her lips purse together. 'It was Angeline's. She had him under her spell.'

'She didn't hold him against his will,' I say quietly.

'As good as! Women like Angeline have no respect for family or commitment. My dad was a decent man and an excellent husband and father. And then Angeline turned his head.' She tears some grass into long strips. 'We were the perfect family until Angeline came along.'

I know for a fact that this isn't true. Monica's mother and mine were in the Women's Guild together. I have clear memories of my mother telling my dad how negligent Peter was, how he was never there for his daughter and how he never gave Margaret enough money to run the house.

'My dad went round to help Angeline with her accounts for that beauty business she started.' She tilts her head towards me. 'He was good that way. Lots of small businesses relied on him. You ought to have seen all the cards we received when he died! Praising his care and his attention to detail. But Angeline – she mesmerised him. I wouldn't be surprised if she put something in his tea.'

Monica keeps talking, reliving imaginary moments in her childhood when her father was perfect, a happy family mythology that absolves him of any blame: much better to see him as the hapless victim of a conniving witch. Angeline was the whore and the wrongdoer. All her father suffered from was being too trusting to see it coming.

Ironically, reinventing her past like this gives her something in common with Angeline. But for Angeline it's about manipulating other people – better that Murray sees her as faithful – whereas for Monica, life becomes bearable when her father is blameless. Because a man who chooses his mistress over his wife and child is not a man who loves his family and can ever be loved in return.

Euan and me. The parallels are obvious. But we will never fracture two families. And we do love our partners and our children. We have beaten this thing before and we will beat it again. Paul will be accepted for his sabbatical in Australia and then I will leave the village and temptation will cease.

'It's important to understand why things happen, Grace.'

'That's not always possible.' This whole conversation feels too close to home and I am holding myself together by the skin of my teeth. 'Sometimes it's just bad luck and worse judgement but it doesn't have to cloud the good times and the good decisions and the day-to-day commitment.' *That's what I tell myself, anyway.*

'You're right.' Monica smiles at me. 'My father did his best. My mother? Well.' She shrugs. 'She was drinking long before the affair.' She looks upwards and breathes deeply. 'Orla isn't a threat to me. I expect that's the last we'll see of her.'

If only. I realise I have to tell her. She'll only find out from someone else. 'Orla is moving back to the village.' I watch her smile wilt. 'I only found out this morning.'

'She can't!' She falls back a few paces. 'She can't do that.'

'She can and she is. She's renting a cottage. I don't know how long for.'

She takes hold of my wrist and grips it so tightly that her nails pierce my skin. 'I have to stop her.'

'Monica! You need to keep this in perspective!' I extract my wrist from her fingers and shake her gently. 'I know she brings back memories of your parents and I know that hurts, but now, in the present, you have nothing to fear from Orla.' Her eyes say otherwise and as she looks into mine I see that she is close to telling me something. 'What is it, Monica? What is it?' My scalp tingles. 'Is it about Rose?'

Her eyes glaze over. 'I was warned about this. I was warned—'

'What are you talking about? Warned by whom?'

'Grace!' she hisses. 'Do you have any idea how much damage she could do?'

I give a short laugh, not because it's funny but because I have to let some emotion out.

'The status quo should never be underestimated. Life, ticking along. It might seem boring at times but . . .' She looks up to the right and seems to pluck her words from the air. 'Orla is dangerous. She will cause havoc and then she will leave. We have to stop her.'

'Believe me, I don't want her around either.' I take her hand. 'Tell me what's troubling you.'

'I can't.' She pulls free. 'I can't break a confidence.' She takes a few steps backward. 'Can you find out what Orla wants? Can you do that?'

I already have. 'I'll do my best.' I try to look optimistic. 'I'll let you know.'

'Good.' She recovers her composure and gives me an awkward hug. 'I may not have been popular at school, my home life was in meltdown, but hey!' She looks around her, takes in the sea and the sky and all the space in between. 'I have a great career, two wonderful children and I married the man I love. I consider myself very lucky. Well, he's lovely, isn't he?' She smiles. There isn't a trace of guile on her face. 'But then I don't need to tell you that, Grace, do I?'

14 May 1999

I've been sharing space in Euan's cabin for over a year now. It's cold outside and the heating is on. When I arrive I peel off my scarf, coat and hat, then stand opposite my half-finished canvas and warm myself over the radiator. I look at the canvas then across at the photographs I'm working from: the sky at dusk, clouds gathering over the sea, an epicentre of swirling black clouds rising up from the horizon. When I look back at the canvas I immediately see where I'm going wrong. The painting is taking shape but the contrast between light and shade is poorly defined and I've lost all sense of the encroaching storm.

Euan arrives. He's whistling. 'Morning,' he says. 'Nipped out for some croissants.' He takes one out of the bag and puts it on the table next to me.

'What is your eye drawn to in this picture?'

He has another croissant in his hand. He takes a bite then stands back to consider. 'This here.' He points to the edge of the canvas. 'What is it?'

'At the moment just a splash of red but it will become the slate roof of a house.' I shake my head. 'There's no movement in it.'

'In the house?'

'In the painting. There should be movement, drama, with the storm at the centre. The light's all wrong.'

'Coffee?'

'Please.'

The room is warming up. I take off my cardigan, roll up the sleeves of my blouse and re-examine the photos. This is always the hardest part. I know the painting is not right and chances are I'll make it worse before I make it better. Euan hands me coffee then sits down behind his desk and leans back, putting his hands behind his head. I'm looking the other way but I can feel him thinking. I know he's about to speak.

'Grace?'

'Mmm?'

'Do you ever imagine us making love?'

He says it, just like that, as if it's a perfectly normal Monday morning question to ask of a workmate. I'm glad I'm not facing him. I take a breath in but have trouble letting it out. I don't answer and after a few seconds, he repeats it.

'Do you ever think about us making love?' He comes over, stands beside me. 'Grace?'

'I'd rather not answer that,' I tell him.

'Why not?'

'Because.' I wave my hands around the room. 'We're making this work. Why spoil a good thing?'

'Be honest.' A look passes across his face, too quickly for me to read it. 'Please.'

'Why?'

'I want to know.'

'Why?'

'I want to know what to imagine.'

I stare up at him and try to hold on to the moment so that it won't slip away from me but the simple truth is that I can't deny him anything. 'Yes, I think about it,' I say quietly.

'Do you know why I came back to live here?'

'Euan, please.' I think I know where this is coming from. Mo died less than three months ago. It's taken its toll on the whole family. Euan has been one minute restless, the next angry, the next subdued. 'We've all had a difficult time lately. You more than any of us.'

'This isn't about Mum.' He takes hold of both my elbows and lifts them upwards. My head tips back. 'I came back to live here because of you. I came back for you.'

I want to cry. In all my life I can't remember anyone ever saying anything that meant so much to me. I don't know what to answer so all I do is look into his eyes and keep breathing.

'I think about making love to you all the time. I just want you to know that.' He drops my arms, turns away and walks back to his desk.

I stand still. I feel like the air is alive and if I move I'll push my life in a certain direction and I don't know which way to go. Pressure builds in my chest. I swivel round. 'That's it?' He's sitting behind his desk riffling through papers for all the world like nothing has happened. 'You drop a bombshell like that and just sit down?'

'It's hardly a bombshell.' He bites on another croissant and takes a drink of coffee. 'It's been running between us for months, years, decades, since we climbed out of our prams.'

'But you've just crossed a line by talking about it,' I point out. 'Now we can't put it back.'

'I don't want to put it back.'

'Well, maybe I do. Did you think of that?'

'Do you?'

'Yeah.' I nod emphatically. 'I would like to put it back because now I feel like you're going to make a move on me.'

'I'm not.'

'We work in such a close space.' I look around the room. 'How are we expected to carry on now?'

'This room is over five hundred square feet and anyway' – he shakes his head – 'I'm not going to make a move on you.'

'Why not? Why bring it up just to do nothing about it? Because we're married? Because you don't want to spoil a good friendship? Because you *can't get it up?*'

'You think I can't get it up?'

'Well, can you?'

'Do you want me to make love to you?'

'No. I want you to prove that you can get it up first.' I lean back against the desk, purse my lips, fold my arms. My heart's pounding but I'm angry as hell. I expect him to back off, apologise.

But he doesn't. He opens his trousers. 'Will you help me?'

I don't answer. I'm busy trying to regroup and then I look at him, wonder when he was circumcised.

'Undo your blouse,' he says.

I do it. I'm wearing a pretty lace bra that I bought in the January sales. It's a midnight blue, balconette style, lays my breasts out like panna cotta on a dessert plate. He doesn't touch himself, just looks at me.

'When were you circumcised?'

'When I was twelve. Tight foreskin.'

'You didn't tell me.'

'I'm trying to concentrate.' His eyes flash up to my face. 'I believe I have something to prove here.'

I smile in spite of myself and then I laugh because what we're doing is ridiculous. It sets my breasts wobbling. He likes that. I watch him grow hard.

'Satisfied?' he asks me.

'In a manner of speaking.' I back away, do up my blouse, hear him zip his trousers. The phone rings. He answers it and talks like it's any other day. I sit down behind my desk. What was *that* all about? I'm shaking.

When he finishes the phone call he looks over at me. 'Is that it?'

My heart swerves. 'Is what it?' I say.

'I thought for a minute there that we were playing I-show-you-mine, you-show-me-yours.'

'What's brought this on, Euan?'

He shakes his head as if it should be obvious. 'We're a long time dead.'

I hold his eyes, see desire in them and tenderness and a flicker of fear. I stand up, walk over, stop in front of him, pull down my trousers and my pants, not elegantly, that will come later. I yank them down. I have my eyes closed. Inside me a voice screams: *What the hell are you doing?* It tries reminding me that I am a mother. It shows me my two girls running off into the playground, the pompoms on the back of their hats bobbing in time with their running legs.

When I open my eyes, Euan is staring between my legs. His mouth is slightly open and I can see the tip of his tongue between his teeth. I begin to tingle, heat spreads down into my groin and I know in a couple of minutes I'll crave him so badly that I'll beg. 'Is that enough?' I say.

'You tell me.'

I'm falling. It feels heady, a rush of sweetness and light. One last try. I think about Paul, how he will be sitting with his students patiently talking them through their dissertations, the way he looks at me when he comes in from work, hugs me to him, asks me about my day, encourages me, makes love to me, gives me money and time and gives me himself. I think of my girls, holding my hand, falling asleep beside me, drawing hearts, big and red to present to me, blowing kisses, shouting, *I love you, Mummy!* into the wind. I think about Mo, how she cried at my wedding, how she looked after me as if I were her own and how much she loved us both.

'If I could go back in time I would do things differently,' I say. 'When you went to Glasgow I thought about looking for you. I imagined myself turning up at your uncle's house and surprising you. I imagined you walking away from me—'

'I wouldn't have walked away from you.' He pulls me on to his lap. 'I would never have done that.' He starts to kiss me so gently that I can barely feel it. My skin sings.

I reach my hands up under his T-shirt. His chest is warm and I tangle my fingers in the hairs.

So it begins.

We make love that first time and all the waiting, the wondering and the imagining ignite with the touch of our bodies like oxygen to a flame. I am shameless. I can't open my legs wide enough. I want to show him all of myself. He takes me so completely that I feel like my body is his. Like he made me. My feelings for him stretch to the corners of myself and back again. He feels strong, warm, delicious, intoxicating.

The minute I leave the cabin to go home for the evening, the guilt starts. Why did I do it? *Why?* I love Paul, I love my children and I love my life. Sure, sometimes it's humdrum but the attachment to my family is deep and satisfying.

In the end I put it down to a flash of pure lust. It won't happen again. I'm better than that. I shower for almost fifteen minutes. I feel like I am coated in him and I'm afraid that Paul will smell him on me. I make a quick family meal then go to bed early, feigning tiredness.

I don't go into work the next day. At ten o'clock Euan calls me.

'Are you coming in?'

'No.'

'Why not?'

I screw my eyes up tight. 'I'm too scared.'

'You have one hour and then I'll come and get you.'

I go. We do it again and again. We take risks but we

minimise them. Monica almost never comes down to the cabin but, just in case, I buy the same sheets and when we've spent the afternoon in bed, I change them. I even make sure we use the same soap powder. We never send texts to each other. We don't email, we don't phone unless it's to do with the children. We limit ourselves to once a week. We double-check that Sarah and Tom are not likely to arrive home unexpectedly.

Sometimes I dig and push. I can't help it. I want to understand him. I want to know why he loves me so that I can protect it, keep it safe, nurture it so that it never dies.

'Why did you marry Monica?'

'Monica's a good person, Grace. She works hard. She's loyal and kind. I love her for that.'

'More than me?'

'Different.'

I can't stop. 'But if you had to choose one of us?'

'I don't know. She's the mother of my children.'

'Does that mean you'd choose her?'

'It means I don't know.'

I still can't stop. 'In your heart me or her?'

He looks at me for a long time. I wait and in the waiting it comes to me that I don't want to know the answer. I cover my face with my hands and peek through my fingers. 'I'm sorry,' I say. I see that I have hurt him. 'I'm sorry,' I say again. 'I'm so sorry.'

'I think we need some rules.' He takes my wrist, kisses the back of it. 'We don't talk about our partners. Ever. That has to be a boundary.'

'I understand.'

So we make rules:

1. We never talk about the sex we have with our partners.

2. We never talk about the future and what would happen to either one of us if we didn't have the other.

3. We resist all pressure from our partners to spend time together as families.

Marriage should be about love and trust, loyalty and honesty. I know that. What I'm doing is wrong, dangerous and ill-advised. But, oh, so hard to stop. I know we have the edge on marriage. We never experience the deadening effect of endless days of mundane arrangements. Euan is always a man to me, never a husband, or provider, someone to put out the rubbish or stop off for dog food. The high-octane mix of love and loss fuels us. I'm not interested in whether he can cook an omelette or remember to put his clothes in the laundry basket. I'm interested in making him smile, stroking him, loving him and working out what makes him tick.

It's not the nineteenth century. We could leave our families and start afresh together. It would be messy, nasty even, but that doesn't stop a lot of people. We think about it and then we talk about it. Just the once. But I can't do anything else wrong. Having an affair is wrong, I know that, but it's the lesser of the wrongs than splitting up two otherwise happy families.

After eight months we agree to give each other up. There is no future in it, the pain of discovery would outweigh the pleasure and we can't keep pushing our luck. I know that it's the right thing to do and I go back to being an honest wife and mother. I have done what's good and proper and I should feel pleased but I don't, I feel utterly desperate, incomplete, raw inside. I can't sleep and spend the small hours doubled up on the bathroom floor.

Euan is no better. He looks drawn, fatigued, snaps at his clients and sighs for no reason. We still work in the same space but keep our backs turned and our heads down.

It gets easier. I work from home more and Euan has a huge project in Dundee that keeps him in the office on site. We manage this for four years. And then one day, I'm feeling low. Paul's mother has died and Ed has been diagnosed with Alzheimer's. I'm at work, trying not to think about Paul's grief and the life that's ahead for Ed. Euan and I reach for the kettle at the same time and our hands touch and hold. I start to cry. He takes me into the bedroom and we spend the whole day in bed, luxuriate in each other's body and make up for time lost.

Three weeks of loving each other again and then a jolt, a near miss. Sarah and Ella are moments away from catching us in bed together. We stop again. It's difficult and painful but we do it. Another four years pass and then Orla comes back.

12

I have a recurring nightmare and whenever I'm stressed, it visits me with a religious vengeance. There's a knock on the door. Two men are on the doorstep, their hands are in the pockets of their black overcoats and then they both pull out ID and hold it up to my face. One is young with an angular jaw; the other is an older man, taller, tough and jaded with an ugly scar running from his temple down the edge of his left cheek like the silver trail left by a slug.

'Are you Mrs Grace Adams?'

I nod.

'Would you be good enough to accompany us to the station?' the tall one says. 'We have reason to believe you were involved in the death of a young girl back in 1984. Ring any bells, Mrs Adams?'

He has a leering, jeering face that morphs into a demon with horns and burning coal for eyes. His scar breaks open and a slug climbs out. Its antennae are long and feel the air then lunge for my eyes.

When I wake my hands are covering my face. I expect to feel slime but I don't. It's just me, myself, my own skin and bones. I don't want to disturb Paul so I slither out of bed and go downstairs, make myself some tea, sit on the sofa with my legs underneath me and wait for my nerves to settle. It's just one of those things, I tell myself. I'm prone to nightmares, lots of people are. No point in analysing it. No point in examining the guilt and the regret. It doesn't help.

It's two o'clock in the morning and I'm wide awake, pumped full of adrenaline. I know there's no point in me going back to bed yet so instead I go into the kitchen and make the pâté, set out the picnic cutlery and glasses.

Orla was right – I am stuck. Just like she said, forever sliding backwards, remembering Rose, reliving that night, catching hold of Euan, seeing myself in his eyes; the self that existed before Guide camp, the self that is straightforward. I have tried to assuage my guilt with a life of family and love and commitment. I have made Rose's father happy. Paul loves me and I love him. And yet what have I really been doing all these years? Delaying the moment when I have to pay for what I did. And all the while increasing the stakes. I could still be living abroad – but no, I came back to the village. Not only do I live in the heart of where it happened but I married Rose's dad. I couldn't have sealed my fate quite so spectacularly if I had deliberately planned it that way.

And Euan. When he returned my call yesterday, he already knew that Orla was living in the village. Monica told him immediately after I met her on the beach. I asked him why Monica was so upset. Was it about her father's affair or was it more than that? He didn't know or didn't

want to talk about it, I don't know which, because the
very word affair brought us right up close to what we
have both restarted. He asked me when I was coming
into work. I said I thought we shouldn't be alone together.
I told him that we couldn't repeat Monday. He said, of
course not. He knew that. But we should talk about Orla.
I told him that Paul and Ed are going away for the weekend
fishing and the girls and I will go to Edinburgh. So that
leaves Sunday free for him to meet Orla and bribe her?
Persuade her? Leave that to me, he said, and we both
hung up.

When the picnic is organised, I go back to bed, turn
towards Paul and shape myself around the curve of his
spine. He doesn't wake but his body yields to mine. I close
my eyes and hope for emptiness but instead I see Angeline,
with her potent mix of charm and sexuality, attracting
men like moths to a flame. Her wanton seduction of
Monica's father, the repercussions far-reaching: a girl
without her dad, a wife without her husband.

I tighten my grip around Paul's chest and wipe all
thoughts of parallels from my mind. It's only two hours
until I have to get up and tackle the day and when I finally
nod off, my sleep is fitful. I wake up as Paul leaves the
bed.

'I thought we could go up to the graveyard for eleven,
Grace.'

'No problem.' I swing my feet on to the floor. 'I'll make
us all some breakfast first.'

The day is warm, the sky high and clear. The family

join me for breakfast and afterwards we all climb into the car. Ed sits in the middle of the girls, bolt upright. For the last day or so he has been avoiding me. Every time I look at him, he looks away. I don't know whether it's something to do with the Alzheimer's. I tried to have a word with him about it but when I asked him what was wrong, he gave me a withering look and said, 'If you don't know, then I'm not the one to tell you.'

We gather in front of Rose's grave. Paul, the girls and I sit on the grass. Ed is busy digging up the small plot in front of her headstone and is arranging some bedding plants in the newly turned soil. Emotions swirl around inside me like a sea gathering to a storm. Coming to the graveside reminds me that my whole life revolves around Rose and what happens next is dependent on keeping what happened all those years ago a secret.

'Mum!' Daisy calls. 'You keep drifting off. Is everything okay?'

Paul is watching me. Everybody is. 'I'm fine.' I pull my lips back into a smile. 'I'm sorry, what were you saying?'

'How did you two end up getting married?' Daisy says. 'You've never really told us.'

'We met in La Farola a few months after Rose died,' Paul says. 'Well, in fact, it wasn't La Farola's then. It was called Donnie's Bites.'

'Donnie's Bites? Sounds like a greasy spoon.'

'It was better than that, wasn't it, love?' He looks over at me and I nod.

'Donnie was a bit of a gourmet on the quiet,' I say.

'Ahead of his time, was Donnie,' Paul continues. 'He had quite a cordon bleu repertoire for a dyed-in-the-wool Scot. No haggis or stovies for Donnie. He had an Italian mother-in-law if I remember rightly.'

'She lurked in the kitchen in her black headscarf,' I say. 'And the only English she ever uttered was "you lazy girl" or "you good-for-nothing boy".'

'Your mum was a waitress. She wore a dinky little uniform that showed off her legs.'

'Do you still have it, Mum?' Daisy says. 'It might come in handy for fancy dress.'

'It's probably in the attic somewhere.'

'It's my birthday coming up,' says Paul. 'As a special treat, perhaps?'

I laugh and Ella screws up her face. 'Do you *mind*?'

'So?' Daisy says, leaning across and shaking Paul's knee. 'Did you eat there a lot?'

'I had nothing to go home for. And as you know, I'm not much of a cook.'

'You can say that again,' Daisy says.

'I'm not much of a cook.'

She laughs obligingly.

'I spent a couple of nights a week in there. We got talking.' He looks at me and smiles. 'We found out that we had a lot in common. We started to play squash together, went for long walks, your mum would bring her sketch-book, I always had a camera with me.'

'Not the most exciting of courtships then?' Ella says. We all ignore her.

'And were Granny and Grandad okay about you marrying so young, Mum?'

'They didn't take much persuading.' Paul holds my eyes. 'When they saw how much we loved each other' – he leans over and kisses my lips – 'any reservations they had melted away.'

'Can we go easy on the mush?' Ella says. She is pulling the petals off a buttercup. 'And anyway, shouldn't we be talking about Rose?'

'I remember Rose,' Ed says, swivelling around on his knees. 'She had her own little set of garden tools and she would wash them down with the hose so that she could take them up to her bedroom at night. She loved to help me in the garden.'

I stand up to stretch my legs while Paul takes up the story. The path ahead is clear, all the way to where the land slopes down to the sea. In the other direction is the church. It's stone-built and weather-worn and has stood on the hill battling the elements for more than two hundred years. It's the church I was married in and in my mind's eye I can still see Paul standing at the altar, turning around to take my hand, holding my gaze all through the cere-mony. I loved him so completely then, so utterly and completely. And I love him still. But it isn't the same. And I was the one to spoil it, not him. When Euan came back into my life, part of me was reborn. I can't explain it even to myself but he gives me something, a feeling, a love, an affirmation that is nigh-on impossible to live without. How can I love two men at once?

As I turn to walk back towards my family, I notice that someone else is there – a woman. The way she is standing, the tilt of her head, jolts me back into the past. Angeline. The holiday we shared in Le Touquet when Orla and I were fourteen; Orla suppressing her agitation as her mother chatted to men and then disappeared for days without so much as a word.

But this woman can't be Angeline – she is too young. She is wearing red three-quarter-length trousers and a white blouse. Her hair is straight and lies loose around her shoulders – that's why I don't recognise her immediately. She's straightened it and, with no curls to soften the edges of her cheekbones, it makes her face more angular. As I draw closer, I see that not only has she dropped the plain clothes but she is wearing make-up. Her eyes are grey across the lids, her lashes long and curled with black mascara. Daisy and Ella are both admiring her shoes and she holds on to Paul's arm as she slides them off her feet. Ella immediately puts them on and starts to parade up and down.

'You look fantastic in them!' Orla exclaims. 'I can tell you the name of the shop where I bought them.' She claps her hands. 'Even better! Why don't I take you both on a shopping trip? Now that I'm home to stay, your mum and I can be friends and I can be—'

'Like a surrogate auntie?' Ella says, handing the shoes to Daisy.

'Exactly!'

'Mum?' Daisy spots me watching them. 'What do you

think?' She walks towards me. 'She could come with us on—'

'Orla! What a surprise,' I say, interrupting Daisy before she mentions Sunday's shopping trip. 'Back in the village.'

'Where else?' She turns a full circle, her arms out, eyes closed. 'There's nowhere quite like it.'

'We felt the same when we came back.' Paul looks towards me. 'We lived in Boston when we were first married, didn't we, Grace?'

'Yes.' I am tight-lipped, both hot with fury and cold with a steely, focused anger that I have never experienced before. The feelings alternate inside me, rising and falling with my breath.

Orla reaches forward and hugs me, brushes my hair aside with her fingers and whispers, 'Relax! I won't tell him. Not yet.'

I hold myself still, stop short at pushing her away.

'A picnic!' she exclaims. 'How wonderful! Is this a special day?'

'It's the anniversary of Rose's death,' Paul says.

'Of course. I'm so sorry.' She lays a hand on Paul's forearm. 'How stupid of me.' Her expression is solemn as she looks around at all of us. 'I'm intruding on family time.'

'Not at all,' Paul says. 'We were just about to walk down to the beach and enjoy our picnic. Why don't you join us?'

'I couldn't possibly. I'm sure Grace is a wonderful cook' – she throws me an admiring glance – 'but I really don't want to intrude.'

'You won't be intruding,' Paul says, looking to me for confirmation. 'Grace has packed more than enough, haven't you, love?'

'I'm sure Orla is busy with her move,' I say. 'Perhaps another time.'

'Grace is right. The cottage will need a lot of work done to it before I can call it home.' She sighs happily. 'But I'm not planning on moving anytime soon so I have all the time in the world.'

I don't react. She really is laying it on thick, each comment set to scare me further. But it isn't working. I feel strangely powerful as if I can tackle anything, anyone.

'Rose was such a lovely child,' she says, her eyes on Paul. 'Grace and I enjoyed looking after her at camp, didn't we?'

I say nothing.

'Do you remember how much she loved that song we were all singing? What was it again?' She pretends to think. 'It was a folk song. She wanted to learn to play the guitar.'

'I didn't know that.' Paul looks at me quizzically.

'I'd forgotten,' I say, knowing full well that Orla is lying but I'm damned if I'll contradict her and open myself up to more games. Ed and the girls start to drift down towards the beach and I follow them with my eyes.

'Yes, we must be off,' Paul says, lifting the picnic basket up off the ground. 'Did you mention Sunday lunch, Grace?'

'I haven't but I will.' I put my arm through Orla's. 'I'll walk you to the gate,' I say, allowing her a few moments for a quick goodbye before I steer her uphill and away from the beach. My forcefulness surprises her and I am able to move her out of my family's earshot before she shakes herself free.

'Do you mind?' She glares at me.

'About Sunday,' I say, determined that she should still keep the lunch appointment and come up against Euan instead of Paul and me. 'We were wondering whether you have any dietary considerations: vegetarian, vegan, peanut allergy. That sort of thing.'

'Really?' She crosses her arms.

'Yes, really.' I match her body language. 'Do you have any?'

'No. But I wonder.' She taps her foot. 'You hustled me away pretty quickly just now. Something you're not telling me?'

She's second-guessing me again. I smile through my irritation. 'All that nonsense back there – we weren't singing folk music at camp.'

'No, but it sounded good. And it made Paul happy. That's what you do, isn't it? Make Paul happy with a lie?'

'I have never lied to him.'

'Not even by omission?' She tips her head to one side and her hair slides across her shoulders. 'The clock is ticking, Grace.'

'Is it money? Is that what you want?'

'You think I'm doing this for money?' Her laugh is derisory, contemptuous.

'Why then? Because of some letters I didn't read?'

She doesn't answer.

I try the obvious. 'A guilty conscience?'

She laughs. It's a cackling noise that sets my nerves vibrating. 'I'm not driven by guilt. I didn't push her. You did.'

'Why then, Orla?' I'm right in her face. 'Why are you doing this?'

She thinks for a moment. 'Because I can.' She looks beyond me, down to the shore. 'I had a lot of time to think when I was in prison. One of the first things I did when I came out was to come back to the village – just the once – to check up on you. I saw you and Euan walking on the beach. And you looked so' – she searches for the right word, her face twisted with a manic look that is unsettling – 'so fucking happy.'

I take a step back. 'This is about me and Euan?'

She doesn't answer me. I watch her. She goes to speak, stops, bites her bottom lip. Her eyes are black, fathomless. Her thoughts are somewhere else. I can see her playing a memory through her mind. I know that this is it. If she doesn't level with me now she never will.

'You know what?' Her head jerks towards me. 'I hope that when Paul discovers the truth, he chucks you out on to the streets. I hope your girls never want to see you again. I hope that you are shunned by everyone.' Red spots highlight her cheekbones. 'And I hope the regret eats away at you until there's nothing of you left.'

Her hostility is palpable but still I have no trouble taking a breath. 'You hate me that much?'

'I don't hate you. I despise you.' Her saliva spits on to my face. 'You are nothing more than a pawn to me.'

I wipe the back of my hand over my cheek and keep my face lowered as anger swells inside me then drops back and settles to a simmer in the pit of my stomach. 'I never saw it before, just how much of a spiteful, vindictive trouble-maker you are. And always were.' I look up at her. 'You need to stop now before this gets out of hand.'

'Are you threatening me?'

'It's more of a warning.'

'Are you going to set Euan on me?' She makes a scathing sound and I wonder just how come she is always able to work out our next move. 'Is he going to have a quiet talk with me? And if that doesn't work, will he progress to not-so-gentle persuasion?' Her eyes sparkle. 'I know! Why not kill me?' she whispers.

'I don't want you dead,' I say flatly. 'I want you gone.'

'Euan was always good at doing what had to be done, wasn't he?' She paces around me, leaning into my body as she speaks. 'You can hold me down and Euan can do the deed. Then his hands will be dirtier than yours. You've lived with one death all these years. Hell! Why not make it two? I won't struggle.' She crosses her heart with her fingers. 'I promise.' Then she walks away, laughing, turns to face me again and blows me a theatrical kiss.

November 1983

'This is a critical year for all of you. The make or break year. Time to separate the wheat from the chaff.'

We're in assembly. We're fifteen going on sixteen. It's our O-level year. The headmaster has been talking for fifteen minutes. The urge to fidget is almost overwhelming but two of the teachers are eagle-eyed, writing down the name of anyone whose back slumps or attention wanders.

'Hard work is of the essence. No lateness to lessons. Homework in on time. Have we all got that?' Nobody answers. 'Good,' he says. 'Now let's show some effort.'

We file out along the corridors in silence. Walk on the left. No running. Ties straight, blazers buttoned. Fountain pens. Trigonometry tables. Avogadro's number. I'm given a lunchtime detention in French for not learning my vocab and the physics teacher deems my work as 'worthy only of a cretin'.

The home-time bell can't come soon enough. Orla and I sit together on the bus. It's a twenty-minute ride back to the village and we talk about the up-coming school disco; what we're going to wear, whom we're going to dance with, whether or not we'll be able to smuggle in any vodka. Halfway home, the bus driver has to stop because the boys down the back are smoking. He reads us the riot act, marching up and down the aisle like a military general, threatening all sorts of punishments that we know he doesn't have the power to enforce and then drives

on to the village hall where we all spew out on to the pavement. Orla goes one way, me the other. I promise to call
her later and then run to catch Euan up. He's walking
uphill towards our houses, cracking his fingers, one by
one, left hand and then right. It's something he does when
he's anxious or in trouble.

'Our mums went down to Edinburgh today Christmas
shopping.' He's walking at a fair pace and I'm puffing to
keep up with him. 'I'm hoping for a new record player.
How about you?'

He doesn't answer. His face is solemn, guarded, as if
he's thinking something through and I'm not welcome to
know what it is. He's still cracking his fingers and the
sound sets my teeth on edge. I catch hold of his hands.

'Macintosh!' a voice roars from behind us.

I look back. It's Shugs McGovern, the boy everyone
fears. 'Don't turn around, Euan,' I say.

Euan pulls his hands away from me and turns around.
Stops. Waits. I wait too. Shugs catches us up. Acne spots
are dotted across his face, some of them enormous, scarlet,
angry, pushing pus out on to his skin. 'You're claimed,
Macintosh.' He moves an index finger across his own
throat and then points at Euan. 'After footie.' And then
he goes back towards the village hall where half a dozen
boys are waiting for him.

My heart freezes. Euan's lips are tight like he's
about to be sick. I take his arm. He shrugs me off.
'I'll tell my dad and your dad and they'll go to the police,'
I say in a rush.

'No way!' He looks scathing. 'That will only make it worse.'

'You can't fight him!' I hiss. 'He's a bastard. He'll kill you.'

'Just leave it.' He points a finger at me. 'Don't dare tell anyone. I knew it was coming and I know what to do.'

'What?' I push him against a hedge. I'm feeling frantic. My face is hot and I know I'm about to start crying. 'You can't do anything against him. He doesn't know when to stop. You'll end up in hospital.'

'I'll get him before he gets me.'

'But, Euan . . .' I grab the lapels of his blazer and lean into him. He smells of school desks and cigarettes and his own particular smell which has been a source of comfort to me for as long as I can remember. 'You can't let him hurt you.' My voice is muffled. I wipe tears into his shirt.

'It's just the way it is. If I don't do it now, I'll have to do it in a month or in a year. I might as well get it over with.' He puts his arm around me and we walk the rest of the way home like this, leaning into each other. When we get to his gate, he lets me go and I wobble back on my heels.

'I'll come with you.'

'No. You mustn't.' He rubs my hands. 'You might get caught up in it. I'll be fine.' He walks up his front path and shouts back, 'Nice that you care though.' As he goes through his front door he smiles at me.

I'm convinced that's the last time I'll ever see him smile. I'm sure he'll end up brain-damaged, in a coma or a wheelchair or, at the very least, all his teeth will be knocked out. Shugs is known for violence. If he's not torturing small animals then he's picking fights. He's often in trouble with the police, most recently for giving a boy a broken collarbone. And last year he was suspended from school for drug dealing and spent two months in Edinburgh, in what my mother euphemistically calls 'the home for bad boys'. Since he got back, he's been settling old scores – he thinks Euan told on him – and when Shugs claims you for a fight, refusal isn't an option.

Youth club football starts at seven o'clock. At quarter to seven I'm standing at my bedroom window and I see Euan leaving his house, a lonely figure, kitbag over his shoulder, walking off down the hill by himself. I'm not very good at praying but I spend the rest of the evening on my knees begging God to look after him.

By nine o'clock I'm on tenterhooks and when the door-bell rings I hurtle down the stairs and almost knock my mother over. It's Euan. I join him outside, scan his body and see that he is intact. I even feel along his face and arms and torso just to be sure.

'I should get in a fight more often.' He is laughing.

I hug him hard and he doesn't even wince. 'What happened?' I stare at him in wonder. 'You're not hurt at all!'

'Like I said, I got him first.'

'How?'

'When he was bending down to do up his boots, I brought my knee up into his face. One shot. Got him hard. Felt his nose break.' He swivels on the balls of his feet. 'It was me or him and it wasn't going to be me. Fancy an ice cream?'

'You felt his nose break?' I am disgusted. 'Shit, Euan.'

'I did what had to be done,' he says. 'Sometimes that's just the way it is.'

I grab my coat and we walk down to the village, arm in arm. Callum is already there and he's telling everyone about what happened. It sounds like Shugs has been badly hurt but in the dog-eat-dog way that boys have, Euan has earned his respect so there won't be any reprisals.

I feel proud of Euan but at the same time I see there is a side to him that I don't know anything about, a ruthless side that is foreign to me.

When we're walking back home he says, 'You were really worried about me.'

'I was scared. You're like a brother to me.'

'A brother?'

'Not exactly a brother,' I backtrack. 'But more than just a friend.'

'In that case' – he adopts a bashful swagger – 'you can kiss me if you want.'

It's pitch-dark by now; the sky is cloudy and starless and the moon is nothing more than a sliver. I'm not sure I want to kiss him. I've tired myself out with all the worrying but, worse than that, hearing the story of the fight has unsettled me. It's not the Euan I know. It's not that I think what he did was wrong, more that there had to be another way, one that didn't involve violence. I didn't want him hurt but I didn't want him doling it out either.

Anyway, I kiss him because he's been brave and he's happy and if I don't kiss him I think he'll find some other girl who will. And I don't want that.

13

It's Thursday. One week since I met Orla in Edinburgh. And though it's already three o'clock in the afternoon, I haven't been in to work. I have spent the day out and about. My mobile is off – I'm still avoiding Euan – and I have been putting the time to good use, walking Murphy and thinking about the past and the present, trying to join the dots between what happened then and what is happening now. But I need more information and there's only one place to get that.

I call Murphy and we go back to the car. He settles down to sleep on his blanket and I drive along the coastal road back to the village. The cottage Orla is renting is positioned on the headland looking out towards the North Sea. I stop some distance from the obvious parking spot, noticing as I do that Orla's car isn't there. Good. I pat Murphy goodbye, lock my car and walk the hundred yards or so down the grassy bank to the front door.

From the outside, the house looks as if it has suffered years of neglect. The stonework has taken a bashing from the wind and salty sea spray and is crumbling at the corners and under the windows. Roof tiles have slipped in places

and some lie broken on the ground. The garden is over-
grown with dock leaves and nettles and coarse, almost
knee-high grass. The door-knocker is hanging on by one
screw. I support the top of it and bang hard with the
bottom. No answer. I try again, just to be sure, and then
I put my hands up either side of my face and peer through
the dirty window. I can't see anyone inside.

I have never broken into a house. I wouldn't know how
to go about it. I imagine that, without smashing a window
or taking an axe to the door, it involves twisted pieces of
wire in keyholes or credit cards that slide effortlessly into
the space between the door and its frame and trigger the
lock to jump free. In any event, I don't have to do either
because the key is in a similar place to where Orla's mother
used to leave it when we were children: underneath a
medium-sized stone beside the front step.

I slip it into the keyhole, taking a furtive look behind
me as I turn it and go inside. The interior is just as dilapi-
dated and gloomy as the outside suggests. There is a stale,
dank smell lingering in the air as if the place hasn't been
cleaned or aired in years. Wallpaper is peeling off in the
hallway and there are brown stains from water leaks
running across the ceiling and down one of the walls. The
living room curtains are hanging by only a few hooks; the
carpet is worn and covered in animal hairs. The fireplace
is obscured with dust and grime and looks as if it hasn't
been lit for many years. It's made of cast iron and has two
child-unfriendly spikes at either end of the plinth.

There has been no attempt made at home-making. There

are no pictures or photographs, no personal items spread over the mantelpiece or dining table, no keys or magazines. Nothing. The sum total of recent habitation amounts to two empty whisky bottles and the remains of a carry out.

I come out of the living room and into the kitchen. The old-style porcelain sink is tea-stained, the cooker thick with grease. I don't hang around – Orla could return at any moment. I have a cursory look in the bathroom and then open the door of the last room: the bedroom. What I see stops me short. I blink several times and tell myself that I must be imagining it. I even close the door and then open it again, expecting to see something different, but I don't. Orla has recreated her teenage room. The duvet is a faded blue and yellow flower print that I remember us choosing from a catalogue, likewise her slippers, and her bedside cabinet is the very same solid oak unit with three drawers and a cupboard and even the bedstead is the one she had as a teenager, with stickers placed randomly across it and her jewellery hanging on a hook at the edge.

I walk into the room feeling like I am stepping through a hole in time. I am barely breathing. The posters are the very same ones she had on her walls back then: Tears for Fears, Guns 'n' Roses and more. We used to write and draw around the edges of them: comments, messages and love hearts. I recognise my own handwriting: *Saw you on Top of the Pops! Great look, Morten!* written in red felt-tip pen down the side of the a-ha poster.

My legs feel hollow and I fall back into a sitting position on the bed. I can't believe she kept all this stuff.

Twenty-four years on and she still has the bed, the cabinet, even the snow globe that she threw to the back of the wardrobe when she was twelve. I pick it up and shake it, watch the fake snow as it falls down around the Eiffel Tower.

The house is completely silent, eerily so. It feels creepy, sitting amid all these memories: creepy and dangerous, like being here will surely invite disaster. The nape of my neck tingles and I keep turning around to make sure that no one is behind me. I stand up with the intention of leaving but the heel of my shoe catches on the handle of a suitcase and pulls it out from under the bed. I bend down to take a look inside. Just a quick look. That's all. I open it.

It doesn't contain clothes or a wash bag. It contains a large and expensive digital camera with a hefty zoom lens. Next to it there are half a dozen A4 manila envelopes stacked one on top of the other. I don't hesitate. I look in the first one. It contains a wad of twenty-pound notes, as thick as a paperback book. I put it back and look in the second envelope. Three brand-new syringes and needles still in their cellophane wrapping and a small packet of brownish powder. I think about what Angeline said about Orla being a drug addict. Heroin? I don't know. I wouldn't know what it looked like. The third envelope contains photographs. I tip them on the floor, spreading them out with my hands. I see myself and Paul, Euan, Ella and Daisy; Euan and me with the dogs, Paul outside the university, Ella and Daisy coming out of school, crossing the road, smiling.

I know that Orla visited the village months ago but to see it like this . . . And Paul and my girls . . . It makes me feel sick to my stomach and I hold my hand over my middle until the nausea recedes. This is much worse than I thought. This isn't just run-of-the-mill spite, a sudden urge to stir up a hornet's nest, this is a sustained obsession, far outwith the realms of normal. She has been secretly, stealthily plotting and gathering information.

There's a chattering noise and I realise it's my own teeth. I am cold inside but now that I've started looking I don't want to stop. I empty another envelope on to the floor. Newspaper clippings. I pick up one. It's from a Canadian newspaper, dated seven years ago. The article is in French. I can't understand every word, but the gist of it seems to be that a man was arrested for the murder of another man. The murdered man is called Patrick Vornier. I scan the text for Orla's name and see it halfway down. She is the dead man's wife. As I thought, I misheard Angeline, thinking she said Fournier when in fact she said Vornier, hence the reason Euan found no record of Orla's crime on the Internet. And then I read further and see that she was arrested for being a *complice de meurtre* – an accomplice to murder.

As I'm trying to translate the next sentence, I sense the blur of a shadow dart past the window. I freeze for a moment then immediately put everything back where I found it, apart from two of the newspaper clippings which I put into my pocket. Then I jump to my feet and look outside. I can't see anyone. I move my head from left to right and stand on my tiptoes but there is no one there to interrupt the roll of the grassy land as it slopes down to the shore. Satisfied, I turn back into the room just as a face jerks into view, filling the small window with a blank stare. I scream. It's a man. He is grinning; I am not. Two of his teeth are missing and the others are twisted and rotten. His head is shaved and he has a row of earrings from his left earlobe, upwards around the rim. It is Shugs McGovern, looking just as menacing as he did when we were teenagers.

I run through the house and try to get to the front door before he does. I don't make it.

'All right, Grace?' We meet in the hallway. He comes inside, closes the door behind him. His voice is a croak and his right eyelid ticks repetitively. 'Looking for someone?'

'Orla.'

'Still a friend of yours, is she?'

'Not exactly,' I say, wondering what gives Shugs the right just to walk inside. As a child Orla hated him and took every opportunity to let him know it. And then the reason jumps out at me. 'Delivering drugs, are you?' The words leave my mouth before I can stop myself.

'She's been telling me a thing or two about you.' He is closer now and he shows me his teeth again. I step backwards. 'You're not quite the prissy little wife you pretend to be, are you?'

My stomach turns over. I give him what I hope is a vague, unconcerned smile. 'I'm leaving now.' I walk purposefully towards the door but he stands his ground between me and the only way out.

'Where are you going?'

'I really must be heading home.' I stop, try to keep my

voice from shaking but I don't think I succeed. 'Paul will be wondering where I am.'

Again, I try to get past him but he barges me with his shoulder and I lurch back against the wall. 'Oops!' He widens his eyes in pretence of an apology then takes hold of a handful of my hair. 'Still a natural blonde?' Snake tattoos wind down his forearms and around his wrists like rope. His fingers, like the rest of him, are squat and strong. He runs them through my hair from my scalp to the ends. I don't stop him. I have lost the feeling in my arms and legs and my brain is a muddle of fear and noise.

'You always thought you were better than the rest of us, didn't you, Grace?' He is right up close. There's a yellowed bruise beneath his left eye. He smells of stale beer and cigarettes. I want to gag. 'Snooty bitch.' His face is in my neck and he whispers, 'Time for me to get my share. How about a kiss for Shugsie?'

The horror of his mouth on mine galvanises me. My knee comes up into his groin and he groans, doubles up. I reach past him to the door handle. His head is down and one hand clutches his groin, his other grabs in my direction but I'm through the door and up the hill as fast as I can. I'm not normally much of a runner but I'm fuelled by adrenaline and revulsion. I get to my car and lean on the bonnet, catch my breath and look back at the cottage. Shugs hasn't followed me. He is standing outside the door lighting up a cigarette.

As I go to open my car I notice that the window has been smashed and broken glass is scattered across the seats. 'Shit!'

I say out loud and look back down at Shugs who is leaning up against the outside wall. 'Bastard,' I say, under my breath this time, and then I see a small patch of blood on the floor. Murphy. He isn't in the car. 'Dear God.' I look back at Shugs and then up and down the road, hoping that Murphy is on the grass verge, sniffing out rabbits or foxes but he isn't and although I spend the next couple of minutes whistling and calling, he doesn't appear. 'What have you done with my dog?' I scream at Shugs but my voice is lifted away in the air and he makes no sign that he has heard me.

Murphy knows this area and could find his way home from here except for the fact that he has no traffic sense. He has simply never appreciated the danger of cars. I have visions of him lying bleeding by the roadside and I quickly brush the broken glass off the driver's seat on to the floor and start the engine. I drive home at a snail's pace, scanning the pavements and the side streets, the grassy patches and the shop fronts. Wind blows through the space where the window should be and I gulp back the tears, grateful for the sea air cooling my face.

When I get home, I park haphazardly and go inside to get help. But as I run through the hallway to the back of the house I see Murphy lying on the kitchen floor. Daisy on one side of him and Ella on the other. He is loving the attention and when he sees me he doesn't bother to get up but settles for a thump-thump of his tail on the ground. I fall down on to him and rub my face in his coat. 'You came home!' He licks me appreciatively. 'Clever, clever boy.'

'We tried calling you but your phone is off.' Paul comes

over to greet me. 'Did Murphy run away from you? What happened?'

'My car was broken into.' I lean back on my heels to look up at him. 'The window was smashed and there was blood inside. Is he hurt?'

'Your car was broken into?' Paul touches my forehead. 'Are you okay? Did they take anything?'

'I'm fine and no, they didn't take anything.' I give the dog another hug. 'Murphy must have escaped through the window.'

'He just has a small cut on his head but it's stopped bleeding now. Wasn't it lucky that Orla found him?' Daisy says and my spine snaps up straight. 'He could have been run over.'

I get up quickly, turning as I do so. She is standing there. She is wearing a summer dress, off-white, off the shoulder. It has blue forget-me-nots around the hem. She looks fresh and flirty. She is holding one of my best crystal glasses, twirling the stem in her fingers. She goes to the dresser, takes out another glass, fills it up and hands it to me.

'Champagne,' she says. 'I wanted to celebrate my return to the village. I hope you don't mind?'

Anger is rising inside me like a geyser. She is in my house, fraternising with my family, pretending to have saved our dog. She must have come back to the cottage for her meeting with Shugs and seized the opportunity to break into my car and steal Murphy. The knife block is to the right of me. I could reach it without even moving my feet. I could grab the biggest one; the one I use for slicing through pumpkin and squash. I could hold the wooden handle and push the blade into her. I could push until her blood flows. I wonder what it would feel like, whether I would have to push hard or whether the blade would slide in easily. I wonder whether she would scream. 'Where did you find Murphy?'

'Out on the pavement.' She takes a sip. 'Lost.'

'How did you know he was our dog?' My tone is flat, unfriendly. I feel Paul and the girls looking at me and then looking at each other.

'He has a collar with your surname and phone number on it.'

'Well, thank you.' I take the glass from her hand. I think about the photos of my family on the floor of her bedroom: the shrine to her teenage self. 'You can go now.'

'Grace!' Paul laughs uncertainly. 'I invited Orla to stay for a drink.' He puts an arm around my shoulders and shakes me gently. 'She just did us a huge favour bringing Murphy back like that.'

'Actually, Paul, she hasn't done us any favours.' I sound cool. Inside I am boiling. 'She should leave now.'

Orla touches Paul's arm, lightly, almost a stroking movement. 'I don't want to cause any trouble.' She makes wide eyes at him, manages to look both innocent and vulnerable and while Paul is nobody's fool, Orla's act is Oscar-winning.

As I watch his face soften, a bitter taste washes through me. 'You really are a piece of work.' I make a decision. I know I'm risking her upping the ante – if I take a stand against her then she might shout out the truth about Rose's death – but what I've just seen in her bedroom, the damage to my car and the way she's worming her way into my family's affections, feels more urgent than a twenty-four-year secret. I point towards the front door and say quietly, 'Get the fuck out of my house.'

'Grace!'

'Mum!'

Paul and the girls are staring at me. The girls are open-mouthed and Paul is frowning and shaking his head. Orla reels back as if she's just been struck, her face fearful, her eyes filled with tears.

Paul takes my arm and leads me into the hallway. 'What on earth has got into you?'

'Orla is not our friend,' I tell him. 'She's dangerous and she's, she's' – I think of an appropriate word – 'unstable. She's unstable, Paul. And she's manipulative and deceitful. She is twisted and evil and would happily have killed our dog. She will destroy our family without batting an eyelid.'

'What?' Paul is incredulous. 'Where is this coming from?'

'She smashed my car window. She hurt Murphy.'

'How can you know that? Did you see her?'

'No. But I know what she's capable of and there's no one else it could be,' I say, agitated now. 'And Shugs McGovern was at her house. He had gone there to sell her drugs.'

'That seems remarkably far-fetched.' He is struggling to believe me. 'How would you know that? And as far as your car is concerned, there have always been occasional acts of vandalism in the village. I'm not sure why you want to blame Orla for this one.'

'Because she did it!' I clasp my hands together and briefly

consider whether I should tell him about her room, the photographs and the rest. But then I remember that if I tell him that much, it will inevitably lead to me telling him about Rose and I can't do that. I hold his hand and say, 'I know this seems ridiculous. I know it looks as if I'm making it up but I'm not, Paul. I'm really not. Please trust me. Will you?'

He starts back and then half smiles at me. 'Of course, I trust you.'

'Then, please, ask her to leave.'

He holds my eyes for a couple of seconds. 'Okay, I will.' He sighs. 'But let's try to do it politely.'

We both go back through to the kitchen. The girls have recovered from my outburst.

'Look, Mum!' Ella is holding up a patterned T-shirt. 'Look what Orla bought us!'

Daisy has one too, a different colour and design but the same expensive cut. And when they notice the label, Ella squeals and Daisy runs over to give Orla a hug.

'Belated birthday gifts,' Orla says, light as a humming-bird, brazen as a vulture. 'And for you, Paul.' She kisses him, once on each cheek and holds out a glitzy, book-shaped package. 'I was going to bring this on Sunday to thank you for your hospitality but' – she gives me a pointed look – 'I bumped into Grace's mum this morning and she told me you're going fishing.'

I don't react. So she has found out that Sunday lunch is off? No problem. Euan and I will arrange some other time to meet her, deal with her, do what has to be done.

'Well . . .' Paul inclines his head but doesn't take the

present from her. 'I appreciate your generosity, Orla, but we have things we need to press on with here.'

'What things?' Ella says. 'Just open it, Dad!' She takes it from Orla's hand and tries to put it into his. 'It's a present!'

I have an almost overwhelming urge to grab the package, push it back at Orla and bundle her out on to the pavement, but I daren't because I have to let Paul handle this. He has asked me to be polite and while I'm desperate to be rid of Orla before she does any more damage, I don't want to alienate Paul in the process.

Ella, impatient with the delay, tears the wrapping off the package. His present is the autobiography I bought for him and mistakenly left underneath the table in the restaurant in Edinburgh. 'That's such a good choice!' Ella says. 'Dad wanted this book, didn't you, Dad?'

I catch Orla's eye as it lights up with triumph.

'I did,' Paul acknowledges and Orla preens herself in front of him, managing to look both coquettish and angelic. She has quite a range and I can't help myself say, 'You've missed your calling. You belong on the stage.'

Paul gives me a troubled look but Orla carries on as if she hasn't heard me. 'And this is for you, Grace.' She tries to hand me a box. 'For old times' sake.'

I push her aside. 'I'm not prepared to accept it.'

'But it's just right for you! Here.' She removes the lid and holds it up to my face. As soon as the scent hits the back of my nose, it jump-starts a memory so intense that my heart stops and my stomach turns over. I can't breathe or speak. I can do nothing more than stare at her.

'Is it okay? It was always your favourite, wasn't it?' She acts stricken. 'Lily of the valley. I haven't got it wrong, have I?'

I'm next to the pond; Orla is screaming. Rose is lying on the ground. Her face is bloated and the blue veins across her temples stand out against her grey pallor. Limbs dense, chest still, eyes staring at nothing. Dead. Because of me.

Dizziness closes down my thoughts. I take a laboured breath and feel beads of sweat break out on my forehead. For a few seconds I lean forward with my hands on my knees and then I snatch the box of soap from her, open the patio door and throw it out into the garden.

When I turn back into the room, Paul is addressing Orla. 'I don't know what's going on here but clearly you are upsetting Grace and I'd like you to leave now.' He turns to the twins. 'Girls, give me the tops and go upstairs.'

'But . . .' Ella clutches hers to her chest. 'Do we have to?'

'Give them to me and go upstairs.' This time his tone is stern and both girls respond at once. He holds the gifts towards Orla. 'Take these and leave now.'

Orla doesn't move. 'What do you say to that, Grace?'

Tension is cramping my stomach and I can do no more than stare at her. Paul, impatient now, takes her by the shoulders and marches her towards the front door. I wait for her to shout out the truth but she doesn't. She lets him lead her out on to the front step and close the door behind her.

It's quiet. I'm breathing. It's not the end of the world. My legs are wobbly and I collapse down on to an easy chair.

Paul pulls another one up opposite me, sits down, our knees touching. He takes both my hands in his. 'So are you going to tell me what's going on?'

'Orla is a bad person,' I say slowly. 'When we were young she was involved in all sorts of stuff—'

'Last week,' he interrupts me. 'When we were talking. Before Sophie came to see Dad. You were upset. Was it because of Orla?' His fingers find the curve of my wedding ring and he moves it gently then strokes the palms of my hands. 'Is she the one who knows something about you?' I freeze. He feels the tension in my hands and he rubs them harder. 'You don't have to tell me,' he says. 'But it might be easier if you did.'

I can't look at him. The room is completely silent. All I can hear is the sound of my own blood pounding through my ears. I remember one of the phrases from the newspaper clipping: 'Recently . . . well . . . she's been in prison. She was an accomplice in her husband's murder.'

He tilts back in his seat, his forehead creased with concern. 'Honestly?'

I nod. 'It was in the newspapers. Wherever she goes she makes trouble. It's what she does. And—' I stop. I don't want to tell Paul about the bedroom. I can't let him know about that. I stand up. 'I'll go and clean the glass out of my car and take it along to the garage to be mended.'

'Sweetheart, I'll do that for you.' He urges me to sit back down again. He takes the brush and dustpan from the kitchen cupboard and goes outside.

I relax into the chair and close my eyes, think about

what just happened and more particularly what didn't happen. She's smart, Orla. Everything she's doing, she's doing for a reason. Just now, she had the chance to tell Paul all about Rose, but she didn't take it. She is biding her time. Clearly she has something else in mind for me and whatever that is, I have to make sure she is stopped before she can carry it out.

May 1982

'Shugs McGovern is a weirdo,' I say.

We're lying in the sand dunes, sheltering from the winds, tearing up strands of marram grass and then tossing the pieces over our shoulders.

'He's worse than a weirdo, he's a psychopath,' Orla replies. 'Being cruel to animals – it's one of the first signs. I read about it. Most psychopaths start by torturing and killing animals.'

'Faye's going to tell her dad so he'll do something.'

'We should do something.'

'What?' I think of the poor cat, his tail set alight and I shiver then jump up and wipe the sand off my shorts. 'If we're quick we'll have time for an ice cream before the café closes.'

'Fuck's sake, Grace! This is important! Sometimes you have to have principles, stand up for what's right.'

Since Orla turned fourteen she's taken to swearing a lot. I look around, scared someone is going to hear us. Callum and Euan are running across the sand kicking a

football between them. When they're close enough I hold
up my hands either side of my mouth and shout to Euan,
'Do you know if Faye's told her dad about Shugs
McGovern and the cat?'

'Not yet.' He comes over and throws himself down
next to Orla then puts his arms behind his head. 'Her
dad's still out on the rigs. He won't be home till the
weekend.'

'It'll all be forgotten by then.' Orla is sitting up now
and putting on her shoes. 'We have to do something now!'

'I'm up for that,' Callum says, bouncing the ball up and
down on one foot. 'I've wanted to give him a doin' since
Primary Three when he dobbed me in for breaking the
window.'

'We're not resorting to beating him up, Callum,' Orla
tells him. 'Nothing as crude as that. If he's to learn his
lesson then we have to hurt him long-term.'

'Two wrongs don't make a right,' Euan says. 'We should
just report him to the police. Let them deal with it.'

'Like that's going to work!' Orla is scathing. 'He'll tell
the police it wasn't him and they'll believe him and that
will be that. He'll know he's got away with it. Where's the
justice in that?'

'Yes, but . . . if he's going to be a psychopath then we
can't really stop that, can we? I mean, if he's like that
then . . .' I shrug.

Orla's already walking away, her heels pushing prints
into the sand. 'Are you coming or not?' she calls back.

I look across at Euan. He's back to playing footie with

Callum. 'I wouldn't get involved, if I were you,' he says, heading the ball out towards the sea. 'We're going to di Rollo's for an ice cream. Come along if you like?'

I'm in two minds. I watch Orla's retreating back. She's my friend. I want to run after her, take her arm and chum her wherever she's heading, but I don't because I know that when she has an idea in her mind there's no changing it. I don't know what she has planned for Shugs but I think Euan's right – I'm better staying out of it.

At school next day, Orla seems to have forgotten all about Shugs. Our first lesson is English. While Mrs Jessop is writing on the board, I turn round and try to catch Orla's eye but she's busy copying down the questions. When class is over, we climb the two flights of stairs to the science labs together. She puts her arm through mine and asks me whether I want to go to St Andrews with her at the weekend. Her dad will drop us off and we can go swimming then have a fish supper in the chippie on the high street.

When we get to biology, both teachers are standing at the blackboard with their hands in front of them. Miss Carter looks like she's been crying.

'Everyone sit down, quickly and quietly,' Mr Mason orders. He is visibly shaking. We slide on to our stools and wait. Even the worst behaved boys in the class don't dare make a sound.

'This morning when I came in to work I found Peter dead.'

A couple of girls gasp and then there's complete silence.

Peter is the class rabbit. We have three guinea pigs, a snake and half a dozen gerbils. Mr Mason likes to bring biology to life.

'Only *this* class has access to the room before school begins. Only *this* class feeds the animals. Only *this* class knows the combination to the animals' cages.'

Orla is next to me. I sneak a look at her. She is twirling her hair around one finger, her mouth slightly open.

'Who fed the animals this morning?'

Breda Wallace stands up. 'It was me, sir.'

'Was Peter alive?'

'Yes, sir.' Her voice trembles. 'When I left he was eating a carrot.'

'Sit down, Breda.' He paces backward and forward, his fists clenching and unclenching. 'Does anyone have anything they want to tell me?'

Seconds tick by. No reply.

'Turn out your bags.'

The tension is palpable. We look at Mr Mason, then at each other and then we do it. Books, pencil cases, lunch boxes and gym kit spill across the science benches. We shake every stray penny and empty crisp packet out of the bottom of our bags. A commotion breaks out on the back row and we all turn around.

'I didn't do it, sir. Honest!' There's a knife in front of Shugs. 'That's not my knife!'

Mr Mason uses a tissue to pick it up. 'You're saying this isn't yours, McGovern? And yet it was in your bag?'

'I don't have a knife like that!' He looks at the boys

either side of him for verification. 'Somebody must have put it in my bag.' Nobody comes to his defence. Even worse follows.

'You set fire to that cat's tail, though,' the boy to his right says.

'It was Faye's cat,' someone else pipes up.

I glance over at Orla. She has a hand up to her face and seems to be as shocked as the rest of us.

Mr Mason takes Shugs by the arm and brings him to the front. 'We'll see what the police have to say about this. The rest of you turn to page twenty-six and copy out the diagram of the Krebs Cycle.' He casts an eye over each of us. 'And don't give Miss Carter any trouble.'

He leaves with Shugs, who is all the way protesting his innocence, and the rest of us repack our bags and open our books. There's a heavy silence in the room and then Faye says, 'Miss Carter, what exactly happened to Peter?'

'His throat was cut.' She swallows. 'There's blood all over his white fur. Not a pretty sight.'

There are quiet murmurs of 'That's terrible' and 'Poor Peter' and then we get on with the lesson.

As soon as it's over and we're on the way out of the door I grab Orla's shoulder and swing her around to face me. 'You didn't kill Peter, did you?'

'Me?' Her eyes are the colour of volcanic glass, obsidian, like black marbles. 'Of course not! For heaven's sake, Grace! Save your imagination for English lessons.' She jumps down two stairs at a time and then looks back up at me. 'It was good he got caught though, wasn't it?'

14

Once more I sleep fitfully. My dreams are full of Orla and Rose, photographs, water, lightning and the sickening feeling of regret. By the time I get up in the morning I feel no more rested than when I went to bed. And to make matters worse, although he doesn't know the half of it and, of course, I can't tell him, Paul is genuinely worried about the threat Orla poses to our family. When he comes back with a hired car for me to use while my broken window is being fixed, he tells me that he will cancel the fishing trip to Skye. I try to persuade him that we will all be fine but he is not prepared to leave us. So I promise him that we will join him and Ed at the cottage. I will drive up late afternoon when the girls have had their sailing lessons.

I'm still mulling everything over: *Why didn't Orla seize the opportunity to tell Paul yesterday? Is she planning an elaborate showdown that will publicly disgrace and humiliate me?* And I've yet to translate the newspaper clippings. Euan's French is much better than mine and I decide to meet him later and ask him to help me.

As I chivvy the girls to have breakfast, the post arrives; Paul has been accepted for his sabbatical. We leave for

Australia in less than two months. I couldn't be happier if
we'd won the lottery. Melbourne. Paul breaks open a bottle
of champagne and we combine it with orange juice then
toast our good fortune. My own silent wish is that we will
all grow to love it so much that we won't come back.

The girls go off for a day's sailing with the youth club,
Paul and Ed are packed and ready to set off to Skye and
I'm desperate for some time alone to think. The three of
us are having a late breakfast.

'I'm sorry, Grace,' Ed says. 'My knife is not quite equal
to this bacon.'

'I have overcooked it, haven't I?' I put my own knife
and fork together and take both our plates away. 'More
coffee?'

'It's not that bad, love.' Paul drinks some water. 'Just
takes a bit of chewing.'

He's being generous. I can't concentrate. Ed's face is
serious. He frowns across at Paul. 'Where's your mother?'

'She's not here right now, Dad. Busy, I expect.'

Ed looks up at me. 'You're not my daughter. You're not
Alison.'

'I'm Grace.' He's wearing a crew neck sweater and I
pick some fluff off his collar and smooth it down. 'I'm
married to Paul, your son.'

He laughs. 'Not a bit of it. Aren't you married to that
young man I saw you kissing along Marketgate? It was
the other day when I was on my way to bowls. You were
standing by his gate.'

Instantly it hits me that this memory is true and the air

around me thickens. I try to take a breath. I can't. It was on Monday, after we'd made love. I looked up and down the street but saw no one. Then we kissed. Ed must have been passing by. That's why he hasn't been speaking to me. *If you don't know, then I can't tell you.* He didn't say anything then but now the memory has spilled out.

I don't look at Paul. I don't need to. I can sense that he has straightened his back and is now perfectly still and waiting. I shake my head. 'Couldn't have been me, Ed,' I say. 'I'm married to Paul.' I reach sideways to take Paul's hand but he moves his away a split second before they meet.

'It was you all right!' Ed chuckles. 'And if you're not married to that young architect then you should be!' He helps himself to more coffee. 'Passionate embrace if ever I saw one.' He looks down the table at Paul. 'Took me back to the days when your mum and I were courting. She was the bonniest lassie for miles around. Sweet and bright as . . .' He frowns. 'Where is she anyway? Surely not shopping again?'

Paul is still waiting. I feel his eyes on my face. I need time to dissemble but I don't have it and my face flushes up red and guilty as the sin I have committed.

Ed looks up. 'Have I got it wrong? I'm so sorry.' At last he seems to see us both and he looks from one of us to the other. 'What have I been saying?'

'Nothing, Dad.' Paul stands up. His face has turned a greyish colour and his mouth is trembling. 'Why don't you start packing the car? The tackle's in the front porch.'

'Absolutely, yes, fishing rods, excellent!'

He walks off whistling and Paul turns to me. 'Grace?'

I hope my face has calmed down. I am completely blind-sided. I have spent the past week wondering how to break the news of my involvement in Rose's death and instead I am faced by my other betrayal. I try to buy time. I pick up the plates. He stops my hand, holds both my wrists firmly.

'Were you kissing Euan?'

'No. Not like that! Of course not!' I try to step backward but he doesn't loosen his grip. 'We were hugging,' I admit. 'Yes. Because I have a new commission and he was congratulating me.'

'A new commission?' His head drops to one side. 'Since when? You didn't tell me.'

'A friend of Margie Campbell's.' I try to breathe but even to my own ears my breath sounds ragged and panicked. 'She heard what I was doing for Margie and called me on my mobile.'

'What's her name?' he fires quickly.

'Elspeth Mullen. She lives outside Glasgow.'

'Why didn't you tell me?'

'I don't know.' I shrug. 'It wasn't at the forefront of my mind. There was the girls' party and Rose's day . . .' I trail off. He doesn't believe me. Ironically, it's partly true: the commission part. But, in fact, I hadn't told anyone, not even Euan, because I had more important things on my mind.

Paul lets go of my wrists and folds his arms. 'So if I was to ring Euan, he would know about this Elspeth Mullen and he would have the same story as you?'

'I'd prefer that you believed me.' My voice sounds weak.

I can't look at him. I'm digging myself in deeper and what-ever I say will only make things worse. I feel sick and ashamed. I want to shout – *This wasn't supposed to happen!* – to run into the corner and hide.

'I've always tolerated—' He stops, drums his fingers on the dining table, thinks. 'Not tolerated, encouraged. I've always *encouraged* your friendship with Euan because I know how much you like each other but so help me God, Grace, if you are having an affair with him . . .' He takes a breath and balls his fists. 'If you are jeopardising our happy family life for—'

'Paul, please!' I know that in order to maintain the lie, I need to look offended. I need to work myself into a how-could-you-think-such-a-thing rage that will exonerate me. But I can't. This is not a good moment to find out that when push comes to shove I can't lie to my husband. I just can't. I lift a hand to my chest. 'Paul, you have to know that I love you.'

'Would that be with all your heart?' He is icy. 'Or just part of it?'

'I . . . I'm not—'

'Is this why you wanted to keep Orla out of the house?' His voice cracks. 'Because she knew about you both?'

'No! It's not. Everything I said about Orla was true!'

'So this is something else, is it?' He is leaning over me and he is white with anger, his skin stretched over his cheekbones as if it's about to tear. 'Something else you can't tell me?'

'Please, Paul, let me—'

'Stop there.' He puts his hand up in front of him. 'I think you've said enough.' He turns away, walks through the door, slams it behind him.

I open the door and follow him, trail in his wake like sewage from a freighter. 'Paul, can we at least talk about this?'

'You look to me like someone who's still getting her story straight, Grace. I would have thought a few days would be just what you need.'

'Paul, please!' I reach for his arm but he is too quick for me and then Murphy gets between us and I lose a couple of seconds. When I reach Paul's side of the car, he's already revving the engine and he drives off. I go back inside. It's not yet midday but I pour myself a whisky. I think. I think about my family, my mistakes, my guilty secrets. I am appalled by the mess I have made. I feel desperate. And then I do the only thing I can do. I ring Euan.

'I'm about to go out on the water. You at work?'

'Euan.' I take a deep breath. 'Ed saw you kissing me on Monday. When we were standing at the gate. He blurted it out at breakfast just now.' I start to cry. 'I'm in so much trouble and this is just the beginning.' I pull a tissue from my pocket and blow my nose. 'Paul's furious with me and now they've gone to Skye.'

I don't say anything more and neither does Euan. It feels like minutes pass before he speaks. 'What did Paul say?'

'He didn't say much. He was wounded, cold.' I am whispering, too ashamed for even the walls to hear me. 'He behaved with dignity. I feel like an absolute shit. He is the last person who deserves to be hurt.'

'Christ.' I hear voices in the background shouting Euan's name. 'Grace, I have to organise these kids. Come and meet me at the end of the day, will you?'

'Yes. And I have to talk to you about Orla,' I say, my free hand feeling for the newspaper clippings that are still in the pocket of my jeans. 'A lot happened yesterday.'

We say our goodbyes and I put down the phone, lean my head on the table next to it. Paul and I have been married for over twenty years and in all that time I have never wanted to be without him. I know I am duplicitous. I know that Euan and I should never have started our affair. Some would say that I want to have my cake and eat it. I would say that without Paul I have no place in the world. He is my family, my every day.

And Euan? He anchors me to myself and to the moment. When he looks at me, he sees me as I am. Not the Grace who is a mother, a wife or a daughter but the Grace who is . . . just Grace. He takes me – loves me – as he finds me. No pretence necessary. Is he a luxury? It doesn't feel that way. He feels essential to me, like my own arms and legs.

But the affair is the lesser of the evils. Orla's news on top of this will surely break Paul. I, of all people, know that he has never forgotten Rose. To find out that his own wife is not only unfaithful but was involved in his daughter's death – I don't know what that will do to him.

September 1995

When do things start to go wrong? I can't answer that. Even afterwards I can't pinpoint the exact moment. The first years of our marriage we live in Boston, the girls are born there, we are happy and we make a good life for ourselves. And then we come back to Scotland. It is not good for me. I feel tired. I suffer from one bout of flu after another. I lose my enthusiasm for drawing. The blank page defeats me. I start to feel Rose's presence again. I see her in the shadows, sometimes an indistinct shape, more a feeling than a presence, but other times I see her clearly: her eyes, her smile, her wispy blonde hair. I start to watch out for her, to sense her in the room or on the pavement ahead of me. I know I'm being irrational. I know I need help but I have no one to confide in. I love Paul. He is kind and funny, easy-going, an excellent husband and father but I am never able to tell him about Rose and I come to accept that there is a part of me that I will have to keep hidden, no matter what. Slowly, insidiously, this realisation grows like brambles around clematis and I have no way of stopping it. I become watchful, afraid that I will be exposed for what I am: a fraud and a liar. We've been back in the village eight months, the girls are barely three and I am anorexic and withdrawn.

And the more I watch, the more I see that I am not the only one who is keeping secrets. Paul isn't a man prone to unexplained absences. He is a family man, one hundred per cent. He looks forward to long weekends with the girls and me. On Saturdays, he takes the girls swimming, on Sundays we have family time, walking, visiting castles and parks or spending time with grandparents. But when we're back living in Scotland, I realise that there are times when Paul doesn't go straight to work. This realisation dawns on me over a period of months: a couple of times I call the university but he hasn't arrived yet, even although he's been gone an hour or more; sometimes when he returns home, the car's wheels and sides are mud-splattered and yet there are no dirt roads between our house and his work. And it's always on a Tuesday when he has a free lesson first thing. Clearly, he's spending time elsewhere. As someone keeping my own secret, I feel no entitlement to pry but the mystery gnaws at me. Has he found someone else? Is he having an affair? Is he gambling? *What?*

I could follow him. He drops the girls at nursery and then continues on to work. I could drive behind him, far enough away not to be recognised but close enough to see where he's going. That feels deceitful, like spying, so I make up my mind to ask him outright. I try to find a time to bring it into the conversation. Impossible before the girls are in bed and then, when they are in bed and we're sitting in the living room reading or watching television, the question sounds too large in my head, so bald, so intrusive that it dies before it is spoken. Would the words sound less accusing if said under the cover of darkness? I try it. When we're in bed ourselves, I make an attempt to whisper a question to him but either my voice is too quiet or he is already asleep. A moment of

closeness, I think, that is the perfect time and so after
we've made love, when the mood is tranquil and our
bodies soften into each other, I try to say it. *Where do
you go, Paul? Where?* But again I can't because it feels . . .
dangerous. Me? Asking Paul to share his secret? How
can I? Where might it lead?

So I sit on my curiosity for months, feel it grow into
anxiety and then decide that I will settle it. I will follow
him. Tuesday comes around, I tuck the girls' vests in, pull
up their knickers and tights, button blouses and pinafores,
force arms into jackets and feet into boots, wedge hats on
heads, kiss them both, kiss Paul and wave them goodbye
as usual. Then I start my car and follow him. I see him
deliver the girls to their teacher, letting go of first one
hand and then another, standing on the pavement,
watching them run inside. When he's in his car again, I
move back into the traffic and shadow him up to the main
road but instead of turning right to the university, he turns
left.

We travel away from the sea, into the countryside. We
drive for five miles and when he turns into an unmade
road, my heart shrinks against my ribcage. I drop my
speed, hang back, park in a space fifty yards behind him
then follow him, on foot, along the path that leads directly
to the pond. Unlike all those years ago, it's no longer a
case of fighting through brambles and over clumps of
heather because the path is well trodden. I meet a couple
of dog walkers and a lone jogger but by the time I get
to the water, only Paul is ahead of me. I stop a discreet

distance away, my body concealed by the trunk of a pine tree. Paul is sitting on a rock, the very rock I sat on myself before I noticed the jacket in the water, the jacket that was Rose. In all these years I have never been back here. Some things have changed: the trees are higher and plants grow where they didn't before, but mostly it's exactly as it was and I feel like my life is bending back on itself, like a gymnast falling backward to catch hold of her feet.

I feel sick, ashamed, unworthy. I want to turn and run but I am held in awe of my husband. He is completely still. He is looking across to the far end of the pond where a stream trickles in, the flow of water barely interrupting the glassy, benign surface. Above the trees' reach, the sky is turquoise blue and what clouds there are, are wispy and spiral in the breeze as flimsy as dandelion clocks. Blackbirds call to one another, their tune high and clear, a late summer melody. Nowhere is there any suggestion that a child died here.

Paul pulls a book from his jacket pocket and starts to read aloud. I can't hear the words but his tone is tender and humorous. Now, suddenly, it seems obvious. All those months of wondering where he was going. My suspicion is shameful. Of course, he would choose to visit the site of his child's last moments. Of course, he would come here to sit and remember. How could I ever have imagined that he was over this?

I have a sudden horror of being seen and I retrace my steps as quickly as I can. I drive home and spend the day gainfully employed: housework, cooking, reading to and playing with the girls.

When Paul comes home from work he is as he always is and so am I. Nothing is said. When I wake at three in the morning, as I do most nights, I get up and go downstairs. I take the book from his jacket pocket. It's a hardbacked exercise book with two hundred pages or more. I open the first page. Paul's unfussy hand has written a title: Letters to Rose. I flick through the pages. The book is almost completely full. He has written her a letter most weeks since her death. I read no further, close it and put it back where I found it.

Rose is his secret just as she is mine.

15

Paul and Ed have been gone for almost four hours. Since the phone call with Euan I've sat in the same place thinking about what I've done and what will happen now. My insides are doing somersaults with worry and shame and the fear of impending catastrophe. Paul's face when he left, stiff with pain and disappointment, is at the forefront of my mind. And what of the rest? Orla, unhinged and determined, is going to reveal the secrets of that fateful evening at Guide camp. What of my marriage then? Could I even go to prison? How will the girls be affected? How can they love a mother who cheats on their father? Worse still, how can they love a mother who is careless enough to push their half-sister to her death?

I don't know what to do next. I feel like I am walking a tightrope in the dark. Over the course of the morning I've tried Paul's mobile six times. Each time I have left a message. He hasn't answered and so finally I send him one text and then another, asking him to call me . . . please. I have no right to ask, I know that, but I need to speak to him. I don't know what I'll say but I can't bear that I have hurt him.

Murphy is sitting upright on the couch beside me, staring into my face. Every so often he strokes a paw down my arm. It feels like sympathy but I know that he's angling for a walk. The back garden isn't good enough. He knows our routine and by now he should have had his run along the beach. I pull on my coat and take him outside. He rushes off ahead of me. I throw a stick far out into the sea and he swims out and brings it back, shaking water up in a spray around him, panting and smiling like the happiest dog alive. Usually his sheer joie de vivre rubs off on me but I am turning myself inside out and back to front with the thought of what's to come. The unravelling has begun, my deceit rolling out like a carpet for the world to walk on and it doesn't help to know that it's all my own fault. I don't expect sympathy or understanding from anyone, least of all my husband.

I spend the day marking time and then, at last, it's late afternoon and I drive to the sailing club to meet Euan. I feel bleak but resolute, still and grey as the sea by my side. With each mile covered determination hardens inside me like a rock. No more games. No more Orla. My marriage is damaged enough. It stops now.

I pull into the car park, choose a bay that faces down to the beach. The sailing boats are back. They are small, two-man vessels. I remember learning to sail on something similar myself, never enjoying the experience much, gripping plastic with tense fingers and tense smiles for Euan's enthusiasm. I could never get the hang of it. He would shout things like, 'Windward side! Quick! We're broad-reaching!' And as much as I tried to follow his instructions, it never made any sense.

When I climb out of my car, Callum comes up alongside me. 'I thought I was giving the girls a lift home. Paul brought Jamie back yesterday.'

'I was passing,' I say. 'I need to speak to Euan. Work stuff.'

'They've had a good day for it. Sea's set to whip up a storm tomorrow. Some fierce weather moving in from the north.' We start walking down on to the sand where the boats have been pulled up on to the beach. 'Euan's over there, look!' He points his finger. 'Somebody's bending his ear.'

Euan is about fifty yards away. One of the boys is talking to him and Euan replies, his arms making diagonal and then circular shapes in the air.

'Tacking,' Callum says knowledgeably. 'Takes some of them a while to get the hang of it. He's a good teacher, mind. Patience of a saint. You coming to the September gala?'

'Course,' I say, knowing there's a distinct possibility that I won't. I hope we'll be in Melbourne by then but I haven't told Euan yet and anyway, now – what if Paul decides to go without me? And the girls go too? They're old enough to make up their own minds.

Ella and Jamie are entwined outside the storage hut. His hands are on her backside, pulling her into his groin. I avert my eyes.

Callum has none of my qualms. 'Shouldn't you two be

helping pack up the equipment?' he asks pointedly. They reluctantly separate their faces. 'Shift your lazy arse.' He gives Jamie a hefty nudge. 'There's work still to be done.' He turns to me. 'Would you have snogged a boy in front of your mother?'

'Not likely. I'd have been dishtowel-whipped around the head. Times change, huh?'

'You're telling me. Jammy buggers! Oh, to be a kid again, eh, Grace?'

'Not for me, Callum.' *Unless I got to change things.* 'It was hard enough first time round.'

Callum and Jamie walk off towards the shore. 'We did go sailing, if that's what you're thinking,' Ella says.

'It wasn't.'

'We came in a bit earlier.' She bangs sand off her trainers and looks up through her hair. 'When Monica dropped Sarah off she was asking me about Orla. She doesn't like her either. She *really* doesn't like her.' Her eyes widen. 'What's so bad about her anyway?'

'She's a troublemaker,' I say and then I think about the photos under her bed: photos of my girls, my family. 'You have to stay completely away from her, Ella.' I hold her shoulders so that she's forced to look at me. 'It's very important that you understand that.'

'Fine.' She shrugs me off. 'Whatever.'

I want to say more – in fact, I want to lock up both girls until Orla is gone – but I don't want to scare them and anyway, I don't believe that Orla will go after the girls. It's me she wants to punish – Euan and me. 'And did you do a good job of cleaning out Monica's attic?' I try for a bright tone.

'Well, what do you think?' She has her hands on her hips and is looking at me the way I used to look at her when she was seven and I was catching her in a lie.

'I think you probably did.'

'I did and by the way, don't throw a fit, but I have a box of stuff to bring back home.'

'Ella, not more for your bedroom!' Callum and Jamie are down at the shore lowering the sails but still I speak quietly. 'Not now that we're going to Australia.'

'Well, it won't seem real until I can start telling everyone.'

'And you will. After the weekend. Just like we said.'

'It's torture,' she moans. 'I hate keeping secrets from Jamie. He is going to be allowed to come out and visit me, isn't he? And Sarah?'

'Of course,' I say. Although it's unlikely Sarah will ever come. As Euan's daughter – how would that work? In my heart I feel that I will be saying goodbye for good and I wonder how it will feel to leave all this behind. I will miss it: my friends, the beach, the sky, I will even miss the weather. And Euan: I will miss his company, his smile in the morning, his familiarity, the easy conversations, the easy silences. And, yes, I'll miss making love to him. Losing Euan will be almost unbearable but I stand to gain too – peace of mind, for one thing. You can't put a price on that.

And then there are my parents. I was hoping they would come for an extended stay at Christmas. Then – who

knows? They might like it well enough to live with us for
ever. But if Dad's not well . . .

'Ella, you and Daisy should still go back with Callum,'
I say, taking my mobile from my pocket. 'I'm going to
ring Gran and then I need to talk to Euan.'

'Okay.' She hands me two buoyancy aids. 'Can you take
these back for me?'

'Sure.'

I dial my parents' number and my mum answers at
once. When we've got through the usual pleasantries, I
ask about my dad.

'Well, funnily enough, the doctor called him in to the
surgery. He was seen this morning.'

I mentally remind myself to thank Monica.

'The doctor thinks it might be a stomach ulcer. He's
sending him for one of those things where they put the
camera down.'

'That's good, Mum,' I say. 'Doesn't sound too serious.'
I almost tell her about Australia but don't want to tempt
fate – after all, Paul might not want me to come and first
we have to deal with Orla. I say goodbye to her and start
walking towards the boathouse. Euan is inside packing up.

'I was thinking just now about how you taught me to
sail,' I say.

'It was an excuse to touch you.'

'We were thirteen. You didn't fancy me then.'

'I've fancied you since I was about' – he takes the buoyancy aids from me – 'I dunno, nine? When I had you tied
to the tree.'

'We were eight,' I say, thinking back to those days, building our den, the sense of purpose, our childish plans and secrets that kept us happy all summer long until my mum found me and spoiled it all. 'We had fun then, didn't we?'

'Didn't we just.' He looks at me properly for the first time since I walked into the boathouse. 'You heard from Paul?'

I shake my head.

'Have you seen Orla again?'

I nod. 'She was at my house yesterday when I got home.' I tell him the story backward: Paul asking her to leave, the smell of the soap, her trying to win over the girls, the cut on Murphy's head, the damage to my car and Shugs McGovern. 'He wouldn't let me out of the house. He tried to make me kiss him.'

'What?' He starts back, frowning. 'Why didn't you call me?'

'I don't think he intended to hurt me.' I shake my head. 'I couldn't get away from a man like that. He's far too strong. I kneed him in the balls but not *that* hard. He let me escape. He was just trying to weird me out.'

'Still.' He touches my cheek. 'You should have called me.'

'I think he was there to supply her with drugs,' I say, following Euan to the back of the boathouse. 'Ironic when you think how much she hated him when we were kids.'

'Drugs, prison, violence.' He hangs up the buoyancy aids on hangers strung on a rope. 'They have a lot in common.'

'Talking of which.' I tell him about the bedroom, the posters, the photographs, the money, the drugs and the newspaper clippings. 'She's not right in the head,' I finish. 'She really isn't. Here.' I bring the clippings out of my pocket. 'I understand some of this but you have a try. I misheard her surname. That's why you couldn't find anything on the Internet.'

He takes the papers from my hands and starts to read, translating as he goes. 'Medical experts have begun a post-mortem examination on a man murdered over the weekend in downtown Quebec. Patrick Vornier, thirty-one, was found dead in his bedroom. A neighbour heard a commotion at about 11 p.m. and raised the alarm. Police told reporters that a man named Sucre Gonzalez and Mr Vornier's wife Orla have already been arrested in connection with the death. Mr Vornier is originally from Perpignan in France but has been living in Canada for some time. He is thought to have been stabbed in the chest, probably with a knife. There is speculation that Mr and Mrs Vornier, who had been married for two years, may have been using heroin on the night he died.'

Euan rolls back on his heels and says, 'Bloody hell,' then translates the next article which has similar information, but this time, Orla is cited as an accomplice to Gonzalez and is sentenced to six years in prison. 'So Angeline wasn't exaggerating,' Euan says, handing the clippings back to me. 'I think this proves Orla's capable of just about anything.'

I nod. 'At first I was surprised that she didn't tell Paul

about Rose when she had the chance but I think it's because she's building up to something spectacular. She has this crazy idea that we should be punished. And she hates that we're happy. Not that I am any more.' The memory of this morning, Paul leaving, comes back to me in a wave of shame and anxiety. I hold myself steady while the wave recedes. 'Paul didn't want to leave me this morning because of Orla's behaviour yesterday but now he thinks I only wanted her out of the house because she knew about you. I was going to take the girls and drive up to Skye to join him and Ed later.' I shrug. 'But now I don't suppose I have to.' I look down at my feet. 'Euan, I can't let her tell Paul about Rose. I simply can't.'

'I'll take care of it.' He is wearing a wetsuit and has taken the top off down to his waist. He peels off the rash vest underneath.

'She knows Paul is going fishing so she won't be coming round on Sunday.'

'Okay.' He thinks for a moment. 'Then I'll go round to her place tomorrow.'

'Should I come with you?'

'No.'

'Wouldn't it be better if I was there?'

'No.'

After what we've just found out I feel scared for him. I take his hand and hold it. 'Euan, you mustn't put yourself in any danger.'

He laughs. 'She doesn't frighten me.'

'But what if she comes at you with a knife?' I touch his

bare chest, let my fingers rest over his heart and feel it beating through the palm of my hand. 'Shugs might even be there.'

'Shugs won't get involved. He won't risk prison again. He isn't as tough as he used to be.'

'He didn't look great,' I acknowledge. 'So what time will you go tomorrow?'

'Afternoon probably. I'll text you.' He glances up at me – 'You can be my alibi' – and then away again, back to watching his hands tie some rope.

'Okay.' It's the least I can do. 'Are you sure about this?'

'Yes.'

I have to ask. 'What will you say to her?'

He shrugs. 'I'm not sure, persuade her somehow.'

'I don't think that will work. She—'

He puts a hand over my mouth. It's cold and his finger-tips are shrivelled from the water. 'You don't need the details, Grace. I will deal with her.'

'When I met her in the graveyard, she said that we could kill her,' I say lightly. 'And make it look as if it was an accident.'

'Well, there's an idea.' His tone is dry but there is steel behind his expression and it worries me.

'You're not going to do anything . . .' I hesitate. 'Anything definite, are you?'

'I have to do something definite or she won't go away, will she?'

'Kill her,' I say in a rush. 'You're not going to kill her, are you?'

'What do you take me for?' His eyebrows come together to tell me I'm way off base but I'm not entirely convinced.

'So why the alibi then?'

'In case something goes wrong, but you know what? You're right. Don't worry about the alibi.' He gives me a cocky smile. 'I won't need it.'

He pulls off the rest of his wetsuit and I turn my back, push my shaky hands into my pockets and remind myself that Euan is doing this for me and that if Paul finds out I killed Rose, albeit accidentally, life as I know it will be over. Couples can recover from affairs but Paul will never be able to forgive me for this. As betrayals go, it's enormous.

'I'm sorry.' I face Euan again. He is doing up his jeans. 'Of course I'll give you an alibi. I'm not meaning to sound like I doubt you.' Sand blows up from the beach and I use it as an excuse to try to rub the tension out of my face. 'You smell of the sea. I love the smell of the sea.' I rest my forehead on his chest and feel the warmth spread into my cheeks.

'I need to check on the boats.' He puts his hand on the nape of my neck and gives me the briefest of kisses. 'I'll call you tomorrow.'

I watch him walk away from me then I go back to my car and drive home.

When I come in through the back door both girls are already there. Daisy is making a sandwich and Ella is eating cereal. I step out of my boots and walk into the kitchen in my socks. 'I'm sorry, I hadn't quite got round to making any tea yet.'

There's no room for either of them to sit down. Ella has the stuff from Monica's attic spread over the kitchen table. There are dusty hardbacked books and bits of old clothing, a box of buttons and some old postcards. 'I thought I could sell some of it on eBay,' Ella says.

I pick up an ancient tennis racket and wave it at her.

'It's a collector's item,' she says defensively, grabbing it back from me.

In among the junk, there is a silver charm bracelet. The chain is delicate and is joined at either end by a heart-shaped lock. The six charms hang at regular intervals around the chain. The first is a tiny fan. When opened, one side is engraved with 'Espana', the other 'Malaga'. The second charm is a Welsh dragon, the third a spinning wheel, the fourth a rose, the fifth a child's interpretation of a Viking boat and the sixth is a gondola. Small and perfectly formed, it is complete with gondolier and a couple sitting at the back, arms entwined. Along the prow of the boat it reads 'Venice'. Somewhere in the back of my mind I have an idea that I've seen the bracelet before. I turn it over in my hands and try to think but I can't place it. 'Did Monica say you could have this?'

'Yes.' Ella has finished her cereal and is rummaging in the fridge.

I hold it up. 'But did she actually see it, Ella?'

'Yes. I told you!' She has a juice straw hanging from the corner of her mouth. 'Can we have money for chips?'

I finger the cool silver charms. 'Help yourself to money from my purse. It's in my handbag by the front door. Take enough for a fish supper each.' My fingers seek out the gondola, feel along the spine of the boat. 'And a drink. Take money for drinks.'

'Shall we eat in, then?' Daisy says, filling Murphy's water bowl. 'Should we bring some back for you?'

I shake my head. 'I'm not hungry.' I think of the spoiled breakfast, Ed's words and the repercussions. Bile rises in my throat. I swallow it down and my eyes start to water.

The girls slam the front door behind them and I sit down, exhausted, overwhelmed by the turn the day has taken. I want to cry but I know that when I start I won't be able to stop so I have to wait until the girls are in bed. Although Paul is in Skye, his shadow is everywhere in the house. His brogues are by the door, his shaving stuff is next to the sink and the book he was reading is beside his chair, the bookmark sticking out halfway through. Murphy is padding around looking for him. He goes into his study then out again, upstairs to our bedroom and back downstairs into the kitchen. Finally, he settles down on the rug by the front door and rests his chin on his paws.

I hold the bracelet on my lap. It's still niggling me. Where do I remember it from? I begin to doze, find it surprisingly comforting, drift off into the mesmerising gap between sleep and wakefulness where random thoughts float before me and hang there like pictures on film. I relax further into the sofa, my eyes heavy as lead, and I roam through splinters of memory: the girls as babies, plump, rosy cheeks, podgy ankles, fingernails like pearly pink shells; a weekend in New York, Paul's hand holding mine as we skip over puddles, on and off kerbs, along Forty-Second Street late for a play; Euan sitting in the pram opposite me, Mo telling us my eyes are as green as grass, his as blue as the sky; Ella and me winning the mother and daughter's three-legged race, hugging each other, giggling.

Backward and forward through my life until finally I land where I need to. I reach for the memory, grasp it and make the connection. My eyes snap open. I look at the bracelet on my lap. I hold it up in front of me. My heart hammers a hectic rhythm then seems to stop altogether. The bracelet – I know where I've seen it before.

April 1987

Paul and I honeymoon on the New England coast. We base ourselves in Cape Cod where the weather is kind to us. It's every day the same: sunshine and soft breezes. Perfect. We stroll along the wide sandy beaches, cycle up country paths and visit the numerous lighthouses that stand guard over the coastal waters. On the first night we discover a beach restaurant that immediately becomes our favourite. New England clambake: cod, scallops, lobster and all types of clams covered in seaweed and steam-baked in charcoal pits then served with red bliss potatoes wrapped in wet cheesecloth.

We talk and we laugh and every morning and evening we make love. At first I'm shy, afraid to let go to the rising tension inside me and I automatically squash it back down again but soon I learn to let go and my body wakes up to his. I can't help but touch him, everywhere, all the time. We are seldom parted. He goes into the post office and I mind the bikes. Within minutes I am aching for him. When he comes out I grab him, hold him in a kiss until the ache is rubbed away. I want our honeymoon to last for ever. I want to trap the moments in aspic and jump in alongside them so that I can relive the sense of completeness where all desires are met and past mistakes wiped clean.

We both love living in Boston. We have a home in the suburbs where the garden stretches into an orchard. Paul studies with Professor Butterworth at the State University and we are welcomed into a circle of friends, some of them Europeans like us. Within the year I have a place at art college and start to live out my dream of becoming an artist.

We've been married for four years when we start trying for a baby. Making love is tender, significant, each ejaculation, each long swim: this could be it, this could be our baby, the melding of us both into a completely new and wonderful human being. First month, nothing, second month, I'm two weeks late. Then I wake up and immediately throw up. I ring one of the other wives and she comes with me to the gynaecologist. I'm pregnant: happily, deliriously, unbelievably pregnant.

When I tell Paul he falls to his knees and hugs me, strokes my belly and I giggle. He is a model expectant father. Those first three months, I vomit both morning and evening. He brings me dry biscuits and weak tea in bed. He does all the shopping and cooking; he comes with me for the first scan.

'Well, well, well!' the doctor says, grinning at us both.

We wait, our smiles frozen, not sure how wide we should make them.

'There's one heartbeat and then there's another! Two for one. How clever are you?'

'Twins?' We both look at each other and then laugh, incredulous. It is a shock, a happy readjustment.

I love being pregnant. I feel like I'm incubating a miracle, two miracles, in fact. I spend hours visualising my babies, what they will look like, their smiles and gurgles, the sound of their breathing. And when they start to move inside me it feels like the flutter of butterfly wings and then, as the months pass, their movements become stronger, proper kicks, hiccups that make my growing stomach shake.

The babies are born, time passes and Daisy becomes as summery as butter with cheeks as round as red apples. And she is content. She's in no hurry to grow up. She watches Ella and learns from her mistakes. It isn't Daisy who bashes her head on the side of the coffee table or breaks her wrist swinging from the elderberry tree.

Ella is a cat. She seeks attention on her terms, wants to be mistress of her own fate. She reaches all the milestones first. She smiles first, crawls and walks first. Her first word is dada; her second is dog.

'I think we should have six children,' I tell Paul. 'And live in the country. On a farm with chickens and goats and—'

He's just come home from work and he kisses me quiet. 'Well! There's the thing, Grace. It's time for me to apply for a professorship. And guess what?'

'What?' I help him out of his jacket and hang it over the back of the chair.

'There's a post coming up in St Andrews of all places.' He takes my hand. 'Wouldn't you like to go back home?'

I don't answer. I don't know what to say. I had given up on the idea of ever living in Scotland again. I no longer see it as my home.

'Your mum and dad would be able to help with the twins,' he continues, 'And my parents. Skye isn't so far from the village. Great for holidays, fishing, hill walking. It's an ideal upbringing for children.'

I see the sense in it. But going back? I'm not so sure. We've made a life for ourselves in New England. I'm a different person here.

'So what do you think?'

He is excited. He holds both my hands and waits, smiling. I want to please him. After all he has given to me, I want to give him something back. 'If it's the job you want then we should go for it,' I say.

He twirls me round and then we collapse on the sofa and start to make plans. While Paul's at work, I pack. I'm sorting through some boxes when I find it. It's a close-up photo of Paul and his first wife Marcia. They were married in the registry office in Edinburgh. It's summer and she's wearing a short-sleeved dress. They are both grinning, holding their hands in front of them, showing off their wedding rings. Around Marcia's wrist is a silver charm bracelet. I can clearly see two of the charms: a Viking boat and a gondola. When Paul comes home from work I ask him about it.

'The Viking boat was to remind her of her gran who lived on the Shetlands.' He points to the gondola. 'We went to Venice in the spring before we got married,' he tells me. 'I bought that charm for her at one of the markets in the square. Had to haggle a bit on the price.'

'It's a beautiful bracelet.' I run my finger along the image of the silver chain. 'What happened to it?'

'I'm not sure,' he says. 'When Marcia died I gave it to Rose. She took it everywhere with her but the catch was loose. She had it with her at Guide camp.' He shrugs. 'She must have lost it somewhere there. I went back several times to look for it but I never found it.'

16

'What's going on?' Ella is standing at the bottom of the ladder staring up at me. 'The hall is full of junk.'

It's the next morning and I've already turned out the understairs cupboard and now I'm climbing into the attic. 'I'm looking for something.'

'If you're trying to compete with Monica, I'd give up now. We've got ten times as much junk as her.'

'Do you want to help me?'

She makes a face and goes into her bedroom. Within seconds the thump of music starts. I continue up the ladder until I'm in the roof space. I hook a light over one of the crossbeams and survey the scene. We have more boxes of books and paraphernalia than I would have thought possible. Almost every inch of space is taken up with a box or bin bag of stuff. I wish I had developed a system for cataloguing it all but it was one of those rainy day jobs that I never got around to. I need to find the photograph of Paul and Marcia's wedding and if it means turning the whole house upside down then that's what I'll do. I have to make sure that my memory isn't making links that don't exist. And if it is the same bracelet, then how did Monica get it? And why has she kept it all these years?

I start working through the bags and boxes, trying not to be distracted by everything else I come across, but when I find the photograph taken during my ultrasound scan, Ella and Daisy, their bodies coiled around each other, head to toe, wrapped up in each other's rhythm, I stop and sit for a moment. Sometimes I play that game: if you had to describe yourself in one word what would it be? Nine times out of ten the answer would be mother. I am more a mother than anything else and my love for them remains as solid and true as the day when I first saw the scan and heard the two baby heartbeats. By the time they were born, at thirty-six weeks and five days, I was already smitten beyond anything I could ever have imagined.

And I remember another time. Five months pregnant, waking up in the middle of the night to discover Paul's side of the bed empty, finding him in the living room, fast asleep in his chair, this photograph in his hands. We parent the same children, live in the same house, make love, have fun, and plan for our future. Why wasn't that enough for me?

I put the scan photo away again and get back to it. Wind is whistling through the roof space from west to east and the light swings backward and forward, illuminating first one corner and then the other, stuff that is no longer relevant to our lives but somehow we're unable to throw it away.

I tread carefully over the sheets of hardboard that act as a temporary floor, bending my head under the rafters to bypass cardboard boxes of Paul's old toys, soldiers and Airfix models. There's a plastic bin bag of old clothes. I look through it and see my waitress uniform, think back to Donnie's Bites, serving Paul his dinner, making up my mind to love and care for him.

The final cluster of boxes I come across look like they could well have been there for some time. Since we moved back to Scotland? Possibly, judging by the amount of dust and cobwebs that lie over the top. As soon as I open the first one, I have the feeling that I've struck lucky. It's all the photographs that Paul took before I met him. I scan through the ones on top then decide to look through them downstairs away from the draught.

Ella has just come out of her bedroom and jumps as I drop the box of photos close to her feet. She looks into it, her nose wrinkling at the cobwebs and dust. 'You're just so random,' she says.

I pick up the box and go downstairs.

She follows me. 'Where's Dad, anyway?'

'Fishing with Grandad. They told you already.'

'I'm not putting all that stuff back under the stairs.' She points a plum-coloured fingernail in the direction of the emptied-out cupboard. The hallway is now almost impassable: tennis rackets, raincoats, old shoes, a broken fax machine, a dozen boxes full of the twins' old school books and jotters and that's not even the half of it.

'I'm not expecting you to,' I tell her.

I climb over everything, feel a long thin something-or-other bend and then snap under my foot, keep walking and sit down on the couch. I turn out the box on the floor and take my time looking at each photo until at last I come to it. It's a professional one, about six inches long and four inches wide. Paul and Marcia grinning in front of the registry office. I position the bracelet on the table next to the photo and examine them carefully. Both are silver, both chains have a distinctive herringbone weave and the two visible charms on Marcia's wrist are the Viking boat and the gondola, side by side, just as they are on the real bracelet.

It's what I expect but still I find it hard to believe and it sets up questions that, for the moment, have no answers. How did Monica get the bracelet? Why didn't she hand it to the police? Why has she never in all these years given it back to Paul? When I went back to the tent after the argument, Monica was still up. What if Rose went to bed after I pushed her? I may even have unconsciously registered that all the girls were there. She may have got up later, just like Euan has always said.

Could it be that I wasn't the last person to see Rose alive?

The doorbell rings and Ella answers it. 'I have to warn you,' I hear her say. 'She's in a strange mood today.'

The living room door opens. It's Euan. I slip the bracelet into the back pocket of my jeans. He looks around at the mess. 'What's going on?'

'Just tidying.'

'Tidying?' He closes the door behind him. 'Looks like a tornado's passed through.'

'I wanted to sort out some photos and . . .' I give him a breezy smile. 'No time like the present.'

He's staring at me. He looks tired. I want to touch him. 'Are you okay?' he says.

'Yeah.' I shrug, aim for nonchalance.

'What are you hiding?'

'What do you mean?'

He points to my hands. I still have them behind my back. I bring them forward and show him they're empty. He looks around at the closed door then leads me into the alcove of the room so that we won't immediately be seen if one of the girls walks in. 'Has Paul been in touch?'

'No. I've left messages but he hasn't answered them.'

He puts his hands in his pockets and blows out a breath.

'At least he's out of Orla's reach,' I say, trying to see the upside. 'But I'm not sure what he'll do when he does come back home; maybe he'll come to see you.'

I expect him to look worried but he doesn't. He gives me a half-smile, resigned, sympathetic. 'It was bound to come out sooner or later.'

'Are you going to tell Monica?'

He rubs the back of his hand over my cheek. 'One thing at a time. Are you still okay about the alibi?'

'Yes.' I can't pretend that I haven't had some second thoughts. *What if Euan hurts Orla? What if I have to lie in court? Under oath? What then?* But bottom line: Orla has to be stopped and Euan and I have known each other since before either of us had language. Our selves are imprinted on the other. We are close enough to have absorbed each other's moods and morals. I trust him completely.

'I'll text you.'

'Euan.' I pause. The bracelet is burning a hole in my back pocket. 'Has Monica ever said anything about Rose's death?'

'Why would she?' He's whispering. We both are.

'It's nothing really.' I shake my head. 'Just a thought.'

He puts his right hand on my neck, under my ear, starts to massage it with his fingers. 'Tell me.'

'Well . . .' I'm afraid that if I say it out loud it will sound like nothing – scraps of information that I've pieced together to form a shape that is more imagination than truth. 'I'm not telling you this to make trouble, but Monica was out of bed that night too. I saw her when I was going back to my tent.'

'So?'

'When Orla turned up at the girls' party last week, Monica saw me arguing with her and was pretty freaked out about it. And then when I met Monica on the beach the other day she was—'

'Grace.' He takes hold of my shoulders. 'This is a bad situation and I can see why you're clutching at straws.'

'I'm not.'

'Have you eaten anything recently?'

'Well, no, but—'

'This has got nothing to do with Monica and everything to do with us.' He shakes me gently. 'You have to stick to the point. Leave Monica out of it. I mean it. No one will ever find out what really happened to Rose. It's a dead-end.' He leads me through to the kitchen. 'You should eat something and then you should rest.' He takes cheese and ham, butter and pickle from the fridge, slices some bread then puts his arms around me and makes the sandwich with me standing in between.

I shut my eyes and lean into his neck. I could show him the bracelet but I don't want him to come up with a rational explanation. I want to hang on to what I know: Monica had a bracelet that belonged to Rose. She has been on the edge of her nerves since Orla came back to the village. It does add up to something. I can feel it in my bones.

Euan hands me a bulging sandwich and I offer him half back. He shakes his head. 'I'm meeting Callum in the Anchor for a pub lunch.'

'That's nice.' I take a bite.

'He's thinking of buying the disused fish store down at the harbour. It could be developed into apartments. He wants me to go halfers.'

'Right.'

'Grace?'

'What?'

'Monica had nothing to do with Rose's death.'

I take another bite and keep chewing, look down at my feet.

'Why don't you come along to the pub?'

'My stomach will be full in a minute.'

'You can just have an orange juice. Keep a couple of old men company.'

'No, you're right.' I smile, pour a glass of water and take a drink. 'I need to have a lie down.' I drink the water and hold the glass into my stomach.

Euan is pacing, thoughtful. Then he comes to stand in front of me. 'You're going to break it, squeezing so hard like that.' He takes the glass from my hand and puts his mouth close to my ear. 'Just remember who's the enemy here.' His teeth tug my earlobe. 'I'll text you late afternoon.'

I follow him into the hallway and watch from the window. When his car turns the corner, I start up my own car and drive off in the other direction. I should be able to have it out with Monica before Euan gets back from the pub. I am driving towards their house and am almost there when, just for a second, my resolve wavers. I slow the car right down to a stop. Perhaps I shouldn't do it. Perhaps I've dug around enough. Rose is dead. Twenty-four years dead. Do the details really matter?

Yes. To me the details are everything. They are the foundation on which I have built my life. Maybe the bracelet means nothing, maybe Monica will have a reasonable explanation for how she came to have it but I'm not missing the chance to find out. Angeline said that the past doesn't matter but it's the past that I'm wrestling with and this might be a chance to make sense of it. I won't let this moment pass. Not even for Euan.

I park, lock the car, take a deep breath and ring the bell.

Monica opens the door and stares at me. She looks as

if she's been crying, as if she's suddenly aged ten years. 'You'd better come in,' she says.

The house smells of burned toast. I follow her through into the kitchen and sit down on one of the stools. The kitchen is a mess, an ordinary family mess, piled-up plates, bottles of ketchup and relish, sticky knives and forks. I have never seen it like this before.

I want to blurt out, *What's going on, Monica? What happened to Rose? What, Monica? What?* But something inside me says to slow it down, slow it right down. I am in finger-touching distance and I don't want Monica to clam up on me. 'Is everything okay?'

She stares at me. Her eyebrows are raised as if it's a stupid question and she's waiting for the next one. She might just deign to answer that.

'Is this about what happened when we were all sixteen?'

Nothing. Just that look.

'That year, 1984?' She still doesn't answer so I answer with another question. 'This?'

I bring the bracelet out of my pocket and lay it on the breakfast bar.

She glances at it and then walks over to the kettle. 'Coffee?'

'If you like.' I look around the room. There is a picture on the wall that I drew four years ago. It's a simple pencil drawing of Murphy and Muffin when they were both puppies. Sarah loved it and stuck it up there between the door and the window. It's always surprised me that Monica hasn't taken it down again. I know she doesn't think much of my drawing – a hobby – not real work like doctoring. In most ways we are opposites: Monica is disciplined, driven, ambitious and controlling. My ambition is limited, I'm more laissez-faire than driven and I don't have her issues of control. But something is upsetting her and I'm determined to find out what.

She puts a cup of coffee down in front of me. 'We never really escape our pasts, do we?'

I stretch my hand across the breakfast bar, don't quite reach her but leave it there anyway and say, 'What's troubling you?'

'It's not me so much . . .' She drifts off, sips her coffee and sighs.

'We all have regrets. Things we would change.'

She laughs. 'What regrets can you have, Grace? You always seem so perfectly well-adjusted, perfectly happy with Paul and your girls and your painting.'

'We all have our dark times.' I tap my finger next to the bracelet. 'This bracelet. I've come about this.'

She looks at it again. 'I don't know anything about that.'

'Pick it up. Look at it closely.'

She does. She lets it dangle on the end of her fingers, holds it up to the light and watches it move. 'It's tarnished but still very pretty.' She puts it down next to my hand. 'However, there are much more pressing matters on my mind.'

'It was in your loft,' I say lightly. 'Ella said you let her have it.'

'Did I?'

'Yes, you did.'

She shrugs. 'So?'

'It belonged to Rose.'

'Paul's Rose?'

I nod.

She gives it another cursory glance. 'Well, I have no idea how it came to be with my stuff.'

'She had it on the camp.'

'Well, there you go then. It must have got mixed up in my camping gear.'

'But you weren't even in her tent.'

She looks exasperated. 'What do you want me to say? That I took it?'

'Paul always wondered what had happened to it. She was never without it. It belonged to her mother. When her mum died, she kept it on her at all times.'

'Well, I will go and see Paul and apologise to him.' Her tone is impatient. 'But in the meantime can we please talk about Orla?'

'I have spent the last twenty-four years thinking that I was the last person to see Rose alive,' I say quietly. 'Thinking that if I'd only listened to what she was saying I might have been able to prevent her death, thinking, Monica, *thinking*, that when I pushed her away, she fell into the water and drowned.'

She goes over to the sink and looks back at me. 'What are you talking about?'

I stand up and come alongside her. 'Orla and I had an argument that night. Rose came to me for help. I pushed her away. The next day I found her in the water exactly where I had pushed her.'

Monica's arms are folded and she is tapping her foot. 'Have you been drinking?'

'No!'

'You think you killed Rose?'

'Yes.'

We stare at each other.

'This is what Orla has on you?'

I nod.

'Christ!' She topples backward, catches hold of the worktop and looks at me as if I'm mad.

'I know.' I hold up my hands in acknowledgement. 'It's horrendous. But just recently, well, something isn't adding up and I need to get it clear in my head. The sequence of events. Did you see Rose that night? Did she come to you?' I point to the bracelet. 'Why did you have her bracelet?'

Monica's eyes look past me as she winds back the clock. 'So around midnight when I was putting away the supplies and you came back to the tent—'

'I had already pushed her.'

She gives a perfunctory shake of her head. 'Then you didn't do it. Rose came back to the tent about ten minutes before you did.'

For a second I am completely still and then I grab Monica by the shoulders and say loudly, 'You're absolutely sure about this?'

'Yes! Otherwise I would have told you that one of your patrol was out of bed.'

Ever practical Monica. Of course she would have made sure the girls were in their tents before she settled down for the night. She took her role seriously. While Orla and I were off fighting over Euan, Monica was being responsible.

I start to tremble. My knees give way and I sit down hard on the stool. *I didn't do it. I didn't kill Rose. It wasn't me.* I need some air and I push past Monica to the back door, breathe slowly and deeply. After a few minutes I go back inside and pour myself a glass of water. 'Are you absolutely sure?' I say again and immediately visualise Rose's body, bloated and blue by the time I found her. I put my hand over my mouth, clench my teeth and concentrate on letting the wave of nausea recede.

'Yes. For heaven's sake! I told the police that at the time.'

'You did?' On the one hand I feel a lifting, an elation, a lightness, a disbelief, a need to laugh, a need to cry, a need to shout my innocence from the rooftops. On the other, I feel a crushing, debilitating sense of loss. Years of guilt and reproach and all for nothing. If only, at the time, I had gone to the police, they would have told me that it couldn't possibly have been me.

'Grace, you married her father! You couldn't really have believed you pushed her to her death! She must have got up later and then she fell in the water. These things happen.' She sits down opposite me. 'Now please! Can we talk about Orla?'

'She has nothing on me,' I say. 'Nothing.'

'Yes, well . . . you're lucky then, aren't you?' Her face is pinched. She leans on the breakfast bar and stares at me. 'Orla must not be allowed to stay in the village.'

'Why not?'

She hesitates, doubt flashes across her face and then she says, 'Do you promise this will just be between you and me?'

I nod, hardly breathing. I hear my phone beep with a text message but I ignore it, primed for what's coming next.

She looks beyond me. 'I love Euan, Grace. Even when we were at school, I loved him. I know I didn't rate. I know I wasn't one of the in-crowd but he has always been, and still is, the only man I've ever wanted.'

I say nothing. I am grateful that she is not looking at me because guilt is written all over my face. I can feel it, shining like a beacon.

'History repeats itself. When I was young, Angeline wrecked my family and now Orla will do the same to my children.'

'I don't understan—'

'She's come back for Euan,' she says quickly.

'She's come back for Euan?' I almost laugh. I think of his face at the convent. He is not attracted to Orla. Not at all. I know he isn't. Sure, he had sex with her once, age sixteen, but never again. He said so and I believe him. I hold Monica's shoulders. 'Euan and Orla? Never in a million years! If that's what you're worried about then I honestly think you've got the wrong end of the stick.'

She breathes deeply. 'I know we've never really been friends but I need you to help me look out for him.'

To my shame, I nod. The irony of Monica asking me to look out for her husband is not lost on me but I want this conversation to be over. I want time to accelerate a month, six months, whatever it takes for me to get past this moment. I want to think and to appreciate and to bask in the knowledge that I didn't kill Rose. I want to make it up to Paul and I want to live in Melbourne and enjoy being with my family.

Monica is still talking. 'She could ruin Euan's life. And for what?' Her mouth is trembling. I watch as she forces her lips steady. 'It was Mo who told me. She said to me, *I have a bad feeling about that girl. This isn't the last you'll see of her.* And Mo was right, just as she always was.'

In a distant part of my brain a bell goes off. 'What was Mo right about?'

'Orla being a threat. Coming back for Euan. Not letting it drop.'

'What drop?' The house is so quiet I can hear the sound of the sea through the double-glazing.

'When she was sixteen—' She stops. Tears spill on to her cheeks. She lets them fall then pushes her shoulders back and says loudly, 'When she was sixteen, Orla had an abortion. The baby was Euan's.'

I am too shocked to speak. My mouth is open. At first I don't believe it, everything inside me says that this can't possibly be true and then connections start to form in my head: Euan being so sure Orla's intentions were spiteful, their heated exchange in the convent, Orla spitting in his face. *Why didn't he tell me?* Slowly it sinks in. This isn't just about me. She is taking her revenge on Euan too. 'When did she have the abortion?'

'The end of August 1984.'

Euan told me he'd only slept with her the once when they went potholing for geography O-level. That was towards the end of April. By August, she would have been more than sixteen weeks pregnant. That would explain her erratic behaviour at Guide camp. She must have known then. And I suppose that's what was in the letters. The ones I never read.

'Euan has always been convinced that the baby wasn't his,' Monica says. 'That was one of the things that set Orla off. The fact that he wouldn't believe her. You know she attempted suicide?'

I nod.

'Remember when Euan went off to live with his uncle?'

I nod again.

'Orla was causing him loads of problems, phone calls, letters, turning up at the door. They moved to England but still it carried on. She sent him pictures of dead babies in the post and wrote to the headmaster at school. So Euan went to live in Glasgow where she couldn't reach him.'

I am speechless. How could I not have known about this? Euan and I were closer than most siblings but I was oblivious to the fact that he was in trouble. I was so wrapped up in what happened to Rose that I didn't see any of it. I can hardly believe it and yet, at the same time, it rings true. Orla is out to punish both of us because neither of us helped her and the fact that we're now having an affair has made it all the richer.

'You will keep this just between us, won't you?' Monica says.

'Of course.' I wish Euan had told me about the abortion but I am the last person to condemn anyone for keeping secrets.

I put the bracelet into my back pocket and stand up. I need to find him, tell him that Orla has nothing on me and in truth – what does she have on him? Perhaps he didn't support her the way she wanted him to but so what? Even if she publishes the truth in the newspaper it can't damage him much. He's a grown-up and, me aside, the way he's behaved since then has been exemplary. He is well respected and well liked. Orla can't put a dent in that.

17

No secrets. For the first time in twenty-four years I have nothing to hide. There won't be a knock on the door. I won't be marched off to the police station. I no longer have to protect my family from what I thought was the truth.

I didn't kill Rose.

I sit on the step outside Monica's house and stare straight ahead. The air smells salty and wet. The wind is whipping in from the sea and I pull my coat around me. Random thoughts and pictures pass through my head: Rose at the bottom of my bed, lily of the valley soap, Mo's voice telling me that my eyes are green as summer grass, seeing the jacket in the water, holding my girls for the first time, running after Euan along the beach, Paul on our wedding day.

I didn't do it. My adult life has turned on an event that didn't happen. I walk back to my car and settle into the seat. 'All these years I thought I killed her and I didn't,' I say out loud. 'I didn't kill Rose.'

It's impossible to describe how much of a weight has lifted and I'm enjoying the feeling of light and air inside me. My marriage is still in trouble – I haven't forgotten that – but adultery is the lesser crime.

Euan. I can't believe that he didn't tell me about the abortion. I don't understand it. He was only sixteen: the age for mistakes. I would have helped and supported him. For almost two weeks now, I have been banging on about Orla and motives and the fact that this was my problem, not his, and all the time he was keeping a hefty secret of his own.

A ginger tom jumps on to the bonnet of the car. Silent and sleek, he sits licking his paws then rubs behind his ears. He is perfectly in sync with himself. He stops washing and stares through the windscreen at me. 'My marriage is in meltdown but at least I didn't kill anyone,' I tell him. 'It's all relative.'

For the first time since Orla got back in touch, I have lost the sense of impending doom. I watch the cat. He's walking backward and forward across the bonnet looking ahead into the street. Every so often he gives a plaintive meow then suddenly he jumps off and slithers through the hedge into the neighbouring garden.

Before I start the engine, I remember to look at my phone. There's a text from Euan. I check the time he sent it and then look at my watch. Forty-five minutes ago. I try to phone him but his mobile is switched to message service so I drive to Orla's house. Euan's car isn't there but there are lights on inside. It's only three in the afternoon and yet the sky is dark with clouds. It's raining a few miles out to sea. Wind heralds the rain's approach and the waves are jumping skittishly as if they know what's to come. The air vibrates as gulls flock together, beaks open, wings flapping and gliding, before coming to land, feet perched precariously on inches of ledge.

I knock on the door. Orla answers it. 'Well! Look who's here!'

She is dressed up to the nines. She is wearing a red satin dress that grips tightly over her breasts and hips and has a thigh-high split up one side. There is a black, beaded choker around her throat and matching earrings that drop almost as far as her collarbones. Her hair is piled up on her head in a seemingly random manner but curls escape at just the right places to highlight her cheekbones. I wonder whether she knew Euan was coming.

'I'm not here to see you,' I say. 'I need to speak to Euan.' I can see him standing beyond her.

He doesn't look pleased to see me. He comes outside and we move away from the house a few feet. 'What are you doing here?'

'I found something out just now. It was Monica who told me. I couldn't possibly have killed Rose,' I say breathlessly. 'She came back to the tent before I did. She was in her sleeping bag when I climbed into mine.' I expect him to be pleased but he shows no emotion. It's as if he hasn't heard me. 'Euan?' I shake him. 'Did you hear me?'

His face is expressionless. 'Is Monica sure?'

'Absolutely! She was there. She remembers it clearly. And you know Monica; she doesn't get stuff wrong. Isn't it brilliant?' I shake him again. 'Euan?'

'Yeah, it is.' He says it without enthusiasm and looks

beyond me to where the storm is gathering pace, coming across the sea towards us.

I feel the first spots of rain land on my hair.

'Don't you see what this means?' He is still staring at the horizon, preoccupied. 'We can both walk away from this.'

No response.

I reach for his hand. 'You could have told me.'

His eyes snap back to mine.

'The abortion,' I say. 'I wish you'd told me.'

His jaw relaxes. If I didn't know better I would think it looked like he was relieved.

'I didn't think we had any secrets from each other.' In this light his eyes have darkened from cornflower blue to the lilac-blue of verbascum. It makes him look sad. 'I'm the last one to criticise anyone for keeping secrets but I never had any from you.'

He clears his throat. 'It was a long time ago and I never really believed the baby was mine. I wasn't the only boy she had sex with. You know how much of a liar she was.'

I nod. 'I understand. It was a heavy price to pay. Like you said, you only slept with her once.' I pause and try to catch his eye again. I have a feeling there's something he's not telling me. 'It was only once, wasn't it?'

'When we went potholing.'

'You know . . .' I hesitate. The rain is falling steadily now and I'm tired and I'm desperate to go home. I want to get right away from Orla, but first, I need to tell Euan that it has to be over between us. 'I have always loved you and a part of me always will.' I hold his hand. 'I want to stay married, Euan. I want Paul to forgive me.' *And we're moving to Australia.* 'I want to make things right again.'

'This sounds like goodbye.' He tries to laugh. 'What's going on?'

'We have to move on.'

'From each other?' His expression merges hurt and scepticism. 'We've tried that before.'

'I know. But Monica loves you and you love her. I know you do. This thing between us?' I shake my head. 'There's nowhere for it to go.' I breathe in. 'I'm hoping that Paul will forgive me and that we can be a family again. He's taking a sabbatical year in Melbourne. We'll be moving there in August.'

He steps backward and then almost immediately towards me again. 'Grace?'

'When we were young we had our chance. We didn't take it. Nothing can make this right.' Wind is whistling around our ears. I lean in towards him. 'If we sleep together the guilt eats away at us and if we see each other every day but don't sleep together then it's a different sort of torment. We have to get right away from each other.'

'The kids are almost grown—'

'We've talked about this!' I am almost shouting. 'Neither of us wants to let our partners down.'

'Grace.' He puts a hand under my chin. 'I love you.'

It would be a lie to pretend that I'm not tempted just to give up the fight, leave Paul and set up home with Euan. But in my heart, I know that this would be foolhardy. These things rarely end well. The children are teenagers but still they need parenting and stability. And there is nothing wrong with either of our marriages. I can't leave Paul, I love him and anyway, I don't want Euan if he has to break Monica's heart to be with me. I want to move on. I want to start over in a new country where I can be a better version of myself. 'We have to give each other up.'

The rain is falling heavily now and he pulls me inside Orla's cottage.

'You have to let me go, Euan.'

'Lovers' tiff?' Orla is watching us. She has her shoulders against the wall but is pushing the rest of her body forward provocatively. Her pupils are like pinpricks and her head is loose on her shoulders. 'Is she trying to dump you, Euan?'

'Mind your own business,' I tell her.

'Isn't it time we told her?' she says, her voice like warm treacle. 'Do you want to or shall I?'

Euan isn't listening. He's staring at me intently as if by doing so he will change my mind. 'I already know about the abortion,' I say to Orla. 'I'm sorry you had to go through that but—'

'She's sweet, isn't she?' She moves towards us and runs her fingers down my wet cheeks. 'Sweet and innocent.'

'And I also know that I didn't kill Rose.' I try to hold her eyes but she seems to be having trouble focusing and her gaze slides sideways out of reach of mine. 'She was in the tent when I went back there.'

She shrugs. 'That's only the half of it.'

'So you have nothing on me,' I finish. I feel strong. I've been running a marathon and now the finishing line is in sight. One last burst of energy and I'll be there. 'Game over, Orla.' I open the front door. 'Time for you to go off and bother someone else.'

'You never quite get there, do you? Don't you want to find out what really happened to Rose?'

I turn back to them both just in time to catch a look that passes from Euan to Orla. It's a warning look, a don't-you-dare glance that makes my scalp tingle and my stomach turn over. And then he cracks his fingers, one by one, left hand and then right. 'Euan?' His face has shut down again.

'Shall we give her a clue?' Orla says.

'Go home, Grace.' Euan grasps my elbow and tries to urge me through the door but I push him away from me. His eyes beseech mine. 'Please.'

I look from one of them to the other. My instinct is to trust Euan. Orla is poisonous, unhinged, malevolent. Driving a wedge between Euan and me would please her no end – I know that. But still.

'No.' I close the door and walk back into the living room.

They both follow me. We stand together in the centre of the room. A triangle. Orla is beaming, excited and I realise that this is what she's been waiting for.

'So tell me, Orla,' I say. 'Let's just get this over with.'

'Well, when you went to bed,' she says, her eyes wide

open and staring, 'I stayed by the pond for a while. I'd arranged to meet Euan there. We were going to talk about the baby.' She touches her flat stomach protectively as if she's still pregnant. 'I told him the week before that I was expecting and I was hoping . . .' She gives a laugh. It's as brittle as smashed glass. 'I was hoping he was going to support me, but no! He accused me of trying to trap him.'

'You were promiscuous,' I say. 'You had sex with loads of boys.'

'Lying about the baby's father? Do you think I would do that to a child?' She shudders. It runs through her body from head to foot like a bitter wind. '*My* child?'

'Yes, I do. I think that getting your own way is more important than anyth—' I stop talking as thoughts collide in my head: Euan was also there that night; Rose's bracelet was found in the loft; Monica said Euan had lots of stuff up there too, stuff he hadn't looked at in years. I take the bracelet from my back pocket and hold it up. My hands are shaking. I throw it to him.

He catches it. He can't look at me.

'Ella came home with that. It was in your loft. Monica had no idea how it came to be there.' I lurch to one side and then say quietly, 'Please, Euan. Just fucking tell me it wasn't you.' I'm so afraid of the answer that I keep my eyes tight shut and wish myself somewhere, anywhere but here.

'Yes, go on,' Orla says. 'And don't spare us any of the details.'

Seconds tick by and still he doesn't speak. I open my

eyes and look at him. He is standing with his arms by his side, shoulders back and hands loose. I sense that this relaxed pose is forced. Inside he's dying. I would stake my own life on it.

'Just tell me what happened,' I say. 'Please.'

His eyes narrow and then reluctantly meet mine. He wants a reprieve. He doesn't have to ask; it's written all over his face.

But we're not kids any more and I'm losing patience. 'Just get on with it,' I say curtly.

He stares up at the ceiling where cracks weave across the plaster from one corner to the next. 'I had a lot to drink. I saw Rose twice: earlier in the evening before I was too far gone and then again later.' His voice falters. He clears his throat. 'First time I saw her she told me she had lost her bracelet. I said I would look out for it and less than five minutes later I found it in a patch of grass. The storm started up, I drank some more vodka and then I met Orla by the pond.' He shrugs, gives me a look that's half helpless and half disbelieving. 'It didn't go well. She was determined to have the baby, tell my parents—'

'Don't blame me,' she cuts in. 'You were the one who couldn't face up to your responsibilities.'

'Shut up!' I swivel towards her. 'This isn't about you.'

'Second time I saw Rose, Orla was hassling me, following me. It was late and I was well on the way to paralytic,' Euan continues. 'The storm had just passed through and I was trying to find my way back to my tent but the ground was slippery and I was too drunk to realise I was going around in circles. She asked me again if I had seen her bracelet and I said I had found it but—' He stops. His mouth is trembling. He puts his hand up to his face then says quietly, 'It was a case of finders keepers. That's what I said to her. Finders keepers, losers weepers and I kept on walking.'

I flinch. 'Euan, the bracelet belonged to her dead mother.'

'I know.' I watch years of self-reproach flood into his eyes. 'And that's not the worst of it.' His tone is uneven as if the words are being squeezed from a half-blocked tube. 'I told her that if she wanted it, she'd have to find it and I pretended to throw it into the pond. I didn't for one moment think that she would go in after it.'

I feel incredibly still inside like the blood has stopped flowing in my veins. 'And did she?'

'I honestly don't know. Eventually, Orla left me alone and I found my way back to my tent. I didn't think about it again until you said you thought you'd done it and slowly I started to remember that night and then, weeks later, when I finally emptied out my rucksack I found the bracelet and knew that what I barely remembered had actually happened.'

'So all these years you've known she didn't die because I pushed her?'

To his credit, he looks me in the eyes when he answers, 'Yes.'

My heart contracts to a tight fist. My bones feel heavy, my insides grabbed by gravity and I drop into a chair. I start to rock myself backward and forward. I wish I could cry but my eyes have never been drier. I want to wash it all away: the memories, the nightmares, the guilt and now this – Euan. I trusted him. Implicitly. I have made love to him, cried for him, held him, defended him, longed for him. God help me, I have even thought of running away with him. I have hurt Paul and threatened my girls' happiness and all this time he knew I had nothing to do with Rose's death.

I look up at him. 'Why didn't you tell me?'

'I tried.'

'Well, not hard enough.' Rage peaks inside me and I stand up, slap him across the face, once and then again. He doesn't defend himself and it doesn't make me feel any better. 'You shit! You spineless shit,' I hiss. 'You're as bad as her.'

'You have every right to be angry—'

'I'm not angry,' I shout. 'I'm furious and hurt and betrayed and . . .' My voice gives way. I shake my head and start to walk the floor.

'When would have been the right time to tell you?'

'Any time was the right time!' I stalk around him. 'When I couldn't get out of bed and was plagued by nightmares, when I was ill and you came back to Scotland. Hell! Even just two weeks ago when Orla turned up.' I lean into him. 'But not like this, Euan. Not me finding out from her.'

Orla is standing in the shadows. She lights a cigarette and walks towards me. 'He really has betrayed you, Grace. Hasn't he?' She tries to lay an arm on my shoulder.

'Get off me!' I push her roughly and she wobbles on her heels. 'Do not touch me.' I look at Euan. 'Either of you.'

I stand by the window. The sky is almost completely dark now. The storm is directly overhead. Hailstones are hammering against the windowpane, on and on like an extended drum roll. Some of them are the size of golf balls. As kids Euan and I would run around outside, jumping with pleasure and pain as they smacked our faces and bruised our skin.

'I fully intended to tell you before I went to university,' he says. 'But mum told me you were engaged. I thought you had moved on. Like loving Paul had wiped it out somehow.'

'And when you came back to live in Scotland?' I turn back to him. 'Why not then? You saw the mess I was in.'

'You were ill. I didn't—' He stops, sucks in his cheeks.

'Christ!' I read the truth behind his reluctance. 'You were afraid I would tell on you?'

'You weren't yourself.'

'Jesus! I would never have done that!' I start pacing again. 'And all the years after? It didn't occur to you that perhaps you should be truthful?'

'Before Orla turned up, you hardly talked about Rose.'

'Euan, there are photographs of Rose in my house, I married her father, she has never been far from my thoughts. Never.' I try to keep my voice steady. 'And last week when Orla called? You couldn't have said something then?'

'Look, I'm not proud of this.'

'Proud?' I push both my hands against his chest. 'You should be ashamed of yourself! I would never have believed this of you.'

'His mother didn't help,' Orla cuts in. 'She was a control freak if ever there was one.' She saunters over to stand beside us again. 'Ruthless when it came to protecting her boy.'

'Mum, she—'

I point a finger at him. 'Don't blame this on Mo.' And then another penny drops. 'Mo knew?'

'I had to tell someone.'

Like a pendulum swing, I lurch from anger back to grief again. It catches in my throat and I moan. Mo knew about this. She cared for me and loved me and was almost as close to me as my own mother and yet she also let me down. It's too much to take in.

'She didn't know that you thought you'd done it,' Euan says quickly. 'She wouldn't have chosen between us.'

I want to believe him but I can't. It's not that I blame Mo for putting Euan first – of course she would choose her own flesh and blood over me – I just wish that she had told me. 'Why did you keep the bracelet?'

'I always intended to give it back.' He looks apologetic, desperate even, but I don't feel for him. Not after what he's done. 'I wanted to tell you. At Mum's funeral—'

'It's too late,' I say sharply and turn to Orla. 'Did you see Rose go into the water?'

'Don't be ridiculous! I would have stopped her. I was following Euan.'

'And next day. When we found Rose's body. You knew it couldn't have been me, didn't you?'

'Yes.' She makes a petted lip. 'I'm sorry about that but I was protecting Euan. He was the father of my child. Then later when I realised he wasn't going to support me I wrote to you but—'

'So both of you knew.' I look from one to the other. If it wasn't so tragic it would be funny. 'My boyfriend and my best friend and neither of you saw fit to tell me.'

'Well, what could I do?' Orla shrugs her shoulders, feigning innocence. 'I had to put Euan first.'

'And the best way to do that was to pin it on me?' Anger spikes inside me. 'You were the one who told me I'd killed her. You were the one who made me believe that I'd done it when you knew perfectly well that she was still alive after I went back to my tent.'

'And you might have done it. You did push her after all.'

'What sort of twisted logic is that?'

'Well, if you'd read the letters—'

'Fuck the letters!' I'm shaking with rage. 'You convinced me that I was guilty. *You*, Orla.' I point my finger into her face. 'I have spent twenty-four years thinking I killed a little girl.'

She smiles, triumphant, delighted with her own deceit. I want to slap her hard but my anger is being sapped by a profound sadness. Rose died because none of us helped her, and while Euan's actions were more final than mine, I know that I also let her down. Perhaps, if I had listened to her, I could have changed the course of events, but I was too caught up in my fight with Orla.

I stand by the window again and look out to sea. A ship's light shines bravely through the storm. I imagine the men on board battling the waves, listening to the deck groan and heave as it plunges down into the water, reaches a low point and is forced up again, praying the deck doesn't split or the cargo shift. Hanging on in there until the storm passes.

'So what to do, Grace?' Orla is a vulture waiting for a turn at the carrion.

'I'm doing nothing. I'm walking away.' I feel drained. 'I never want to set eyes on either of you again.'

'But you're missing an opportunity!' She throws an arm out towards Euan. 'He's the villain here. Why don't we turn the tables on him? Why don't we give him what's coming to him? You and me? What do you say?'

'I say – fuck you.' I lean towards her. 'I say you're a manipulative, twisted bitch who needs psychiatric help.'

She flinches at this but it's through her in a moment and she's back on track. 'I expect you agreed to let him deal with me.'

'We're not killers.'

'Correct me if I'm wrong but I saw you thinking about it.' Her eyes are piercing and I turn away from them. 'The knife block in your house. You imagined sticking a knife in me, didn't you?'

'I did.'

'So why didn't you?'

'I've told you.' I look back at her, raising my voice. 'Unlike you, I'm not a killer.'

She throws back her head and laughs at this. It's a mirthless sound that echoes the mania in her eyes. 'I'll destroy you, Grace.' She tilts her head and purses her lips regretfully. 'You have to strike first. Really, you do.'

'I don't have to do anything. You're not my problem. He's not my problem. In fact' – I shrug my shoulders – 'I can walk out of here with a clear conscience.'

'But you've spent twenty-four years thinking you killed Paul's daughter.'

'Well, now I can say with conviction that I didn't.'

She is circling me, breathing heavily. 'I'll tell Paul you've been having an affair.' She is using the best piece of leverage she has left. 'I'll tell him you've been at it for years.'

'You're too late.'

That stops her short.

'Paul already knows.'

'Should we tell Daisy and Ella too then? Or is truthtelling selective?'

I'm tired of this. I'm not blameless; I know that. But Orla is an arch-manipulator and I've had enough of her games. 'You have no control over me.' I start moving towards the door and she follows me.

'You are not going to walk away from me!'

'Oh yes, I am.' I'm inches from her face. 'I'm going to

find Paul and I'm going to grovel and beg and hope that he has enough compassion to forgive me.'

'I'll keep watching you.' Her mouth is crippled with an ugly smile. 'I'll come after your girls.'

'Why?' I shake my head. 'Why pursue me?'

'Because I'm not done with you yet.' Her tone is adamant. 'You can't just throw me off like this. I won't let you.' She flashes a glance across at Euan. 'I spent a lot of time in prison thinking about you both and then when I came back to Scotland and found out that you were playing happy families, I made up my mind not to let you away with it. You think you deserve to have perfect lives when I have nothing?'

Her eyes are bright with enmity. Her hand is around my throat. Her forearm stretches the length of my sternum and she pushes me back against the wall. She is surprisingly strong, strong enough to stop me breathing and no matter how much I try, I can't get any air into my lungs. Panic overwhelms me. I struggle against her, digging my nails into her hand and kicking out with my feet. My lungs are fit to burst and I want to scream but I can't. Pressure builds at the back of my eyes but just before I close them I see Euan pull her away from me, hard. She falls back, almost in slow motion, her arms windmilling, her eyes wide with surprise. Her head strikes the cast-iron fireplace. The sound is like nothing I've ever heard before: a cross between the thud of a football against a wall and the cracking of a very large nut. I don't move and neither does Euan. Her eyelids flutter once and then stay closed.

A weighty silence swells to fill the space around us and then Euan crouches down beside her. 'Orla! Can you hear me?' He tries to feel the pulse in her throat then gives up and lays his ear against her chest. He looks up at me. 'She's not breathing.' He starts mouth to mouth, then finds the base of her sternum, moves his hands up her ribcage and pushes hard where her heart should be. Just like I did for Rose. Fifteen compressions and two breaths, over and over.

Time slows right down. I watch Euan and I watch Orla. Blood is leaking on to the floor. I walk around her body to better see where it's coming from. Her skull has been opened up by one of the cast-iron points at the edge of the fire surround. Blood and a spongy, grey mess is oozing from a deep cut in the base of her skull. I put my fist in my mouth. The air around me judders. Lights flash and I slide into a memory. Euan has me tied to the big tree and I've fallen asleep. I'm dreaming about us flying. We're holding hands and we're flying over the village. Me and him. I can see our back gardens and I shout, 'Look, Euan! There!' And we fly back down to earth, land with a bump.

I'm on the floor. Someone is whimpering. Me. It's a weak, insipid sound that says nothing about how desperate I feel. My eyes are smarting, my head pounds and I cough and then immediately wince. My throat feels as if it's lined with cut glass. I crawl around Orla's body and grab hold of Euan's trousers. 'Her head,' I say, and then try to stand up but my legs tremble uncontrollably and I end up on all fours again.

Euan leans over her body. He feels the back of her skull then says something under his breath and sits back on his haunches. There is blood all over his hands. The smell is metallic, iron-rich and cloying. It catches at the back of my throat and I retch. I crawl back towards my handbag and my mobile phone. I will call an ambulance. Of course I will. They might be able to save her. They can work wonders nowadays. They have all sorts of cutting-edge techniques that save lives and restore people back to full health. But hard as I try, I can't press the numbers. My hands are shaking and my vision is blurring. I start to cry, hacking sobs that shake me inside out.

I don't know how much time passes – one minute or five, I can't say – but finally I get up on to my feet again. Euan is standing now and is looking down at Orla's body.

'Is she dead?'

He nods.

I steel myself to look at her. People often say that the dead appear to be sleeping. But Orla doesn't look like she's asleep. Her face is bleached of colour. Her body is eerily still. Her dress has risen up at one side and I can see marks on the inside of her thigh.

'Track marks,' Euan says. 'From where she's been injecting heroin.'

The pinkie finger of her left hand is bent backwards. I move it in line with the others. It won't stay. It juts out at right angles to the one next to it.

Euan sits down in the armchair and I sit on the floor close to his feet, pull my knees up to my chin. Part of me is disengaged like a chain separated from the cog that turns it. The other part of me is asking: What now? Orla is dead. It's over. My stomach shrinks. It's like she said in the graveyard: *Euan was always good at doing what had to be done.*

I twist around to face him. 'Did you mean to kill her?'

'No.'

'Are you sure?'

He looks hurt then says flatly, 'I didn't know the spike was there and even if I had, I could hardly have judged it so accurately.'

I consider this and then say, 'Why did you never tell me about Rose?'

He raises his eyebrows. 'Cowardice.'

I shake my head. 'You're not a coward.'

'Then you pick a reason.' He stands up. 'For now we have to deal with this.' He points to Orla's crumpled body, blood spreading across the floorboards in a meandering stream. I am resigned to calling the police and telling them the whole sorry tale, beginning with Rose and ending with Orla's death but Euan says, 'Grace? Look at me.'

I look.

'This is what you have to do. Go back to your car and wait there. If anybody comes down the path to her cottage call me. Can you manage that?'

'What will you say to the police?'

'We can't call the police.'

'Why not?'

'I could end up being prosecuted.' He looks stern. 'We both could.'

'We can't cover this up!' I stand up beside him. 'It was an accident! Self-defence. She was trying to strangle me and you stopped her.'

'Maybe so but it doesn't look good,' Euan continues. 'There will be an inquiry and the police will be bound to discover that we had reason to shut her up.'

I almost agree with him and then I think about the years stretching ahead of me. Fearful. Looking over my shoulder. What if someone has seen my car and tells the police I was here? What if Orla told someone that she thought we were going to harm her? What if Euan, years down the road, decides to blackmail me? He's not someone I can trust any more. He's almost as much of a snake as she was. He deliberately withheld information that would have turned my life around.

'Just go, Grace.' He tries to touch my arm, thinks better of it when I glare at him. 'Walk through the door and don't look back.'

I reach for my mobile. 'Well, there's the thing.' I hold his eyes. 'I would always be looking back.'

'Stop! Think,' he says, urgent now. 'Think about the girls and Paul, Ed, going to Australia.'

'No.' I shake my head. 'I've been down this road before. I can't keep another secret. Not again.' I call emergency services and ask for the police. I expect Euan to take the phone from me but he doesn't. He walks into the kitchen and washes the blood off his hands. When he's finished he comes back to join me by the window.

'What are you going to tell them?'

'I'm going to tell them the truth.'

'All of it?'

I don't answer.

'We have to tell the same story,' he says. 'Grace?'

I turn away and when I see the lights of the police car arrive at the top of the footpath, I walk out into the rain to meet them.

Once more a police station. Once more I am wet and have a blanket around me but this time Orla is not opposite me. Orla is dead. Euan sits opposite me instead. Neither of us speaks. We are taken to separate rooms and questioned. I tell the truth. It isn't the whole truth: I don't mention Rose and I don't mention the fact that I thought about killing Orla, albeit only for moments. I always give them the same answers: she was obsessed with me and my family and with her teenage self. She had been hounding me for almost two weeks and I came to the cottage to try to reason with her. She attacked me. I have bruises from her fingers around my throat and her skin is under my fingernails. I confirm Euan's story that all he did was pull her off me and that she fell awkwardly. No one could have predicted that.

Paul and Ed return from Skye at once. Paul stays beside me, supporting me through the questioning and the whispered speculation that inevitably follows. For those first two weeks after Orla's death, he is constantly with me. To all intents and purposes he is one hundred per cent on my side but when we are alone, I see and hear how he really feels.

'I'm doing this for the girls,' he tells me. 'You. You, Grace.' His eyes are shot through with betrayal and I keep my head low, too ashamed to look at him. 'I will never understand, first, why you were having an affair with Euan and second, why you didn't tell me about Orla's obsession with you.'

'I couldn't—'

'But you could tell Euan?' he snaps back.

I say nothing. The truth is – I have no defence. There is nothing I can say that will make it better. If I was completely truthful, I would only make matters worse. I search my conscience but I truly believe that there is nothing to be gained from telling Paul the exact sequence of events that led to Rose's drowning. It's too late to help Rose and it will reopen an old wound for Paul. I don't feel like I'm protecting Euan and I don't feel like I'm protecting myself. I feel like I'm doing the only thing I can do by accepting that what happened all those years ago can never be made right and I have to live with that.

Daisy and Ella are both visibly horrified when they find out about Orla's obsession with me. Ella fluctuates between tears and being over-protective of me, making me cups of tea, filling the dishwasher, emptying the tumble drier. Daisy is confused. 'I don't understand how it happened,' she keeps saying. 'Why did she want to hurt you? She seemed nice.'

I worry that Shugs will come forward to give the police another angle but he never does. I worry that fellow diners in the Edinburgh restaurant might read about the case, recognise Orla's photograph and come forward to say that they heard me threaten her, but that doesn't happen either.

In the end, Orla seals her own fate, and two weeks after her death the police come to the house to inform me that neither Euan nor I will be prosecuted. There's the bedroom – evidence that her obsession was a real and powerful one. Her history of poor mental health, her drug addiction and her conviction for the part she played in her husband's murder. (I find out that while she didn't actually wield the knife, she paid the man who did and then stood watching as her husband died.)

When the police leave, my feeling of relief is heartfelt but tempered by the growing rift between Paul and myself. We are to move to Melbourne as originally planned but gone are the moments of shared decisions: where we will holiday, where we will live, what we will take with us and what we will leave behind. Paul makes the decisions himself. He is polite but cold. He doesn't seek my company. He no longer includes me in his thoughts. We don't make love any more.

I throw myself into packing up, glad to have something else to focus on and one morning when I am at the front of the house emptying the garage, a car pulls up. My stomach turns over when I see Murray and Angeline climb out. I meet them halfway along the front path and see at once that Angeline has changed. She is immaculately dressed, as always, but her walk is less confident, her gaze less assured.

'Grace.' She stops a pace away from me. 'It seems I misjudged you.'

'I'm sorry for your loss, Angeline.'

'Are you? Are you really?'

'Yes, I am.' I keep my voice steady. 'I did not want any of this to happen. I absolutely didn't.'

'And yet it did.' She leans towards me. 'Look me in the eye and tell me that neither of you wanted my daughter dead.' I look her in the eye but before I speak she says, 'I thought as much.' She starts to shake with rage. 'I will not forget this. You may have fooled the police, both of you, with your plausible story but you have not fooled me.'

'Angeline.' Murray takes her left elbow and as he does so she lifts her right arm and slaps me so hard across the face that my teeth shift in my jaw. I lurch backward, my hand automatically raised to my cheek. Murray turns Angeline around and they go back to the car.

I go inside, my vision blurred, my heart pounding, my face stinging with pain. I pull Murphy up on the sofa beside me and stay there for the rest of the afternoon, dry-eyed and empty inside. No one disturbs me. The girls are not coming home until late evening because they are rehearsing *Romeo and Juliet* – Ella is Juliet and Daisy has found her niche backstage. Ed isn't due to come home either. He has been staying with my parents since Orla died. All three, in spite of their initial shock and subsequent anxiety as the details came to light, support me unreservedly. 'Don't you worry about us – we're all rubbing along well together,' my mum tells me, her voice high-pitched with optimism. 'And we're looking forward to Australia.'

I'm pleased that my mum and dad are coming out with us. My dad's stomach has settled since he started a course of treatment and they are planning 'an adventure', my mum says. 'We won't come for the whole year; just to see you settled. And then we might do a spot of travelling. I hear you can walk up and over the Sydney Harbour Bridge. I might even persuade your father into shorts.'

Paul will be back for tea, I hope. He is tying up loose ends at the university and I can never be sure quite when he will be home. I have made his favourite chicken casserole. It's in the slow cooker, ready, just in case.

At just after six he comes through the front door and Murphy goes to greet him. I stand up, stretch out my stiff legs and touch him lightly on the arm. 'The table is set,' I say.

He doesn't look at me. 'Give me fifteen minutes.' He goes upstairs for a shower and I stand at the kitchen window, watch the waves break over the sand and try to think of nothing.

When Paul comes to the table I sit opposite him and dish up. When I take the first forkful I realise that I can barely swallow, my face is numb, my teeth feel like they belong in someone else's mouth.

'Are you going to tell me how you got that mark on your face?'

The sound of his voice makes me jump and I drop my fork. 'Orla's mother.'

'She came here?'

I nod.

He leans across the table and tenderly touches my cheek. 'My God, she really hit you.' He comes around to my side, stands me up and turns my face up towards the light. 'Why didn't you call me?'

'I thought you would think . . .' My voice gives out. I try again. 'I thought you would think that I deserved it.'

His jaw tightens and then he gives me a small, sad smile. 'No, I don't think that.'

He runs his hands across my hair and down my shoulders and my arms.

At once I start to tremble and then to cry. Silent tears stream down my face. 'Please, Paul,' I whisper. 'Just tell me that there's a chance you'll forgive me.'

'Of course there's a chance.' He pulls me into his chest and holds me there. 'Give me time, Grace.'

It's more than I could have hoped for and I can barely breathe for fear that he will change his mind and push me away. But he doesn't. Food forgotten, he takes me upstairs. We lie on the bed together. He keeps his arms around me and we talk. I tell him how sorry I am, how much I love him, how much I want to make it right between us and how hard I will work to make our family happy again.

The evening's performance of *Romeo and Juliet* is just days before we leave for Melbourne. My face is still bruised but I do a good job of covering it with make-up. We collect my parents and Ed and go in to St Andrews to watch the play. Paul holds my hand as we walk up the steps. We sit in the second row, right in front of the stage. I am in the middle, Paul on one side, my mum on the other.

Just before the performance starts, my dad realises he has left his glasses in the car. I take the keys from Paul, go back through the foyer and past the last few stragglers who are just arriving. I find Dad's glasses and head straight back inside only to bump into Monica and Euan. I haven't spoken to either of them since the day Orla died.

There are an awkward few seconds while we each appraise one another. Monica looks remarkably well: her hair, her make-up, her smart trouser suit and crisp white blouse. She has hold of Euan's arm in such a way that makes it look as if she is the one keeping him upright. Euan's face is strained. Clearly, he hasn't shaved in days and there is a tremor in his jaw. I don't know what goes on in their private moments but, in public, Monica has behaved like Paul. She has stayed by Euan's side, supporting him, warding off idle gossip and nosey neighbours. And I don't know whether she knows about the affair, but if she does, she hides it well.

'It hasn't started, has it?' she asks me.

'Just about to, I think.' I sidle past them both.

'Grace?' His voice sounds sore. I turn back and find that I can look him in the eye without hating him, without loving him, without, in fact, feeling anything at all. 'I'm sorry.'

I don't answer. I walk back down the centre aisle, just as the curtain begins to open and slide into my seat next to Paul.

'Did you get talking to someone out there?' he says.

'There's nobody out there.' I rest my head against his shoulder. 'Nobody at all.'